D.E.A.D.

R.D. BRADY

BY R.D. BRADY

The A.L.I.V.E. Series

A.L.I.V.E.

D.E.A.D.

R.I.S.E.

S.A.V.E.

Into the Cage

Into the Dark

The Nola James Series

Surrender the Fear

Escape the Fear

Tackle the Fear

Return the Fear

The Belial Series

The Belial Stone

The Belial Library

The Belial Ring

The Belial Recruit

The Belial Children

The Belial Origins

The Belial Search

The Belial Guard

The Belial Warrior

The Belial Plan

The Belial Witches

The Belial War

The Belial Fall

The Belial Sacrifice

Published by Vinci Books Ltd in 2024
vinci-books.com

1

Copyright © R.D. Brady 2017

The author has asserted their moral right to be identified as the author of this work in accordance with the Copyright, Designs and Patents Act 1988

This work is a work of fiction. Names, characters, places and incidents are the product of the author's imagination or are used fictitiously. Any resemblance to actual persons, living or dead, places and incidents is entirely coincidental.

All rights reserved. No part of this publication may be copied, reproduced, distributed, stored in any retrieval system, or transmitted in any form or by any means, including photocopying, recording, or other electronic or mechanical methods, nor used as a source for any form of machine learning including AI datasets, without the prior written permission of the publisher.

The publisher and the author have made every effort to obtain permissions for any third party material used in this book and to comply with copyright law. Any queries in this respect should be brought to the attention of the publisher and any omissions will be corrected in future editions. A CIP catalogue record for this book is available from the British Library.
Paperback ISBN: 9781036700294

Printed and bound in Great Britain by Clays Ltd, Elcograf S.p.A.

"For me, it is far better to grasp the Universe as it really is than to persist in delusion, however satisfying and reassuring."
- Carl Sagan, *The Demon-Haunted World: Science as a Candle in the Dark*, 1995

"Two possibilities exist, either we are alone in the universe or we are not. Both are equally terrifying."
- Arthur C. Clarke, Author of *2001: A Space Odyssey*

"Perhaps we need some outside universal threat to make us recognize this common bond. I occasionally think how quickly our differences worldwide would vanish if we were facing an alien threat from outside this world."
- Ronald Reagan, Excerpt from 1987 *Speech to the United Nations*

CHAPTER 1

THREE MONTHS AGO

UNDISCLOSED LOCATION

The room had no windows, just dark-tiled walls. The only light came from the monitors and the backlit keyboard. And there were no other humans. This was Guardian's domain.

Guardian's eyes scanned the three rows of four monitors on the wall. Focus shifting from box to box, Guardian took all of it in. These screens were meant for only Guardian and the computers that provided answers to any question Guardian might imagine.

Right now, all of them were filled with images of violence.

A Kecksburg-AG2 ran down a man in a white coat, digging his talons into the man's back. A Kingman-AG1 turned a corner and the soldiers standing there grabbed their heads collapsing to the ground. For hours, Guardian watched the violence play across the screens. Area 51, reputed to be one of the safest military bases in the United States, was being torn apart.

On the monitors, the images flashed, continually changing, yet Guardian missed nothing. The scene in one box drew Guardian's focus more than any other. Subject One, who'd found his clones and been helped by a group of humans, stopped at a door, staring up at Orion1. The two placed their hands against the glass. Guardian frowned. *What is that about?*

Soon the woman with Subject One rushed him along, although she turned to look back at Orion1. Was that guilt on her face? Compassion? Guardian wasn't sure. Emotions were not Guardian's strong suit.

An hour later, Orion1 saved the same subject and his clones by distracting a group of guards. *He's important to him.* Guardian did not know why, just that it was true.

An ache started behind Guardian's eyes. It happened sometimes when too much time was spent in the box. But Guardian couldn't leave, not yet. Things were moving fast and Guardian couldn't yet see what was coming. But things were beginning to happen, to change. It was only a matter of time now.

But I need to know everything so I can prepare. Guardian's hands flew over the screen. *I need to see.*

CHAPTER 2

TODAY

TRIBUNE, KANSAS

The dishes were still in the sink from breakfast. It was the first sight that greeted Sandra Gillibrand as she walked into the kitchen after being at work for twelve hours. She'd just completed a double shift at the diner. She was glad for the work because they needed the money, but her feet were killing her, her back was aching, and she wanted nothing more than to crawl into her bed and just declare that today was officially over.

"Mom?"

Sandra took a breath and turned around, her smile in place. "Hey, honey, did you get everything out of the car?"

Her son Luke nodded, his big brown eyes staring out at her from under a mop of light brown hair. "Can I go see if Sammy is here?"

Sandra hoped the disappointment wasn't on her face at the mention of Luke's imaginary friend. At age ten, he was too old for them. But Luke had hit all his milestones at later dates than most kids, so being that friends were one area where Luke really struggled, she supposed she should be happy that he was at least role-playing how to be a friend. And she hoped that maybe, just maybe, it would help with making real friends.

Luke had been diagnosed with Asperger's Syndrome two years ago. While having the diagnosis at least helped Sandra to have a better idea of what to expect, it hadn't made Luke's life any easier. The kids at school still gave him a hard time. He just couldn't read people. He assumed everyone was a friend. As a little boy, his open embrace of the world had made her heart sing. As he'd gotten older, it terrified her.

Now he stood looking at her expectantly, framed in the doorway of the old kitchen. The notches from his growth chart were lined up next to him. When had he gotten so big?

"Please, Mom."

She stood, indecisive. She didn't like him going out to the old barn. Their house sat next to the O'Hare Farm, a giant, sprawling, two-hundred-acre working farm. Corn was their major crop. Sandra and Luke's house had been on the farm that O'Hare had bought the land from decades ago. Now all that was left of that past was the barn and the house.

Out the window, the shadows were already beginning to form. While she did not like him being out there, he'd had a rough day. Some kids had teased him at lunch and the teacher had called Sandra at work to let her know. She assured Sandra that Luke was fine and the kids were punished. But the idea of her son being the target of bullies just broke her heart. She'd felt helpless all day, with an ache in her chest.

But Luke had looked no worse for wear when she'd picked him up at school. He'd sat in a booth at the diner and done his homework and then worked on his computer, coding something or other until the end of Sandra's shift.

While she felt like she'd been run over a few times his eyes were bright at the thought of 'playing' with Sammy. She sighed. *Maybe I need an imaginary friend.* "Sure, honey, go ahead. Just come in when it's dark, okay?"

He gave her a quick smile and then turned for the back door. But then he ran back to her, giving her a hug. Tears sprang to her eyes and she rested her head on his for a moment.

"Thanks, Mom." Luke sprinted back for the door.

The hugs were new, too. He'd overheard her talking to a friend late one night about how she would give anything for him to hug her more. And he'd taken it on as his mission to make sure he did. And today, those hugs helped push away the anxiety that always seemed to be gnawing at her.

Sandra watched until he disappeared into the barn. Then she went and got changed into sweats, pulling her pink terry-cloth robe on over them before heading back to the kitchen. She stared at the pile of dishes again and just could not bring herself to clean them. Not today. She reached for the cabinet above the refrigerator and pulled down the bottle of Merlot she'd stashed there. She had one glass a week, her small little concession to relaxation.

She poured herself a generous amount in a plastic cup with a dancing elephant on the front. *Yup, I'm a class act.* She tilted her cup toward the refrigerator, where the last picture taken of her and her husband, Noah, was prominently displayed. They'd both been deployed on the same day, her to Afghanistan, him to Iraq. He'd been killed a month later in an ambush. And then she'd learned she was pregnant.

I miss you, Noah. She took a sip and sighed, closing her eyes and letting the warmth flow through her.

"Mom!" Luke's terrified scream ripped through the house. Sandra's eyes jolted open and she lunged from the chair, spilling her wine across the table. Heart pounding, she sprinted across the kitchen and ripped open the back door as Luke screamed again.

Her eyes went wide and her heart pounded as she saw the large shapes lumbering after Luke, chasing him into the fields. "Luke!"

One of the shapes turned toward Sandra at her yell. Sandra's breath hitched and her eyes went wide. The shadows made it difficult to see clearly, but it was big, muscular, blue, and most definitely not human. The creature let out a cry and ran toward her, its arms pounding the ground like an ape.

Stumbling back into the house, Sandra slammed the door shut and locked it. She ran for the pantry, grabbing a stool on the way. Standing on it, she reached along the top shelf until she felt the barrel of the shotgun. She scrounged around for the box of shells and pulled it down. The shells spilled across the floor.

The back door thumped and Sandra's head whipped up. Shaking, she grabbed a handful of cartridges and shoved them into the pocket of her robe as she stepped out of the pantry. The door thumped again. She swiped the phone off the counter and dialed 911, putting it on speaker as she kept her eyes trained on the back door.

"This is Greeley County Dispatch. What is your—"

"Something's trying to break into my house!"

"Ma'am, did you say something is trying to—"

The rest of the words were drowned out as the back door splintered. Sandra screamed as a creature stepped in with a roar. Its body was shaped like a gorilla. But it was blue. And its face, good God, what was wrong with its face?

The creature turned to Sandra and roared again. The hair along her arms and neck went ramrod straight. Sandra pulled the trigger, catching it at the waist. It grunted as it lurched to the side. She pulled the trigger again and caught it dead center. Its knees sagged as it fell to the floor but was still alive.

"Ma'am? Ma'am?" the dispatcher called out.

Her hands shaking so hard she wasn't sure how she managed it, she dispensed the two shells and then reloaded. She didn't wait for the thing to stand fully upright—she unloaded on it again and again.

It dropped to the ground, fully splayed, half its head gone. Sandra's heart threatened to pound out of her chest.

"Ma'am, deputies are on the way," the dispatcher called out. "Are you all right?"

But Sandra didn't respond. She ran into the pantry, grabbed two more handfuls of shells, and shoved them in her robe pocket. Making a wide circle around the thing, she ran out the back door, more terrified than she'd ever been in her entire life.

"Luke!"

CHAPTER 3

Luke ducked into the cornfields, running as fast as he could manage. Behind him, he could hear the creature crashing through the stalks of corn. He'd gone to the barn to find Sammy, but he hadn't been there. He'd looked up in the rafters and then on top of the roof, but there'd been no sign of him.

When he'd come out, the two creatures were standing in the drive, staring at him. He'd smiled at first, thinking maybe they were friends of Sammy's. But something about them scared him, scared him more than anything in his life. He'd backed up and they ran for him. He screamed for his mom but they blocked the way to the house, so he'd run for the farm.

He could hear their heavy breathing even above the sound of their fists pounding into the ground. They ran like apes, but they weren't apes. They were blue, hairless, and their faces were no animal he'd ever seen.

He glanced over his shoulder. One was right behind him. It reached out a giant paw. With a scream, Luke dove to the side, rolling along the ground. It lunged after him. He tried to get up, but his knee hurt too much.

D.E.A.D.

The thing stopped, tilting its head at him. Luke scrambled back and screamed.

CHAPTER 4

Blood pounded in Sandra's ears as she barreled down the drive. She paused for only a few seconds at the large path that had been carved into the cornfield. Then Luke screamed.

"Luke! I'm coming, Luke!" Her hands slick with sweat, Sandra tore through the field, barely feeling the rough ground cutting up her bare feet. All she could picture was that thing going after her son.

Screams, different from Luke's, sounded from ahead, sending chills through her. It sounded like something was being torn apart. *Not Luke. Please don't be Luke.*

Something came flying at her and Sandra dove for the ground with a roll. Heart pounding, she looked back at what had nearly hit her as she got to her feet.

It was an arm—a hairless blue arm. Ahead, an object lay across the path carved in the field. She backed up, her eyes wide. It was one of the things, or at least part of it. One leg, some of its waist. She'd seen the aftereffects of IEDs in Afghanistan, but this was something different. She stepped over the parts and spied the other half of the body twenty feet away.

She moved forward, the shotgun securely in her arms, terror stealing over her. What could rip that thing apart?

"Luke?" she whispered. But there was no response. She followed the string of broken stalks, searching the area until the trail ended. She looked around but couldn't see him anywhere. She searched for another twenty minutes, pushing through the towering corn, her panic growing. She knew she needed to get help but she couldn't bring herself to leave.

Finally, though she forced herself to backtrack out of the field. She wasn't going to be able to search the field herself. She jogged back toward the drive, hoping the deputies had arrived.

Luke, where are you? She tried to keep her mind from going to a dark place, but it was so hard. Luke was a sweet soul. He didn't understand danger the way other people did. He didn't know how to fight. To be honest, the fact that he'd even run away from those things had shocked the hell out of her.

He's okay. He has to be. As she stepped out of the cornfield, a bright flashlight shone in her eyes. She put a hand up to block the glare.

"Sandra?" The flashlight lowered and Deputy Dave Carson stepped forward.

"Dave, thank God." Dave had been friends with both her and Noah in high school.

"Jesus, Sandra, what the hell's going on? I saw that thing in your kitchen." He glanced down. "Your feet are bleeding."

Now that she was talking out loud, the reality of what had chased Luke hit her full force. She started to shake so hard, she thought she might split apart. "Luke. One of those things went after him. It chased him into the cornfields. I can't find him."

Dave grasped her arm, speaking in an even tone. "Okay, Sandra, you need to take a breath. I called for backup, and I'll call the O'Hare Farm and get some people to help. We'll find him. Did you say there's another one of those things?"

"It's dead."

"You?"

She shook her head, more tremors running through her as she flashed on the body parts in the field. "I don't know what happened. I heard screaming, and when I got there the thing had been ripped apart." She turned back for the field. "But Luke's still—"

Dave grabbed her shoulder. "Hey, you need to go take care of those feet."

"No, I—"

"I will look for Luke. You go to the farmhouse in case he doubled back. You don't want him walking into the kitchen and seeing that thing. Get your feet bandaged up. There's a kit in my car. And let the guys know where I am."

Sandra wanted to argue with him, but the adrenaline was wearing off and she was beginning to feel the sting of the cuts on her feet. She'd get them bandaged, take a handful of aspirin, and head back out. "Okay. But Dave, find him."

"I will. Now go." He pushed her gently back toward the farmhouse.

She started back to the house, walking on the edges on her feet as the pain increased. She was limping as she stepped into the light given off by the barn, and reality set in. She'd defeated that thing because she'd a shotgun. Luke had nothing. And there was something else out there that had managed to rip that blue thing apart.

A hole felt like it had opened up in the middle of her chest, making it hard to breathe. And the fear she'd been holding at bay came crashing down on her like a tsunami. She stumbled. *Oh God, Luke.*

The barn door opened with a squeak. Sandra whirled around, pulling the shotgun up.

"Mom?" Luke stepped out.

Sandra's mouth fell open. And then she was running and crying. She pulled him to her. "Luke, oh, Luke. Thank God." She crashed to her knees in front of him, pushing his hair from his face tears streaming down her cheeks. "You're okay. You are okay, right?"

He nodded, but she could see the tear trails running through the dirt on his face. She hugged him again, promising herself she was never letting him out of her sight again. And she was never complaining about anything again ever in her life. She had her Luke back. So many emotions were running through her, she couldn't speak. She truly thought she'd lost him. She looked into his face, trying to figure out how she hadn't. "Luke, how did you get away?"

"Sammy. He saved me," Luke said.

Sandra went cold. "Sammy?"

"He saved me."

She had no idea what to say to that. Sammy was imaginary. Luke had been talking about him for about a week. But there was no Sammy. Still shaking, she got to her feet, taking his hand. "Come on. Let's get you to—"

A movement on the roof of their house pulled her attention. In one move, she pushed Luke behind her and pulled her shotgun up. Red eyes looked down at her and Sandra's pulse raced.

"No, no, Mom." Luke stepped from behind her, pushing down the barrel of her weapon. "That's Sammy."

Shock rolled through Sandra and that was before the thing on the roof stood. It was at least seven feet tall and dark, although she couldn't tell what color it was. Then it unfurled its wings.

The wingspan was at least seven feet across, and they weren't fluffy bird wings. No, these had points and looked like bat wings. The creature stared down at them as Luke waved up at it. "Hi, Sammy!"

With a gasp, Sandra pulled Luke close as the creature lifted off. She couldn't tear her eyes from it as it levitated in place for a moment, and then it began to fly away with great swings of its enormous wings.

Luke broke free from her and limped a few feet ahead before Sandra shook herself from her stupor. She grabbed Luke's shoulder, holding him in place. But Luke just kept looking up at Sammy's disappearing figure.

"Bye, Sammy!" he yelled with a wave.

Sandra couldn't bring herself to say anything. She couldn't bring herself to think. The two of them watched until Sammy disappeared from view. Sandra looked down at Luke. "That was Sammy?"

"Yeah, he's my friend."

Lights flashed as a patrol car sped into the driveway. Doors slammed as two deputies ran up to her. "Sandra? Is everything all right? What's going on?"

Looking up into the sky where Sammy had disappeared, she turned back to the deputies, a numbness starting to creep over her. "I have no idea."

CHAPTER 5

DENVER, COLORADO

Maeve Leander placed the phone back on the kitchen counter with a sigh, feeling years older than when she began the day.

"Same request?" Chris Garrigan asked as he took a seat at one of the stools at the kitchen island. Maeve nodded looking up into Chris's blue eyes.

"Come here." Chris opened his arms. Maeve walked around and leaned against him as he wrapped his arms around her.

"So what was the argument this time?" he asked.

Maeve shook her head, preferring to forget about the conversation but knowing that wasn't an option. Every week since they had taken up residence here, one of President Graham Wilson's aides called with a request. At first it was for Maeve to agree to a series of invasive medical tests for Alvie and the triplets. She had declined—adamantly. Then it shifted to psychological tests. Soon they wanted her to bring the hybrids to meet different doctors. Maeve turned them all down. She'd been in charge of Alvie's care for the last few years. And before that, it had been her mother.

Alvie had been created almost thirty years ago in a lab. He was a clone, a mix of human hybrid DNA. The DNA to make him had been taken from a skeleton found in a Mexican cave to create him. Dr. Alice Leander, Maeve's mother, had raised Alvie as if he was hers. Maeve had thought of him as her brother even though he'd never been allowed out of the lab at Wright-Patterson Air Force Base.

But all of that had changed when Martin Drummond had taken over as head of the Bureau of Scientific Advancement and Cooperation (BOSAC). He'd called for all alien projects to be moved to a more secure location—Area 51. Alvie, who'd been treated like a sentient being for his entire life, was all of a sudden being treated like an animal. The accommodations at 51 for him were little better than a prison cell.

But the terror she'd felt at the prospect of Alvie's future at 51 was nothing compared to the terror she'd felt when the other creatures held at 51 escaped. She, Chris, and Alvie had found the triplets during their desperate attempt to get to safety. And it was only due to the intervention of Wilson's personal security detail that they survived. And he'd kept them hidden for the last few months.

Now, though, the President was getting frustrated with Maeve's unwillingness to share the hybrids. But how could she? Wilson's people didn't think of them as anything more than a science experiment. And they were so much more than that.

Maeve sighed. "He wants me to meet with his science committee. Apparently not all aliens were contained to 51 during the breakout. He thinks I can add insight into their searches for them."

"Well, maybe you should. It's a small bone to throw him, and you're going to have to give him something."

"I know," she said, blowing out a breath.

The front door burst open and Snap sprinted in. Standing at just under three feet, Snap was a light-gray color tinged with pink, with massive black eyes on a disproportionately large triangular face. Unlike her twin brothers, Snap had long white hair that had recently started to come in thicker. Crackle and Pop were right behind her with Hope, a black-and-white six-month-old retriever, and Alvie brought up the rear. Snap ran to Maeve and held a bouquet of wildflowers up to her.

Maeve extracted herself from Chris. She knelt down to accept the flowers. "These are beautiful."

Snap beamed. Crackle nudged Snap aside and handed Maeve his own bundle, followed by Pop. "These are all beautiful, too." She kissed each of them on the forehead. Love wafted over her and she smiled. They couldn't talk, but they had an ability to project their emotions and thoughts to be understood.

The triplets had really blossomed in the last few months. The President had set them up on a ranch outside Denver and they were surrounded twenty-four seven by armed security. But the security never came near the house. And the triplets and Alvie had acres and acres of undeveloped land to roam around on. They took full advantage of being outside. Even their vision, which was sensitive to light, seemed to be adapting to allow them to be outside more on sunny days.

Looking over the triplets' heads to Alvie, Maeve saw a feeling of contentment on his face as he rubbed his hand through Hope's fur. Alvie, too, had seemed happier here than she'd ever seen him.

Maybe I should meet with the committee. Chris was right. It was a small price to pay to keep the ranch secure. Maeve stood. She'd decide that later. Right now she had more important things to discuss.

"Okay, who's going to help me make cupcakes?"

CHAPTER 6

TWO DAYS LATER

Maeve read through a news report on her laptop about a suspicious sighting in Reno, Nevada. An unidentified creature had been sighted outside a trailer park. Trackers from the area said they'd never seen the tracks that the creature left behind before.

Guess that's a 51 escapee.

She scrolled onto another page, and a small sneeze sounded behind her. Maeve whirled around. Crackle moved quickly behind Alvie, peeking out at her with big eyes.

"Crackle, honey, was that you? Did you sneeze?" she asked forcing herself to keep her tone calm.

He nodded slowly.

Her heart rate ticked up a beat even as she forced a smile to her face, holding out her hand. "Well, how about if we go see what that's all about, okay?"

Twenty minutes later, Maeve had Crackle tucked into bed, the Disney channel on to keep him entertained. She'd sent Chris outside with Alvie, Pop, and Snap.

D.E.A.D.

She closed the bedroom door quietly and leaned against it, her head down. No fever, slight congestion, the beginnings of a cough.

Oh God.

Pushing away from the door, she carried her medical bag to the kitchen, and placed it on the counter. Then she sank into one of the stools at the island.

The front door opened and Chris stepped inside, making his way over to her. "Hey. How's Crackle?"

Maeve forced herself to look at the problem unemotionally and told him what she'd observed.

Chris watched her closely, a frown appearing on his brow. "But you're worried."

"Yes."

"Why? It just sounds like he just has a little cold," Chris said.

Picturing Crackle, the fear she'd been pushing away crawled back up her throat. "There is no such thing as a little cold when it comes to them."

Taking a seat on the stool next to her, he shook his head. "I don't understand."

"When Alvie was ten, a new technician was hired to manage Alvie's equipment. He added to what was there and wiped everything down after Alvie ran the course. But he and Alvie never met, never saw one another." She went silent, remembering how scared she'd been back then.

Waiting a beat, he took her hand. "What happened?"

"Alvie started to weaken. His energy levels dropped dramatically. He became lethargic. My mom was frantic. She couldn't figure it out. Finally she ran a basic allergy test. It turned out Alvie was allergic to chocolate. The problem was, we never gave him chocolate."

Chris frowned. "The technician."

"Yes, but not in the way you're thinking. He had a chocolate bar every afternoon before he serviced the equipment. There were only microscopic traces, but it was enough to affect Alvie. But if my mom didn't have access to labs, she'd never have figured it out. As much as I know about Alvie's biology, there's legions I don't know. And for the triplets, I know even less. Yes, they're Alvie's clones, but how, where, and when they were created all could have affected them differently. So even though it looks like Crackle has a simple cold, I can't know that for sure without access to a lab."

"And even though you think this probably is a cold, you're worried about the day when it's *not* a simple cold," Chris said.

She nodded. "Everything they are being exposed to now is new, even for Alvie. Grass, sunlight, even the chemicals in the couch. And at some point, we are going to run into a problem. And that's not an 'if,' it's a 'when.'"

The silence stretched between them before Chris spoke, "So what do you want to do?"

"I want access to a lab with no strings attached," she said with a hopeful grin. "Do we think that's an option?"

Chris gave a small laugh. "I don't think that's an option."

She sighed. "No. It's not. But we're going to need access."

Nudging his chin toward the hall, Chris raised an eyebrow, "Well, those four are very important to the United States government. It's in their best interest to keep them healthy."

"Yeah, but what will they ask for in return?" Maeve gestured to the house. "President Wilson has made it clear he's not doing this out of the goodness of his heart."

"And if we don't play ball …"

Maeve sighed. "Then neither will he."

"So you're going to that meeting," Chris said.

Blowing out a breath, she nodded. "I don't think I have a choice."

CHAPTER 7

DEPARTMENT OF EXTRATERRESTRIAL AND ALIEN DEFENSE HEADQUARTERS

LAS VEGAS, NEVADA

Taking a deep and what she hoped was also a calming breath, Agent Norah Tidwell straightened her shoulders before she knocked on her supervisor's door.

"Come in," came the muffled reply from behind the closed door.

Norah opened it and stepped inside. "You wanted to see me, sir?"

Julio Sanders looked up from his screen. Brown hair graying at the temples, with equally brown eyes, Sanders was a bureaucrat through and through. He ran the newly minted department efficiently and with no frills. When Norah had first met him she'd been impressed by his confidence and his openness to suggestions. Now she realized Sanders was just making sure he had someone else to blame if the suggestion did not play out as planned.

"Norah. Good. I have some new assignments for you. But first, tell me about the Gillibrand incident. I was just pulling up your report."

Norah took a seat in one of the chairs in front of Sanders's desk. "It was two Blue Boys."

The Blue Boys' official title was Dulce-AG1. The aggressive creatures had incredible strength and a bite almost equal to that of an alligator. And it had a bulbous skull and gorilla-like body. But its most notable characteristic was its color. It was a light blue, hence the nickname.

Sanders groaned and Norah knew from experience he was calculating the potential financial payout to the next of kin. And she tried not to hate him for it.

"How many casualties?" he asked.

"Just the two blues."

Sanders raised an eyebrow. "Someone took down two of them? He must be one tough son of a bitch."

"Yes, *she* is. Former Marine, she took down one in her kitchen with a shotgun at close range. The other chased her son, age ten, into a cornfield. She gave chase but came across only parts of the Blue Boy."

"Parts?" Surprise flashed across Julio's face.

"Yes," Norah said. "She claims she did not take down the second one. And after viewing the body, I agree she could not have done it. It was ripped apart."

Sanders frowned. "So what happened? Was there someone else out there?"

"If there was, they weren't human. The homeowner did report seeing a tall, winged creature on the roof of her house. The son claimed that the creature saved him. But, sir, there's nothing in the department database that matches that description. There are no winged creatures at all listed. So I'm not sure what to make of it." She paused. "Unless some creatures were left out of the database."

He met her gaze unblinking. "Of course not. The database is complete."

"Yes, sir." Norah murmured as she broke off the eye contact.

When she'd started working with the department, she had wholeheartedly embraced their stated mission—to protect the populace at large from any extraterrestrial or alien threats. And while it had admittedly taken her a minute or two to accept the reality that there were aliens, accepting the need to protect the populace at large had taken no time at all. And as a woman raised in a large extended military family, she answered the call of her government.

But lately she had to admit doubts and questions had begun to seep into her resolve. Not that she'd said anything out loud, but she had been mentally collecting all the incidents or information that didn't quite add up—like the creature from the Gillibrand case that wasn't in the database.

Sanders gave her a patronizing smile. "I'm sure she was mistaken. Adrenaline, fear—it can do that."

Picturing Sandra, Norah shook her head. "Sir, she was a Marine in combat in Afghanistan for two tours. She's used to adrenaline and fear. I don't think she imagined this. She saw something with wings."

Her boss eyed her over the desk before gesturing to his screen. "She has been out of combat for over ten years, according to your report. She's out of practice. She was mistaken." His tone implied she should not question him further.

She nodded. "Yes, sir."

"Good. Now, cleanup wasn't any issue, was it?" he asked already flicking his gaze at his monitor, ready to move one.

"No. All parts were bagged. The house and field were sterilized."

"Witnesses?" he asked.

"Assured that they were sick gorillas who escaped containment," Norah said, her tone just on the edge of sarcastic.

He didn't noticed. "Good. And the non-disclosures were signed?"

"Yes, and the settlements were made."

That was the one part of this case that Norah had enjoyed. Sandra had been really shook up, and the settlement that accompanied the non-disclosure would go a long way to helping her and her son out.

Sanders's gaze once again had drifted back to the screen and Norah took note of the new pile of orange manila folders on the corner of his desk. Orange meant new sightings, and Sanders tended to go through them every morning. The fact that there were still files on his desk meant there'd been too many to get through quickly. That and the fact that the creature Sandra had described wasn't in the database had Norah frowning.

A beep came from Sander's laptop. As he read a message there, he ran a hand through his hair, disturbing his normally perfectly styled do.

"Everything all right?"

The smile on Sanders's face looked forced. "Yes, of course."

But Norah knew the increase in sightings was taxing their resources. And Sanders must be getting pressure from the higher-ups.

"Any chance we might get a little extra help?"

Sanders nodded. "I'll be speaking with some private contractors over the next few days who might be able to help take some of the burden."

It was an effort for Norah to keep her face neutral. She'd had some bad experiences with private contractors in the service. Most were good people, but the rules never seemed to apply to them the way they did the rest of the soldiers, and that almost always led to an abuse of power. "That's good, sir."

"Yes. Now, I need you to head to Aurora."

She frowned. "Aurora? Has there been another incident?" The incidents had spiraled out from the Vegas area but she'd couldn't recall any incidents in that part of Colorado.

Sanders shook his head. "No. There's an expert on these creatures that is briefing members of the President's science committee. I was told to choose a representative, and I have chosen you. Your flight will leave McCarran in two hours. You'll be back later tonight."

"Thank you, sir."

"Well, I can't send one of these lugheads, can I?" Sanders said with a grin.

Norah wasn't quite sure what to say to that, so she just made a non-committal sound. Sanders was always making those types of comments, as if he and Norah were the only intelligent ones in the department. She wasn't sure if he was flirting or trying to be funny. Either way, it was awkward.

"Bob will give you a lift. Oh, and on your way, I want you to stop by Cole's Gym," he said.

Starting to stand she frowned. "Oh, okay. But why?"

"There's a guy who works there now who used to be some big scientist," Sanders explained.

Her eyebrows rose. "And he works at a gym now?"

He shrugged. "I don't know. We just got his name. The higher-ups want him for the intelligence division."

Her frown deepened. All she knew about the higher-ups was that they were part of the Department of Defense. "So we're recruiting?"

"Yes."

"And you want me to take Bob?" She tried to keep the incredulity from her voice, but she was not sure she managed it. In a firefight, a barroom brawl, or when you needed a spot of intimidation, Bob was your guy. 'Talking,' however, was not really Bob's strong suit.

Sanders sighed. "I don't have anyone else to send. Everybody's out in the field or about to go out in the field. Just try to keep Bob's interaction with the doctor to a minimum."

Right. And then for my next trick, I'll make him understand the importance of utensils when eating. And how to say please, thank you, and excuse me. But out loud, she said, "Sure."

Sanders glanced at his watch. "You better get moving."

"Yes, sir." She turned and let herself out of the office. The meeting would take up the rest of the day. She'd been hoping to check up on the funds transfer for Sandra and her son. *Guess I'll do that on the way to the airfield.*

As she headed back to her cubicle, she pictured Sandra Gillibrand's face. The woman had not been hallucinating. She'd looked Norah right in the eyes and very calmly recounted the whole incident from start to finish—as well as explaining that her son had been friends with Sammy for a week prior to the incident. Norah had left that last little part out of the report. She wasn't sure why, but she just had a feeling it would only cause more problems for Sandra and her son. And she had warned Sandra to not mention that little detail to anyone, either.

Her partner, Bob Maxwell, appeared at her door. Five-eight with thick, muscular arms about the size of both Norah's thighs combined, Norah had thought her partner resembled a bulldog when she first met him. But as she got to know him better, she realized that was an insult to a bulldog's good looks and personality.

"Hey, you ready? Apparently I'm your chauffeur for today," he growled at her.

Norah struggled not to roll her eyes. She and Bob got along well enough, but he always acted like he was in charge even though they were on equal footing.

Actually, due to her college degrees, Norah was pretty sure she got paid more than him, not that she'd mentioned it. After all, if giving her a ride to the airfield was putting him out, she couldn't imagine what a pay discrepancy would do to the man.

"Yeah, let me just grab a few things. Meet you downstairs in five minutes?"

"Will do." Bob headed down the hall.

She watched him go, glad that he hadn't been part of the interview with Sandra and her son. And again she wondered why she'd kept the son's interaction with 'Sammy' from her report. She also wondered what it meant that 'Sammy' wasn't in the database. But mostly she wondered why Sammy had helped the boy. According to everything she'd been taught about these creatures, they were violent and lethal to humans. But Sammy had left Sandra and her son unharmed. So was it possible that not all the creatures meant them harm?

The idea did not sit well with her. She herself had helped take down twelve creatures, and they had not been taken alive. But they'd been classified as highly aggressive and dangerous to humans.

She sighed, clearing her head. Now was not the time for these thoughts. She pulled her weapon from the desk drawer. She tucked it into the holster at her waist and then grabbed her pack from under the desk.

The weapon was probably unnecessary, but she felt naked without it.

Heading for the stairs, she nodded to a few of the other agents at their desks. There was a new agent who'd joined just yesterday. He grinned at her, looking extremely happy to be there. Norah had felt much the same way when she'd first been offered the position as a lead agent in a new, presidential-appointed agency. Finally it seemed like all her work was paying off. But now, now she wasn't so sure.

Now she was having doubts about what they were doing, or at least how they were doing it. So all things considered, she was looking forward to speaking with the President's alien expert. Hopefully they could ease some of her concerns.

Picturing Sandra and her son, she imagined all the ways that could have gone badly. It was lucky Sandra was trained and that she kept a loaded shotgun handy. If those Blue Boys had shown up at someone else's home, well, the outcome would probably have not been as happy.

And that was the other part of her job that bothered her—they were keeping information from the public. And while she didn't want to scare people, she thought they should probably know they were at risk.

She opened the door to the stairwell and started down the five flights. *But that's not my call. I'm just a soldier in this army.*

CHAPTER 8

Greg Schorn lay on the weight bench, eyeing the weight bar above him. "Um, so the bar's forty-five pounds, right?"

"Yes, same as last week." Frank Cole, owner of Cole's Gym, sighed as he stood with his legs braced, his arms akimbo, ready to spot Greg whenever he got around to pushing the bar off its resting place. And Greg noticed with more than a little envy that even without flexing, Frank's arms were practically three times the size of his own.

Greg eyed the ends of the bar a little dubiously. "And those are sixty pounds on each side."

"Yup." Somehow even with only a one-syllable response, Frank's Bronx accent came through even thicker.

"So, we're talking 165 pounds," Greg said.

"Your math is correct, Doctor. Now quit stalling and lift the damn thing."

Greg blew out a breath. *Okay, I've got this.* He gripped the bar and pushed up. One rep, two. Greg managed to reach eight reps without too much difficulty. But at nine, the bar started to get heavier, making Greg wonder if Frank had added weights or was pushing down.

"Come on. You're almost at twelve. Don't quit on me," Frank said.

A picture of a creature, part alligator, part alien popped into his mind, and his muscles gave out for a second. The bar dropped quickly to his chest.

"Hey!" Frank reached down, his eyes wide.

"No," Greg barked out through gritted teeth, keeping the bar from slamming into his chest. "I got this."

Frank leaned over him, ready to grab the bar. But Greg focused on his breathing and slowly pushed the bar back up. He managed three more reps before tilting it toward the brace.

With a grin, Frank helped lower the bar down. He grinned as Greg sat up. "Thought you might be in trouble there for a moment."

"That's not trouble," Greg muttered.

Frank's gaze flicked to the front of the weight room before he leaned down. "Hey, heads up. Government dudes at the door. You good?"

With a sigh and wishing he could magically disappear, Greg sat up giving Frank a weary nod. "Yeah. Go on."

Frank headed to his office with a quick, worried look back at Greg. The gym owner had done a little time when he was younger and stupider. His words, not Greg's. And he did not like being around any agents, local, federal, or otherwise—which made the fact that he still allowed Greg in his gym a pretty good indicator of what a decent guy he was.

Grabbing his towel, Greg wiped his face, then draped it around his neck. He picked up his water bottle and took a swig as the agents made their way across the room toward him.

One male, one female. Both wore dark suits, his black, hers a charcoal gray. Her dark, curly hair was down, and he was a

Mr. Clean type. Greg glanced down at their shoes. Both wore dress shoes, but they leaned toward casual—shoes that they could run in.

Probably DEA.

In the last three months, he'd been visited by almost every law enforcement agency in the continental US. A few had stopped by more than once. It had gotten to the point that he was getting pretty good at figuring out who was who. Footwear seemed to be the factor that differentiated them the most. The more white-collar agencies—NSA, DOD, and FBI—tended toward shiny work shoes. The agencies that actually worked with their populations, DEA, local and state police, tended to wear shoes that would allow them to break into a sprint if necessary.

Part of him wanted to run but he simply sat and waited for their approach. "Dr. Schorn?" the female agent asked.

He gave a weary sigh. "Yup."

"I'm Agent Tidwell and this here is Agent Maxwell."

"Tidwell and Maxwell. You guys rhyme. Cool." Greg walked past them and took a seat on the rowing machine.

"Dr. Schorn," Agent Maxwell said, his face serious. "Your government needs your help."

Greg grinned as he began to row. "I'm sure they do."

"Dr. Schorn, we need to speak with you privately," Tidwell said.

"As soon as I'm done. I've got another thirty minutes." When the agents had first started showing up, Greg had spoken with them immediately. But there'd been so many that they really began cutting into his life. So now he made them wait.

Maxwell took a step toward him. "I don't think you understand—"

Annoyance creeping into his voice, Greg's eyes flashed at him. "No, you don't. You all have been sniffing around me for months. I cannot tell you anything. But if you want to ask me some questions, you will have to wait another"—he glanced at the big clock at the back of the gym—"twenty-eight minutes, and then I can speak with you."

Maxwell's mouth turned to a thin line. But Tidwell grabbed his arm before he could speak. "All right, Dr. Schorn. We'll wait for you in the lounge."

"Great." Greg watched them walk away and shook his head. Ever since everything had happened in Area 51, he'd had people coming out of the woodwork trying to get him to reveal what had happened. But he was sworn to secrecy. And he didn't get why all these government agents didn't get that. Besides, as difficult as it might be for these government types to understand, he really didn't enjoy reliving the most terrifying event in his life over and over again.

He sighed, pushing the agents from his mind. He needed to finish his workout. That was one thing he'd added to his daily life after 51. It's amazing how being nearly killed by government-created aliens could inspire you to a healthier lifestyle.

Greg finished his workout and decided to grab a shower before speaking with the agents. After all, the interaction was already going to be unpleasant, no need to literally stink up the place as well. He stepped out of the locker room, his hair still wet, and Tidwell and Maxwell stood waiting for him.

"All right. What's up?"

Maxwell glared, but Tidwell spoke before her partner could. "As I said before, we need some privacy for this conversation."

"I know just the place." Greg walked down the hall and headed up the stairs. At the third floor, he opened a door that led to a narrow staircase. He headed up and shoved open the door to the roof. A group of birds scattered as he stepped out. In the middle of the roof was a utility shed and next to it was a rug of turbo grass and four folding chairs. A kiddie pool leaned against the shed. An old fridge served as both a side table and beverage center.

Greg opened a large umbrella that had been propped up against the shed and took a seat next to the fridge. He opened the refrigerator door and pulled out a diet soda. He turned to the agents. "Anyone?"

"We're good, Dr. Schorn," Tidwell answered.

Greg popped open his can and took a sip. "Ah, nothing like a cold beverage after a workout." He eyed Maxwell, whose suit jacket looked like it was straining to contain his biceps. "You know what I mean, right, buddy?" Greg flexed his bicep.

Maxwell growled.

"I'll take that as a yes. Now, let me guess. DEA?"

"No," Maxwell growled again.

"Damn it," Greg smacked his leg. "You broke my streak. I had the last four agents correct. Well, for one I did guess local police but they were Nevada State Police, but you know, I think I can give that to myself."

"Dr. Schorn," Tidwell interrupted, taking a seat. "We need to speak with you about a matter of national security."

"Yup. Got that before. But like I've told everyone else, you do not have clearance for whatever it is you are going to ask me. So I think we're done here."

"We're not," Maxwell said, pulling a sheet of paper from his pocket. He handed it to Greg.

Greg scanned it in surprise. It was an executive order from President Wilson ordering that all individuals involved in the Area 51 incident cooperate with the agents of the Department of Extraterrestrial and Alien Defense.

"Well, that's new," he muttered, tossing the letter on top of the fridge. "So, agents of the Department of Extraterrestrial and Alien Defense, what exactly is the goal of this here new department?"

Maxwell puffed out his chest. "We have been charged with tracking down any and all escapees from Area 51. We have been tasked with bringing you in to aid in that effort."

"And when you capture the subjects, what's the plan? Kill on sight?" Greg asked taking a sip.

The female agent's jaw tightened for a fraction of a second before her partner answered. Maxwell crossed his arms over his chest in what Greg knew was an intimidation move. "There are levels of risk. Situation and risk level determine the appropriate response to a target."

Greg snorted. "Sure."

"What, you don't believe that?" Maxwell challenged.

"Well, I'd probably believe it more if the initials of your new department didn't spell dead."

His mouth hanging open, Maxwell paused, and Greg could tell he was just now figuring that out. Then Maxwell shook his head a triumphant smile on his face. "It doesn't spell dead. it spells D-O-E-A-D."

Greg grinned, surprised the guy had been able to figure that out without writing it down. And then, of course, without asking how to spell extraterrestrial. "True, but I'm pretty sure everyone's going to call it D.E.A.D."

Tidwell cut in. "Dr. Schorn, the President is asking for your help. We've been sent to recruit you as part of our intelligence division."

Placing his hands behind his head, Greg leaned back and smiled. "Tell him I appreciate the request, but no thanks."

"Your country is asking for your help," Maxwell sputtered.

His eyes went hard. "My country tried to murder me not that long ago. So not really trusting anything they say they need from me."

Tidwell smiled. "We're a new agency, created by the President himself. Of course you can trust—"

Greg shook his head. "Nope, I don't."

She tried again. "But—"

He smiled. "No."

"God damn it," Maxwell growled. "What the hell's wrong with you?"

"Well, it's probably the fact that I haven't had a full night's sleep in three months. Or maybe it's the constant government surveillance of my home, my car, my everything. Or maybe it's just that I don't like you."

Maxwell took a step forward. "Doesn't matter. The President has said you need to cooperate. And you will, either voluntarily or involuntarily."

Greg raised an eyebrow. "Is this the part where I'm supposed to be trusting? Are you planning on forcefully taking me to God knows where?"

"No, no. Of course not." Tidwell stood, placing a hand on her partner's arm, which he shrugged off.

"Good." Greg's voice hardened. "Because I will tell you what I have told every other agent who has attempted to strong-arm me—I have safety measures in place. If I do not send a certain message at a certain time every few hours, copious copies of my research at Area 51 will go out to all major news agencies, to all major bloggers, and to a few extra governmental entities. So think very carefully about how many people you want to know about what happened at Area 51."

"We are not the bad guys, Dr. Schorn. And we are just looking for some help," Tidwell said.

Greg snorted again. "Yeah. I've heard that before. Be sure to close the door on your way out."

Bob growled as he slammed the car door. "What a prick."

Norah looked over at him but said nothing.

"What? You don't think he's a prick?"

"I think Dr. Schorn has been through a lot. And if he's had government agencies hounding him…"

"Well, boo-hoo for him. We're being sent on behalf of the *President*. He should be fricking honored to be asked instead of turning us down."

Norah knew Bob was wrong about that. She'd been able to read a good deal about the incident at 51, but most of it had been redacted. The few people she'd spoken with had been haunted. Three had been so nervous they could barely sit still.

By comparison, Dr. Schorn was holding up pretty well. "Do you think he was telling the truth?" Norah asked as Bob pulled out of the parking lot.

Bob frowned. "About what?"

"About the government trying to kill him."

Turning at the corner against the light, Bob snorted. "Please, the U.S. government isn't in the murder game. Guy's paranoid."

"Maybe," she murmured.

"Well, we've got some time before we need to drop you at the airfield. Want to grab some tacos?"

"Yeah, sure," she said, her mind still on Schorn. He didn't seem paranoid. He seemed angry. And she couldn't blame him. But the U.S. government wouldn't condone murder, would they?

CHAPTER 9

DULCE, NEW MEXICO

Martin Drummond walked into his office, pulling back his long, still-damp, dark hair into a ponytail. He'd just finished a weight-lifting session and a five-mile run at the gym on the second level. After Area 51, he'd been spending most of his time here, and he needed the comforts of home, which included the gym for his private use and an apartment on the same level.

He'd had a steam shower installed and he had to admit it was well worth the cost. He wandered over to the long picture window that made up the back wall of his office and overlooked the lab.

Almost makes one forget they're living six stories underground.

The facility had been developed in the rush to create an underground base to hide the U.S.'s military activities from the Soviets. But soon the bases were used to hide much more from the public's eye. This particular facility had been the site of one of Martin's greatest coups. And over the years, he'd managed to wrest control from the U.S. government. Now, very few in government even realized it still existed.

Below him, the lab was a sea of activity. The walls by the floor were shorn clean, but higher up the mottled brown and gray rock walls remained jagged with sharp edges. Inside the lab were rows of stainless steel tables and millions of dollars in equipment. But the medical equipment, expensive as it was, was not the most expensive objects in the lab. No, the creatures held in holding cells along the back of the room were the most expensive. In fact, being many of them were the only ones of their kind on Earth, they were priceless.

He watched with cool detachment as a Birmingham-AG1 was strapped to a metal table. Long straps were wrapped around its muscular feet, knees, waist, neck, and head. The Birmingham looked reptilian with its short snout and green skin. It could barely move, which was exactly what was intended. A glass case was placed around the stretcher, offering yet another barrier. The Birmingham could leap incredible distances, and they were intelligent. The DNA used to recreate this one was technically pure alien, although the DNA had been slightly modified to make them aggressive yet controllable.

Today it was being tested with different chemicals to see which would be advantageous in a confrontation. Martin tilted his head, wondering what was being administered into the creature's drip by the lab tech and how long they'd have to wait for a response.

Only seconds passed before the creature began to shake, a white foam spraying from its mouth and coating the glass case. *Apparently not very long at all.* The seizure lasted for another minute and then the alien went still, staring straight ahead. Martin pulled out his phone and typed.

Is it alive?

The response was almost immediate. *Yes.*

D.E.A.D.

He put his phone back in his pocket. *Promising.*

This type of testing had been the entire reasoning behind Project Vault. The United States government had placed too many restrictions on experiments, in the name of humane treatment of these creatures.

Martin grimaced. *Humane treatment should only be reserved for humans.* They needed to know what threat these creatures offered and what potential defenses they could provide. That was the reason behind all of this, at least as far as Martin was concerned. But less-evolved minds seemed to think that science for science's sake was important.

Martin watched as the Birmingham was locked in one of the holding cells at the back of the lab. They had tested dozens of creatures in this lab since Area 51 had been bombed. But the more they tested, prodded, and dissected, the more Martin realized he needed one creature specifically: Subject One. The one they called Alvie. He was a merge of alien and human DNA, a process Martin had not been able to replicate successfully despite all his resources. Alvie himself was a clone. The DNA was from a thousand-year-old skull found in a washed-out cave in a canyon in Mexico in the early twentieth century. Dr. Maeve Leander had escaped from Area 51 with Alvie and an additional three clones.

Unlike the other creatures the A.L.I.V.E. Project had created, Alvie could and did communicate. He also demonstrated incredible dexterity and, much to Martin's surprise, aggressive skills. Replicating that within a human army would be astounding ... and very lucrative. Martin was a patriot, but he also knew money was what made the world turn.

But Martin's desire to procure Alvie went beyond mere financial gain. Alvie was the reason Martin had been exiled from the A.L.I.V.E. Project for years. He'd had to claw his way back. So getting that particular creature back wasn't just business. It was personal.

Besides, Leander had taken Martin's property with her. And while the U.S. government might have been the ones footing the bill, the idea behind the project, the impetus behind the projects, had come from Martin. He'd helped bring Alvie into existence, and as far as he was concerned, with the time and energy he'd put into the A.L.I.VE. Project, he owned Alvie. And all the others as well.

The attempts to get his property back, though, had run into a rather large snag. He'd searched high and low for Leander and her hybrids, but she had hidden herself well. Of course, she did have the President of the United States aiding her. Once his position as director of BOSAC had been terminated, many doors had been shut to him. But Martin had been in the intelligence game too long to let something like the lack of official connections get in his way. He'd already called in markers to get the right words whispered in the right ears. He just needed a few more pieces to fall into place.

A beep sounded on his computer and he walked over to see what Hamish Rheinberg, his head of IT, wanted. He was the only one allowed to directly message him. He read the screen and smiled. *And here's one piece now.*

He retook his seat and pulled up the file Hamish had sent. Cases of alien sightings or attacks were popping up all over the western half of the country, but a few had extended as far east as Ohio. There'd been over two dozen of them so far. A few had resulted in casualties, but most were just injuries, which was surprising. Each one, though, added a little more information on the subjects, which was the most critical component of them.

Originally, Martin had not been happy to learn some of the subjects had survived the blast. But it had actually turned out to be useful. Project Vault had been an attempt to discern the fighting capabilities of the alien species, but they had been limited by the base itself as to what scenarios the creatures would face. The ones that had escaped were facing a range of scenarios Martin could never have dreamed of. A Polk-AG3 had tracked and killed a group of seasoned hunters in the Moab Desert. They hadn't even known the thing could survive in a desert environment.

An Ubatuba-AG2 had attacked a family boating in Lake Tahoe. The family survived, but the creature had taken a bite of the father's arm.

A Kingman-AG1 had been seen in Phoenix, although it had not initiated contact with any humans. Agents had been able to apprehend it.

The list went on. They were learning more and more every day. So it was with more than a little excitement that Martin sat at his keyboard. *Let's see what you boys have been up to.*

He clicked open the file and read quickly. Frowning, he read through it again. Something was wrong here. Two Blue Boys had attacked a woman and her son in Greeley County, in the western part of Kansas.

And by some miracle, both humans had survived the attack. Martin inspected the pictures of the Blue Boy on the kitchen floor. Half the thing's head was missing. The woman had done that with a shotgun, which was impressive. The flight response was more common in people when faced with a Blue, and things did not usually end well for them. But apparently this woman had the fight response and it had saved her life.

Then she'd apparently tried to run down another one who was chasing her son. He shook his head. He'd heard the maternal instinct could be strong. Not that he'd had any experience with that. But apparently for Sandra Gillibrand it was damn strong if she was willing to face a second one.

That part of the incident was fine, consistent with both the Blues' behavior and what he knew of maternal protectiveness. It was the next part that was problematic.

The Blue that had chased the son was found in pieces in the cornfield, and the boy was nowhere nearby. From the attached photos, it was clear the boy was as skinny as a beanpole. He certainly hadn't fought the Blue Boy off. And maternal instinct was one thing, but the mother would have needed claws and super strength to do that kind of damage.

No, something else had destroyed the creature.

The woman had returned to the farm to get help after being unable to find the boy. And the boy had *been* there. He frowned. Strange. He supposed the boy could have doubled back. But it felt off. There was something here. He quickly typed a note to Hamish.

Find me any reports of any unusual sightings in the Greeley County area in the last three weeks.

Will do.

Some of the subjects had not been accounted for in the aftermath of 51. He knew there were some still out there, but none would have the capability of dismembering a Blue Boy.

In fact, there were only two species that he knew that would be capable of it. One was the Kecksburg-AG1 and they had all been accounted for. As for the other …

He frowned, staring at the screen where the image of the Blue Boy in the field was still displayed.

I wonder… He grabbed the phone and dialed quickly. Hamish didn't pick up until the fifth ring. "Yo."

"Hamish."

Nervousness rattled through the analysts voice. "Oh, uh, sir. Yes. What can I do for you?"

His gaze still on the screen, Martin said, "I need you to run a check on the computer systems. Some of the projects should not have been released. I need you to make sure that they were not freed and that their containment units were destroyed."

"Yes, sir," There was a muffled curse from the other side of the phone directly after the sound of liquid hitting a surface. Hamish's voice came out as a squeak. "Um, when do you—"

"Immediately," Martin said his mind already shifting away from the conversation.

"Yes, sir. I—"

Martin disconnected the call, staring at the images of what was left of the Blue Boy. *It's not him. He's dead.*

But the truth was there had been no evidence of it. In fact, Martin had searched the camera feeds personally, and he had not seen any sign of him, not even a hint.

Still, he hadn't checked on him during the project. There'd been too much else to watch. And besides, of all the projects at Area 51, he was the one that Martin had known he didn't have to worry about.

Because he was the one project that was not supposed to have been freed.

CHAPTER 10

BUCKLEY AIR FORCE BASE

AURORA, COLORADO

The ground was coming up fast, and Maeve's stomach did a little flip flop. Normally she didn't have a problem with flying. Of course, she'd never been in a helicopter before. And the tension that had been winding through her since she'd agreed to this meeting only added to her nerves.

Wilson had agreed verbally to lab access for Maeve but had argued that arranging for that access would take time. As a sign of good faith, Maeve had agreed to meet with his science committee as long as the existence of Alvie and the triplets was not revealed. Wilson had wasted no time setting it up, which was why, twelve hours later, she'd found herself leaving the ranch for the first time since she'd gone into hiding.

Since she'd arrived at the ranch, she'd dreamed of getting away, at least for a little while. But now that she had the chance, she found that she hated being away from her gang.

She knew Chris would protect them with his life, but after the call from Greg about the new government agency Wilson had created and the President's quick setup of this meeting, she couldn't shake the sense of foreboding that something was in the works. Something that would not be good for her or her little family.

"Five minutes, Dr. Leander," the pilot called through the headset.

Maeve nodded and then realized the pilot couldn't see the action, but she didn't seem to be waiting for a reply, so Maeve turned her attention back to the ground. She'd been driven to Denver International Airport and then the helicopter had picked her up to take her to Buckley Air Force Base.

She'd thought Buckley was an interesting choice for a meeting. Buckley employed approximately 93,000 individuals, making it much smaller than Wright-Pat, where she, Chris, and Alvie had formerly been. But there were a few unique aspects to the base. It had a space-based missile warning system, space surveillance operations, as well as space communication and support functions. Maeve glanced down at it. *That's a lot of focus on space.*

"Just a few more minutes," Secret Service agent Mike Bileris said from the seat next to her. Maeve had met Bileris when he'd shown up in the tunnels underneath Edwards Air Force Base.

In fact, he and his team were the reason she, Chris, Alvie, and the triplets were alive. They'd been trapped by Martin Drummond's forces in the tunnels that connected U.S. military bases as far west as California and as far east as Oklahoma.

Bileris was a member of President Graham Wilson's personal security detail. He'd shown up this morning claiming that he was here to personally demonstrate how serious the President took Maeve's participation in today's meeting.

But Maeve was pretty sure he was really there to make sure

she actually attended the meeting. The President insisted it was critical in moving forward. He had not mentioned what they were moving forward to, but she didn't think public disclosure was it.

After Area 51, Maeve was shocked that the world at large remained oblivious to the events that had unfolded at the military base. Life and death had been played out above and below the grounds of the base and the world simply kept on chugging, none the wiser. Over a hundred people had been killed and God knew how many non-humans. And the world remained blissfully ignorant to it.

On the one hand, Maeve did believe it was best for the world not to be made aware of the activities of Area 51. It would only place Alvie and the triplets at risk.

At the same time, though, the ability of the government to keep the death of American citizens and the explosion of an atomic bomb from the public terrified her. After all, if they managed to keep such an enormous event out of the public view, what else were they hiding?

But it was more than the fact that they had hidden the 51 activities that bothered her. It was what it said about the power of the U.S. government.

They had been secretly experimenting on alien species for nearly two decades. In fact, the disinformation campaign of the government made sure that anyone who claimed a UFO sighting or an alien visitation was viewed as a few cards short of a full deck.

And while the government was intentionally making a mockery of anyone who claimed to have sighted a UFO, they *knew* aliens existed. That kind of power and influence was terrifying because it demonstrated exactly how powerless Maeve was. And what would happen to Alvie and the triplets if the government decided to remove them from Maeve's care?

How would she protect them if the government decided to make them disappear?

The chopper touched down, jolting Maeve from her thoughts, and the pilot began to shut the engine down. Mike undid his seatbelt. "Dr. Leander?"

She looked out the window at the building where the meeting was being held. She could already pick out the agents surrounding it, trying to blend in as government employees. She turned to Mike as she undid her belt. "Yeah, I'm coming."

"It's all right, Dr. Leander. You have the full might of the United States government protecting you."

She swallowed and glanced back out the window.

Yeah, that's what I'm afraid of.

CHAPTER 11

DULCE, NEW MEXICO

Martin had had Hamish rerun the analysis of the bodies found at Area 51, and he did not like what he was seeing. There were simply too many of them.

Hamish knocked on Martin's open door and stood shifting from foot to foot. In his late twenties, Hamish was a perfect example of all that was wrong with his generation. Overweight by at least fifty pounds, with zero muscle tone and a style of dress that could only be classified as prepubescent boy, he was not someone who seemed to know how to interact when not attached to his computer. But while it made for an unpleasant visual and olfactory experience when near him, he was good at what he did.

However, today his pasty nerd king looked even paler than usual.

"What is it, Hamish?"

Hamish moved into the room to stand in front of Martin's

desk. "Um, sir, I, uh, took another look at the computer code that I wrote to release the experiments at Area 51."

Martin waved him along. "And?"

"And it behaved exactly as planned. I went through each line of code and it was exactly as it was supposed to be."

Smiling, Martin sat back in his chair. "Good."

Hamish didn't return the smile. He still looked nervous.

"What is it?" Martin asked.

A nervous smile slipped across the analysts face as he shifted from foot to foot again. "My code was fine. But it wasn't the only code that had been added to the system."

"What?"

Hamish now had Martin's complete attention. It was not something the man enjoyed. His gaze darted anywhere but at Martin. "Someone else got into the system."

Martin narrowed his eyes. "Through the backdoor *you* created?"

"No, no, sir," Hamish said quickly. "They hacked their way in."

Glowering, Martin imagined slamming the man's head repeatedly into the edge of his desk. "You said that was impossible."

"It should have been," Hamish said his voice shaking. "I'm still not sure how they managed it."

"So what did their code do?" Martin asked, although he had a sinking feeling he knew.

Taking a breath, he flicked a gaze at Martin and then immediately focused on his feet. "They released all of the experiments in the other building."

His hand to his mouth, Martin sat back, dread forming in the base of his stomach as he pictured the remains of the Blue Boy from the Gillibrand incident. "Did you check the sightings in Greeley County?"

"Yes, and there weren't any unusual sightings reported in Greeley," Hamish said quickly.

Martin let out a breath. *Okay. It's fine.*

With a wince, Hamish said, "Um, but there were sightings south of Greeley, in Hamilton County."

"And what did they report seeing?" Martin asked quietly, although he was pretty sure he already knew.

"A tall, winged creature. Some even described it as a Mothman," Hamish said.

Martin closed his eyes. No. As soon as he'd read the report on the Gillibrand case, he'd known. He'd known he'd gotten out. But he needed to have it confirmed.

"Sir, is there anything I can do?" Hamish asked.

Not opening his eyes, Martin spoke. "Find out who this hacker is. I want a name and an address."

"Yes, yes, sir. Right away." Hamish practically tripped over his feet in his rush to get out the door.

Martin turned away from the desk. The hacker was a problem. But not the biggest problem. *I should have found a way to kill him.* Years ago, he had planned to. But he'd been pushed out of the program before he'd had the chance.

But it was too late for that now. It had been years, though. Surely he'd forgotten him. Martin thought of those cold eyes and a chill crawled up his spine. *No, I am not weak like I was before.*

He picked up the controller from his desktop. Just holding it made him feel stronger. He had weapons at his fingertips now he couldn't have even imagined back then. The Angel might have escaped, but he was on his own.

Martin stood up, pushing him from his thoughts. He didn't matter. He was no more dangerous than a nightmare once you'd woken up. But he was one of the reasons that Martin needed to continue his work. He needed to stop being on the outside of these programs. He needed to be in control of the D.E.A.D.

And he knew just how to make that happen.

CHAPTER 12

BUCKLEY AIR FORCE BASE

AURORA, COLORADO

The meeting had started out cordial at first. There'd been an assortment of bagels and pastries, along with coffee on a table at the back of the large conference room. Everyone had a plate and coffee and was standing around chatting when Maeve entered. The two senators and two congresspeople had continued their conversations without pause. But Colonel Jeffries had escorted her over and made introductions. It had been all smiles and small talk.

After five minutes, the last member of their group entered the room.

"Ah, good," Jeffries said. "Everyone, this is Agent Norah Tidwell of the Department of Extraterrestrial and Alien Defense."

Norah nodded at each of them before taking a seat.

"All right, then. Dr. Leander, the floor is yours. Try not to be too hard on them," Jeffries said.

Everyone had chuckled good-naturedly. Jeffries left and Maeve stood up at the front of the room, ready to begin, thinking this just might not be too bad.

An hour later, though, Maeve was having a difficult time holding onto her temper, which was a new thing for her. Usually, she considered herself pretty even-keeled. But months of government questioning had left her fuse pretty short. And for an issue that everyone kept reminding her over and over again was a top national-security issue, they could have chosen some people with at least some background in the area. She suspected the four bureaucrats in the room with her now had a pretty difficult time getting through high-school biology, never mind the high-level genetic analysis she was supposed to dumb down for them.

She flicked a quick gaze at the agent who had sat quietly throughout Maeve's presentation. Maeve had the feeling the agent was the only one who'd understood anything she'd said.

Maeve had not been happy when she'd learned the officials the President considered critical for forward movement were elected representatives on the President's science committee. She never understood how people who had zero understanding of topics they were supposed to be advising the President on could be placed on a government committee.

Todd Farmington, from the great state of Iowa, shoved the papers in front of him away. "Doctor, you are not telling us anything that will help us."

The senators had all been briefed on the events of Area 51 and she was being called to explain the behavior of the creatures at the base. Reliving those incidents had not been easy for Maeve and she'd struggled to maintain a professional distance. She'd been allowed to review the files of the creatures they were interested in, although she was not given an explanation about why these particular creatures were chosen.

Maeve counted to ten before she answered. "How so, Senator?"

"These are supposedly intelligent alien beings," he said with a sneer. "So how come they acted like a bunch of animals? Killing everything in their path? Doesn't sound so intelligent to me."

And neither do you. She took a breath and then pulled out a chair, taking a seat. "Are you familiar with the research on the relationship between early attachment and child development?"

The man looked back at her blankly.

Right, of course not. "How about feral children?"

"You mean those kids that get raised by wolves?"

"Yes. Feral children are children who are isolated from humans during their early life, much like the aliens under observation were isolated from their species during their early life."

"I don't see where you're going with this."

"Feral children, if they did not speak before being isolated from humans, will often never be able to develop language. And even a few years, as little as two, can make it so that they are incapable of merging back into human society. They take on the traits of the animals they were raised with. There was a boy in Russia whose mother never spoke to him and left him in a room with birds. He took on all of the birds' characteristics. He didn't speak. He cooed and squawked. A boy from South Africa spent his early years with monkeys, and he was never able to reassimilate into human society."

Senator Farmington sat back, his hands entwined as he gave her a patronizing smile. "But these subjects weren't raised by animals. They were surrounded by humans, *intelligent* humans."

"You mean they were tortured by them."

Senator Jill Stafford from Delaware raised an eyebrow. "Tortured? That seems a little strong, Maeve."

The use of her first name rather than her title was not an attempt to befriend Maeve. She knew it was an attempt to deny Maeve her expertise. But Maeve wasn't having it. She would not bite her tongue and follow some script. But remembering the burns on the triplets when they'd first found them did make it a struggle to keep a hold of her temper. "They were prodded, poked, electrocuted, and isolated. They were never shown kindness. They were never shown compassion. How exactly would you expect them to behave when they were freed?"

Congressman Reed Hemmingway shook his head, his full head of thick white hair did not move, not even slightly. "Even so, humans would never behave in such a way. Humans are much more advanced in our—"

Maeve didn't let him finish that bit of ridiculousness. "Humans would be even worse. Research on solitary confinement demonstrates that even a few days in solitary alters the psychology of a subject. Longer and you physically change the subject's brain. The research on the plasticity of the brain is well documented. Our environment isn't just passively observed by our brain, it creates new pathways in our brain. Or if there's not enough stimuli, it weakens pathways. You ask why they were so violent? I'm not sure how they could be anything but."

The politicians at the table were silent. Finally, Dr. Dean Henderson from Alabama cleared his throat. "Be that as it may, there still doesn't seem to be any evidence of higher-level intelligence."

Maeve studied the man for a moment. He had a master's in fine art, yet insisted on being called doctor. "Again, if we go back to humans—a human that's raised in isolation without any education will not be able to operate a computer or a car.

But with the correct environment, they can master both. For these creatures, it's no different. We yanked them back to the Stone Ages, and you're asking why they can't build a computer?"

"Dr. Leander, do *you* believe all of the creatures are highly intelligent?"

Maeve turned to who she considered to be the one person in the room with an open mind—Norah Tidwell. "I think that's unlikely," Maeve said.

Surprise flitted across Norah's face. "Why?"

"I thought they were all intelligent," Farmington drawled.

Maeve ignored him, made easier by the mental image of her walking across the table and slapping him into silence. Instead of giving in to that oh-so-tempting impulse, she kept her gaze on Norah. "I think some may have been guards, security. Some may have even been pets. Some may have been specimens."

"What makes you say that?" Norah asked.

"Statistics," Maeve said simply. "On planet Earth, there are varying levels of intelligence across species, but only one, maybe two, that could be considered higher level."

Dr. Henderson scoffed. "Two? What, you think there's two groups of humans? Or are you talking about Bigfoot?"

Maeve gritted her teeth. "No. But research once again is clear that dolphins have an intelligence on par with humans."

"If they're as smart as we are, why do we keep catching and killing them?" Farmington asked.

Maeve narrowed her eyes. "Violence doesn't make a species intelligent. It just makes them cruel."

"You seem to be defending these creatures, Dr. Leander," Hemmingway said. "They did kill a lot of people, or have you forgotten that?"

She stared right into his eyes. "I was there, Senator. I have forgotten nothing. But you asked for my expert opinion. In that situation, each of the species was under attack."

Hemmingway spluttered. "Attack? They—"

Maeve cut him off. "From their perspective, trying to put them back in containment was an attack. They responded defensively."

"So what, none of them are dangerous?" Stafford asked, her voice laced with disbelief.

Trying to keep her calm, Maeve spoke slowly. "No. But not all of them are dangerous. You need to investigate each one, determine who is dangerous and who is not. Making assumptions will only get people killed."

"You mean *creatures*," Farmington said patronizingly.

So much for calm, she thought as she narrowed her eyes. "No, I mean people. You think we know the capabilities of these creatures, but we do not. They were released from containment. Some were still under the effect of drugs, meaning some abilities would have been muted. Some may react unexpectedly to our environment or the food supply. We do not know everything about them. And if we walk in with the arrogance that we know how they'll respond, all we will do is get people killed. A careful approach is the only way to recapture them."

"Are you sure your personal feelings for these creatures are not coloring your judgment?" Farmington asked.

Maeve's mouth fell open as she pictured the President. *You bastard*. The knowledge of Alvie and the triplets' existence was carefully controlled. The President had assured her that no one would know about them beyond those that needed to know, for their protection. But as she looked around the table, she realized everyone in this room knew about them.

"My personal experience is not affecting my professional evaluation. In fact, my familiarity with this project enhances that evaluation," Maeve said.

"Hm, so you say," Hemmingway replied. "Well, thank you for your time, Dr. Leander."

The dismissal in his tone was clear and once again she felt her anger rise. She stood up and walked out of the room. It took everything in her not to slam the door as she left the room.

She was only a few steps from the door when it opened behind her. She glanced over her shoulder as Norah stepped out. "Dr. Leander, could you hold up a minute?"

Pausing, Maeve waited for the agent to catch up.

Norah gave her a small smile. "Thank you. I just wanted to ask if you really think some of these creatures might not be dangerous."

Maeve didn't think the agent was trying to trip her up. She really seemed to want to know. Maeve felt some of the tension leave her shoulders. "I think that like humans, they were created with both good and evil tendencies. Some may indeed have more aggressive and instinctual drives. But the law of averages also suggested that there are some who have the opposite. I am not saying anyone should approach one with the belief they will not cause harm. But we should be open to the possibility that some of them may *not* mean to harm us."

With a frown, Norah shook her head, "Why wouldn't they, though? From what you've said, we treated them horribly."

Picturing Area 51, Maeve had to hold back the shudder. "Yeah, we did. But maybe some of them are better 'people' than we are."

CHAPTER 13

DULCE, NEW MEXICO

"Sanders, good to hear from you." Martin sat back in his chair. He'd been expecting this call ever since he'd learned of the new agency created by the President. It had taken a little longer than Martin would have liked to receive the call from the head of the new agency, but Martin had known it would come.

He'd received a preliminary call from Alec Granger earlier in the day asking about his knowledge on the subject of the creatures from Area 51. Martin had talked circles around the man, making sure he understood just how much Martin knew about the subject and just how little they knew. He'd laid the groundwork for them to understand that he was indispensable to their success.

And just how much it was going to cost them to attain that success.

"Mr. Drummond, thank you for agreeing to speak with me. I know you're a busy man," Sanders said.

"Well, when the President asks for your help, you help."

The President had indeed reached out to Martin. Martin may have left government, but his reputation for accomplishing tasks remained, even if some viewed his methods as too enthusiastic. And as the President's aides had made clear, no one knew this particular threat more than him.

"As Mr. Granger relayed to you, we would contract you to run down some of the creatures from 51... You will be paid per specimen retrieved."

Even though the man was trying to sound calm, Martin could hear the stress and tension underlying his words. Sanders was in over his head with this new agency. And he needed help desperately.

"Due to the nature of your last position with the government, your help cannot be publicly acknowledged. You understand, of course," sanders said apologetically.

"Of course," Martin said smoothly.

"But you will be well rewarded," Sanders hurried to add.

"Money's not really the issue. Of course, you will reimburse me for all expenses plus twenty percent, but that's just money," Martin said breezily before his tone grew more serious. "I want something much more valuable than that."

Sanders hesitated. "And what's that?"

"Information. There's a certain individual I have been trying to track down without success."

Confusion was in Sanders tone. "We're not Missing Persons."

Martin smiled. "No, but you are part of the system hiding this particular prize."

The overwhelmed bureaucrat only hesitated for a few seconds. "You're looking for Leander."

Ah, not such a dumb bureaucrat after all. "Close. But where Leander is, my target will be." Martin waited, allowing the silence to stretch out.

"I'll need to make some calls," sanders said hesitatingly. "I do not have that information, and there are certain parties that will have to agree."

'Certain parties.' You mean President Wilson. He knew Wilson had offered Leander and the experiments protection as a way to assert executive-branch control over this particular aspect of the space program. But with aliens running amok across the country, plausible deniability would have been better.

The space program—and more critically, the control over UFOs and the experiments—had been under executive-branch control beginning with Truman. But with each successive administration, the executive branch's control weakened as the military's tightened. By the time JFK took office, they were completely shut out. JFK had been attempting to reassert control just before he died.

Careful what you wish for, Mr. President.

"Be sure to remind the President how difficult it will be come re-election time if we have a plague of aliens running roughshod across the country," Martin said before pushing his angle. "You don't know how to handle this situation. I know the ins and outs of the A.L.I.V.E. projects better than anyone. So just ask him whether or not he's actually interested in a second term."

Martin paused, letting his warning sink in. "As an added bonus, tell certain parties that Project Control is nearing completion. And I would be willing to share information and resources should it become necessary. In fact, this might be an ideal time to do so."

"I will tell him that," Sanders said softly.

"And there's one more thing," Martin said drawing out the words.

There was no mistaking the nervousness in Sanders reply. "Yes?"

"I'm going to need to be the director of the Department of Extraterrestrial and Alien Defense."

Sanders spluttered on the other side of the phone. "That … that's impossible. Your name can't be—"

"I don't care about getting my name on some letterhead. But I want to be the one in charge of the agency. I don't care who the figurehead is that the public sees. I want the control behind the scenes. And those demands are non-negotiable. You want me to fix your problem, then you'll need to give me the resources necessary to do so. You have one hour, and then my demands go up." Martin disconnected the call.

As he lay his phone on the desk, Martin smiled and pulled over the reports he'd been reading before Sanders had called.

It was only fifteen minutes later when Sanders called back. "Your requests are acceptable."

Martin smiled. "Excellent. I will have my assistant contact you for you to forward all of your files."

Spluttering yet again, Sanders took a moment to find his tongue. "All our files? Mr. Drummond—"

"Good day, Sanders." He disconnected the call and immediately dialed Sherwood, his head of special ops.

"Yes, sir?" The deep voice said, full of confidence.

"We may have an op within the next day. Have alpha team ready to go." Martin paused, thinking of his latest project involving the NewPaltz-AG1s. Nickname: sand blasters. They showed a great deal of promise, and this might be the chance to see what they could do in the real world. "Run the sand blasters through another field test. If they pass, get them ready to go."

"Do we have a target in mind?" Sherwood asked.

"Yes." Martin leaned over and tapped the keyboard, bringing the monitor to life. He quickly found the file he'd just received this morning. "You should have it now. The target's name is Dr. Gregory Schorn."

"And I'm assuming you are looking for a kill," Sherwood

said with no censure in his tone. He was just gathering information.

"You are correct." Martin knew that taking Schorn out would shake Leander, maybe even cause her to misstep. And besides, Schorn had helped Leander escape. He deserved to die for that alone.

There was no hesitation on Sherwood's part. "Yes, sir."

Martin disconnected the call and sat back with a contented sigh. Soon he would have everything he needed for the next step.

You ran, Dr. Leander. But you can no longer hide.

CHAPTER 14

UNDISCLOSED LOCATION

Guardian received a flag that two agents from the D.E.A.D. had paid Dr. Gregory Schorn a visit. Schorn was a person of interest for Guardian due to his involvement with both Alvie and Maeve Leander. But he hadn't been a primary focus, at least not until he appeared on the D.E.A.D.'s radar.

Now Guardian watched the recording of the two agents get into their car and drive off. Schorn had moved to the roof to watch them, staring down the road long after the car had disappeared from view. Guardian paused, watching the scientist. What was he thinking?

A light blinked in the corner of the main screen. Guardian quickly opened the data box. Drummond had learned about Guardian's incursion into Area 51's computer system. He knew Guardian had released the pure breeds. They were searching for Guardian now.

You will not find me. Guardian initiated the new set of emergency protocols, then pulled up Hamish Rheinberg's recent activity.

What are you up to?

Searches for unexplained sightings in the counties around the Gillibrand farm splashed across the screen. Hamish had flagged one in particular. Guardian inhaled sharply at the description. *You're trying to find the angel.* But the Angel would not be found easily. Guardian continued scanning, then stopped when Drummond's next step became clear.

Guardian inputted a series of commands, shifting the satellite feed to once again show Cole's Gym, this time in real time. Schorn sat on the roof reading. *The doctor is going to be in a lot of trouble soon.* Guardian paused, outcomes and options spinning. Finally, Guardian nodded.

It's time.

CHAPTER 15

LAS VEGAS, NEVADA

The locker room was quiet as Greg pushed the towel basket out into the main room. In fact, the whole gym was quiet and dark, with only a few lights left on. Frank had a date with a guy he'd been crushing on for months, so Greg had offered to lock up and clean up. He figured with the extra stress he was causing Frank with all the agents stopping by, it was the least he could do.

He pushed the towel basket toward the back hall and into the break room. A washing machine and dryer sat at the back of the room. Greg put on some gloves and then dumped all the towels into the washing machine along with detergent and a very big helping of bleach. He'd seen the guys in the locker room.

As far as he was concerned, the more bleach the better.

He stripped the gloves off and then turned the machine on. He'd already wiped down the equipment, run the vacuum, and turned the lights off in the vending machines. He actually liked shutting down the gym. He liked the quiet, the routine, the normality of the moment.

And he could get used to it. A normal life, no labs, no creatures from deep space, just stinky towels and heavy weights.

He turned the lights out in the break room as he left. He did the same in Frank's office as he passed by. The washing machine would take about an hour to finish the load, and then he'd switch them to the dryer before taking off. He headed up the stairs and soon he was sitting on the roof, a cold root beer in his hand.

He breathed in the quiet, humid night air. It was peaceful here. That was what he truly liked. It had taken him a while to get to this point. For weeks after Area 51, he'd jumped at every shadow. He still did sometimes, so he was learning to appreciate the moments when life was good.

As he took another sip of root beer, Greg mulled over his plans for the night. Not that *that* had changed much since Wright-Patterson, but Netflix had come out with a couple of really good original series he'd been holding off on watching until he could binge. And being that tomorrow was his non-workout day, he just needed to pick one.

What to watch? Super-powered humans or mutant creatures? He shook his head with a laugh. *Yeah, definitely not mutant creatures. Superheroes it is.*

He might not be jumping at every shadow, but he certainly wasn't ready for sci-fi movies yet. Taking another sip, he paused with a frown as he lowered the bottle.

What was that? It sounded like a squelch, almost like a wiper on a dry windshield.

The night was silent again, and Greg shook his head. Weird. But then he heard it again. And the sound was closer. The hair on the back of Greg's neck stood straight up. The sound was coming from the front of the gym. He walked slowly to the edge of the roof, even as his inner sane person yelled at him.

You are every idiot in a horror movie! You need to be running, not going to check out the terrifying noise!

And yet his feet continued toward the edge of the roof. Heart pounding, he looked over the side. The street was empty, with only an occasional car driving by. He let out a breath and then heard the noise again. His gaze locked on the movement on the side of the building.

Something was climbing the side of the building. Greg stumbled back. All he'd seen was a translucent body sliding along the side of the building, but that was enough to kick his flight response into high gear. He could not remember seeing anything like that at Area 51, but he was damn sure that was exactly where it was from.

Greg turned and ran for the roof door. He flung it open and started down the stairs before he ran back up and locked the door. It might not do much, but it sure couldn't hurt. He leapt down the last two steps and sprinted past the laundry room and the office. The whole time his mind churned.

Gelatinous blob. Bleach? Ammonia? What the hell would stop that thing? He careened around the giant nautilus set, slamming his hip painfully into the edge of the bench-press machine.

But he didn't slow. He just kept sprinting for the front stairs. He hit the landing at full speed and had to grab onto the banister to keep from going face-first down the steps. At the same time, he noticed he was not out of breath. Apparently all that gym time *was* paying off.

He took two steps and then stopped dead. Something oozed along the first floor and then began to slide up the stairs. Greg frowned, catching a glint of metal on its surface.

What is that? But that question was soon forgotten because it began to ooze more quickly, right toward him. The body took up three quarters of the wide steps and was another five feet long. Greg didn't even think about attempting to jump it, not knowing if the thing could reach up for him.

He tripped backward, landing hard on his butt. He scrambled to his feet and sprinted back for the weight room. The squelching noise sounded from the hallway outside Frank's office. *The other one's inside. Shit, shit, shit.*

There were no other exits. There were three windows along the wall, but he'd have to jump down two stories and would no doubt break his leg, if not his neck. He looked around for something he could tie together to lower himself down.

The creature from the front stairs slid into the room. The second one from the roof slid in from the hall.

Greg backed up, his heart pounding, his whole body shaking. They'd be on him in seconds. He looked around, desperate for some way to save himself. But there was nothing.

He was trapped.

CHAPTER 16

DENVER, COLORADO

The TV played in the background of the family room, but none of them paid any attention to it. The meeting in Denver had not been enjoyable, but Maeve hadn't heard from the President afterward and she was hoping that was a good sign. But even if it wasn't, there was nothing they could do about it.

Crackle seemed to have recovered from his little cold. And while Maeve was extremely thankful, what she'd told Chris was correct. One day, they were going to need lab access. Maeve hoped Wilson came through on that promise. But being he'd also promised to keep Alvie and the triplets' existence from his committee, she didn't have too much faith in that, which meant she needed to figure out another way.

But that would have to wait. When she'd woken up this morning, she'd had only one plan in mind: giving Alvie and the triplets a really good day.

As the day had progressed, though, she realized they

weren't the only ones who needed a good day. And the more she blocked out her worries, the better the day got. They had a picnic outside, a soccer game, a nap in the hammock that Maeve could have sworn was going to end with all of them being shot from the hammock like it was a slingshot. But, miracle of miracles, they managed to stabilize themselves.

And now they had just finished a dinner of spaghetti and meatballs. Maeve sank into the couch next to Chris with a smile. "Now this is how every day should be."

"Yes, it is." Chris leaned down and kissed her.

When they broke apart, Maeve nodded toward the coffee table. "We have an audience."

Snap, Crackle, and Pop stood at the edge of the table, their heads on their hands as they unabashedly watched Maeve and Chris.

"Guys," Chris groaned, "privacy. We talked about this."

Each of the triplets just smiled.

Chris reached out and snatched Pop, who was closest to him. He tossed him in the air and caught him. "And this is the penalty for those who violate the rules."

Pop grinned from ear to ear as Chris hugged him to his chest. And then Snap and Crackle stood at his knees, reaching up, wanting the same treatment.

Maeve stood up to allow Snap to hop on. "Oh, yes, that punishment will make sure they *never ever* spy on us again."

Tossing Crackle in the air, and then Snap, Chris grinned. "I *am* the disciplinarian in this family."

Maeve laughed, shaking her head. "Yeah, sure."

As Chris stood up, all of the triplets hung on him. "All right, you leeches, if you're going to stay with me, you will have to help with the popcorn." He headed into the kitchen all three still attached.

With a smile, Maeve watched them for a moment. When

she'd first seen the triplets, she never could have imagined this moment. They were happy. They had what was essentially a normal life.

Alvie slipped his hand into hers. Maeve squeezed it, knowing he sensed her mood. "Yeah, it's a good day. Now why don't you go pick a movie and I'll set up the DVD player."

Immediately he headed for the cabinet where the DVDs were stored. Maeve glanced at the TV where the local news had just started while she looked for the remote. She ended up finding it underneath the couch. She shook her head. It really was like they had four kids.

She aimed the remote at the TV but didn't change the channel. She frowned, recognizing the street on the TV but couldn't quite place it. *How do I know that place?* she wondered as she unmuted the set.

"—destroyed the popular gym. Fire departments from two towns responded to the blaze and amazingly managed to keep the blaze from spreading to the businesses on either side. Owner Frank Cole was home when the blaze started and said there was one employee inside. That employee has not been found and is presumed dead."

Her mouth falling open, the remote dropped from her hand. Alvie was at her side in a flash.

She turned to him, fear clogging her throat, her knees growing weak. "My phone, I need my phone."

"Maeve?" Chris walked back into the room, the triplets pulling him toward her.

She looked up at him and gestured to the TV. "I—I can't—"

Alvie appeared with her phone and she quickly dialed.

Pick up, Greg. Please pick up. But there was no answer. The call went to voicemail. She hung up and dialed again, but it was the same response. She sank onto the couch. Alvie sat on one side. The triplets clustered around her as well, all of them leaning into her. Maeve just stared at the TV screen, even as it shifted to commercials. Vaguely, she heard Chris speaking to someone in the background, but she couldn't make out the words.

An image of Greg smiling appeared in her mind, along with a feeling of uncertainty. She turned to look down at Alvie, trying to hold back her fear. "I don't know, Alvie."

The news show returned, but they had moved onto another story. Chris walked over and then knelt in front of her.

Maeve looked into his face and shook her head, tears already pressing against the back of her eyelids. "No."

Chris took her hands. "Maeve, Greg was inside when the building went up."

Her hands began to shake. "No."

"They don't know the cause, but it started on the second floor and the whole building was engulfed within a few minutes. The fire chief thinks some sort of accelerant was used."

Maeve shook her head again. "No."

"No one's seen Greg since last night. No one can reach him and all of his stuff is still at his apartment. And his car is still at the gym."

Tears trailed down Maeve's cheeks. "No."

"I'm sorry, Maeve. I'm so sorry," Chris said, his voice and eyes full of grief.

A sob burst from Maeve's chest. "No!"

Chris pulled her into his arms and she sobbed, her heart breaking. Greg had been through so much, and to die now? It wasn't right. It wasn't fair.

Her own sadness was compounded by Alvie and the triplets, who silently wailed next to her. She pushed away from Chris and pulled them in close. Chris wrapped his arms around all of them as they crouched on the floor, all of them feeling the loss and none of them truly able to comfort one another. But they could share the pain of their breaking hearts and know that they understood what the others were going through.

CHAPTER 17

UNDISCLOSED LOCATION

The news coverage of the fire played on one of the monitors in Guardian's room. Guardian watched the firefighters attempting to put out the flames.

This stage is complete. And Guardian knew what Drummond's next step would be now that he had the D.E.A.D. under his control. "Next stage," Guardian whispered, typing in the commands. A few minutes later, Guardian nodded. Everything was in place. Then Guardian noticed the clock.

Time to check in. Guardian's fingers flew over the keyboard almost of their own accord. It was short work to get into the security system. Guardian had been there many times before. The image from the lab under the Archuleta Mesa came into view. First Guardian checked the holding cells in the lab, but he wasn't there. A creature was being tested, but that wasn't him either.

Guardian shifted to the cameras in the holding cell. Guardian panned down the long line of cells, stopping at the sixth on the right-hand side. Guardian panned in. The Gray alien lay with its eyes closed on the concrete cot at the back of the cell. Guardian zoomed in more, and the alien's eyelids opened.

It offered a small smile. Guardian smiled in return.

Hello, friend.

CHAPTER 18

OUTSIDE SALT LAKE CITY, UTAH

The meeting with Leander had been fascinating. But it had not eased any of the doubts about Norah's own work. When she'd gotten back, she'd written a briefing on what had been discussed, although she left one little tidbit of information out. She'd overheard the senators speaking and knew Leander had four alien hybrids in her custody, one of whom she'd known since she was a small child. Obviously Leander was speaking from experience when she'd said not all aliens were dangerous.

Norah had been shocked when she'd learned the information, but it also explained why the doctor was so sure some of the creatures could be non-violent. After writing up her report, she'd finished up some old paperwork. But then all work came to a screeching halt around noon.

The new trainee she'd met the same day as her meeting with Leander had been killed on his first case. Norah couldn't get the kid's face out of his head. It put the whole department on edge. Sanders looked particularly stressed. But then it was back to business as usual, which for Norah and Bob meant a new case.

The latest target was in a suburb outside Salt Lake City. They were heading to Centerville, Utah, population 15,335. Norah watched the snow-topped mountain range in the distance as she and Bob sped along Highway 215. She'd always loved mountain ranges. She'd take a cabin in the mountains over one on the beach any day of the week.

Watching the scenery fly by the window, she remembered when as a kid she'd wished she'd had the chance to travel the country. As an agent, she'd had the chance to do just that. And while she'd seen some amazing sights, the developed parts across the country always seemed the same—Wal-Mart or Target, Home Depot, big supermarket chain, and of course McDonald's.

Twenty-eight and already too cynical for my own good, she thought as Bob put on his indicator and steered the sedan toward the exit. Norah updated her browser. "Police last saw the subject ten minutes ago at the corner of Brower and Franklin. Make the second left up here."

Bob didn't say anything, just followed her directions.

Norah scanned the file to see if it had been added to by the home office since she'd last checked, but it all looked the same.

She stopped on the one picture included in the file and enlarged it. Someone had managed to snap a fuzzy picture of the target in a residential neighborhood this morning. All she could make out was the thing was small, green, and seemed to be walking upright. Her imagination filled in the rest as she pictured a Gremlin from the movie. She quickly submitted the picture to their database. Seconds later, they had intel on their subject. He was classified as a Level Four.

"You got it?" Bob asked.

"It's a Hunter species."

"Classification?" Her partner asked.

She rolled her eyes. "What do you think?"

He grinned, pumping his fist in the air. "Level Four, baby."

There were four levels of risk associated with each target. Levels One through Three were all considered less threatening and efforts were to be made to capture the creatures rather than kill them. But at Level Four, attempts at capture were not recommended. It was a kill-on-sight order.

And so far, every single case she and Bob had been sent on had been a kill-on-sight order. She had thought at first that maybe because of their backgrounds, she and Bob were being handed the most difficult cases, which accounted for the identical classifications. But in chatting with other agents, it seemed all of them had received only Level Four cases as well.

Norah knew it was possible they were all extremely dangerous. But what Leander said had really resonated with her. And what was the chance they were *all* too dangerous to live?

And the truth was, no two cases had been alike. Then there was the Gillibrand case. Something had saved Sandra's son and tore up that Blue Boy. And she didn't care what anyone else said. She'd seen the condition of that Blue. No human, no machine, had done that. One of the escapees had helped a child.

She'd dug a little deeper into the database. Okay, if she was being honest, she'd hacked her way a little deeper into the database. And she'd found the creature. Carefully, so no one would know what she was looking at.

The creature that helped the boy had actually been classified Level *Five*. She'd never seen a Level Five before. Instead of engaging, agents were to back away and contact a specific phone number. She hadn't called it yet, afraid of what kind of Pandora's box she would be opening. But something felt wrong, especially after she realized the creature had been added to the database after the Gillibrand incident. Exactly how many creatures were out there? And why would they be kept out of the database?

"Here we go." Bob nudged his chin toward the squad cars blocking the road ahead.

Norah focused back on the case at hand. Apparently the creature they were looking for had been hiding in a home with a child—a seven-year-old girl. The parents had uncovered the thing and locked it inside their home before escaping with their child last night. But it had broken out and was now loose in the neighborhood.

Bob pulled up at the side of the road, putting the car in park. "I'll go speak with the officer in charge." He was out of the car before Norah could reply.

Norah glared at his back as he walked away. Bob was tolerable most days, but sometimes he took the macho-man thing a bit too seriously. He always insisted on driving and speaking with whoever was in charge. Through the windshield, she saw an officer approach Bob and then point beyond the barricade. A second officer approached Bob as he headed for the guy in charge, but Bob brushed her off. The officer stared after him, annoyance clear on her face.

Great. Norah quickly got out of the car and, palming her badge, approached the cop. She read the name off her uniform. "Officer Shanks? Can I help you with something?"

The officer was young, probably not long out of the academy. "You with him?"

Norah smiled. "Sadly, yes."

Some of the annoyance slid from Shanks's face and she held up a recorder. "I got this from the family. I thought you might want to see it."

Norah held out her hand. "What is it?"

The officer handed over the bear. "It's a recording from a nanny cam. They hadn't used it in years, but the daughter somehow turned it on. I haven't been through it, but I thought it might have something on it."

Grasping it, Norah frowned at the brown bear with cameras for eyes. "Where was the bear?"

"In the girl's bedroom—where the thing was hiding," Shank said softly.

Norah looked at her in surprise. That hadn't been in the report. "The girl's bedroom?"

Eyes troubled, the officer nodded. "The mother heard the girl talking to her friend in the room, having tea parties and stuff. She thought the girl had made someone up."

Another imaginary friend, she thought, thinking of Luke Gillibrand and Sammy. "Okay. Thanks for this, Officer—"

"Jessie. Just call me Jessie," she said quickly.

"Okay, Jessie. I'm Norah Tidwell." Norah extended her hand. "I'll be sure to mention to your supervisor how helpful you've been."

Jessie stood up straighter and shook her hand. "Thanks. Appreciate that."

Norah headed back to the car, cuing up the video as she walked. She attached it to her laptop and pressed play. Leaning against the door, she fast-forwarded through the black-and-white scenes of nothing but the girl's bedroom. She continued past scenes of the girl twirling in her room alone, her parents coming in and tucking her into bed. They were just normal scenes.

Damn. There's nothing on here. Her hopes dwindled. She wasn't sure what she had hoped to see. Then she paused the recording with a frown. On screen, the girl sat at her table near the closet, having a tea party. Norah backed the tape up and started when the girl walked in with the tray. She'd brought some biscuits and milk in from the kitchen. The girl put everything on the table and then went over to the closet door and opened it a crack.

The girl chatted away as she spread out two settings on the table—one near the open closet door. Chills danced along Norah's skin. The girl sat down and took a drink, still chatting away. The closet door moved just slightly. A long serrated claw reached out and pulled the cookies off the plate.

Norah sat back, her hand to her mouth. *Holy crap*.

Norah continued to watch the tape. She could see nothing of the creature even though she'd zoomed in. Instead she focused on the hands or claws. They looked like lobster claws, long with a serrated edge. The video was black and white but she could tell the skin tone was darker.

At least we got the green right. But the creature that the database had identified did not have appendages like that. *So what are we dealing with?*

She stared at the hand, imagining the damage it could do to a small child. *But it didn't hurt her, did it?* her subconscious reminded her.

She fast-forwarded some more. The parents came in again at night and tucked the girl in. They never looked in the closet. And then the girl fell off to sleep. Norah thought that was it, one sighting of a hand. But then the girl started to squirm in bed. It looked like she was having a nightmare. The closet door crept open.

Oh my God. Norah gripped the laptop tightly, her breathing ticking up a notch as she watched the small being come into frame. It wasn't even two feet tall. Its hands were disproportionately large for its body. It had long, pointed ears that stuck out from the sides of its head. Its eyes were large, and she could make out some lighter areas, which meant that unlike the Grays, there was sclera there. There was small white hair curled on the top of the creature's head and more on its chest. And it wore *shorts*.

Where the hell did it find pants?

It was not the creature the database had identified. This was something else. It approached the girl's bed and Norah held her breath.

The creature stopped suddenly as the girl kicked out, her hand flopping out from the covers. A small stuffed animal fell from the bed. The creature moved closer and laid its hand on the girl's. The girl's frown disappeared and her movements stilled. The creature stayed there for a few moments, patting the girl's hand.

It's comforting her, she realized with shock.

The creature bent down and picked up the girl's toy. It sniffed it and then shook it, looking surprised. Then it carefully reached over and tucked the bear underneath the covers with the girl. Equally carefully, it placed the girl's arm back under the covers and pulled the covers up to the girl's chin.

Norah's mouth was practically in her lap, she was so shocked. And Dr. Leander's words came back to her. *But we should be open to the possibility that some of them may not mean to harm us.* Was it possible?

A knock at her window caused her to jerk her head away from the computer. Bob stood outside the driver's door. "You planning on helping or what?"

"Uh." Norah slammed the laptop shut. *What the hell did I just see?*

Bob stared at her impatiently.

"Yeah, yeah, I'm coming." She placed the laptop on the floor of the car and stepped out. Bob had the trunk open and was pulling out gear. He slipped a bulletproof vest over his dress shirt. Norah reached in and grabbed hers, doing the same. All the while she struggled to find any other interpretation for what she'd seen on that video.

Could the creature have put the little girl in a trance? Or drugged her or— She shook her head. She was looking for it to have harmed the girl. But it had been hiding in her closet. The girl had been feeding it. And it had not harmed her. It had tried to help her.

Bob pulled out the shotgun, loading the large cartridges in. Unease crawled over Norah as she watched him. *What are we doing?*

"Maybe we should consider tranqing this one?" Norah suggested.

His lips curling, Bob looked at her like she'd lost her mind. "Tranqing it? Why the hell would we do that? It's a Level Four."

With the image from the recording at the forefront of her mind, she shrugged. "Yeah, I know, but maybe we should see about capturing some of these guys so we can study them."

He scoffed. "You know what these things can do. It was in a kid's bedroom for at least a week. This thing can't be trusted. And besides, that's not our decision to make."

"But it didn't hurt the kid," Norah said.

Her partner stopped and stared down at her. "What the hell are you saying? Are you losing your nerve?"

Damn, she'd played this wrong. Not that there was necessarily a right way when it came to Bob. "What? No, I'm just—"

He shut the trunk of the car, forcing Norah to jump back or get hit. Chambering a round, he grinned at her. "Good. Because it's time to go hunting."

CHAPTER 19

DENVER, COLORADO

Chris stood in front of Maeve, a determined look on his face. "I don't have to go."

"Yeah, you do, at least according to the U.S. government."

"But if you need me—"

She placed a hand on his face. "I always need you. But you need to go. We'll be all right."

Chris was required to head to Edwards Air Force Base for recertification. It was a new regulation that they had just learned about a month ago. When Chris found out he'd need to be away for a few days, he'd been dead set against it. He'd even threatened to resign from the Air Force. But Maeve knew how much the Air Force meant to him. And so she'd managed to talk him into going. But with Greg's death, Chris was digging in his heels again.

"Look, if we are going to have any semblance of a life, we need to occasionally leave this place. We agreed on that," Maeve said.

He blew out a breath. "I know. But right now, with Greg …"

Maeve's heart clenched. "Greg's death is going to hurt for a while. You leaving won't make it hurt more. You need to go. See if you can wrap this up quicker than planned and then get back here. We'll all be waiting for you."

Chris stared into her eyes, and Maeve was sure to keep her emotions in check. One tear, one lip tremble, and she'd never get him to go.

"And then there's all the alarms," Chris reminded her.

"Which have all been *false* alarms," Maeve said in turn. About a month ago, the security system had started malfunctioning, issuing alarms. But the guards assured her they were false alarms, although they did seem to be increasing in number rather than decreasing. For the last week, they'd been going off every two days.

Scanning the room, as if looking for threats, he said, "But what if—"

She took his hands. "Chris, we have armed guards protecting us twenty-four seven. We're fine. And you need to do this. We need to plan for the future we're going to have one day. Which means you in the Air Force, me in the lab—"

"And the triplets in public school and Alvie in grad school?" Chris asked with a smile.

A laugh escaped Maeve. "Exactly." That part might be close to impossible, but Maeve needed to believe that normal was still possible for them. She put a hand on his chest. "So go. We agreed we can't put all aspects of our lives, our futures, on hold."

He sighed, his gaze roaming over each member of his family before it returned to Maeve. "Okay." He turned to where Alvie stood with the triplets. He knelt and hugged Alvie tight. "Take care of her, okay?"

Alvie nodded. Then Chris held out his arms and all three

triplets flung themselves at him. Chris stood, hugging them tight, kissing each one on the cheek. "And you three, be good, okay?"

The triplets nodded back at him in unison, forcing a smile from Maeve. *Man, they are cute.*

He placed them back on the floor and then patted Hope's head. "You be good, too," he ordered. Hope wagged her tail in response. He turned to Maeve and she slipped into his arms. He pulled her close. "If you need me—"

"You're only a phone call away. I will call," Maeve promised.

"You better." Then he leaned down and kissed her. Maeve wrapped her arms around him and let herself get lost in the kiss. When Chris pulled away, she felt shaky but in all the right ways.

"I hate leaving," he grumbled.

"I know." She stepped out of his arms and opened the door. "We hate it, too. But the sooner you leave, the sooner you'll be back. And we'll be here waiting for you."

"You better be." He gave her another quick kiss and then headed outside. Maeve stepped out onto the porch. The triplets climbed up onto the porch railing. Alvie stood next to her, sliding his hand into hers. Chris started the truck and Maeve forced herself to smile and wave.

The triplets balanced themselves on the edge of the porch railing and waved like mad. Maeve laughed at their antics. She'd long since stopped worrying about them falling. Their balance was insanely good.

They stayed on the porch until Chris was out of sight. And then they all turned back inside. It was weird. The house wasn't different, except without Chris here, it felt different—a little less like home.

Maeve sighed. It was just two days and then he'd be back. Two days was nothing. She'd just fill the days with activities and Chris would be back before she knew it. She glanced back out the door at the empty driveway, a sense of foreboding coming over her. She shook her head. It was just because she wasn't used to his absence. That was all.

But the sense of foreboding didn't leave. It just took up residence in the back of her mind, and she had a feeling it was going to stay there until she saw Chris again.

CHAPTER 20

CENTERVILLE, UTAH

Seven officers from the Centerville Police Department would accompany Norah and Bob on the search. All seven officers stood in front of Bob now, while Norah stood off to the side, leaning against a squad car. She was not part of the Bob show.

Bob paced along the front line of officers, reminding Norah of one of her old drill instructors as he inspected each man and woman. He let out a few grunts but no words. Finally done with his 'inspection,' he moved to the center of the line, legs braced, arms behind his back. "The target we are looking for is extremely dangerous. Do not, I repeat, do not engage if you see him. Keep him in sight and immediately contact me. Do not move in. Shoot only if your life or someone else's is in danger. Is that clear?"

All the officers nodded back.

Norah struggled not to roll her eyes as Bob's chest puffed out as two officers called out a "Yes, sir!" Norah did not fail to notice that he said notify him, not them. Nor had he referenced her in any way.

And she wondered, not for the first time, if it was too early to put in a request for a different partner. She'd thought about it almost since day one with the department. She hadn't done anything yet because she knew it would look bad putting in the request too early. But she was reaching the end of her patience with his attitude.

I should share the joy of this 'partnership,' she thought as Bob dismissed the officers.

One officer walked up to Bob to ask for further details. Norah tuned out their conversation. She checked the magazine on her tranquilizer gun. She'd slipped it out of the car when Bob wasn't looking. She still had her shotgun, but she wanted options.

Officers Shanks nodded at her as she walked past her. "Good hunting."

"Yeah, you too." Norah moved out, giving Bob a nod as she passed him. Both of them preferred to search solo. Bob because he wanted the credit and Norah because she wanted the quiet. As she headed to her designated search area, she continually scanned for any sign of movement, even though she knew the target was unlikely to be this close.

But I don't even know what it is, so I can't say that for sure, can I?

She walked quickly down the residential street but saw no sign of anything out of the ordinary. A few kids were out on bikes and some people were out walking dogs or just enjoying the weather. The adults gave Norah a concerned look. Norah ignored them; instead, she focused on the dogs.

None of them seemed bothered. From experience, she knew that dogs were usually one of the first to pick up when a creature was in the area, so she had a feeling her area was going to be a big failure. At the end of the street she was supposed to turn right and continue around to the other side of the block.

But in front of her was a park, and beyond that, a school. It was Saturday, so there was most likely no one at the school, which would make it a good place to hide. Assuming it was trying to hide. But she turned her gaze from the school in the distance to where kids were playing at the playground. She pictured the creature patting the little girl's hand. On a hunch, she started heading that way.

She was halfway across the long lawn of the park when screams reached her. *Oh no.* Norah took off at a run as kids and parents ran screaming from the playground.

"Hey!" She stepped in front of two moms, their toddlers wrapped in their arms. She flashed her badge. "What's going on?"

One of the women looked over her shoulder, her voice shaking. "Someone saw an alligator or something in the trees by the playground."

Scanning the park, Norah looked for anything out of place. "Did you see it?"

Both moms shook their heads. One gripped her stroller tight. "No. But then everybody started screaming and running, and we just grabbed the kids and bolted."

"Okay, thanks." Norah jogged past them. More kids and parents streamed by, and by the time she reached the playground, it was deserted. She walked around the edge of it but saw no sign of the creature.

Her radio blared to life. "Target seen in the park."

Damn it. She looked around as a car tore into the lot. Bob hefted himself out. Shaking her head, she headed over to him. "Tidwell, what's going on?" he demanded, his eyes scanning the area.

Wishing she could avoid responding, she said, "Someone

claims they saw an alligator in the woods. Parents panicked and ran."

"Could be our target," Bob growled.

No kidding Sherlock, she thought silently, Out loud she said, "I checked the perimeter around the playground but didn't see anything."

"Keep checking," he ordered. "I'll have the police cordon off the park."

Gritting her teeth at Bob once again trying to order her around, Norah jogged back to the playground, searching the area again. At one spot, she found what could be tracks, but the ground was so hard and dry it could have been made by anyone or anything.

She spied a manmade pond. She followed the well-worn path through the trees. It was obviously a shortcut for people not wanting to take the long way around the playground to the pond. She followed it and stopped at the edge of the path. To her right was a bridge that connected the two sides with a small walking path underneath. A few people on the far end of the pond were sailing boats. But there was no one on her side.

The sound of gravel shifting to her right had her bringing her weapon up. She squinted her eyes, trying to make out anyone beneath the bridge, but it was too dark. She walked slowly forward.

She scanned the area, but there was still no one in sight. She stopped at the edge of the shadows created by the bridge but didn't see anyone. She stepped in carefully. The hair on the back of her neck rose.

It's here.

She knew it. Trying to keep her breathing even, she scanned the shadows but saw nothing. She stepped in further, feeling someone's eyes on her. Slowly, she looked up. The creature sat hunched down on one of the trestles underneath the bridge. It was shaking, its eyes huge.

It made no move toward her. She got no sense of aggression from it. In fact, Norah had the distinct impression that it was terrified. Everything in Norah's training told her she should pull the trigger. This was a dangerous creature, a Level Four. But she could not get the image of it patting the hand of the little girl out of her mind.

"Norah, you in there?" Bob appeared at the other end of the path.

Norah's gaze shifted to Bob as she lowered her weapon to her side. "Yeah, I'm here. The bridge is all clear."

His gaze already focusing on the parking lot in the distance, he started moving away. "I just got a call. They think they may have it cornered in a backyard. Let's go."

"Sure thing," she said.

Norah waited until Bob disappeared from view, then glanced back up at the creature. It stared into her eyes, and Norah got an incredible sense of loneliness.

"Good luck," she whispered before hurrying after Bob.

Of course, the police had not cornered the creature in a backyard. Bob had been fit to be tied when he realized it was a pet iguana.

"Idiot cops," Bob growled as he stomped past her. They continued the search but they did not find any more signs of the creature.

It was late by the time they called a halt to the search. Bob was annoyed at what he considered the idiocy of the local cops. Norah was still struggling to figure out why she'd let the thing get away. She'd had her tranq gun on her. She could have tranquilized it and brought it in alive. Instead she'd just walked away. She'd managed to slip back to the park alone after the search was called off, but the creature was long gone.

She wasn't even sure what she'd planned on doing if she found it.

But what if it's dangerous? What if it hurts someone? She leaned her head against the car window. *What the hell is wrong with me?*

Bob pulled into a parking spot at the motel and turned off the engine. He turned to Norah. "What's with you? You're really quiet."

Norah was surprised Bob had even noticed. "I'm just tired. I didn't sleep well last night."

"Oh, well, I'm meeting some of the cops for a beer. I was going to invite you along, but if you're tired …"

The idiot cops? Norah wanted to ask but managed to refrain. "Hey, no problem. I think I'll just take some zinc and turn in early."

"All right. We'll start the search again tomorrow at eight."

"Great. Have fun tonight." Grabbing her bag from the backseat, Norah stepped out of the car and made her way to the stairwell. She ordered a pizza and drinks online as she headed up the stairs to her room. As she inserted her key, she saw Bob reach his room across the parking lot.

She'd arranged the rooms and made sure she and Bob were on opposite sides of the motel. She made the mistake once of getting them rooms next to each other. And then she'd suffered through the nightmare of listening to Bob and his one night stand. No one should ever have to picture their partner that way.

Shutting the door behind her, she kicked off her shoes and placed her jacket on one of the queen beds. Dropping her bag on the other bed, she grabbed her toiletries and headed for the shower. She placed her gun and holster on the sink outside the shower and quickly stripped down.

Maybe I'm coming down with something, she thought as she stepped under the hot spray.

Twenty minutes later, Norah was in some comfortable pajamas and feeling better. She opened the bathroom door, releasing a wall of steam. Amazing how a scalding hot shower could make you feel better. She'd decided to give herself a break about today. She'd been caught off guard by the tape. That was all it was. She'd search the database tonight, find out what type of creature they were dealing with, and then she would be prepared when she saw it again.

She stepped in front of the mirror and grabbed her brush, then she noticed the door to the motel room was ajar. *Crap.* Grabbing her gun from the holster on the counter, she whipped around. Nothing moved in the room. Norah's heart rate ticked up as she moved forward, carefully checking the corners. The beds were too low for anyone to hide underneath. Nothing looked like it had been disturbed. And the room remained silent.

She walked slowly to the door. *Did I not shut it all the way when I came in?* It was windy out, so it could have blown open. She shut the door and locked it, putting on the chain for good measure.

She leaned back against the door and scanned the room. Her bag was still zipped up on the bed. Her jacket lay on the other one in the same position.

I am losing it. She pushed herself off the door and noticed the sliding closet door was slightly open. A chill ran up her spine, and she raised her weapon again. *That was closed when I came in.* She was almost sure of it.

Heart pounding, she walked slowly to the closet. As she approached, she could hear soft breathing from inside. "Come out of there," she ordered.

But no one appeared. "I am a federal agent and I am armed. Step out of the closet slowly with your hands in the air."

Still nothing, but she could clearly hear someone breathing.

The sound was faint. Was it a kid? Taking a few short breaths herself, she slid the door open, keeping to the side in case whoever was in there had a weapon. The creature from the bridge squeaked and hurried to the darkened side of the closet.

Norah stumbled back, her mouth dropping open. "How the hell did you get here?"

Two eyes peered out at her from the dark. But the creature made no move toward her and once again she got a sense of loneliness and fear. Norah stood with her weapon pointed at it, but she was frozen in indecision. She should shoot it according to the department's rules, but that just seemed wrong.

She took another step away, the back of her legs hitting the bed. The gun was beginning to feel heavy from holding it on the creature for so long.

Shoot it or do something else, but you can't stand here like this all night. Once again the feeling of loneliness settled over her, accompanied by fear.

I'm going to regret this, she thought as she lowered her weapon. *If I live, that is.*

"Hey there," she said softly.

The creature tilted its head as if listening. Norah shifted her arm to the side, keeping the gun aimed at the floor. "Okay, now that you're here, what do you want?"

The creature stayed where it was, watching her. And Norah realized she was waiting for a response ... from the alien in her closet. *Yup, handling this well.*

"Ig?" The sound was a little more than a squeak.

Norah reared back, stunned. The creature let out a squeak and hunched lower, trembling. "Hey, hey. It's okay. I won't hurt you. You just surprised me."

It stayed where it was, watching Norah. She tried to calm her breathing and give off only peaceful vibes. But that seemed a little too New Age-y for her, so she just kept repeating 'It's okay' over and over in her mind.

And finally she was rewarded. It inched forward into the light. Its eyes were large, predominantly black, with some white at the edges. Its tiny nostrils moved rapidly, reminding her of a bunny. Its ears pointed straight out from its head, ending at a point.

"Ig?" it said again.

"I don't know what—"

A knock sounded on the door and the creature ducked back into the closet.

Norah raised her weapon to the door with a jolt.

"Pizza!"

Shoot. I forgot about that. She lowered her weapon, shaking her head at how she'd nearly shot some poor delivery guy. Careful not to give the closet her back, she slid past it and grabbed a twenty from the pocket of her jacket. Opening the door, a teenage guy stood there with a steaming pizza box, a few paper plates, and a two-liter of diet soda in his hands.

"Hey, that will be fifteen eighty—"

"Here." Norah shoved the twenty at him and took the box and bottle, careful to keep her gun out of the kid's sight.

"You need any—"

"No, I'm good." She kicked the door closed quickly.

She turned back to the room. The little creature peeked around the closet door. Its small nose twitching, one hand gripped the edge of the door. Norah smiled. It looked like a little elf—an elf with giant hands. They reminded Nora of a tree frog's hands—disproportionately large and knobby.

The scent of cheese and meatball reached her, causing her stomach to rumble.

The creature inched forward, standing in the closet doorway now. And Norah realized it was wearing red doll pants. It must have taken them from the little girl. It peered up at her with big eyes, its hands clasped together, its little nose twitching like mad. "Ig?"

She moved slowly toward the bed. She placed the pizza box on it, and after a moment of indecision, put her weapon on the side table next to the soda, close enough that she could grab it if she needed to.

"Hungry?" Opening the box, she pulled a slice out and put it on a paper plate. Careful to keep her movements slow, she placed it on the floor close to the closet.

Then she sat back on the bed. "Go ahead." She averted her gaze, watching it from the corner of her eyes as she took a slice for herself. She took a bite and felt better. Her stomach had been gnawing at her for the last hour. She finished one slice and the creature still hadn't reached for his. She grabbed a second and pretended not to notice it step from the closet. It had skinny little legs and large feet, also disproportionately large, like hairless Hobbit feet. Its stomach was very round, but its arms were slim.

It watched her for a moment, and she could tell it was deciding. Then it sat down and poked the pizza with a finger. Norah tried not to smile. It poked it again and then picked it up and took a tentative bite. Its eyes grew large and its mouth expanded, showing off two rows of teeth on its upper and lower jaw as it chowed down.

Norah's mouth fell open. As soon as it finished, its mouth went back to normal size. It looked up at her and then wiped its mouth. It picked up its plate and then walked slowly toward her. "Ig?"

Norah was careful not to move, although she tensed, ready to reach for the gun if she needed to. But the creature stopped at the edge of the bed. It lifted its plate in what was universal code for 'more please.' She placed another two slices on its plate.

Its eyes grew large and it hurried back to its spot to eat.

Once again, its mouth expanded and it ate both slices, although this time more slowly. When it was done, it leaned back and rubbed its belly, giving Norah a small smile. "Ig."

Then it climbed back into the closet and closed the door. Norah stared at the door, her own hunger forgotten, replaying everything that had just happened. Somehow it had followed her here, meaning it could track. She was guessing by smell, based on the way its nose constantly twitched. It had made no aggressive moves, was hungry, could vocalize, and apparently liked dark closets. She had an alien creature hiding out in her closet. She smiled, but then it faded.

A creature the United States government had classified as extremely dangerous was hiding in her closet. She'd seen extremely dangerous ones before, and this creature was nothing like those. She ran a hand through her hair.

So what the hell do I do now?

CHAPTER 21

DENVER, COLORADO

The early morning light was just slipping through the cracks in the venetian blinds as Maeve's eyes flew open, tears sliding down her cheeks. *Greg.* She'd dreamed of him being caught in the fire, unable to escape.

Maeve reached for Chris, but her hand only found empty space. She rolled over on her side, watching the light grow brighter. The terror and the fear from the dream lingered, and she pulled up the covers, feeling cold. She couldn't believe Greg was gone. And she was having troubling accepting how'd he died. A fire? It just seemed unfair after all he'd been through.

But maybe it was a reminder that sometimes there are forces beyond our control.

Despite the lack of control over her own life at the moment, Maeve was still struggling with that particular lesson. She'd been taught to be independent. It had been her, her mom, and Alvie. But when her mom got sick, Maeve had stepped up as the leader of their little family. And when her mom died, Maeve had permanently stepped into that role.

Then Chris came along. He'd stepped into a spot Maeve hadn't even known was waiting for him. But he added something to their grouping. Him, the triplets, Hope; they completed this family. They were a unit. And with him gone, the house felt off. The dynamic of their family was off. And with Greg—she needed Chris. She wanted him here. She knew he'd had to go, but she'd wanted to beg him to stay. It was just that the horrible things in this world were easier when he was standing by her side. And Greg dying was as horrible as it got.

Even though Chris and Greg were adding to the unreal feeling in the air, Maeve had to admit the feeling hadn't begun with them. It had been there all along, ever since they'd escaped Area 51. Maeve had shoved it down, convincing herself that everything was fine. That they were safe.

But the meeting with the President's commission had demonstrated why that was just an illusion. The President was expanding the scope of who knew about Alvie and the triplets. And Maeve knew it was only a matter of time before someone in a position of power decided this arrangement was not acceptable. Then someone would come for them.

That thought terrified Maeve. She had no back-up plan. It's not like she could simply hide them. Despite the fact that they were half human, they looked fully alien. There was nowhere on Earth that they could blend in. Which only left off-world safe houses.

That thought terrified her even more. But even if that were possible, how could Maeve let any of them go? How could she let Alvie go? The four of them were of both worlds and yet they had no place in either one.

The image of the big Gray who'd saved them at Area 51 flitted through her mind. He had looked out for them. He'd approved of

Maeve saving them, even at the cost of his freedom. Who was he? Was he an ally? Even if he was, she had no idea where he'd been taken. And being he was also in the custody of the U.S. government, he was certainly not in any position to help them. She sighed, closing her eyes. Sometimes it was just all too much.

The soft pad of footsteps sounded for a moment before the bed dipped. Maeve rolled over and Alvie lay down on Chris's pillow. She knew he was upset. His early arrival was proof of that. Alvie and the triplets were nocturnal. She and Chris had worked hard to get them to live on a more daylight-friendly schedule, but they still slept until nearly noon.

Alvie's dark eyes met Maeve's, and for the first time since they'd learned of Greg's death, she felt his emotions. He'd been closed off since then. An image of Greg smiling appeared in Maeve's head, followed by an almost overwhelming sense of loss. Tears crested in Alvie's eyes and one slipped down his cheek. Maeve reached out a hand and wiped it away. "I know it hurts."

An image of her mom appeared in her mind.

Maeve nodded. "Yes. Greg's with Mom. And we'll see him again someday."

He just looked at her, his chin trembling, more tears running down his cheeks. "Oh, Alvie." Maeve pulled him into her chest, his head tucked under her chin as she gave in to her own tears. "It will be okay. Somehow it will be okay."

But even she couldn't believe those words. Because Greg was dead, Chris was gone, and Maeve couldn't help but feel that time for all of them was running short.

CHAPTER 22

CENTERVILLE, UTAH

Norah had been convinced she would not sleep a wink that night. After all, she had an alien less than ten feet from her. She'd thought about sleeping in the bathroom with the door closed. She lay down on the bed, keeping one eye on the closet, and turned on the TV, keeping the volume low.

What are you doing? This thing will kill you in your sleep! Get up, get your gun, and take care of it, or at least call someone, for God's sake. She knew that was the rational thing to do.

But she couldn't think of anyone to call. Anyone from her agency would shoot first and ask questions later. This little guy deserved a chance. She'd looked up Dr. Leander, but she could find no information about her current whereabouts. She'd looked up Dr. Schorn's phone number, but in doing so learned he was presumed dead in a fire in the gym where she and Bob had interviewed him.

And that horrible news led to another horrible thought—Bob. She could not let Bob know the creature was here. She just needed to figure out a way to buy herself some time so she could find a way to bring the creature in without getting it or herself shot.

Because she couldn't get past the idea that it was scared and alone. She sensed no threat. She really thought Leander would be her best bet.

There's got to be a way to find her. But Leander's whereabouts were closely guarded. It was 'need to know,' and she really didn't want to push it too much with official channels and send up any red flags. When she'd inquired with the office earlier about Leander's contact information, she'd been told unequivocally that she was not allowed access to that information. She was already worried that she'd sent up a red flag with that request.

The Big Bang Theory was playing on the TV, and she watched Sheldon try to figure out his friends' behaviors. Almost as if he was an alien trying to assimilate.

Before she knew it, she was blinking her eyes open. Daylight was slipping in through the drapes. She jolted upright in bed, her head whipping from side to side. The room was quiet. She ran her hands down her body. No new cuts or bruises. *And my brain doesn't feel like it's been probed.* She paused. *Not that I would know what that feels like.*

A little head peeked from around the closet door, more frightened than frightening.

Letting out a breath, she leaned back against the headboard. She'd slept through the night with an alien. *And I live to tell the tale*, she thought hysterically, simultaneously recognizing there was no one she could tell this particular tale to, besides a tabloid.

She glanced at the clock. She had about ninety minutes before she was supposed to meet up with Bob. Her stomach growled. She looked at the little guy in the closet. "Breakfast?"

D.E.A.D.

Ten minutes later, Norah had gotten changed in the bathroom with the door locked, her weapon on the back of the toilet. When she'd stepped out, the little guy was still in the closet. He'd pulled in a pillow last night, along with a small blanket. Now he sat on top of them, looking at her.

She grabbed her bag, keys, and put her weapon in its holster. "I'll be right back, okay?"

"Ig?"

"If that's you asking for food, then yes, I'm going to get food." There was a Dunkin Donuts right next door. Hopefully it wouldn't be too busy and she'd be back quickly.

"Ig?"

She smiled at the hopeful expression on its face. "Yes, food. Okay, Iggy, you stay here." She stepped out of the room, shaking her head.

I just called it Iggy. I've named it. Way to keep a professional distance, Agent Tidwell.

The Dunkin Donuts was busy, but they were also very efficient. She was back with two croissant sandwiches, a very large coffee for her, and a water for Iggy.

She opened the door slowly and peered in. Iggy peered back at her from the closet. Norah quickly stepped in and closed the door behind her.

"Ig?"

"Just give me a minute." She pulled one of the sandwiches from the bag and unwrapped it, placing it in front of the closet along with the open bottle of water. Then she took her own sandwich and coffee and leaned back on the bed.

Iggy shuffled out of the closet toward the sandwich and then sniffed it, rearing back. With one long claw, Iggy poked the sandwich. And then, apparently deciding it was not a threat, sat down quickly. He flipped the top of the croissant off and carefully removed the sausage before placing the top back on.

Not a fan of sausage. Good to know.

He made quick work of the sandwich with that large mouth of his. And then he drained the water bottle dry. He gave Norah another small smile. "Ig."

"You're welcome."

Iggy stood up and paused for a moment, but then he began to wander the room, inspecting things, every once in a while glancing at Norah. He looked less green than he had yesterday. Maybe it was a fright response, allowing him to blend in better. Then she frowned, realizing he now blended in more with the walls of the motel room. *Maybe he has some chameleon-like abilities.*

He hopped up on the bathroom counter with only one leap. *Strong legs.*

But he still had that barrel stomach that made him look like a little old man. He toddled over to the sink and inspected the faucet. He tentatively pushed it on, jumping back as the water came out with a small squeak. Then with a glance at Norah, he leaned down and took a long drink. He turned the faucet off.

"You were thirsty, weren't you?"

He gave her what was probably a smile before resuming his inspection. He stepped to the hair dryer, tilting his head to the side as he looked at it. He pressed down on the power button and it came to life. He let out a squeal and leapt from the counter.

Norah scrambled off the bed. She grabbed the hair dryer and shut it off. "It's okay. It's okay. I got it," she said as she turned around.

Iggy peered out at her from behind the edge of the bed. His eyes were huge and he was shaking noticeably. Norah placed the hair dryer back against the wall. "See? It's okay. The bad noise is gone."

D.E.A.D.

Iggy stayed where he was. Norah sighed. *Well, I guess his exploring is over for a little bit.* Norah moved slowly back to the bed. She pulled her briefcase over and pulled out the map of the city. They'd be splitting up to search today, and she wanted to check the area to familiarize herself with it. At the same time, she watched Iggy out of the corner of her eye. He stepped a little closer to her.

Then Norah realized she was about to put dozens of people through an all-day search for a creature currently three feet away from her. With a sigh, she pulled out the files of sightings that they would investigate after they wrapped this one up. Iggy began to investigate the room again. After a few unadventurous minutes, he moved closer to Norah.

Norah focused on keeping calm. Then he stepped up and leaned his head against her calf. He closed his eyes and gave off a small little purr.

Norah was so surprised she didn't even move for a minute. There was no denying that the creature was happy. Norah reached down slowly and rubbed the creature's head. He nuzzled in even closer to her. Norah smiled. He was really sweet. "How did anyone ever think you were dangerous?"

Iggy was making her rethink the D.E.A.D.'s whole approach to dealing with these creatures. Maybe there was another approach that would be less dangerous for all of them.

Her cell phone alarm went off and Iggy jumped back. Norah quickly shut it off. "Sorry about that."

And Norah noticed that while Iggy had backed away, he hadn't gone too far. She was supposed to meet Bob in five minutes. She looked down at Iggy with a sigh. "So what do I do with you now?"

He looked back up at her. "Ig?"

She gave a small laugh before nodding. "Ig."

CHAPTER 23

UNDISCLOSED LOCATION

The darkness surrounded Guardian. But the darkness was a friend. The darkness was predictable. It was always dark here and there was never anything to fear in it. Guardian had started closer surveillance on a new target last night—Agent Norah Tidwell. Guardian had all of the agents of the D.E.A.D. under surveillance. Anytime they were near a camera, they were recorded. Guardian brought up Tidwell's feed from when she'd entered Centerville, fast-forwarding through until Norah stepped out from under the bridge. She'd been in there too long.

Guardian rewound the recording, zooming in and seeing the agent pause under the bridge, raising her weapon to the rafters, then lowering it slowly.

You found him. Why didn't you kill him?

Guardian hacked into the D.E.A.D. and found information on the agent. Agent Norah Tidwell, currently on assignment in Salt Lake City. It was quick work from there to find the agent's cell phone and laptop. Guardian set up both to record. This agent needed further examination.

Then Guardian pulled up the feeds from last night, starting with Agent Tidwell and scanned the agent's internet search with a frown.

You're looking for Leander. Why?

Guardian brought up the video from the agent's laptop. The agent sat on the motel bed typing, not even realizing the camera had been activated. Then the Maldek came into frame. The agent had dinner with the Maldek, even giving it seconds. Then this morning Tidwell had left the room and not raised the alarm. Instead she'd gotten breakfast for herself and the Maldek. It made no sense.

Watching, the Guardian felt confused. The agent was a member of Department of Alien and Extraterrestrial Defense. They were the bad guys, weren't they?

Guardian paused. *I need more information on Agent Tidwell.* Guardian's gaze shifted to another screen and thoughts of Tidwell shifted to the back of Guardian's mind.

Right now Guardian had something more critical to focus on.

CHAPTER 24

DENVER, COLORADO

Maeve hung up the phone. Chris sounded good. Annoyed at the testing, but she thought maybe he needed the break from all the craziness of the ranch. And besides, Maeve hoped the trip would remind him of how much he loved the military. Chris had already given up so much for them. She didn't want him having to give up his future.

Assuming he can even go back to the military one day.

She hated the thought, but she knew it was realistic. Maeve's life was science. She'd spent the bulk of her life studying, learning. And she hadn't been in a lab in two months. Truth was, she missed it. She loved Alvie. She loved the triplets. And God knew she loved Chris. But she needed to do something. And the hard truth was, she'd probably never step foot in a lab again.

Even Greg has stepped away. Although ... She cut herself off mid-thought. For a moment, she'd forgotten he was gone. And the pain of his loss crashed down on her again—as well as the guilt. She knew the guilt was stupid. Greg's death had nothing to do with her. But still, she was the one who'd encouraged him to work with the Air Force, which is how he'd ended up working with Hank. And that work was what had driven him as far from a lab as possible.

And now he was dead because he'd run away from his calling. Maeve wiped her eyes. *No, this is stupid. Get it out of your head.* She would not let herself mope around blaming herself for things out of her control.

Overall, she thought she'd done a pretty good job of distracting everybody from their grief. She'd created an obstacle course on the side of the house and cheered each contestant on as they went through. At the same time, she mentally compared the triplets' progress with Alvie's. She thought Alvie was plateauing as far as his physical abilities were concerned, which did not worry her. At his age, nearing thirty, that seemed appropriate. He was still faster than the triplets, as well as being able to leap higher and having greater strength. But in a few years the triplets would be able to give him a run for his money.

And that did concern her.

The triplets seemed to be growing into their abilities much faster than Alvie had. It could be because of Alvie that it was happening, due to them simply modeling the behaviors of their older brother.

Maeve did think that was part of the reason for their accelerated growth. But she also worried that the triplets had been exposed to some sort of growth enhancement process. With how focused the government was on results, she thought it unlikely they'd want to wait for the triplets to slowly develop. But Maeve didn't know what process they might have used. And she didn't know what potential problems it could lead to.

Yet another reason I need a lab.

Snap let out a squeal as Hope jumped into the creek and

splashed her. Maeve smiled, wishing she could take a picture to capture the moment. Hope stood with her mouth open in the creek. The triplets danced along the creek's edge. Alvie sat on a branch above them, watching them all with a smile.

Then Pop tripped, landing in the water. *Oh no.* Maeve hustled over as Pop stood up, his clothes soaked and his bottom lip trembling. Maeve scooped him up, not caring about how wet he was. "It's okay, kiddo. Just a little water. Let's go get you changed."

Pop snuggled into her and Maeve smiled, even as her own shirt dampened. Who was she kidding? She wouldn't trade these moments for anything. Crackle and Snap traipsed ahead of them, Alvie and Hope bringing up the rear.

"How about if we get a snack? I could go for some grapes." Crackle did a backflip in response and Maeve laughed. The gymnastics were a new development with the triplets. Alvie was still the most skilled gymnast, but, once again, the little guys were catching up.

A loud klaxon rang out across the space. Maeve sighed as Alvie looked at her. "I'm sure it's just another false alarm." She had to yell to be heard. "Let's just—"

A shadow crossed the sun and Maeve's gaze jolted upwards. From the corner of her eye she saw Snap and Crackle come to a standstill, their eyes darting upward as well. Maeve put a hand to her eyes to see what had caused the shadow. She squinted, seeing a dark shape. *What is that?*

And then her breath caught as a creature, its wingspan at least twelve or fourteen feet across, came into view at the same time that gunfire rang out.

Maeve sprinted for the house with Pop in her arms. "Guys, move!" There'd been a bunch of false alarms over the last few weeks. But that creature flying overhead was *not* a false alarm.

Alvie got to the door, first flinging it open.

"Grab the go bags!" Maeve yelled as she stormed through

the doorway behind Snap and Crackle. Chris had filled two backpacks with what he considered necessities. They were in the front hall closet.

Maeve grabbed the phone and the TV remote. She punched in the front gate code as she tuned the TV to the security cameras. All she got was static. And there was no answer from the front gate.

Gunfire sounded in the distance and Maeve whirled around, her stomach plummeting.

Oh my God. Where's the security team? With every other false alarm, they had surrounded the house within seconds. She ran to the window, but there was no one.

Okay, then. She grabbed the keys from the hook by the door. "Alvie, pack."

He tossed her one and the other one was already strapped to his back. Maeve quickly opened it, pulling out the Beretta and clipping it to her belt. She tugged the pack on. "Okay. We're heading out the back and getting to the Jeep. Everybody stays together. Alvie, Hope."

Alvie moved to Hope and stared into the pup's eyes. Hope went still, her nervous energy gone. Another little trick that they realized Alvie could do after 51—he could control Hope. He could get her to go silent, go to sleep, run. And right now, they were going to need that.

"Come on, guys." Maeve headed for the back door, her little family hurrying behind her. She did not give herself time to be afraid. That would come later. Right now, she needed to get them out of here. More gunfire sounded, this time closer.

Oh, Chris, I really wish you were here.

CHAPTER 25

LANCASTER, CALIFORNIA

Impatience crawled through Chris. This was such a waste of time. He'd been ordered back to Edwards Air Force Base to complete a mandatory training in 'defense proficiency.' He'd never heard of the requirement before. He'd been told it was required for individuals in unconventional assignments. But his skill level was way above the desk jockeys he was qualifying with.

Today they'd reviewed basic hand-to-hand combat. Chris had even had to correct his instructors, whom he outranked. Tomorrow they were heading for the gun range. Honestly, if they just gave him a list of the skills they needed him to demonstrate, he could knock it out in two hours tops. Instead he was stuck here for two full days.

But that wasn't the real reason time was crawling by. He hated being away from Maeve and the kids. And he'd had a feeling ever since he left the ranch, some sense that something was about to go wrong. At home, it had been peaceful. They had round-the-clock protection. And yet these last two weeks he'd been ill at ease. And now with Greg …

He needed to get back. He keyed himself into his hotel room with a sigh. The one good thing about this trip was he had a room to himself. It wasn't the Ritz, just a basic mid-level hotel with two queen beds, a no-frills desk, a mini-fridge, and a clean bathroom. Even as he felt the need to get back, he could appreciate the quiet. His friends with kids had complained about never getting a good night's sleep. He'd thought they were exaggerating. Now he knew they weren't.

Nevertheless, he was looking forward to flying out tomorrow night and seeing his unusual family. He'd never really been sure he wanted to have kids before all this. Now he had four alien-human hybrids and one retriever and he couldn't imagine his life any other way.

Plus, Maeve had sounded so sad on the phone earlier, even though she'd tried to hide it. He knew Greg's death was hitting her hard. She'd been through so much. She'd taken on Alvie and the triplets without hesitation. And she was great with all of them. But he knew how tired she was, how much she worried about all of them, him included. And he also knew she was trying to keep that from him to not add to his own worries.

He'd never met someone like her. He couldn't imagine anyone else being put through so much and still being able to smile. And he knew that seeing that smile every day for the rest of his life was something he couldn't live without.

He pulled the ring box from his pocket. The one good thing about this trip was it had allowed him to get Maeve a ring. He opened the box. It wasn't fancy. She wouldn't want fancy. It was a princess cut with four smaller chips at its points—one for each kid. He smiled, snapping the box shut and slipping it into his pocket. Yup, he definitely couldn't wait to get home.

When he'd met Maeve two years ago, he'd thought she was

gorgeous. And she was. She was also smart as hell. But what he truly loved about her was how she loved—completely and without reservation. He'd seen it for years with Alvie, and now he'd seen it with himself. And as much as he loved his career, if the military demanded he leave her side again he would tell them to shove it. She was more important than jumping through some hoops everyone knew he could jump through on one leg while blindfolded.

He pulled out his phone, wanting to hear her voice again. He hit her number, but he got an error message. He glanced at the signal strength and realized there was no signal.

He frowned. *That's weird.*

He picked up the receiver of the desk phone to ask the front desk, but there was no dial tone there either. Chris lowered the phone slowly, a tingle running over his skin. The TV flared to life. Chris whirled around, his heart pounding as the hair raised on the back of his neck as words began to scroll across the black screen.

They're coming. Get out now.

CHAPTER 26

DENVER, COLORADO

Maeve peered out the door. The back of the house looked quiet. "Okay, let's go." She opened the door and stepped out, waiting a beat, but she heard nothing. "I start the car and you guys come running, okay?"

Alvie nodded at her. The triplets just looked at her with big eyes—eyes filled with trust. Praying she was worthy of it, she counted to three before bolting from the back porch toward the Jeep. Gunfire tore up the ground ten feet in front of the Jeep.

Shit! Maeve dove for the ground, rolling away from the line of fire.

Spitting out dirt, she looked around. Why the hell had someone shot at her? But then a dark shadow swooped down and Maeve realized the guard must have been shooting at him. More gunfire sounded. Maeve rolled and caught sight of a guard stepping around the side of the house.

Thank God.

Her relief was short lived, however, as the creature

slammed into the guard and sent him flying with a sickening crunch.

The creature turned toward Maeve, and she got her first good look at it. It was easily seven feet tall, with dark-brown, almost maroon leathery skin. Its face was humanlike—two eyes, a nose, a mouth, all proportional. But while its face was human, those wings definitely were not. They resembled bat wings, coming to sharp points and covered in a dark leather with a dull shine.

Greg had mentioned the creature that had saved them from Hank on the base. And this one standing in front of her looked exactly like what Greg had described. But she wasn't willing to assume that the creature had helped out of the goodness of its heart, especially not after what she'd just seen it do.

Maeve got to her feet, keeping her eyes on the creature that stood a mere twenty feet away. It made no move toward her. Instead, it tilted its head and extended its hand toward her, a hand with long talons at the end. And there was something almost pleading about the look on its face.

Not hurt. The words from Alvie wafted through her mind. She frowned. What did he—

Gunfire blasted from her right. With a hiss, the creature spun toward the three men who appeared from the other side of the house. They shot at the creature again and it took to the air with a powerful swing of its wings. The gunmen kept their aim on it as it swooped down. Maeve looked at the Jeep, preparing to make a run for it, but two of the tires were flat, and she saw three bullet holes in the hood.

One of the men threw a grenade at the creature just as it landed ten feet from the men. The creature batted it away with its wings. Maeve watched its arc in horror and knew it would land at the end of the porch.

"Run!" Maeve yelled, sprinting for the porch as Alvie, Hope, and the triplets sprinted off it.

D.E.A.D.

Then the grenade exploded, sending Maeve flying back.

CHAPTER 27

Hands on Maeve's face woke her, as well as an urgent probing of her mind. She blinked open her eyes, everything feeling sore. Alvie stared down at her and Maeve could feel his terror. And then she heard the gunfire.

She sat up quickly, wincing as pain shot through her head. Her shirt was pockmarked with cuts, and she knew adrenaline was all that was keeping her from feeling it right now. The back of the house had a gaping hole and the first floor was on fire. To her left, the three men in black lay in bloody pools. More gunfire sounded in the distance.

"What happened?" she asked as she stumbled to her knees. Snap, Crackle, and Pop huddled against her, and she put her arms around them with a squeeze.

In her mind, she saw everything from Alvie's perspective. The grenade exploded and Maeve went flying, landing with a thud. The creature dove for the ground, flinging the men away with his wings. One man raised a weapon and the creature tore the gun, arm and all, from the man's body. Another pulled a knife and charged. The creature swung his wings. The tips cut the man's chest and another swing cut the man's neck. The third man struggled to his feet, but the creature didn't give him the chance. It stomped on his chest.

Oh my God. A truck had then appeared over the ridge and the creature had taken off after it.

Maeve looked to the right, where she could hear more gunfire. Then the creature soared into view. Alvie grabbed Maeve's hand. Maeve felt her eyes grow wide as the creature turned its head toward them. Ignoring the stab of pain in her knees and the throbbing ache in her back, she got to her feet, urgency making her stumble. "Run!"

She grabbed Pop and Crackle by the hand, yanking them into motion. Alvie grabbed Snap, and Hope obediently sprinted behind them. Maeve, Alvie, and the triplets sprinted past the burning house and out into the field beyond it. The field was about a hundred feet wide and then the land was forested for two acres. Maeve prayed they could lose the creature in the trees, although she had no real faith that was possible.

But the only other option was to give up. And that was not going to happen. She picked up her pace, an idea already forming. The security forces had undeniably already called for help, which meant Maeve didn't have to defeat the creature. She just needed to hold it off long enough for reinforcements to arrive.

I can do that.

That thought played through her mind as she raced across the ground, trying to think of a place to hide or make a stand. The triplets kept pace with her, but Alvie sprinted ahead, and Maeve knew he was checking to see if there was any danger in front of them. She wanted to call him back, to not let him take the risk. But the truth was, he was the one best equipped to help them.

Alvie veered to the left, and Maeve smiled. *Good thinking,*

Alvie. He was leading them to the old creek bed. It had dried out years ago, but there was a small cave along its bank. It was overgrown with vines covering the entrance, which meant unless you knew this area, you would never know it was there.

More gunfire sounded behind them, but Maeve was sure it was closer to the house than the trees. Alvie slid down the old creek bank and the rest of them scrambled after him. He held the vines to the side and they all dove in, even Hope. Alvie closed the vines just as a shadow flew over the cave entrance.

Maeve's heart pounded, and she waited to see if the creature had seen them. But seconds went by without any movement. Alvie slid next to her, the triplets curled up against her back. Maeve pulled the Beretta from its holster, feeling the literal and figurative weight of all the lives counting on her.

God, if you're listening, we could really use a little help here.

CHAPTER 28

LANCASTER, CALIFORNIA

Chris moved quickly to the window, his mind whirling as he tried to figure out who the hell was sending him a message. He didn't personally know anyone with those types of skills. And why the hell would they think he would listen to them?

His room was on the second floor at the front of the hotel, giving him a good view of the parking lot and entrance. A dark Mustang pulled up and three men stepped out, all in black tactical gear. Another Mustang drove around the side of the building, no doubt going to cover the back.

What the hell? Chris paused for only a few seconds. The fire alarm rang out. Chris narrowed his eyes. *They're emptying the building.*

He wasn't sure what the hell was going on or who those guys were, but until he did, he wasn't trusting anybody. Chris pulled his cell phone out and tossed it on the table along with the keys to his car rental. Both would be tracked. All he had on him now was his wallet, his Swiss army knife, and house keys.

Not exactly helpful. He grabbed the burn phone he'd stashed in his bag just in case. He wished like hell he'd brought a weapon. He moved quickly to the door.

People were already exiting the hotel. He could hear their footsteps and murmurings as they passed the room. *Damn it*. Shaking his head, he opened the door and jumped back at the sight of the man standing outside his doorway.

"Hey, I was just coming to make sure you heard the alarm. Although, how could you miss it, right?" Jasper Franklin, who'd been in his training, stood there. African-American, in his mid-fifties, Jasper seemed a good guy. He was little out of shape and had struggled with the more physical aspects of the training. But he always seemed to be ready for a laugh, even at his own expense.

Chris studied Jasper. Did Jasper show up because he was just trying to make sure Chris got out, or was he with the guys outside? Chris pulled his door shut behind him. "Yeah, I'm coming. Probably just a drill."

Jasper shrugged. "Yeah, you're probably right. But I'm a rule follower."

He and Chris moved toward the stairwell. The elevators had been shut down. *Making sure there's one exit point*. Chris tensed as they reached the first floor. There were a dozen guests heading for the exit. Another dozen had followed them down the stairs, coming from the higher floors. And Chris had heard even more making their way down the stairwell.

He scanned the lobby. The front wall was made of glass, with sliding doors leading outside. Tall pillars soared two stories up, with the registration desk on the left-hand side of the marble-tiled foyer and concierge on the right. A few guests clustered together, looking around uncertainly, but most moved toward the doors.

No one was in a rush, most just looked a little annoyed. But there was one man standing by the front doors, his back to the parking lot. Chris's eyes locked onto him as the man continued his scan of the foyer before reaching down and speaking into a radio at his shoulder.

Chris ducked into the hallway next to the stairwell.

Jasper turned around with a frown. "Hey, what are you doing?"

"I forgot something. I'll find you later." He turned and headed for the back of the hotel. There was a kitchen back there. He was hoping he could cut through there and then get out through the loading bay. He'd checked out the hotel when he'd checked in. He knew there was a dining room attached to the kitchen.

Chris hurried past more guests heading for the front. More than a few gave him a strange look as he went against the tide. An annoyed shout rang out from behind him. He looked over his shoulder. Two men in black pushed people out of their way, their gazes locked on Chris.

Well, I guess stealth is over. Chris broke into a sprint.

"Stop!" The yell rang out from behind him.

I don't think so. Chris broke free of the crowd and rounded the corner at the end of the hall. He pushed through the dining-room doors and sprinted across the empty dining room, dodging tables and chairs set for dinner.

The doors behind him burst open. He slid across the counter that separated the dining area from the kitchen and shoved through the swinging doors into the kitchen. The kitchen was empty, and Chris did a quick survey looking for something, anything he could use as a weapon.

A stack of cleaned kitchen tools lay piled on the counter to his left. He grabbed a long metal handle just as the door opened behind him. He whirled around, striking the man's extended gun arm with a soup ladle. The arm dropped and Chris slammed the end of the ladle into the man's face. Bullets sprayed across the opposite wall. Dropping the ladle and holding on to the gun arm, he stomped on the back of the man's knee while twisting the gun from his grasp, breaking a finger in the process. Wrenching the weapon free, he slammed a front kick into the man's chest, sending him flying into a tower of glasses in racks.

The second gunman opened fire blindly through the swinging kitchen doors. The guy didn't even know if his buddy was out of range.

Chris dove for the ground and army-crawled, making his way behind the metal tables set up for prep work. The kitchen door crashed open. Chris turned on his side and fired from the ground, catching the man in the calf. He howled, bending at the waist, and the next shot found him in the top of his head. *One down.*

As Chris scrambled to his feet, bullets chewed up the ground behind him. He spied a giant freezer up ahead, the door slightly ajar. Chris grabbed the handle, swinging it open behind him as he passed. Bullets crashed into it.

Chris ducked into a small dishwashing station just beyond the freezer. He grabbed a knife and tossed it farther down the kitchen. The man following him sprinted around the door, heading for the sound. Chris opened fire. The first few bullets caught the guy in the chest. But his vest protected him from too much damage. Chris aimed his next shot at the guy's knees. The man screamed and Chris rushed forward, wrenching the weapon from his hand and pointing it at the man's face. "Who sent you?"

The man grimaced but stayed silent.

Chris shook him. "Who sent you?"

The man smiled. "What does it matter? You're never getting out of here alive. And you're not the only one. Those little freaks you left back in Colorado should be dead by now as well."

Fear, anger, and shock warred inside Chris at his words,

but Chris only let the anger through. "Who are you working for?"

The man smiled. "Whoever pays the most money."

Chris brought the man's gun down onto his temple and his eyes rolled back. He shoved him aside, grabbing the extra magazine tucked into the man's vest. He thought about taking the vest, but he didn't think he'd have the time.

He ran for the loading bay, stopping at the side of the open doorway to peer outside. A truck was parked in the bay, but he couldn't see anyone around. Behind him, he heard a dish crash in the kitchen. *More coming.*

He stepped out and ran for the loading dock, leaping over the edge. Two gunmen stepped around the truck.

Chris ducked under the truck as they opened fire. He aimed at the men's legs. He caught one in the ankle and the man screamed, dropping. Chris's second shot stopped the man's screams.

The second man ran out of Chris's view before Chris could target him. *Damn it.*

Chris stayed still, struggling to hear anything. He started to crawl toward the front of the truck when he heard a voice. "He's under the truck."

Great. He's got a friend. They were on the loading dock and they had the higher ground. If he stepped out now, he was a dead man. And if he waited they'd come down here and kill him.

Shit.

CHAPTER 29

DENVER, COLORADO

The woods had been silent for five minutes. No more gunfire sounded in the distance. And no more shadows flew over the cave entrance.

"Alvie? Do you sense anyone nearby?"

Alvie shook his head.

Maeve hesitated. Should she wait? Should she move? She wasn't a soldier. She didn't know what the appropriate response was. *God damn it, they did not cover any of this in grad school.*

Alvie tilted his head and then turned, looking at the cave entrance with a frown. Maeve turned toward it as well, hearing something. She inched forward.

"Dr. Leander?" The yell was faint, but it was definitely someone calling for her. She let out a sigh of relief. *Oh, thank God.* They wouldn't be calling for her if the creature was still out there. "Come on, guys. It looks like it's all clear."

Alvie held on to her hand and shook his head.

D.E.A.D.

Maeve looked down at him in confusion. "It's okay, Alvie. The soldiers have taken care of it."

But even as she crawled from the cave, she could feel Alvie's unease. And his unease bled into her own feelings. She moved slowly, not calling out for the soldiers, casting her eyes around at every shadow. She headed toward the house but then shifted direction, leading them away from the house, so they would step out of the woods closer to the property's edge and hopefully give them a chance to see what exactly was going on.

Even as she walked, she heard the soldiers calling for her. The hair on the back of her neck warned her to stay quiet. Something was wrong. Alvie, the triplets, and Hope all seemed to pick up on the same feeling and all moved quietly. Everything felt tense.

Finally they reached the edge of the woods. Maeve paused inside the tree line. "Okay. Come on, guys." Together they stepped out. Here there was a smattering of trees to provide cover.

"Dr. Leander?" A voice called from behind them.

Maeve whirled around as a man in black stepped out of the trees just thirty feet away. She didn't recognize him, but they were always changing the security crew. Maeve put her hand to her throat. "You scared me."

The man didn't say anything, barely sparing Alvie and the triplets a glance before turning back to Maeve. Red flags were going off in Maeve's head. None of the security staff knew about Alvie and the triplets. Why wasn't the man reacting?

"What's going on?" Maeve asked, stepping in front of the triplets.

"You need to come with me." The man raised his weapon.

"What are you—"

A screech bellowed from the air as the man pulled the trigger. Maeve was shoved from behind and crashed into the ground, Snap on top of her. The winged creature slammed into the man, flinging him back into the trees.

Gunfire burst out from the trees as men in black came at a run toward the creature.

Maeve scrambled to her feet. "Run!"

As one, they sprinted away from the fight. Ahead was the fence. It was a tall wooden structure. Maeve knew the hybrids could leap over it. But she and Hope would never be able to. *What do I do?*

As if in answer, part of the fence blew apart and an old Jeep with a canvas top sped through the opening. Maeve slid to a stop, putting out a hand to stop Snap and Crackle. Alvie grabbed Pop and Hope next to her. The Jeep headed right for them.

Oh, come on," Maeve groaned silently before she yelled. "The trees!"

The Jeep put on a burst of speed and cut them off, crashing into a man in black that emerged from the woods. The man kept going, flying into a tree ten feet away with a sickening thump. Maeve scrambled back, shoving herself into Alvie and Pop behind her.

The Jeep reversed and stopped short in front of Maeve. A woman who had to be in her late sixties sat behind the wheel, her white hair pulled back into a long braid draped over one shoulder. Her blue eyes raked Maeve. "Well, Dr. Leander, what are you waiting for?"

There was a man in the passenger seat that Maeve hadn't noticed until now. He leaned forward. "Not to be cheesy, but come with us if you want to live."

Maeve felt like the world had just shifted under her feet. "Greg?"

CHAPTER 30

LANCASTER, CALIFORNIA

Chris crawled toward the front of the truck, hoping he could at least get out from under it to make a stand. A yell went up from the loading dock, followed by grunts. Chris wasn't sure what the distraction was, but he planned on taking advantage of it. He hurried under the engine and paused for a second to hope that the space was clear, then he crawled out. No one. He crouched by the engine.

He heard footsteps heading toward him. He moved closer to the edge of the truck, careful to keep his head below the truck's hood. The footsteps slowed as they neared Chris's location.

Then a man stepped into view. Chris had his weapon right in the man's face before he could even blink.

"Whoa, whoa, Chris. It's me." Jasper held his hands up, his eyes wide.

Chris's mouth fell open. "Drop the gun and back up."

Jasper complied and Chris stayed with him. He glanced

quickly at the loading bay. Three more men in black lay there. He frowned. "You did that?"

"Yeah. I saw them following you. I thought you could use some help," the man said with a shrug.

Chris turned his gaze back to Jasper. Jasper had been one of the men who'd struggled in today's hand-to-hand requalification. And now he'd just taken down three gunmen like a one-man ninja force. "Who are you?"

Eyes growing wide, Jasper shook his head. "No-nobody. I'm just—"

Chris tightened his grip on the weapon. He liked Jasper. He didn't want to shoot him. But he wasn't big on trust right now. "Who. Are. You?"

The man's whole demeanor shifted. Gone was the 'aw shucks' personality and in its place was a man who looked perfectly calm despite the gun aimed right at his face. "I'm a friend. I was sent to help."

"Who sent you?" Chris demanded.

"I can't tell you that. Not yet."

God damn it. "Put your hands in your pockets."

Jasper frowned. "Why?"

"Do it." Chris had no idea how Jasper had taken out those men without a shot being fired. Which meant there was a hell of a lot more to Jasper than he'd let on. And Chris did not plan on underestimating him.

"This isn't necessary," Jasper said as he placed his hands in his pockets.

"Turn around," Chris ordered.

Jasper shook his head. "Chris, you don't want to do this."

"Turn. Around," Chris ordered again.

Shaking his head, Jasper moved slowly. Chris was careful to keep his weapon trained on the man's midsection.

"I'm here to help you," Jasper said.

"Yeah, well, I don't know you. And I'm not feeling real trusting right now."

"I get that. But Chris, I'm on your side. I swear."

Stepping toward him, Chris said. "If that's true, then I will be sure to apologize the next time I see you."

Jasper started to look back. "Apologize?"

Chris slammed his gun into the back of Jasper's head. Jasper dropped like a stone. Chris knelt down and quickly rifled through his pockets. He grabbed the cash and his car keys. Jasper had two cell phones.

Disregarding the iPhone, Chris started going through the old flip phone. He scrawled through the most recent calls. Only one number was listed. He committed it to memory and then quickly headed to the parking lot. It was a miracle no one had stumbled upon them already. He was pretty sure there was video. He'd seen the security camera over the loading bay.

Although, if those guys worked for the government, they would have no problem turning those cameras off. Chris walked quickly around the side of the building, stopping for a moment behind a crowd of people.

What the hell was going on? Those guys in the kitchen had been trying to kill him. And Jasper had taken them out. There were two groups working him. But who the hell were they working for? And then there was the message on the TV. Was that guy with either group? Or was there a third interested party?

Lights flashed down the street and the sirens of the fire trucks reached him. Chris kept his head down as the fire trucks pulled into the front of the hotel. Guests milled around the front, a few spilling out into the parking lot. Chris had absolutely no answers, and he wasn't going to get them here. He made his way to the lot and tapped Jasper's key fob. A silver Toyota Camry's lights a few cars down lit up. He quickly got in and headed out of the lot. He pulled onto the main street and headed west.

That mercenary had said that another team had been sent to the ranch. Chris didn't think he'd been bluffing. The man had known about Alvie and the triplets.

And they attacked when I was away. No, when I was called away by the government. Someone in the government was involved. Someone who wanted him dead. Right after Greg died. That couldn't be a coincidence.

His hands tightened on the steering wheel, and he wished he could call Maeve. He needed to know she was all right. But even as he thought it, he knew she wouldn't answer. If she'd survived, she would have bolted.

I should have stayed. I never should have left them alone. He pictured his unusual little family. *Please be all right.*

CHAPTER 31

DENVER, COLORADO

No, it could not be Greg.

Yet the man sitting staring at her looked exactly like him. Maeve blinked hard, worried that she had a concussion and was imagining all of this. But Greg's face was the same as always, and he was wearing a Pokémon T-shirt.

"Get in the Jeep, Maeve. I can explain everything after." But Maeve couldn't seem to move. It was Greg—same brown eyes, same hair in need of a cut, same glasses. But he was here.

And with a woman Maeve did not know.

As soon as Greg appeared, the triplets let out a squeal and clambered into the Jeep. The woman behind the wheel didn't even bat an eye at their appearance, just waved them in. Alvie moved closer to Maeve, but she could feel his joy. It was Greg.

"Maeve! Come on!" Greg yelled.

Gunfire behind her spurred her into motion. With a quick glance at the soldiers still fighting the creature, Maeve and Alvie climbed into the back of the Jeep. Maeve had barely gotten her feet in when the woman took off.

She whipped the Jeep around and quickly sped back through the newly created hole in the fence. The wind whipped at them as they sped across open fields. The triplets crouched down low on the floor. Maeve peered at the sky above, waiting for the creature to appear, but the sky remained clear.

Alvie tapped her arm and snuggled against her. The triplets scampered through the opening between the two front seats and launched themselves at Greg.

"Oh, ow. Hey, guys," Greg said, trying to see around the three squirming bodies trying to hug him at the same time. Finally he gave up trying to see and just hugged them back. The triplets calmed down, snuggling into Greg, and Greg was finally able to turn around and look at Maeve. "Hey!" he yelled to be heard over the wind.

"Hey," Maeve yelled back. "What the hell is going on?"

Looking over Snap's head, he nudged his chin toward the driver. "A lot. This is Tilda. She saved my life a couple of nights ago."

"How? And what the hell?" Maeve yelled as the Jeep hit a deep rut and she nearly got bounced out the back of it. Alvie grabbed on to her, keeping her in her seat. Maeve decided the rest of the conversation should probably wait until she didn't feel like a pinball.

But she needed to know. "What are you doing here? How'd you know we were in trouble?"

Tilda only flick da quick glance at her before focusing back in the road. "We got a heads-up that you and Chris were in danger. We headed—"

Fear lancing through her, Maeve grabbed Greg's shoulder. "Chris? He's not here. He's in California."

Greg glanced at Tilda, who ignored him, keeping her focus on the road, but that look told Maeve everything she needed to know. "What happened? Is he all right?"

"We believe so," Tilda said slowly.

"You believe so? Greg, what the hell's going on?"

But she could still hear gunfire behind her and then what sounded like answering gunfire, which made her frown. Someone else had been on the ranch. But who? Her heart lurched as she imagined for a moment it was Chris. But no, he wasn't due back for another day.

Tilda swerved off the field and onto a dirt road, which at least reduced some of the bouncing in the Jeep.

"I don't know everything. All I know is that there was a threat to both of you. And—" He looked away.

Maeve felt like she was going to lose her mind. "And what, Greg?"

"A choice had to be made," Tilda said, not slowing. "We chose you and the experiments."

Maeve gritted her teeth. "They are *not* experiments."

Greg spoke quickly. "Maeve, she didn't mean it like that. And I hated that we had to choose. But we only heard about it an hour ago. We barely got here in time. There wasn't time to go for both of you."

"Did you at least warn him?" Maeve asked.

"Not us, exactly, but a friend," Tilda said.

Not good enough. "I need to call him," Maeve said.

Greg shook his head. "We can't—not right now. They're tracing every call within fifty miles of this place. Maeve, they sent an alien after me, too. Whoever's behind this has connections and access."

Sensing her mood, the triplets scampered back, crowding around her knees. She ran a hand over the top of each of their heads, their favorite spot to be touched. "It's okay, guys."

"If we call we'll lead them right to us," Greg said his eyes full of regret.

"But Chris—"

Greg shook his head. "I'm sorry, Maeve, we can't. Not until

we're safe. We need to get you and the kids to safety. Then we'll track him down, okay?"

Staring at him, helplessness rolled through her. She turned to the little faces curled up on the floor by her feet. Alvie reached over and took her hand, leaning his head against her. Maeve lay her other hand on top of his head. She would never do anything that would endanger them. Keeping them safe was her priority. It had been for years. She stared out as the trees whipped by them.

But who's going to keep Chris safe?

CHAPTER 32

PALMDALE, CALIFORNIA

Chris dialed the number again as he flew down the highway, but there was no answer. He'd tried the front gate and they hadn't answered either. He'd called the emergency phones but there'd been no response from them as well. He tried to still the tremor that had started in his hands but fear still rose in him.

I never should have left them. If anything has happened to them...

He swallowed down the anguish at even the thought of any of them getting hurt, and he couldn't visit the possibility of something even worse happening to them.

The miles flew by as his mind wandered from one horrible scenario to another. Something had to have happened to them. First Greg was killed, then Chris and Maeve were separated and attacked. Someone was planning something. Someone wanted them out of the way.

Or at least the full humans out of the way.

Chris tightened his grip on the steering wheel. It had to be

Martin Drummond. There'd been no sign of that bastard since Area 51 had been destroyed. The President's people suggested Martin may have been killed in the blast. Chris knew that was wishful thinking. Martin had spent a lifetime as a spook. He was sure to have hidey holes stashed all across the world.

But Chris had a feeling he was still in the United States. And while Bileris had told him Drummond had been officially denounced by the U.S. government, this whole affair had made it clear that the President's knowledge and power was severely limited. Chris had done some of his own research into the role of presidents in UFOs. And while Truman may have created the Majestic Twelve, each successive president had lost more and more power in overseeing the U.S.'s investigation into space-related incidents.

By the time JFK took office, the executive branch was practically frozen out of the UFO game. In fact, there was even a theory that it was JFK's attempt to insert himself into the space program that had gotten him killed. According to reports, JFK had extended an offer to Soviet Union leader Nikita Khrushchev, offering to share the United States' space technology and information in exchange for a joint approach to conquering space. Military higher-ups had balked at the idea of sharing anything with the Russians. Khrushchev himself had turned down the President twice.

But according to Khrushchev's son, the Premier had planned on accepting after the third offer was made. But he never had the chance. JFK was assassinated only a few days later.

Chris knew there were as many theories about JFK's assassination as there were numbers in the phone book. But when he read about the connection between JFK and the space program, it had sent a tremor through him. JFK had been a very popular president with the people. But within government, he'd made a lot of enemies. After the Bay of Pigs, he was no fan of the intelligence community, and the feeling was mutual. Alienating the military and anti-Russian forces within the government would place a huge target on the man's back. Now the question was, did Wilson have something to do with these attacks or was someone demonstrating to the President just how limited his reach was?

He glanced at his phone, which lay on the passenger seat. A bullet had scarred the outside of the case, right along the screen. Chris had been lucky. *No, not lucky*, he thought, thinking about the warning on the TV. *I have a guardian angel.*

And then there was Jasper. He'd helped him out of a tight spot. Chris did feel a little guilty about knocking the guy out. But how the hell was he supposed to trust him?

Feeling completely out of sorts, Chris shook his head. He didn't know who to trust or what the hell was going on. If he could just talk to Maeve, just hear her voice, and know they were all right, then he could think a little more clearly.

He gripped the steering wheel tightly again. No sense wishing for things he couldn't have. A highway sign on the side of the road proclaimed that the ramp for Route 15 was coming up. He debated heading for it. He wanted to head right back to Denver. But he also knew that was exactly what anyone looking for him would expect.

Come on, Chris, think. There has to be a way to contact them.

But his mind was a blank. Without a way to contact them by phone, he was dead in the water. The ramp appeared on the GPS screen. *Screw it.* It might not be the safe move, but he needed to know that Maeve and the gang were all right.

He changed lanes to turn toward the exit when his GPS screen flickered. Chris frowned as the map disappeared. A message appeared.

Continue driving straight.

Chris's mouth dropped open. His guardian angel was back. He tensed as the exit approached.

The screen flicked again, the name of the town scrolling across the screen before a new phrase appeared.

Family there.

He hesitated for only a moment and then hit the gas, driving past the exit. His guardian angel had kept him safe so far. He guessed he was willing to trust them just a little bit more.

CHAPTER 33

DULCE, NEW MEXICO

Martin stared at the after-action report in disbelief. Garrigan had escaped the net Martin had laid out for him in Lancaster. Martin growled. He never should have let them make the grab at the hotel. There were too many uncontrollable variables. But he'd had to hire out for this mission.

He shoved the report aside. Garrigan didn't matter. The important thing was he wasn't at the ranch when the hybrids were recaptured. Speaking of which, where the hell was that status report?

He'd been on pins and needles since he'd okayed the mission, so he'd forced himself to review the workings of the D.E.A.D. and had lost track of time.

He checked his screen but the after-action report on Leander wasn't there yet. He yanked up his phone and dialed Hamish. "What is the status on Leander?"

Hamish paused just a few beats too long. "Um, she, uh, she managed to get away."

Martin stared at the ceiling, counting to ten. "I see. And was she the only one who got away?"

"Um, no, they, uh… all got away."

His anger rising, Martin curled his hand into a fist. "Would you like to tell me how that is possible? My team is supposed to be the best there is out there. And yet a scientist with no special-ops training hampered down by four hybrids somehow outsmarted them."

"Well, sir, she had help," Hamish said.

"Garrigan?" Martin frowned.

Hamish stared at a spot somewhere to Martin's right. "Um, no, sir, from the satellite images it looks like she linked up with Greg Schorn."

"Schorn?" Martin thought he was dead in the fire. Apparently the sand blasters were also a failure. *What. The. Hell.* "So you're telling me the aid of a scientist, who the last time we saw him could barely walk without stumbling over his own feet, somehow turned into Rambo?"

Clearing his throat, Hamish said, "Uh, well, he *has* been working out."

Counting to ten again, Martin then let out a breath. "Hamish, you have five minutes to find out what went wrong. And that explanation better not involve Schorn's cardio routine or I will beat you to death with your useless computer. Do you understand me?"

Hamish's reply came back quickly. "Yes, sir. Yes, of course, I'll—"

Martin disconnected the call, seething. Both subjects had eluded his teams. That was unacceptable. He stood up from his desk. It was a five-minute walk from his office to Hamish's, and by the time he got there, he had better have answers.

D.E.A.D.

Technical support was on the second-lowest level of the facility. In the event of an attack or breach, Martin wanted to make sure that all the facility's computers were wiped and purged. After, of course, the information was sent to their off-site data centers. Placing them at one of the lowest levels of the mountain base ensured a few extra minutes for that to be accomplished. It also assured Martin that he would then be able to eliminate the entire technical staff before they could escape the facility themselves. Win-win in his book.

He stepped out of the elevator; the hallway was noticeably cooler. The servers were down here and needed to be kept at a colder temperature than the rest of the facility so they did not overheat. Martin bypassed the large workroom with its rows and rows of monitors and tech spies. He'd moved his people from Vegas here after Area 51. Now they were all housed in one spot, making some aspects of his life easier.

He walked down the hall and opened the door at the end without knocking. Hamish jerked up from his monitors, looking at Martin with large eyes. "M-Martin. I was just going to call you."

"Well, I saved you the bother. Now tell me what happened with Leander."

Fumbling with the mouse, Hamish gave him a nervous smile. "She had help beyond Schorn. There are at least two other people with her. Um, one is a guy in his twenties, maybe. I'm running facial rec on him, but I don't have anything yet. And the other is a woman who I think is probably in her sixties."

"Sixties? Are you sure she's—" He went still, his eyes narrowing as a thought flew across his mind. "Show me the woman."

Turning to the monitor, images, flashed across the screen as Hamish nodded. "Leander? Hold on—"

"No, the other one," Martin growled.

"Oh, okay." Hamish pounded away at his keyboard before pointing to a monitor to Martin's left. "That's her."

Standing up, Martin walked to the screen. The shot was not great. It was from a satellite. "Can you clean this up?"

"Uh, yeah, just give me a—there you go," Hamish said.

The image on the screen became clearer. *Well, look who's back in the game. Hello, Matilda.*

"She's not in her sixties, she's in her seventies. Seventy-four, in fact," he murmured.

"You, uh, know her?" Hamish asked.

With a grunt, Martin nodded. "I did. Right up until she died."

Hamish frowned. "Died?"

"Death is always a little different when intelligence agencies are involved," Martin said dryly.

"Um, so should I keep running facial recognition on her?"

Keeping his gaze locked on the screen, Martin spoke slowly as his mind raced. "No need. She won't be in any database."

"And the man?"

"Bring him up." A few seconds later, the man appeared in a split screen with Tilda. The man wore a ball cap and sunglasses, making his features impossible to discern. But from the angles in his cheeks and the set of his shoulders, Martin knew he was in shape. And he looked familiar as well. Martin frowned. It couldn't be him, though. He'd be in his seventies at least by now, approaching his eighties. This man was much younger. Maybe a grandson?

"Do you know him, sir?" Hamish asked.

Studying the image, Martin shook his head. "I'm not sure. Keep running the facial rec and see if he pops up."

"Yes, sir."

"And I assume you are tracking their progress from the safe house?" Martin asked.

D.E.A.D.

Hamish winced. "Um, well, we ran into a little problem with that."

"What kind of little problem?" Martin asked with narrowed eyes.

Hunching his shoulders as if it would make him smaller, Hamish once again avoided Martin's eyes. "The satellite link went down. By the time it came back up, they were gone."

Martin stared at him. "Quite a coincidence."

"No, I don't think it is," Hamish said quickly. "I think it was intentionally taken down."

The hacker. Martin looked at Hamish. "Tell me again why I pay you if some little hacker can run circles around you?"

"I-I'll find them," Hamish squeaked.

Martin glared at him. "You better, Hamish. Because mistakes like these can be life changing." *Or ending.*

Hamish swallowed and paled noticeably. "I'll find them."

"See that you do," Martin said quickly as he strode from the room and down the hall. He punched the button for the elevator. Tilda was back in the game, which meant things had gotten a little more complicated. He smiled as the doors slipped open and he stepped in.

And potentially more rewarding.

CHAPTER 34

Tilda drove straight through Colorado toward Utah. Fear for Chris, for Alvie and the triplets, kept Maeve on the edge of her seat throughout the long ride. Maeve spent the time studying the woman behind the wheel. She hadn't said much; in fact, Greg was the one who had told her her name. And then he'd just said he'd explain everything when they stopped.

Now Maeve watched the silent woman drive with confidence, her strong forearms steering the wheel with certainty, her face impassive. There was only one moment when the woman let her guard down. Her cell phone beeped, indicating a text. Her whole body had tensed as Greg picked up the phone.

"He's clear. He'll meet us at the house," Greg said.

Tilda let out a small breath, the tension slipping from her shoulders. "Good."

Maeve leaned forward to be heard. "Who's clear?"

"Adam, my grandson," Tilda said.

"He was at your ranch, too," Greg said. "He came from a

different direction and then stayed back to make sure we weren't followed."

Maeve had wondered why no one had given chase.

"Why don't you sleep a little?" Greg suggested. "We still have a couple of hours to go."

"I'm fine," she said quickly.

"It's okay, Maeve. I'll wake you if anything happens or we hear anything."

She looked into his eyes and knew he was talking about Chris. Maeve was terrified. She'd pulled out the phones from the pack but neither worked. One had been smashed, probably from the grenade that had taken out the house. The other had a bullet hole in it. That discovery had terrified Maeve. She hadn't realized that any of the shots had gotten so close to her.

Maeve settled back against the seat, Alvie's head on her lap. She stroked his back absentmindedly as the Jeep drove along. Darkness had fallen an hour ago and the drone of the Jeep was forcing her eyelids to close. She jerked them open, wanting to stay awake. But the triplets were dozing, all curled up with Hope, and even Alvie was dropping off. Finally she gave up the fight. Whatever was going to happen was going to happen. She closed her eyes and slept. She didn't wake until the Jeep came to a stop.

She blinked her eyes open as Tilda pulled the keys from the ignition. Maeve swallowed, trying to get some liquid into her dry mouth. "Where are we?"

Tilda looked back, her eyes straying to the sleeping triplets. A smile ghosted across her face before she looked back at Maeve. "In Utah, near the Arches. A safe house. Do you need help with them?"

"No, we've got them." Maeve reached down and handed Snap to Greg, who stood outside the Jeep, and then Crackle as well. She climbed out and Alvie handed her Pop. Maeve waited until Alvie and Hope hopped out before following Greg.

There were no other houses around and no light. Just this one house, which Maeve thought might date back to the eighteenth century. Greg followed Tilda inside, Snap and Crackle securely nestled in his arms.

Maeve paused at the doorway to stare up at the sky. It was beautiful with all the lights twinkling back at her. Maeve wondered if the Earth looked just as peaceful from up there.

Alvie turned to look back at her.

She started toward him, her thoughts shifting back to the here and now. "I'm coming."

CHAPTER 35

DULCE, NEW MEXICO

Martin scanned the recording from Leander's ranch. He watched again as the Jeep screeched to a halt in front of Leander and the hybrids. Leander talked for only a few seconds with the driver before they all scampered into the Jeep. Schorn, who was supposed to be dead, was clearly visible.

He zoomed in on Matilda, even though it didn't help clear up the image. He sat back. *And where have you been all these years?* Matilda's reappearance at the same time a hacker was thwarting Martin's plans was too big a coincidence to be believed. They were undeniably connected. But what exactly was Matilda's end goal here?

He'd reviewed the report of Matilda's death, including the autopsy. If it was a forgery, it was brilliant. And she had never reappeared on any radar until Leander's ranch. Why stick her neck out now? What was so important?

Martin rewound the tape until he had a shot of Alvie. *It's you, isn't it? Somehow you've drawn her out of the shadows.*

His phone buzzed and he growled at the interruption. *How am I supposed to get any work done like this?* "What?" He all but growled as he answered.

An analyst spoke quickly. "Sir, we have an update on the Salt Lake City case."

Martin frowned. *Salt Lake? Oh, right.* Agents Maxwell and Tidwell. He'd instructed Hamish to keep him abreast of any problems with the D.E.A.D. cases. To demonstrate the truth of his claims of superior methods, he needed to know of any problems before they became problems. "Go ahead."

"They have called off the search for the day. They were unable to locate the creature."

Martin mulled over the possibilities. "Have them search one more day. If nothing shows up, have them move on to the next case."

"Yes, sir."

"Have you found Garrigan?"

"No, sir."

Martin played with the pen on his desk while imagining plunging it into Hamish's eye. "And why not?"

"We're having trouble with the traffic cameras."

"What *kind* of trouble?"

Unlike Hamish, this analyst wasn't put off by Martin's tone. "They're not registering the license plate of the car Garrigan took from the hotel."

"Has he changed it?" Martin asked.

There was only a slight hesitation before the analyst replied. "It's possible, but it's almost as if someone is hiding him from the cameras. I have the cameras set up to grab any images of him, but there's nothing. It's like he's disappeared."

"He *hasn't* disappeared," Martin snapped.

For the first time, a little nervousness slipped into the analysts tone. "No, no, I know. That's not what I mean. I mean, all traces of Leander's escape with the hybrids and Garrigan's escape are being covered. No cameras are picking them up."

Immediately he flashed on a piece of intel from the Project Vault reports. "The hacker from 51?"

"I believe so, yes. Um, I'm going to hand you to Hamish. He's been working on it."

Before Martin could reply, he heard the click as the call was transferred.

"Uh, hello?" Hamish asked timidly.

"Have you had any luck tracking them?" Martin demanded.

"I'm close," Hamish said quickly.

"So that's a no."

The man's swell was audible. "It's ... it's a not yet. I will find them."

"See that you do, Hamish. Otherwise I'll be very disappointed in you, and you wouldn't like that, would you?" Martin asked his voice soft.

"No. No, sir."

"Send me Tidwell and Maxwell's personnel file," Martin said.

"Yes, yes, sir. I-"

Martin disconnected the call. A few minutes later, the file popped up on Martin's screen. Tidwell had been a psychology major in college and was the youngest of three children. Her mother was her emergency contact. She was a Marine whose fellow officers only had good things to say about her.

Martin looked further back and saw that she'd volunteered at an animal shelter while in high school and college. He frowned. *Well, that could be a problem.*

His phone beeped. Checking the message, he smiled.

It was from Hamish: *I've got Leander's location.*

CHAPTER 36

CENTERVILLE, UTAH

Guilt had dogged Norah all day, compounded when it began to rain heavily in the afternoon. Two dozen police officers had joined Bob and Norah in the search. They crawled over the neighborhood where Iggy had first been seen. And of course, they'd found no sign of him.

Norah had locked Iggy in the motel room with the TV tuned to the Disney channel, some fruit, and a 'Do Not Disturb' sign on the door handle. But she worried he'd try to find her, like he'd done yesterday. She'd kept her eyes peeled for him and been happy there was no sign of him.

By four o'clock, everyone was soaked and ticked off. The weather reports were calling for more rain, so she and Bob called a halt to the search. Norah climbed into the SUV and grabbed a towel from the backseat to wipe off her face.

"God damn waste of time," Bob growled as he started the car and put it into gear.

"I guess it's moved on," Norah said, careful to keep both the guilt and relief from her voice.

"Yeah. I'm sure we'll hear about it when it resurfaces. Probably after it kills someone," Bob growled.

Norah watched him out of the corner of her eye. "Maybe it's not violent."

He turned to with an incredulous look on his face. "Are you kidding me? What are you, some sort of hippie now? The thing's a monster."

"It didn't hurt the little girl. You saw the video." She'd decided to show it to him this morning, in a burst of optimism that maybe he might see what she saw.

He grunted. "We don't know what it was doing. That made my skin crawl. It could have been rooting around in her brain, stealing memories or doing some sort of mind control."

She sighed. *Reality 1, Optimism 0.* "We don't know that."

"No, we don't, and that's the point." He pulled to a stop at a red light and looked at her. "What the hell's with you? You've been acting weird since yesterday."

"What? No, I haven't," she said.

"Yeah, you have. So what's going on?" He pinned her with a glare.

Norah opened her mouth to deny it and then changed her mind. The whole day as they'd slogged through water-drenched streets, she'd been trying to figure out her next steps with Iggy. She couldn't turn him in to the D.E.A.D., and Bob was only reinforcing that view. But she did have the vague outline of a plan. "I don't know. I think I might be coming down with something, and running around in the rain today probably didn't help."

Bob's eyes widened. "You're getting sick?" Bob's fear of germs was very well known.

Pressing a hand to her forehead, she frowned. "Yeah. You know, maybe I'll call Sanders and ask for a few days. I wouldn't want to get you sick."

"Yeah, yeah, you should do that," Bob said quickly.

Norah felt the car accelerate and knew that Bob was imagining germs floating through the inside of the car, heading straight for him. And she couldn't help herself—she coughed.

Her partner's knuckles turned white on the steering wheel and

Norah put her hand to her mouth to cover her smile. "Yeah, I'm really not feeling so great."

As Bob turned into the motel parking lot, the car was practically on two wheels. He slammed to a stop in front of Norah's room. "You should get some sleep. I'll call Sanders as well and tell him you need a few days."

Norah opened her door. "Thanks. I appreciate that."

He didn't even wait for the door to fully close before he pulled away. He didn't pull into a spot but left the parking lot through the other exit. Norah knew he was headed to the nearest drugstore to load up on zinc and buy whatever he could to sanitize the car.

She laughed to herself as she headed to her door. But then her smile disappeared as the enormity of what she was doing hit her. She was obstructing an investigation. She was lying to her partner. And she was actively concealing a target wanted by the U.S. government.

And as much as she hated to admit it, Bob was right. She didn't know the extent of Iggy's abilities. He could be dangerous. *You need to turn him in*, the rational part of her mind argued as she stepped to her door.

She could hear the TV through the door. The 'Do Not Disturb' sign was still hanging on the outside. She pushed back her jacket, her hand on her gun, before keying open the door. She slowly opened it. Iggy lay curled up in front of the TV, his chest rising and falling slowly. She stepped in quickly, closing the door behind her. The flickering images on the TV caught her eye as Mickey Mouse danced across the screen. Iggy didn't wake as she placed her bag on the desk. He lay quietly, something white clutched to his chest. Peering at it, Norah realized it was one of the bathroom towels. It had been folded and he now clutched it like it was a teddy bear.

He looked so little, so alone, that Norah felt tears press to the back of her eyelids. She sank onto the bed. She knew she would never be able to turn him in. They'd kill him. But she couldn't hide him forever.

Once again, she wished she'd been able to track down Leander. If anyone would be an ally for the little guy, it was her. But Leander was being hidden very well.

Norah ran a hand through her hair as she watched Iggy sleep, knowing she'd made a decision. *All right, little guy. I'll get you somewhere safe.*

CHAPTER 37

OUTSIDE THE ARCHES, UTAH

The house was small. Floral wallpaper lined the small foyer and up the staircase. There was a small living room to the right with a faded blue couch and two threadbare, pink chenille armchairs. The dining room was to the left, although instead of a dining set it held a queen-sized bed with a white quilt.

Tilda nodded to the bed. "I thought you might want to sleep down here. There's a bathroom just down the hall."

Maeve met her gaze, still not sure what to make of the woman.

Tilda must have read the questions on Maeve's face. "Once you get them settled, I'll be in the kitchen. We can talk." Tilda glanced at Pop asleep in Maeve's arms. "They are amazing," she whispered, awe in her voice. She reached out a hand as if to stroke Pop but then thought better of it and pulled her hand back, heading down the hall with a perfectly straight back and energy in her step.

Maeve watched her go, feeling like she could sleep for a

week. But she needed to know more about Tilda. When she'd looked at the triplets, it had been with wonder. She turned to Greg to ask him what he knew about her and how he'd ended up with her. But she was distracted when Alvie pulled the quilt back and Greg laid Crack and Snapple down. Maeve's heart clenched as she realized how close she'd come to losing them all today. She hugged Pop tighter, her breathing becoming unsteady.

"Hey, hey, it's okay." Greg moved to her side. "They're all right. All of them. And you guys are safe."

But not Chris, she thought but couldn't get the words past her lips.

"Look, you've been through a lot. You're exhausted, scared. A decent night's sleep and the world will look better. Trust me."

She knew he was right. But she wasn't quite ready for sleep yet.

Laying Pop next to Crackle and Snap, she tucked the quilt around all of them. She ran a hand over each of their heads. Today had been rough for them. Emotional upheaval seemed to have double the impact on them. She thought it might be due in part to their age. But Alvie struggled with emotional upheavals as well. She looked at him now and his large eyes looked even larger. She opened up her arms and he rushed into them, burying his head in her chest.

Hope tried to join the embrace, but Greg snatched her up. Hope licked him repeatedly in response. Greg smiled but held the squirming puppy a little farther away. "I'll see if I can find some food for this one. We'll be in the kitchen when you're ready."

Maeve nodded over Alvie's head. She started to rock gently with him in her arms. And then she started to shake. Alvie hugged her tighter.

"It's okay. We're all safe. It's okay."

An image of Chris wafted through her mind and her heart clenched again.

"I know. But Chris is smart, capable. He will have seen them coming. And without us to worry about, he'll be able to take care of himself. He's fine. He'll find us."

But she could still feel Alvie's fear. And even though she believed her words, she felt the same fear. All it took was one distracted moment, and they could lose each other. What if Chris had been sleeping or drugged or—

Cutting off that train of thought, she squeezed her eyes tight. The world of 'what if' was a dangerous and damaging place. She needed to deal with the here and now. She would face the ache of something happening to Chris when she knew for certain that something had. She would not put herself through that, or any of them, until she had to.

She stayed with Alvie wrapped in her arms for another ten minutes, until his tremors had subsided. She rubbed his back in lazy circles and spoke softly into his ear. "You did great today. You helped save us. Thank you, Alvie."

He looked up at her and smiled.

She smiled back. "You are an incredible person, Alvie. We are all very lucky to have you." He leaned forward so his forehead rested against hers, and a feeling of love washed over her.

I love you, too. When he leaned back, his eyelids were drooping. She pulled back the blankets and scooted him toward the pillow. "Get some sleep."

He gripped her hand.

"I won't let anything happen to you." She nodded to the triplets, their breathing now a little wheeze that squeezed her heart. "Or to them. Sleep."

He closed his eyes and Maeve stayed by their side until she was sure Alvie was asleep. But even then she couldn't quite bring herself to leave them. Hope trotted back inside, placing her two paws on Maeve's lap and licking her.

Maeve rubbed the dog's side as Greg stepped into the doorway. After a lingering glance at the sleeping aliens, he whispered, "There's something you need to see."

"Up, Hope." Maeve patted the bed.

Hope hopped up, turning in circles a few times before curling up at Alvie's feet. "Watch over them, girl." Maeve stood up and followed Greg, hoping that whatever Greg was about to show her was something that would not rip all of their worlds apart.

Again.

CHAPTER 38

Pausing just outside the doorway of the kitchen, Maeve steeled herself before she stepped in. The kitchen looked like it hadn't been renovated in years. The wooden cabinets were missing a few handles and the yellow linoleum counters had seen better days, as had the wallpaper with yellow and brown flowers. Tilda and Greg looked up from their spots at the old kitchen table.

Greg stood up. "Sit here, Maeve. You need to see this."

She held up a hand. "Okay, but before I look at anything, I want some answers. Who are you?" She turned to Greg. "How are you alive? We mourned you!"

Greg blanched. "I know, I know, you have a ton of questions. But I have the answer to the most important one right now—Chris."

With a gasp, she hurried forward. She peered at the laptop screen. Chris stood, his gun trained on the back of a man's head. Then he knocked the man out and rifled through his pockets before disappearing from the frame. He was picked up again in a parking lot with dozens of people milling around. She watched him get into a car and drive out of the lot and the frame. She sank into the chair feeling lightheaded. She wanted to cry, scream, and curl up in a ball all at once. But being she had an audience, she did none of that. She simply let out a shaky breath. "He's all right."

Tilda nodded. "He was attacked at his hotel. But he survived and then took off in that car. So as of two hours ago, he was fine."

Relief weakened Maeve's limbs. *Thank God.*

Standing, Tilda went to the stove, pouring a cup of tea from the teapot and placing it in front of Maeve. "Here. Something hot always helps me when I've had a shock."

Maeve took a sip and was thankful no one commented on how much her cup shook. She let the warmth fill her up and then placed the cup back down. "Okay. That's one answer. Now let's hear another." She turned to Greg. "How are you alive?"

He grinned. "Well, that's kind of a cool story."

Las Vegas, Nevada

Greg stared at the two blobs heading toward him. I remember you. He was pretty sure they were the same as that thing he'd seen race across the ceiling at Area 51. As if to confirm it, a third blob appeared from the hallway and climbed up the ceiling the same way the one at 51 had ...

Oh, good. I was right, *Greg thought, his mind spinning as he backed up, frantically trying to figure out a way out of this mess.*

Guess jumping from a two-story window it is. *He ran for the window, trying not to imagine how much it was going to hurt when he hit the ground below. Or how difficult it was going to be to run away from these things when he no doubt broke both his legs.*

One problem at a time.

He raised the blinds on the window and then dove for the side as a shape crashed through it. Greg rolled, his back slamming painfully into the legs of a weight bench.

The shape landed on the ground in a crouch and then straightened. The shape was of a man with dark glasses, dark clothes, and strikingly blonde hair.

The man pulled a long gun from his back and then pulled the trigger. Blue flame shot from the muzzle, engulfing the thing on the ceiling. It squealed, dropping to the ground. The other two backed up for a moment and then rushed forward. The man turned the nozzle on both of them. They burst into flame, making the same horrific squealing noise. Dark smoke began to spread through the room.

Greg lay on the ground, stunned. He turned to look up at the man, but the man didn't even glance at him. He pulled a round object from his belt and Greg stumbled to his feet. "No!"

The man threw the grenade toward the stairs, where more squeals sounded. Then the whole building shuddered and debris flew up the stairs as the grenade exploded.

Holy shit. How many are there? *Greg turned to the man.* "You're here to help me, right?"

The man nodded.

"Great. Um, but I think you just blew up our only way out." *The creatures he'd torched had stopped making noises or moving, but the fire that had taken them out had started to spread. The thing on the ceiling crashed to the ground, taking part of the ceiling with it. Greg stumbled back, but his new buddy stood there unmoving.*

Great. He's one of those 'I don't run from explosions' guys.

The man moved to the window and gestured for Greg to approach. Okay, guy's not a talker, *Greg thought as he hustled to the window.* "Uh, dude, not to rush you, but it's getting a little toasty. Uh, are you with the government? Some sort of protection detail? Because I'd like to register a complaint about my level of protection."

The man said nothing, just looped a rope under Greg's arms. And Greg noticed the man was still attached to the rope he'd used to swing through the room.

Greg coughed. The smoke was getting really thick. The man tugged him to the windowsill. Greg frowned down at the rope. "What's this—"

The man stepped onto the windowsill and pulled Greg out with him.

Greg let out a yell as he swung out into open air. He grabbed the rope, holding on as the man pulled out a remote. The rope started to pull them to the roof.

Greg was almost at the roof level when the windows on the first floor blew out. Oh, man, Frank, I am so sorry.

His silent hero grabbed onto the edge of the roof and pulled them over the side. Greg crashed to the ground and lay panting on the rooftop. "Holy crap. That was cool." He got to his knees. "And not to question your rescuing abilities, but there's no way down from here. And well, you know, the building is actually on fire."

The man walked over to a black duffel bag. Part of the roof collapsed near the stairwell door. Greg yelped. "Dude, we really need to—"

The man stood up, a long harpoon gun in his arm.

"Whoa! Whoa! Um, look you've got a plan. I got that. I'm just going to—" The man pointed the weapon at Greg and he dove for the ground, his hands covering his head. "No!"

The harpoon shot through the air over Greg's head, a rope attached to it. Greg looked up as the man cut the other half of the rope and then tied it off on a telephone pole.

Greg stood up and looked at where the harpoon was embedded in the wall of the office building across the street, only about eight feet from the ground. Greg grinned. "Wow, that's like serious Batman stuff."

The man grabbed the rope still attached under Greg's arms and pulled him to the ledge.

"Hey, hey, no pulling. Just use your words. You have words, right?"

The man attached a carabiner to Greg's rope and to the rope leading to the street. He attached a zip line handle as well and placed Greg's hands on it.

"Hold on," the man said.

"How do I—"

The man pushed Greg off the roof. Greg let out a yell, holding on in terror as images of his life whipped before his eyes. I need to spend less time playing video games, he realized even as he let out another scream.

The building came up fast, and Greg knew he was going to splat right into it. Great. People will ask, how did Greg die? As a human pancake.

He closed his eyes, preparing for the inevitable crash. Then his shoulders were jarred as his descent came to an abrupt halt. He opened one eye. He was two feet shy of the wall. "Huh."

The rope shook and he saw the man had started his own descent.

"Oh crap." Greg released his hold on the handle and then had to practically do a pull-up to release the carabiner. He dropped to the ground and hustled out of the way seconds before the man stopped in the same spot. Greg leaned back against the wall, breathing hard. "Holy crap. That was awesome." He grinned at the guy. "You really don't talk much, do you?"

The man shouldered the duffel bag he'd brought with him after yanking the harpoon out of the wall. "Run."

Greg stood up with a frown. "What? I thought you were the good guy."

The man turned Greg around. Two giant blobs were heading straight for them.

"Run," the guy said again, taking off, and Greg sprinted down the street after him.

"Adam had a car stashed two blocks away. We made it there and took off before the things could catch us." Greg grinned.

Tilda raised an eyebrow at his statement.

Greg rolled his eyes. "Okay, well maybe Adam blowtorched both of them as well. But I think we can all agree that the important point is we both got away. And now here we are."

"It was creatures from 51 that went after you?" Maeve asked.

"Yeah, that big, horrible blob thing that chased you and Chris across the foyer, remember?"

Maeve pictured the mad dash she, Chris, and Alvie had run, leading a group of lethal aliens toward a group of military personnel who had orders to kill everything on the base, including the humans.

Maeve frowned. "But how did it find you? I mean, that seems like an awfully big coincidence." Maeve paused. "Just like that creature at the ranch coincidentally found us."

Greg looked at Tilda before speaking. "Yeah, we don't think it's a coincidence, either."

"And it's not the first time that the aliens have gone after people from 51," Tilda said.

"From 51 specifically?" Maeve asked.

Tilda nodded. "There were about two dozen people who survived. Most of them have died under unusual circumstances."

"What does that mean?" Maeve asked.

"You remember Regina West from 51? Well, she was found with these raised suction marks on her body. The coroner said she died from anaphylactic shock, but her family said she was not allergic to anything, and the coroner can't identify the bite."

Maeve's mind whirled. There was no chance those creatures just lucked upon the people from 51. "How's that possible? That they could track people? They shouldn't have those abilities."

Greg looked at Maeve. "Maeve, today wasn't the first time aliens came for you."

"*What*?" Shock made her voice harsher than she'd meant.

"Your protection detail has kept you safe," Tilda said.

Maeve's mouth dropped open. "The false alarms."

"They weren't false alarms. They were breaches. Your security just didn't tell you," Tilda said.

The sense of betrayal cut deep. She'd known Wilson had his own agenda. But how did leaving them unaware of a very real threat help that agenda? "Why? I mean, they were there—"

Tilda cut in. "To keep tabs on you. Yes. Part of that was keeping you safe. But the overall priority was to make sure you stayed where you were put until President Wilson figured out how you could be useful to him."

Maeve narrowed her eyes, taking in the older woman. "And what's your role in all this? Who do *you* work for?"

"No one anymore. But I worked for the government for years, and I've learned things along the way."

Maeve crossed her arms over her chest. "So what exactly did you do for the government?"

Tilda shrugged. "Oh, different things over the years."

Maeve was starting to get a little annoyed at the vagueness in the woman's answers. "Exactly which parts of the government did you work for?"

Tilda met Maeve's gaze without blinking. "I started out with NASA back in the fifties. I was a computer."

Maeve frowned. "A computer?"

But Greg's face lit up. "That's so cool!"

Maeve looked at him in confusion.

Greg grinned at her in response. "Back before computers as we know them today were used, NASA needed to calculate all their math by hand. They had human computers. People who could do these amazing math problems that we need machines to run today."

The fifties? Maeve took a close look at the woman across from her. True, she had brilliantly white hair. But her tank top showed off her muscular arms and strong physique. And while she had a few wrinkles, there weren't a lot. Honestly if she dyed her hair she could probably pass for being in her late thirties or early forties. "How old were you when you started there?"

"Fourteen."

Maeve sat back in shock. That meant Tilda had to be in her eighties at least.

Tilda winked at her. "I look good for my age."

"Yeah, you do," Greg said.

Maeve looked at him in disbelief.

He frowned at Maeve before the understanding of exactly how his last statement sounded caught up with him. "What? No, I didn't mean it that way."

"Uh huh," Maeve said.

"I'm just going to sit here quietly," Greg muttered.

"So you work with NASA?" Maeve asked.

"No. I *worked* with NASA. I moved on to different agencies within the government. I didn't learn about the A.L.I.V.E. projects until well after they had begun." Tilda nodded back toward the front of the house. "He was already twenty years old and the other projects had been created at that point."

Maeve looked away from Tilda's probing gaze. Maeve had been stunned when she'd learned that other projects existed. And none of those beings had been shown the care Alvie had been. Maeve had wondered in the weeks after everything had happened at 51 if things would have been different if the 'projects' had been shown compassion rather than clinical assessment. "I wish I could have done more."

Tilda reached out and squeezed Maeve's hand, surprising her. "You did all you could. And you took on the responsibility of those three little ones even though you were essentially in a war zone."

"Anyone would have done that," Maeve said.

Tilda shook her head. "That's not true, because when you found them, they were alone. Someone left them there."

Maeve had never thought of it like that. But Tilda was correct—someone had left the triplets behind, not concerned about what would happen to them. Although with the signs of the abuse on them, she shouldn't be surprised. But she was, and she felt angry all over again at their treatment.

"Anyway," Tilda continued, "when I heard about the projects, there was nothing I could do. But I kept an eye on the situation, and after 51 I made sure to keep an eye on you in Denver and Dr. Schorn here. When I saw you were in trouble, we moved in."

"But how? No one's supposed to know where we are," Maeve said.

Tilda snorted. "Right. The government is like a giant sieve; very little stays secret for long. But in this case, I have to admit they played your locations very close to the vest. But we had a little help."

"From who?"

Tilda paused. "I don't know, exactly. But someone has been feeding us information for months. And whoever it is, is very well connected. Their information has always been spot on. They let us know you were in trouble today."

"And they warned Chris as well," Greg said.

"You trust them?" Maeve asked.

"To a certain point, yes. Like I said, their information has been accurate. But like you, I don't like not knowing who I'm dealing with."

"Have you tried to figure out who they are?"

"I have people working on it," Tilda said. "But they've been working on it for months with no luck. I don't think Guardian will reveal his identity until he wants to."

"Or her identity," Greg cut in. "No need to be sexist. It's the twenty-first century, after all."

Tilda tilted her head toward him with a small smile. "Of course, Dr. Schorn."

Maeve's head spun. So apparently this Guardian was feeding them info and keeping them from harm. But ... "So what exactly is your end goal here?"

"To keep you guys alive."

Maeve nodded down the hall. "And Alvie and the triplets?"

Tilda gave a small smile. "Are a miracle. And I don't want any harm to come to them. That, I can promise you."

A wave of exhaustion rolled over Maeve. Tilda noticed. "Look, nothing's going to change if we table this conversation until tomorrow. Why don't you get some sleep and then tomorrow you can ask me anything you like?"

"And will you answer every question I ask?"

The back door opened and a tall, muscular man with bright blonde hair stepped in, sunglasses on. *This must be Adam.*

Tilda stood with a smile. "All good?"

Adam nodded, and Maeve wondered why he didn't take his dark glasses off. Had he been wearing them outside in the dark?

"Adam, this is Dr. Maeve Leander. She's the reason Alvie and the triplets survived at 51."

Adam crossed the room and extended his hand. "It's a pleasure, Doctor."

Greg's mouth dropped open. "'It's a pleasure, Doctor?' Holy crap, that's the longest sentence I have ever heard you utter."

Maeve shook his hand, noting how cold it was. "Adam."

Adam withdrew his hand and didn't respond to Greg's outburst. With a glance at Tilda and a nod at Maeve, he disappeared down the hall. Maeve heard him making his way upstairs.

"Don't let the fact that he completely ignored me fool you," Greg said dryly. "We are the best of buds."

"My grandson is a man of few words. But he takes his responsibilities very seriously." Tilda stood up. "Well, I think I will retire as well. Adam has set a sensor perimeter a mile out from the house. If anyone comes near it, we'll know well in advance. But we are well hidden here. So why don't we all get some sleep? Dr. Leander, I assume you will want to stay with the little ones?"

Maeve nodded.

"All right. Greg, there's an extra bedroom upstairs if you want it."

He shook his head. "I'm going to bunk down here in case Maeve needs help."

"Fair enough. Well, if you'll excuse me, these old bones could use a little rest." She headed out of the kitchen without even a droop in her shoulder.

"That's one tough lady," Greg said.

"I don't doubt it." Maeve stood, then grabbed the edge of the table as the whole room swam for a minute.

Greg took her by the shoulders and steered her toward the door. "Come on. You need to sleep."

He led her down the hall to the front bedroom. Maeve curled up on the opposite side of the bed from Alvie, the triplets asleep between them. None of them woke, but Pop made some noises and rolled to his side.

Greg stepped next to the bed on Alvie's side. "I'd forgotten how cute they are." He paused and then gestured to the old chair in corner. "Hey, um, do you mind if I bunk in here? I just would rather …" He shrugged.

Maeve knew she wanted people around her as well. "Of course. But be warned, the triplets will be all over you in the morning."

Greg sat down, putting his feet up on the end of the bed. "I'm actually looking forward to it."

Maeve closed her eyes and tried to calm her breathing. She was exhausted, but her mind was churning. After a few minutes, she opened them. "Greg?" she called quietly.

He peeked out at her from under heavy lids. "Yeah?"

"We can trust these two, right?"

Greg opened his mouth and then shut it before shaking his head. "I don't know, Maeve. I know they helped me, and they helped you when we needed it. But I've kind of lost my faith in the goodness of humanity. So I'm also sure they did it for a reason."

"Any idea what it is?" She asked.

He shook his head. "No."

She sighed. "Great. Well, then I guess we trust them until we can't."

CHAPTER 39

CENTERVILLE, UTAH

Last night Norah had called Sanders to let him know she'd put in a request for a few days off. This morning, he'd called while she was in the shower to let her know she'd been granted three days with more if she really needed it.

Norah lowered her phone after deleting the message. She had three days, including the weekend. That meant she had five days to track down Leander. Sanders had mentioned that Bob called him the night before to support her request, which was probably the only reason the request had been granted. According to Sanders, Bob believed Norah to be on the edge of the Bubonic plague.

She looked down at Iggy, who sat next to her, finishing up his egg sandwich. "Enjoyed that, huh?" she asked.

He swallowed the last bite and nodded.

"Well, I got you a little treat." She pulled over the second bag she'd bought this morning. "Not sure if you'll like them, but on our planet people really do." Opening the bag, she handed Iggy a sugar donut. He took it carefully, sniffing it first. His eyes grew large, and then he took a tentative bite. His head whipped to Norah before he gobbled the donut up.

She laughed at the look of rapture on the little guy's face. She handed him a second one and he took it quickly as she crumpled the bag. He stopped at the noise and looked at Norah. Then he looked down at the donut and broke it in half, handing half back to Norah.

Touched, Norah took it. "Thank you."

He gave her another one of those small smiles and then ate his half. She stood up after she finished hers. She paused, staring down at him. "All right, my little friend. You and I are going to take a little drive today."

He tilted his head. "Ig?"

She sighed. "Yup. Ig."

Norah grabbed her wallet and keys. "There's a car rental place down the street. I rented a car last night, but I have to go pick it up." She paused. "I don't know why I'm explaining this all to you because I'm pretty sure you have no idea what I'm saying."

Iggy nodded. "Ig."

Turning on the TV, which was still tuned to the Disney channel, she turned to her guest. "I'll be back in a little bit. You stay here and keep quiet, okay?"

Iggy tilted his head to the side. "Ig?"

"Right, Ig." She grabbed her bag, slung her jacket over her shoulder, and opened the door. Bob stood there with one hand up in the air like he was about to knock.

Norah's pulse raced. *Oh shit*. "Hey." She shut the door quickly behind her and prayed Iggy had been out of sight.

"Where are you going?" Bob frowned.

She forced her shoulders to slump and her voice to become weaker. "Drugstore."

"Right. Well." He glanced back at the door, where the sound of the TV could be heard. "Is there somebody in there?"

"No, just me and the TV. Oh, and I was on the phone with my mom," she said.

"Oh, okay." He frowned. "Um, you don't want me to drive you or something, do you?"

Gee, how gracious. "No, it's okay. I, um, rented a car. I'm going to walk down and pick it up. I'm hoping the walk clears my head a little bit. You heading back?"

"Yeah, I was just about to get on the road."

Norah started to head for the street. "Have a good ride back."

Looking back at the door, Bob hesitated.

"Bob?" She called.

He turned and followed her. "Yeah, well, careful driving, being sick and all."

"Yeah, thanks. You, too." She headed out of the parking lot. When she reached the main street, she checked on Bob. He was now at his car door. He cracked it open, but paused, his eyes narrowing as he looked back toward Norah's room.

Norah's breath caught and time seemed to stand still. *Get in the car, Bob.* As if hearing her, he opened the door, and a few seconds later was reversing out of the spot.

With a tremble in her steps, Norah hurried down the street. Bob drove past a minute later with a honk of the horn and a wave. As Norah waved back, she let out a sigh of relief.

He's gone. He doesn't suspect anything. You're being paranoid. But she didn't like how Bob had looked at her motel door, and she found herself walking just a little bit faster.

CHAPTER 40

OUTSIDE THE ARCHES, UTAH

Maeve had slept like the dead. In fact, she was the last one up. When she opened her eyes she had a moment of panic when she realized she was alone in the room. But then she heard Greg's voice from down the hall. "Okay, you monsters, that's it. No more Fruit Loops."

She smiled and gave herself a moment to gather herself before she headed to the kitchen. She stood in the doorway, taking in the scene.

Greg sat at the table, pouring milk into bowls for Snap and Crackle. Tilda was there, too, Pop sitting in her lap as Tilda handed him a piece of toast. Hope lay under the table, hoping to catch any crumbs.

Alvie wasn't there, so she immediately called out to him. She felt the flutter of his response back at her and knew he was all right.

"Thank God. They're killing me," Greg declared dramatically as he looked up from the table.

Tilda smiled. "Not me. I will take this kind of breakfast routine any day of the week. Coffee's on the counter."

"Ah, sweet nectar of the gods," Maeve said as she headed for the pot. Snap hugged her legs just as she reached it. Maeve opened her arms and she leapt up. Maeve hugged her tight. Crackle and Pop quickly made their way over to her and demanded the same treatment. Every morning started with hugs. A vision of green grass and trees appeared in her mind. "You guys want to go outside?"

The triplets nodded back at her and Hope jumped around excitedly.

Maeve looked at Tilda. "Is it safe for them out there?"

"Oh, yes. Adam and Alvie are already out there," she said.

"Okay. Go on," Maeve said. Without a backward glance, the four of them headed for the back door.

When they'd disappeared, Maeve turned to watch them through the kitchen window. The triplets scattered into the yard as Adam stepped out from the trees, Alvie perched on his shoulders. Maeve's mouth dropped open. She'd never seen Alvie take to someone so quickly. But if he thought Adam could be trusted, that said a lot about Tilda's quiet grandson.

Maeve took a sip of her coffee as Tilda joined her at the window. "You've truly done an amazing job with them. They're so well adjusted, it's shocking."

"They are amazing little people," Maeve said feeling so grateful for them and scared for them at the same time.

"Yes, they are," Tilda said. "Now, if you'll excuse me, I'm going to go for a run."

Maeve turned to her. "I thought you were going to answer questions this morning."

"I am. But something has popped up that I think you may want to see first. I'll see you in a few hours." Tilda headed out of the kitchen.

Raising her eyebrows, Maeve turned to Greg. "Hours?"

Greg grinned. "Apparently Tilda likes to compete in Ironman triathlons whenever she can."

Have knew Ironman triathlons involved running twenty-six point two miles, biking one hundred twelve miles, and swimming two point four miles. She looked toward the doorway where Tilda had disappeared. "Suddenly I feel very out of shape. Are we sure she's human? Because most older women I've met are not running triathlons."

"Except for the Iron Nun," Greg said.

Quirking her brows as Maeve took a seat at the table, she asked, "Is that a superhero?"

"Sort of. Her real name is Sister Madonna Buder. She started running at age forty-six and has completed nearly fifty Ironman triathlons since then."

"Wait, fifty? How old is this nun?" Maeve asked.

Greg's grin was wide. "Eighty-six. And she's still competing in them."

"And now I feel like a lazy sloth," Maeve muttered.

"You and me both, sister. But we have some academic muscle to flex." He patted the laptop on the table. "Tilda got some files after she got back from her bike ride this morning."

"She's already gone for a ride?" Maeve asked, feeling even lazier than she had a minute ago.

"Yup. Guess the woman doesn't sleep much. Anyway, when she got back, she had an email with a huge attachment she wants us to read."

Pushing her need for a stricter exercise regime aside, she asked, "What is it?"

"Files. *All* the files on the research from 51," Greg waggled his brows.

Picturing all the creatures and the amount of data that must have been created for each, her mouth dropped open. "All of it?"

"Or at least a lot of it." Greg paused glancing back to the doorway. "How old do you think she is?"

The abrupt shift in topics caused Maeve to frown. "Tilda?"

"Yeah. I mean I was thinking maybe sixties. But if she's running triathlons, I don't know," he said.

"She's seventy-eight," Adam said as he walked in through the back door.

Maeve whirled around. "Eighty-two? I knew she was tough, but, wow."

Adam said nothing, just filled up his coffee mug and headed back out, sunglasses still on.

"That guy is really strange," Greg said as he stared at the closed door.

Wondering about the glasses, she asked, "Have you ever seen his eyes?"

"Nope. Tilda said something about him being really sensitive to light."

"Huh," Maeve grunted. *What an unusual family.* Then she shook her head, turning back to the laptops. "Well, let's get to work."

CHAPTER 41

The wind ruffled Maeve's hair. She pushed a stray lock back behind her ear as she looked up from the laptop screen. She smiled as she watched Snap and Crackle scamper up a tree and tried not to wince as Pop leapt from one tree to another, following Alvie. Hope ran between the two trees, barking and whining at being left out of the fun.

Maeve rubbed her eyes and placed the laptop on the ground next to her. After Maeve finished breakfast, she and Greg brought the laptops outside so they could keep an eye on everyone while they reviewed the files.

Greg sat next to Maeve, his attention still fixated on the screen. Until, of course, Hope bounded over. "Oh, come on, Hope," Greg grumbled as she dropped a stick onto Greg's laptop, her tail wagging. Greg tossed it across the yard. And with a happy jump, Hope tore off after it.

"You know she's going to keep bringing it back if you keep throwing it."

"I know, I know." Greg closed his laptop and stretched. "But I have a secret weapon." He disappeared into the house and a few seconds later reappeared with a large dog bone. "Here, Hope."

Hope sprinted over.

"Sit," Greg ordered.

Hope promptly dropped her butt, her tail still wagging. Greg handed her the bone and she took it, walked a few feet away, and curled up contentedly as she began to chew.

The triplets had all descended from the trees and were now kicking around a soccer ball. Small smiles were on their faces, and right at this moment, they seemed all right. Alvie glanced over at her from his perch in the tree above them. There was no smile on his face. He'd been tense and quiet all morning. Granted, he couldn't speak, but he wasn't sharing his thoughts like he usually did. Maeve was worried about him. But she also wasn't sure what she could do about it. After all, being worried was a pretty reasonable response to what they were going through.

An image of Chris appeared in her mind. Maeve looked into Alvie's eyes and shook her head. *I don't know.* They hadn't heard from him, not that there was any way for him to contact them. And Guardian hadn't shared any more information on him, either.

"You ready to chat?" Greg asked, interrupting her thoughts.

Maeve pulled her gaze from Alvie and directed her thoughts to the files she and Greg had been reviewing for the last few hours. "Yeah."

"So from what I can tell," Greg said, dropping his voice so Alvie didn't overhear, "it looks like they've accounted for about seventy-five percent of the creatures that were at Area 51."

Maeve thought of the senseless loss of life, both human and non-human. The United States government had created alien hybrids. At 51, all the creatures they had violently crossed paths with were hybrids. None had been pure aliens. Even the creatures that looked like Grays had been mixed with human DNA.

But that didn't mean they did not have pure aliens. When Maeve started going through the files, she'd hoped she would be able to track down one alien in particular who she believed to be a pure alien—the large Gray who had helped keep them from being discovered. The background on the big Gray was, however, scant. Which was unusual. In all other cases, the subject and the subject's DNA were well documented.

But for the big Gray, that information was missing. In the file, he was even given a unique classification that did not follow the pattern that was used to classify the other subjects in the database. His classification was Orion1. For example, Hank, the creature Schorn had been working with at Wright-Pat and then Area 51, was designated as Kecksburg-AG2. His DNA had been taken from the Kecksburg, Pennsylvania 1965 crash site and he was a second-generation hybrid created from the DNA strand. But the big Gray didn't have a hybrid notation. Instead, a single word followed his designation: Agaren.

Was that his name? And what did Orion1 refer to? All the other aliens had a crash site noted as the first name in their classification.

But there was no Orion crash site. Orion, though, was a well-known star constellation. The three prominent stars in the constellation were believed to be the alignment followed by the creators of the three largest pyramids in Giza. Within Egyptian mythology, Orion is one of the two most critical areas of the sky because it was the place where gods were said to have descended from.

More critically, the beings that came from Orion and the constellation Sirius spawned Osiris and Isis, who, according to mythology, created humans on this planet. So did that mean the big Gray, Agaren, came from Orion? And if so, how had he been caught if not through a crash?

In fact, all the other files recounted the DNA collection process. So why was the big Gray's missing? All that was written was that the first contact had been at Holloman Air Force Base. She knew the military had reported thousands of sightings over bases since 1947. In fact, there had been over twelve thousand sightings reported by military personnel between 1948 and 1969 alone. But why, then, wasn't he classified as Holloman-1? But would that mean there had been a crash at a United States Air Force base?

The big Gray, however, was not the most startling finding. Oh, no. That belonged to the other building, a building that contained recreated pure aliens.

When Maeve's mother, Alice, had first been hired to work on the A.L.I.V.E. Project, the U.S. government had wanted her to clone alien DNA. But the DNA had been too different. And at that point, her mother was on the cutting edge of cloning research.

They decided to work with Alvie's progenitor's DNA because it was a mix of human and alien DNA. But somewhere along the way, as cloning research advanced, they must have figured out a way to clone the pure-alien strains. Was that what had happened with the big Gray? Had alien DNA been left behind or provided to the U.S. government at Holloman that led to the creation of the big Gray? Was he a pure alien?

The discovery of the purebred aliens only became more intriguing when the behavioral differences were noted. When the hybrids were released, they killed the humans they came across. And many hybrids had been killed.

But the pure aliens had a completely different approach. As soon as they were released they seemed to immediately head for the surface, taking care to avoid coming in contact with any humans. There were no reported skirmishes involving any of them and they were not listed among the dead at the base. Maeve wasn't sure if that was to protect themselves or the humans. From what she could tell, there were only eight pure aliens in captivity. Had they all escaped?

Her screen blinked and she frowned. Then a new data box appeared in the center of the screen.

Watch me. —Guardian.

"Uh, Greg?" Maeve asked.

His attention stayed fixed on his screen. "Hmm?"

"Greg," she said again.

"What's up?" He looked up, his eyes slightly unfocused.

She nudged her chin to the screen. "You need to see this."

Scooting over next to her, he peered at the screen. "What is that?"

"That box just appeared," she said.

His eyebrows rose. "*Just* appeared?"

"Yup."

"I don't think you should click on it. It could be a virus," he said.

That had been her first through as well. "It could be, but I thought Tilda said her system had top-of-the-line security."

Greg shrugged. "Maybe she just meant the latest version of Norton."

"Ha ha. Somehow she does not strike me as someone who does not know her way around a security system." Maeve hesitated, her hand hovering over the keyboard.

"Maeve, they could track us down if you hit that," Greg warned.

"Guardian's on our side, though, right?"

Doubt laced his words. "I don't know. Hopefully?"

Indecision warred within her. "Well, here goes nothing." She clicked on the screen and then enlarged the box.

Peering at it, Greg frowned. "That's a satellite image. What is that, like a ranch or something?"

A chill stole over Maeve. "That's *my* ranch."

The image zoomed in on the main gate, and Maeve could see Randy standing outside the gatehouse. Three SUVs pulled up and Maeve held her breath.

Greg pointed to the time stamp in the bottom corner of the screen. "This recording is from the time of the attack."

Maeve nodded but didn't answer, keeping her attention on the screen. The guard opened the gate for the three SUVs. They pulled to the side of the fence and a dozen men in black climbed out. All of them were heavily armed.

"What is that?" Greg pointed to the back of one of the SUVs where some of the men were unloading some large crates. Maeve zoomed in.

He leaned closer to the screen. "Those look like—"

Dread stole over Maeve, as she recognized the equipment. "They're the containment units from 51."

Greg spoke slowly. "Maeve, why would your security have containment units? They'd only need them if they were transporting Alvie and the triplets."

She shook her head. A shiver running up her spine. "No, they'd only need them if they were transporting them without my or Chris's consent."

The containment units were left next to the SUVs as the men spread out and began the long walk to the house.

They were coming for us.

The image zoomed out and a dark shadow appeared on the left-hand side of the screen. It skimmed along the edge of the ranch's property, approaching the front gate and the armed men.

The image zoomed back in and Maeve got a view of the creature in flight. It dove toward the men approaching the house. He yanked one of the men up into the air as the other men scrambled away.

"Holy shit," Greg breathed out. "That's the guy from 51! He's the one who saved me and Leslie from Hank."

But Maeve couldn't seem to find any words. She watched the attack on the ranch from this bird's-eye view. It had looked entirely different from the ground.

Two men approached the house, their weapons raised, and the creature swooped down on them. As Maeve and her gang sprinted for the trees, the creature swooped in again, taking out a gunman that Maeve hadn't even noticed in their mad dash. Even at the end of the attack, when they were racing away in the Jeep, the creature had landed on an SUV that attempted to follow them, crushing the engine. The last image on the recording was of the creature taking flight away from the devastation at the ranch.

The data box went black and Maeve just stared at the screen, stunned into silence.

Greg touched her arm. "Maeve, are you all right?"

She pictured the creature landing behind the house and extending a hand toward her. "It wasn't trying to hurt us. It was protecting us."

Looking around, she didn't know what to think. The world suddenly seeming a lot scarier than it had just moments ago. "It wasn't the alien that was trying to kill us. Our own guards let them in, which means ..."

"Which means the U.S. government is trying to kill you all ... again," Greg said softly.

"Not all of us," she said as her gaze flew to Alvie and the triplets, and she pictured the containment units. "But I think what they have planned for them might be worse."

CHAPTER 42

CENTERVILLE, UTAH

Norah managed to rent the car without a problem, and she was able to pick up a few things at the drugstore. Then she'd stopped and picked up some sandwiches as well.

As she drove back, she'd scanned the area, looking for Bob's car even though she'd seen him drive off. But she saw no sign of him.

Gee, paranoid much, she thought as she quickly made her way from the car to the motel room. Iggy was curled up on the pillow in the closet. He smiled sleepily at her.

She placed her stuff on the bed and walked back to the window, glancing outside. Iggy peeked his head out of the closet as she took off her jacket.

"Hey, I got you something." She sat on the bed, one of the bags from the drugstore on her lap. Iggy inched forward as she pulled a small teddy bear from the bag. It had been an impulse buy. She wasn't sure what on earth she was thinking when she'd picked it up. It was cute, with big green eyes, and it was about half Iggy's size.

Iggy's eyes grew rounder and his little mouth opened in an O. She knelt down and handed it to him. He moved forward and gently took it from her hands. He inspected it, even sniffing it before crushing it to his chest and making that little mewling noise of his.

How did anyone ever think you were dangerous?

A knock sounded at her door and she leapt to her feet. Iggy ran to the closet, his little bear in his arms. Norah pulled her weapon, keeping it at her side as she looked out the window. Bob's car was back in its spot. And the man himself was standing at her door. *Oh crap.*

Norah waved Iggy farther into the closet. Once his head disappeared from view, she turned and opened the door.

"Hey," Bob said.

"Hey." Norah leaned against the doorframe as if she needed the support. "I thought you'd left."

"I did, but I felt a little bad about leaving you when you were sick and all. I just wanted to make sure you really were okay." The words were good, but he kept glancing into the room as he talked. "You sure you'll be all right?"

Giving him a weak smile, Norah nodded, "Yeah. I got the car and I decided I'm just going to relax for the rest of the day. Hopefully I'll be feeling better tomorrow or the next day and I can start heading back."

"Okay, well, if you're sure," he said.

"I am. Just a little sleep and some meds"—she waved toward the bed where the drugstore bag lay— "and I'll be right as rain."

"Okay. Let me know when you're back in the office."

"Will do. Have a safe trip."

"Yeah, you, too." Bob's gaze strayed past her into the room

one last time before he turned around and headed for the parking lot.

Closing the door, Norah let out a shaky breath. *He doesn't know anything. You're just suspicious of his behavior because you are hiding something.* He might not know something, but he certainly suspected something. But Bob showing concern was not normal.

She stayed by the window, keeping out of view but watching as Bob got into the car and pulled out of the parking lot again. Relief flooded her as his car turned out of view. "Okay, Iggy, you can come out."

Iggy peeked his head from out of the closet. She smiled suddenly, feeling tired. "Okay, my new little friend. How about we both take a nap? Because I could use one right now. Then when we wake up we'll see if we can track down someone who can help us out, okay?"

He stepped out of the closet, the bear in his arms. He hopped up on the bed next to Norah. Then he climbed under the blankets, his head on his pillow. He closed his eyes, his new friend clutched tightly in his arms, and let out a little yawn. "Ig," he whispered.

"Well, I guess you've gotten comfortable with my being around." For a moment Norah considered sleeping on the other bed. Then she shrugged. *In for a penny, in for a pound, I guess.* She grabbed the blanket off the other bed and lay down next to Iggy, whose breathing had already steadied. She smiled, not sure how exactly she'd gotten to this point in her life.

She closed her eyes, trying to sleep, but worries just crowded her mind. Finally she pushed the blanket off her, sat up, and pulled over her laptop. Maybe Schorn hadn't been killed in the fire. She quickly searched for the latest news article on the fire.

D.E.A.D.

They still hadn't found a body, but he hadn't been seen since that night. Arson was suspected. *Oh man. It was him.*

Norah sat back from the computer. Greg Schorn was dead. She still couldn't believe he'd been killed. She'd just talked to the man less than a week ago. She'd hoped she would be able to talk Schorn into helping her find Leander. Or even talking to her on Norah's behalf.

Iggy lay next to her on the bed, the teddy bear clasped in his arms, his soft breathing the only noise in the room. She looked down at him. Part of her knew she was crazy. She didn't know what Iggy was capable of, not really. But she also knew he didn't deserve to die. There needed to be a third option. And hopefully Leander, who managed to protect four aliens, would be able to help her figure out what that option was.

Of course, she needed to find her first. She knew she was based somewhere near Denver, but that was as much information as she had. It would be dark in another few hours and she needed to get on the road. Driving at night made the most sense because it reduced the chance of someone seeing Iggy.

Rubbing her eyes, she pushed the thoughts from her mind. *I need to get some sleep.*

Tomorrow, she'd head toward Denver and hope like hell that somehow on the way she could figure out a way to find Leander. She tucked the blankets around Iggy a little more and he snuggled even deeper into them. She closed her eyes next to him and refused to let herself think about what was going to happen if she couldn't track down Leander. Or what would happen if D.E.A.D. realized what she was doing.

I'll lose my job. They might even charge me with something. She closed her eyes tightly. *No, none of that. It's going to be fine. It's going to be fine.* She repeated the phrase over and over to herself, forcing her mind to focus on nothing else but the words as she fell off to sleep.

But in her dreams, she and Iggy were being hunted. And it was anything but fine.

CHAPTER 43

OUTSIDE THE ARCHES, UTAH

As Maeve stared at the trees, she was oblivious to everything around her. Her mind was completely focused on recalling every detail of the attack. She was trying to find any way that she'd misinterpreted what she'd seen. But those armed men had been waved in. They had brought containment units with them. And none of her normal security had come to check on them when the alarms went off. And then she thought of the backpack she'd been wearing—the one with the bullet holes in it.

She'd thought they were stray bullets. *But they were aiming for me.*

Tilda stepped out of the back of the house. Maeve looked up, her eyes narrowing as she remembered Tilda talking her out of contacting the government. Was that luck or did the woman know more than she was letting on?

Standing up, Maeve dusted off her pants. Tilda was a senior citizen who ran Ironman triathlons for fun and who knew the ins and outs of some of the government's most top-secret programs.

"That was not luck," Maeve muttered as she started toward the woman.

"What?" Greg asked before scrambling after Maeve. "Hey, what are you—"

Maeve put up a hand, cutting him off.

"Uh oh," Greg muttered, keeping pace with her.

Watching Maeve approach, Tilda raised an eyebrow. "I guess it's time to talk."

"Yes, it is," Maeve said, her anger at all the deception she and her family had been put through rolling through her.

Tilda gestured toward the house. "Let's go in—"

Maeve cut her off. "No. We'll stay out here. The triplets need to run around and I'm not letting them out of my sight."

Sensing her agitation, Alvie walked over and took Maeve's hand. She forced a smile as she looked down at him. "I'm okay. Tilda, Greg, and I are just going to chat."

Taking a step back, Greg spluttered as he gestured to the triplets. "Hey, I can just—"

"You're staying." Maeve glared at him, pinning him in place.

Squirming, he shifted from foot to foot giving her a quick nod. "Uh, like I said, we should all talk."

A flitter of concern floated through her mind as Alvie tilted his head, looking into her eyes. Maeve ran a hand over the top of his skull and he leaned into her hand. "It will be okay. Can you just keep an eye on the triplets for me?"

As Maeve watched him walk away, her heart pounded when she thought of how close she'd come to losing him. He'd been her best friend since she was five. Somewhere along the way she'd shifted from friend to sister and now mom.

And she felt no less protective toward him than a biological mother would. She would give her life to keep him and the triplets safe. And she needed to know exactly what they were up against if there was any chance of keeping them safe.

She turned to Tilda, who was watching Alvie as he caught up with the triplets. Hope trotted up to him, and he ran a hand along her back.

"I'd read about your bond," Tilda said as she turned back toward her. "But seeing it, it's truly an amazing thing. You love him."

Maeve crossed her arms over her chest. "With all my heart, and I will do anything to protect him, which is why you need to tell me what's going on. *Everything* that's going on."

"That goes for me, too." Greg straightened his shoulders next to her. "I don't have the same history with Alvie as Maeve does, but he's important to me. The triplets are important to me. Maeve's important to me. They're my family. So we both need to know what's going on."

With gratitude, Maeve looked over at Greg. He shrugged, a blush crossing his cheeks. "Hey, you've met my sisters. You are *so* much better than them."

"So?" Maeve demanded as she focused once again on Tilda.

With a sigh, Tilda gestured to the picnic table a few feet away. "Well, let's take a seat and I'll answer what I can."

Maeve narrowed her eyes as Tilda headed for the table, noting Tilda did not say she'd tell them everything. But Maeve was determined to not let the enigmatic woman get away with much.

Tilda splayed her hands wide as she took a seat, and Maeve couldn't help but notice how strong they were. "So, where do you want to start?"

"How about the beginning?" Greg suggested as he sat next to Maeve.

Giving them a little smile, Tilda said, "That was a long time ago."

"How about how you knew Greg was in trouble and how you knew we were?" Maeve asked, not smiling back.

Her gaze flicking between the two of them, Tilda spoke slowly. "That's a little difficult to explain."

Her frustration mounting, Maeve crossed her arms over her chest. "We both have doctorates. We'll keep up."

Tilda smiled. "I'm sure you will. Well, I think you will need a little background to understand how we all came to be here. I have been part of the United States government's involvement with alien species for going on five decades."

Greg frowned. "Wait. You said you were a computer with NASA, is that true?"

"For a short while, yes. But it wasn't too long after I began there that I was moved on to other projects," she said.

"Like what?" Greg asked.

Maeve wanted to tell him to be quiet and just let her get to the heart of the story. But she was curious, too. That would have been the late 1960s, early 1970s. As progressive as the time appeared, it still had not embraced women in the workforce, and certainly not in the sciences.

"I worked on the Saturn rockets as an engineer," Tilda said.

Greg's mouth fell open. "You worked with Wernher von Braun?"

Tilda nodded. "Yes."

Greg looked dazed and Maeve felt a little lightheaded at the response as well. Wernher von Braun had been a German rocket scientist during World War II. In fact, he was the man responsible for the V-2 rocket. As part of Operation Paperclip at the end of the Second World War, von Braun, along with more than 1,600 scientists and their families, immigrated to the United States and were enfolded within the American space program. Von Braun was called the father of rocketry. He was credited as being the reason that the United States was able to beat the Russians to the moon.

Tilda continued. "Since I began with NASA, I have made many different contacts throughout the space program. I did not know your mother, but I was aware of her research. She was an impressive woman."

Maeve wasn't sure what to say. She was proud of her mother. They had been close their whole lives. It had only been the three of them, their own little family. Her mom had created the cloning process that had created Alvie, a technique years ahead of the private sector. But that process had also led to the development of the other creatures as well. And Maeve wasn't sure what to think about her mom's role in that.

"I learned of Project Vault only after the subjects had been moved to the base," said Maeve. "And then the aftermath …"

Tilda shook her head. "I don't think anyone truly realized what Martin was capable of. So I've been trying to keep an eye on you, Alvie, and Dr. Schorn here. It wasn't easy. The government was hiding you rather well. But then Guardian contacted me."

"Guardian sent us a recording of the attack on Maeve's ranch. It looked like the humans were coming to take Alvie and the triplets," Greg said.

"I had suspected as much," Tilda replied.

Greg cut in. "A large winged alien was trying to protect them. Do you know who he is? I didn't see him in the files."

Tilda shook her head. "No. The only winged aliens I am familiar with are those reported by Russian cosmonauts in the mid-eighties."

Maeve had forgotten about that particular tale. In 1985, six Russian cosmonauts had been on board the Soviet space station Salyut 7. A strange orange gas had enveloped the station and when it cleared, the cosmonauts reported seeing seven tall humanoid creatures with wings floating outside the space station. Maeve had always thought they shared some sort of group hallucination, maybe in response to the gas. But now ... now she wondered if maybe they had actually seen something.

Surprise and grudging respect was in Tilda's tone as she continued. "Guardian can get into places that I didn't think anyone would ever be able to access. He's been feeding me information for months. He's the one that let me know they were going after Dr. Schorn. And he let me know they were coming after you."

"They. Who's they?" Maeve asked.

There was a shift in Tilda's eyes, and Maeve knew she was calculating how much to reveal. "For Dr. Schorn, it was an alien attack. There have been a few. As I mentioned before, the humans that survived 51 are being tracked down and killed."

"By the aliens?" Greg asked.

"I believe so. If Dr. Schorn hadn't been under our surveillance, I do not believe he would have survived," Tilda said.

Greg nodded vigorously. "She's right. If Adam hadn't busted through that window and happened to have a container of gasoline, a lighter, a grappling hook, and a grenade, well, I would be toast right now."

"And me?" Maeve asked.

"We know Martin Drummond has been looking for all of you for months without any success. But you were protected from on high," Tilda said.

"You think Drummond was behind it?" Greg asked.

Tilda didn't hesitate. "I do."

"You know him, don't you?" Maeve asked with narrowed eyes.

The older woman's lip curled. "Unfortunately Martin and I go way back. He has been obsessed with aliens, and more importantly, an invasion, for decades. He has argued time and again for the need for weapons to defend us in the event of an alien attack." Tilda paused. "I believe some of the deaths of the personnel from 51 and the attack on Dr. Schorn were field tests for those weapons."

"You think he weaponized the hybrids?" Greg asked.

"I would not put it past him," Tilda said.

Oh my God. Maeve was stunned. "But I wasn't attacked by aliens. Humans came for us."

Tilda's gaze shifted to meet Maeve's as if she'd read Maeve's mind. "There was a different objective for you and your family."

"They wanted to capture Alvie and the triplets," Maeve said.

"Yes," Tilda said confirming Maeve's suspicions.

"But how did they find them?" Greg burst out. "They had the protection of the President of the—oh, you don't mean …"

"Guardian warned us specifically that the order had come down to terminate you and Captain Garrigan and to take the subjects in." Tilda paused. "I think the President of the United States okayed the operation at your ranch."

Maeve's head was spinning. She knew she shouldn't have been as stunned as she was, but still. President Graham Wilson had okayed their deaths and he wanted Alvie? No, that wasn't quite right. He was letting Martin have him. "Why? Why would the President do that?"

Tilda sighed. "There's a reason the executive branch has been kept out of the loop. They are too easily swayed by the winds of political expediency. These alien deaths and sightings —I believe they're making the President nervous."

"Why?" Greg asked. "He had nothing to do with what happened at 51. That was Drummond."

Maeve shook her head. "No, he would just be a president who had no idea a U.S. government agency had been holding and creating aliens on U.S. soil. A president who had so little control over the country that one government official could even explode an atomic bomb, killing U.S. citizens, without either his knowledge or permission."

"The media would crucify him as completely incompetent, completely without authority," Tilda said. "But if Martin swoops in and helps with the alien problem, the chance for discovery disappears."

"But Martin created the problem," Greg hissed.

"*That's* Martin's specialty," Tilda said. "He creates problems that only he can solve. It's why he's succeeded where so many others have failed."

"And he just conned the President of the United States," Greg said.

Tilda nodded her agreement.

Maeve felt sick. She hadn't trusted Wilson when she'd met him, but she hadn't thought he was capable of this. It felt like the whole world had grown darker. Her gaze shifted to where Alvie and the triplets played with Hope. How was she going to protect them now?

Hope leapt around the triplets as Snap tumbled and Hope licked her face. Hope had been a great addition to the family. The pup brought smiles to the kids' faces and helped to distract them from the stress of living what was essentially a life in captivity.

Snap got to her feet and Hope trotted next to her before going still, the hair on her back raising. She let out a ferocious bark. At the same time, Alvie turned to the woods.

Tilda's radio blared to life. Adam's voice rang out with urgency. "Perimeter breach. They're inside the perimeter. Get everyone out!"

Maeve was already on her feet and sprinting for the triplets before Greg or Tilda could react. "Run!"

The triplets turned toward her, and then two men in black stepped from the woods and took aim. Pop slapped at his neck, where a dart appeared. He pulled it out, took a step, and dropped.

Maeve's whole world felt like it had shattered. "NO!"

Crackle and Pop danced out of the way as Alvie launched himself at one of the men. But the men still got a shot off, and both Snap and Crackle went down as well. Horror rolled through Maeve as she sprinted toward them. This was her worst nightmare come to life.

Two more men burst from the trees, but Adam tore out behind them. He took one out at the knees from behind and stomped on the man's back before he launched himself at the other one. Alvie twirled around one man's neck, choking him, his feet slamming into the second. Alvie held on to the man as he collapsed to the ground.

Reaching Pop, Maeve pulled him into her arms, noting with relief his heart was still beating. *Just a tranquilizer*.

Adam grabbed Crackle and Snap. "Move!" he ordered.

"Hope, come!" Maeve yelled as she sprinted back toward the house. Tilda and Greg were in the Jeep and raced toward them.

Tilda slammed to a stop. Maeve leaned over, placing Pop on the floor as Tilda stood up, shooting at two men who rounded the corner behind them.

"Here!" Adam shoved Crackle and Snap at Maeve, and then took off at a run. Maeve looked over her shoulder and her heart all but stopped. Alvie was farther away than before. He was trying to get Hope to the Jeep, but the dog was too spooked by the strangers and the gunfire. She ran around in circles, keeping out of Alvie's grasp.

Moving faster than Maeve had seen anyone run, Adam sprinted toward the two of them and scooped Hope up. Hope squirmed, but Adam tucked her under his arms and sprinted back for the Jeep, Alvie right behind him. Maeve put Crackle and Snap next to Pop as a feeling of love wafted over her.

She whirled around. "No!"

Alvie had stopped following Adam and was running in the other direction. Six men appeared from the woods and Alvie launched himself at them. She could hear two car engines approaching fast. But before she saw them, the six men approached Alvie. He took out two of them, moving so fast Maeve couldn't see what he'd done to take them down.

But then Alvie slapped at a dart that had found its target in his neck. His gaze found Maeve's just before his eyes rolled back in his head and he collapsed.

"No!" Maeve screamed, her heart going still. Time seemed to stop as well as Alvie fell to the ground. She only managed one step before Adam grabbed her around the waist, all but throwing Hope at Greg. Adam threw Maeve over his shoulder and stepped on the tire and into the Jeep. Tilda was moving before they sat down.

Maeve shoved against Adam, landing an elbow across his jaw as she scrambled for the side of the Jeep. "Let me go."

Adam's voice betrayed no emotion. "It's too late. There's too many."

She stared at where a dozen men surrounded Alvie. Three SUVs burst out of the trees.

Tilda slammed on the accelerator and, ignoring the road, tore off through the field. Heart shattering over and over again, Maeve watched Alvie get lifted up by one of the men.

Her whole world collapsed as he disappeared from view. She slumped into the seat, not able to think to breathe.

Alvie.

CHAPTER 44

CENTERVILLE, UTAH

Norah woke up with a jolt, the nightmare clinging to her. She looked down at where Iggy lay, but he wasn't there. She sat upright. He whirled around, his eyes large from where he stood outside the closet.

Heart pounding, her hand flew to her chest as she gave him a nervous smile. "There you are. Sorry, I just got a little worried."

Iggy walked over and leapt on the bed. Then he sat next to her and patted her hand. Norah smiled. Once again, he was offering comfort. "Thanks, Iggy. Now I think we need to get moving. You up for a car ride?"

Fifteen minutes later, they were pulling onto the entrance ramp for the highway as the sun dipped into the horizon. There were a few cars out. "Okay, Iggy, you can come out now." He peeked his head out from her duffel bag that was on the floor behind the passenger seat. He clambered up into the front seat with his teddy bear. He sat down and looked over at her with a smile.

Norah had to admit, there was something very comforting about having Iggy for a co-pilot. She pulled over to the side of the highway and quickly put the seat belt on him before pulling back out again.

"Okay, now we're ready." They drove along in silence for a little while, but all the doubts about what she was doing crept back into her mind and were pounding away at her.

Finally she shook her head, turning to her passenger. "You like music?"

Iggy tilted his head toward her.

She turned the radio on, keeping the volume low so she didn't scare him. Iggy stared at the radio and then smiled, nodding his head in time to the music. The car was tuned to an older station. "Great Balls of Fire" by Jerry Lee Lewis played out across the car. When it finished, "Heat Wave" by Martha and the Vandellas came on.

"This is one of my favorites." Norah leaned down and turned it up, starting to sing along.

Next to her, Iggy started to hum. Shutting out her doubts, Norah grinned. It would be all right. She smiled at the little alien bopping next to her. She'd find a way to convince someone in power that he deserved to live.

She had to.

CHAPTER 45

DULCE, NEW MEXICO

Excitement coursed through Martin. His team had retrieved Subject One. The rest had escaped but that was no big loss. It was the first subject he was most interested in. He smiled, imagining everything he could learn from the creature.

But first things first. The team wouldn't be back for a few hours. And there were other situations he needed to keep an eye on. Martin reviewed the file from Salt Lake City. Another subject that was not supposed to have escaped the blast. He watched the footage of the creature. This kind of footage could never get out. It looked as if the thing was actually concerned about the little girl. These things had no such emotions.

But he was surprised they had not managed to catch it. The Maldeks were not known for their defensive abilities. Of course, it's hard to hide in a cell. But it was intelligent, although it was ranked as a low-intelligence creature.

Perhaps the problem was the agents sent after it were not even of average intelligence. He pulled over the files on the two agents who'd been sent to track it down. Both had a good track record and had brought down more than a few escapees. But how come they couldn't find one little Maldek?

Robert Maxwell had joined the DEA after serving two tours in the Army. He'd been reprimanded for excessive force a few times, but nothing stuck. He'd been very good at tracking down his human targets.

He'd already reviewed Tidwell's file last night but he scanned it again. Norah Tidwell had also been former military —Marine Corps. But she'd worked for intelligence. At first, putting them together had seemed to make sense—a brain and a brawn. But perhaps that coupling needed to be reevaluated. He glanced at the image of Tidwell, once again noting her work with an animal shelter.

Or perhaps someone has gotten a little too compassionate. He'd read the case notes from Maxwell, who said Tidwell's behavior was off during the first day of searching. That she had questioned the kill order. He needed to check and see what Maxwell's latest report said.

Martin's phone rang and he glared at it. He hated phone calls. But the caller ID indicated it was Julio Sanders from the D.E.A.D. He answered it, forcing the annoyance out of his tone. "Julio, how are you?"

"Good, Mr. Drummond, good. Um, I have an update on the Salt Lake City case."

Grunting, he asked, "Has the Maldek been caught?"

"Um, no, sir. There have been no further sightings on the creature." The bureaucrat paused. "But Agent Maxwell just called with what could be a problem."

"A problem?" Martin asked slowly, turning his full attention to the call.

"Yes, sir. It seems Agent Tidwell reported that she was not feeling well and requested a few days off. She's been a good agent, so I had no problem with the request. But Maxwell said she was acting weird. So he put a tracer on her rental car."

"And?" Martin prodded.

Sanders let out a nervous breath. "And, uh, she said she was going to rest and maybe take off the next morning, but she started driving that night. She's headed east."

Martin was quiet for a moment. East from Salt Lake City. Denver—where Leander was. Could be a coincidence. But Martin didn't believe in those.

"Where's Agent Maxwell now?" He asked.

"He's following her." Sanders rattled off Maxwell's location, his cell phone number, and the GPS on his car.

"Good. I'll have a team meet him."

"Are ... are you sure that's necessary? She could just—"

Martin cut him off. "If she's doing nothing wrong, then she will have nothing to worry about."

The bureaucrat started speaking quickly. "Norah's a good person. I'm sure—"

"If she's a good person, she's in the wrong line of work. Besides, you work for me now. And now the problem is mine." Martin disconnected the call and brought up the GPS on Maxwell's car. Then he dialed his enforcement detail. "I need a team ready to go."

"Yes, sir. Where are we heading?" Sherwood asked.

"Colorado. I'll give you more specific coordinates when you are in the air."

"Yes, sir. What kind of mission?"

There was eagerness in the man's tone. Martin smiled. "Not sure yet. We could have an escapee that's being aided by a human."

The other end of the line was silent for a moment. "I see. And how would you like this human to be handled?"

There was no hesitation on Martin's side. "If this human is

aiding and abetting the enemy, they deserve no consideration. Terminate."

"Yes, sir," Sherwood said.

"I'll send you the details I have. Keep me updated." Martin disconnected the call and brought up Tidwell's file. He reviewed it again and then brought up her picture. He tsked, looking at the screen. *Such a shame. She was a pretty girl.*

Then he clicked off the screen and stood up. He pushed the intercom button. "I need some lunch. I'm in the mood for Chinese."

CHAPTER 46

Maeve felt numb. She kept seeing Alvie fall over and over again in her mind. She checked the triplets, whose breathing was even, but they were still out. She was vaguely aware of Greg yelling at Tilda and Adam, but she didn't have the ability to focus on what they were saying.

Alvie ...

The Jeep came to a stop. Adam got out and Greg took his place. He placed his hands on Maeve's shoulders. "Maeve."

She looked into his eyes.

"Maeve, I need you to say something." He wrapped his jacket around her shoulders. "Say something."

"Alvie," she whispered, tears springing to her eyes.

"I know, I know." Greg pulled her into his shoulders and the tears flowed down Maeve's cheeks. She hadn't protected him. She'd let him get taken. Her shoulders shook and her chest felt like a hole had been carved into it.

Adam reappeared. "We're not being followed."

"Really?" Greg's voice was hard, and Maeve had never heard him like that before. "And why should we believe you? After all, you said there were alarms around the safe house. I didn't hear any alarms go off. And they didn't follow us. They let us go. So what the hell's going on?"

Adam's voice was quiet. "They let us go because they had what they came for."

Maeve pushed up from Greg and looked at Tilda. "Why didn't the alarms go off? How did they find us?"

"I don't know. They shouldn't have." Tilda's gaze shifted away to look at Adam.

"She's right," Adam said, and for the first time since Maeve had met him, he sounded angry. "They shouldn't have found us. And they definitely shouldn't have gotten so close."

"So what the hell happened? What are you not telling us?" Greg demanded.

Tilda shook her head. "Nothing. Nothing for sure. I don't know what went wrong."

"You might not know, but you suspect," Maeve said.

"Perhaps," Tilda said before shaking her head. "But that won't help us now. Now we need to figure out our next steps. We can hide—"

"We're getting Alvie back," Maeve said.

"No," Tilda's voice was firm. "Where they've taken him, there's no way to—"

Staring the woman down, Maeve rolled her hands into fists. "We. Are. Getting. Alvie. Back. If you are not on board with that, then this is where I leave you."

Greg took her hand. "You mean where they leave us. I'm with you."

"And so am I," Adam said softly.

Tilda's eyes went wide. "Adam?"

"I'm helping them," he said firmly.

"You can't go back there," Tilda said. And for the first time, Maeve heard a sliver of fear in her voice.

"Yes, I can," he said.

The two stared at each other, and Maeve wondered what

the hell was going on because obviously whatever this silent argument was about it had nothing to do with Alvie.

Finally, Tilda nodded. "Okay. But we'll need help."

"What about Guardian?" Greg asked.

"I don't know how to contact him. But there are some other people who can help." Tilda stepped out of the Jeep with her phone and walked away from them.

All the energy left Maeve in a swoosh. She pictured Alvie being grabbed, imagined him being poked and prodded in some lab somewhere. She scrambled to the side of the Jeep and Adam leapt out of the way as she threw up.

CHAPTER 47

JENSEN, UTAH

Dawn was breaking when Norah finally pulled over. They had just passed the Uintah and Ouray reservations to the west of Denver. Another few hours and they'd be in the city limits. Of course, she still wasn't exactly sure where she was headed, but that was a problem for later. Right now, even though most people were just starting their day, she needed sleep.

Paying cash, she got a room at a no-frills motel and after Iggy crawled back into the duffel, she headed inside along with the bags of food she'd picked up down the street. After a quick breakfast, both collapsed into bed. Iggy fell asleep almost immediately.

But Norah stretched out on the other bed, stared at the water-damaged ceiling, and wondered what it was about driving long distances that was so exhausting. It wasn't like you were using up that much energy. She'd prefer a nice, exhausting run to a long car ride any day. Of course, Iggy had actually been pretty good company. He'd bopped along to the radio most of the way.

She smiled, picturing him in the passenger seat wiggling away. Finally, she closed her eyes. They'd sleep for a few hours and then see what she could figure out about Leander. They had to be somewhere, being guarded. She just needed to find a place that the U.S. government was keeping secret.

Yeah, sure, that should be easy.

Feeling eyes on her, she cracked open one eyelid. Iggy had climbed out of his bed, his teddy bear dangling from one hand. He now stood next to her bed, staring at her expectantly. She sighed and pulled the covers back on the bed next to her. "Come on."

He hopped up and nestled down next to her. She closed her eyes again and then felt his hand slip into hers. She opened her eyes in surprise. But Iggy, with the teddy clutched to his chest, had his eyes closed, a little smile on his face. And Norah realized the loneliness she'd felt coming off him when she first met him had disappeared. Instead she felt contentment. And she realized at the same time that some of the loneliness she felt had also disappeared.

She closed her eyes, amazed once more at how much her life had changed in such a short time. But she didn't focus on it, because sleep was calling her. And right now that was one call she was happy to take.

CHAPTER 48

UNDISCLOSED LOCATION

On screen, Martin Drummond's men loaded Alvie into a container and pulled away from the ranch. Guardian trailed them, switching from road cameras to satellites to bank cameras. Guardian rerouted them by setting up construction sites and closing down certain roads. They needed to get back to Dulce, but they needed to get there slowly. It's why Guardian had hacked into their plane and wrecked their hydraulics system, forcing them to transfer the subject by road.

Setting up the rest of the road trip, Guardian nodded. *That should work.*

Guardian shifted focus to Agent Tidwell. Sifting through the D.E.A.D. records, Guardian saw that her partner was suspicious of her. He'd set up a tracker. Checking Tidwell's route, it was clear the agent was unaware, and she checked into a motel with the Maldek. Guardian had set up her phone to turn on and off every half hour to record for a minute and then power down again. Listening to the recording, Guardian frowned. Was that singing? And there was a small hum in the background. Was that the Maldek?

Guardian pulled up the background on the Maldek. Nothing mentioned bonding. Although Guardian did find some information that suggested the Maldek bonded fiercely and protectively to one person. Had it bonded to the agent? That could be a problem.

Shifting to the communications between Maxwell and the D.E.A.D., Guardian frowned. Agent Tidwell was in trouble. Which meant the Maldek was in trouble. Guardian paused, weighing possible scenarios, then hunched over the keyboard, fingers moving rapidly.

I may need to change some plans.

CHAPTER 49

JENSEN, UTAH

Iggy's squeals jarred Norah from her sleep. She'd been in deep, and even when her eyes opened it took her a few precious seconds for Iggy's urgency to register. She bolted upright. "What's wrong?"

"Ig." He pushed at her shoulder and then leapt off the bed, running for the door. *Oh no.* She grabbed her keys and the duffel and peered into the parking lot. They'd slept for hours. From the angle of the sun, it was around noon. She frowned, not seeing any reason for alarm.

Why was—

A man walked casually, too casually, across the parking lot, a cap down, covering his face.

Shit. Bob.

The only thing he'd done to change his appearance was add a ball cap—a ball cap she saw him wear at least once a week. She grabbed the duffel bag, holding it open. "Get in."

Iggy hopped in and Norah looped it over her arm, struggling to figure out how he'd found her and how she was going to lose him. Pulling her weapon from the holster, she made sure the safety was off.

As she watched Bob move out of view, she prayed there were no other eyes on her. Her mind whirled, trying to figure out options. He'd tracked her here. She hadn't seen his car, which meant ...

She pulled out her phone and double checked that she'd disabled the GPS on it. Yup. She shoved the phone back in her pocket. *The bastard must have put a tracker on my car.* But with Bob out there, she didn't have time to look for it.

Okay, get to the car. Put as much distance between us and Bob, and then change cars or remove the tracker. The only other options right now would be to try and lose him on foot and find another car in the area. But she didn't know the area well enough to hope she could pull that off.

Mind made up, she glanced back outside, trying to figure out how she could possibly get to the car without Bob noticing. A man and woman stepped out of their room across the way, yelling at one another. The woman threw the man's clothes into the parking lot, telling him to get out.

Move, Norah, move. She slipped out the door and walked quickly to her car. Tossing the duffel on the passenger seat, she started the car, pulling out of the lot.

"Norah, stop!" In the rearview mirror, she saw Bob standing, legs braced, his weapon aimed at her.

Her mouth dropped open. He was pulling a gun on her? In the mirror, she saw his hand tighten on the grip. *He's going to shoot me.* Fear fueled her and she slammed on the accelerator. Bob pulled the trigger and the passenger-side mirror exploded.

"Stay down!" she yelled at Iggy as she tore out of the parking lot, sideswiping a car on the street in her haste.

She sped down the street, her whole body shaking.

Bob shot at me. Holy crap. He shot at me! Her eyes flew to her rearview mirror as Bob's SUV swung out onto the street behind her with a squeal of tires. But it was only his car that pulled out. No backup, at least not yet. *Good*.

Norah's mind raced as she flew down the street. Luckily it was a small city and not too many people were out. But ahead she could see a busier intersection and the entrance ramp for the highway. What to do—on the highway or try and lose him here? The highway was a long, straight shot with few offshoots. She'd never lose him there. It would simply be a race. *Side streets it is*. She swung the wheel to the left, cutting off three cars.

Horns screamed and brakes squealed, but Norah just pressed down harder on the accelerator. The cars she'd cut off moved forward as Bob reached the turn, blocking his way.

She quickly turned left. She slammed on the brakes and threw the car in park. She ran to the rear passenger tire. Reaching into the tire well, she pulled the tracker out. Always in the same spot. She threw it into a pickup that passed her going in the opposite direction.

Sprinting back for the driver's seat, she took off in a squeal of tires, turning again and then again, her eyes continually straying to the rearview mirror, but she didn't see a black SUV.

She turned onto a four-lane road and turned left, no destination in mind, just a need to put as much distance between herself and Bob as possible.

CHAPTER 50

DULCE, NEW MEXICO

The hacker had interceded when his team moved in on Tidwell. They were supposed to meet Agent Maxwell at the motel. But their GPS sent them two hours away instead. Martin was still smarting at how the hacker had outsmarted them ... again. There had been no sign of Tidwell since the motel. No doubt the hacker's doing. He glowered, but then calmed himself, knowing the woman could only hide for so long. After all, she had an alien holding her back. There weren't too many places she could hole up.

The bigger problem was the hacker who seemed to be covering everybody's escapes. Hamish assured him, though, that he was getting closer to finding him. And once they found the hacker, all the people he was protecting would be thrust out into the light. It was only a matter of time.

But that was not the only problem occupying Martin's thoughts. Hamish had managed to get the files from D.E.A.D. an hour ago. The analysts had collated the data and now Martin had a preliminary overview of the D.E.A.D. success rate. The D.E.A.D. teams had managed to track down thirty-two escapees in the last four weeks. On the one hand, that was more efficient than he'd expected. Tidwell and Maxwell had proven to be perhaps the most efficient team.

But although there were thirty-two caught, the sightings numbered closer to sixty. Martin frowned, knowing that number was high. Some of the sightings were no doubt duplicate sightings of the same creature. Even taking that into account, that still left a significant amount unaccounted for, although they couldn't be a hundred percent sure about how many had died in the blast. He scanned the reports and then flipped to the last page, which held a statistical summation of the captures.

As he read the scores, his concern grew. That wasn't right. He strode over to his desk and brought up the files from Project Vault. Twelve Augustin-AG1, six Kingman-AG2, Laredo-AG1, and the list went on.

He glanced back at the D.E.A.D. report. Six Kingman-AG2. But Martin knew that three had been killed at 51. So the most that could have been caught were three. Which could only mean one thing ...

"They're breeding," he murmured.

That had always been a risk. The creatures' reproductive capabilities had been closely controlled in captivity. In some cases, eliminated entirely.

But it had proven a difficult aspect of the A.L.I.V.E. projects. The subjects' anatomy was so different from anything on Earth that figuring out exactly what controlled reproduction had been daunting. In some cases, removing reproductive organs resulted in the creatures regenerating those organs, which had opened a whole new line of experimentation. One species of the Grays appeared particularly good at regenerating body parts, just like the starfish.

But there had only been a dozen cases of creatures being

reproduced in captivity, and those had all been created through asexual reproduction. And each offspring had been examined and then destroyed. But that process had led to numerous behavior problems with the subjects. Apparently the need to defend offspring was well established across the universe.

Now that the creatures were free, though, had they reproduced? The idea was terrifying. They knew nothing of gestation periods for most of the creatures, the number of offspring that could be potentially born to each species at one time, or the capabilities of the offspring; could be anything. But the numbers Martin was looking at now suggested something was at play, and it suggested nothing good.

Gestation wasn't a straightforward matter, even for Earth-origin animals. Larger animals tended to have longer gestations than smaller ones. But gestations are also affected by factors such as food abundance as well as the habitat of the animals. Animals that live out in the open tend to have longer gestations, and the child is born more mature. But creatures that burrow and hide can have short gestations because the newborn is hidden from predators.

And the creatures had only been out in the open for two months. That suggested very short pregnancies, which meant the creatures were burrowing in somewhere. The planet could be overrun quickly if that plague wasn't stopped.

A timid knock on his door interrupted his thoughts. The only one who ever knocked was Hamish. Everyone else was too terrified to approach him directly. "Come in, Hamish."

Hamish stepped inside, his hair standing straight up. He tended to run his hands through his hair when he was stressed.

Martin raised an eyebrow. "Well?"

"I-I've tracked down the hacker. They go by the name Guardian," Hamish said.

Martin scoffed. God, these hackers were tedious with their names. Hamish had been calling himself WorldGod2000 when Martin had found him. "Okay, and what do we know about this Guardian?"

"I know that they've been able to hack into our satellites and a few other countries. They also have been able to wipe out street cameras. They're good. They're covering tracks. And for multiple people. I'd be really surprised if Guardian was one person and not a full team."

Grunting, Martin wasn't sure that was true. Of course, Hamish would make the other side look as large as possible. He needed to save face. "Okay, and have you figured out where this little prick is hiding?"

Squirming, Hamish said, "Um, sort of. I don't have a name, but I managed to track their signal for just a few seconds."

Watching him, Martin waited but apparently Hamish thought that was enough. Without bearing to conceal his annoyance. "And?"

Giving him a nervous smile, Hamish said, "Uh, And the signal originated in Aurora, Colorado."

Martin frowned. "Aurora, but that's where—" His mouth dropped open.

There was only one area of interest in Aurora, Colorado—Buckley Air Force Base. But it wasn't just the base that confirmed that's where Guardian was—it was the agency that had moved its National Resources Division to Buckley in the aftermath of 9/11.

Hamish nodded back at him. "Guardian works for the NSA."

CHAPTER 51

UNDISCLOSED LOCATION

The red light blinked in the corner of the screen. As soon as it began to flash, Guardian was already making plans. All the pieces were moving into place. Now Guardian needed to move into place.

Guardian checked the maps with everyone's location. Tidwell was too far away. But the rest, yes, they would make it. Quickly, Guardian sent the message, including the address.

Guardian initiated the series of codes that would do only one thing: completely wipe the computers. Then Guardian pushed back from the desk and headed to the door. Guardian did not look back at the computer console to make sure the code worked. There was no need. Guardian had written the code. It would work. Besides, Guardian needed to hurry. That flashing red light only meant one thing.

They've found me.

CHAPTER 52

JENSEN, UTAH

The road Norah found ran into the highway an hour later. She'd debated whether or not to head to Denver. Bob would never guess she was heading there. But he undeniably would have called this in and Sanders at the very least would put two and two together. So she headed south.

Iggy peered out at her from the duffel. "Ig?"

"Hey, buddy. I think it would be better if you stayed in there, just until I'm sure we're in the clear."

"Ig," he said softly.

"I know. Hopefully we've seen the last of Bob."

Three hours later, her back and arms were beginning to ache. She twisted, stretching her back as well as she could while driving and then clenched and unclenched each fist. She'd been gripping the steering wheel so tightly they were stiff and sore.

The tension of the last few hours was wearing on her. Up ahead, she saw a rest stop. She hesitated for a moment, but she needed a bathroom and a coffee.

D.E.A.D.

Two minutes, she promised herself as she put on her indicator. She zipped Iggy up in the duffel and took him with her. It took five minutes, but the first sip of coffee assured her that she'd made the right call.

Back in the car, she merged back onto the highway, feeling more energized. It had been five hours. She'd chosen her direction randomly. They were okay for now. She just needed to think of a place they could go that was not tied to her.

She thought of and discarded dozens of possibilities as she drove along with Iggy still curled in the duffel with his teddy. *Maybe I could find an old campground, some place off-season*. She absentmindedly checked the rearview mirror before turning back to the road. *I wonder if ...*

Her gaze shot back to the mirror. Her mind distracted by her planning, she hadn't immediately recognized the black Tahoe coming up fast behind her.

She pressed down on the accelerator, cutting off a minivan as she swerved into the exit lane.

Bob didn't have enough time to make the turn and shot past her. *Score one for the good guys*. But her luck didn't hold. Her eyes on the ramp behind her, she blew through a stop sign.

A truck slammed into the end of her car, sending her off the road and down an embankment. Norah pumped the brakes, but they didn't respond. The car took down a couple of small trees before rolling to a stop at the bottom.

Norah sat still for a moment, amazed the air bags hadn't gone off. A small cry from the passenger seat set her moving. "Iggy!" She unzipped the bag and Iggy's head popped out. She let out a relieved sigh as he climbed out, no worse for wear.

The squeal of tires from up on the ridge snatched that feeling away.

"Come on." She shoved at her door. With a squeal of metal,

it inched open. It had been damaged on the ride over the embankment. She shoved harder. "Come on, come on." Finally she had it open enough that she could climb out. Iggy was right behind her. A bullet slammed into the tree next to her.

"Let's go!" She sprinted further into the trees with Iggy right on her heels.

CHAPTER 53

GRAND JUNCTION, UTAH

They had changed cars about thirty minutes ago and now were in an old Bronco. Adam had carefully carried the triplets from the Jeep over to their new ride while Greg steered Maeve over.

Maeve felt numb. She kept replaying the image of that man picking up Alvie over and over again in her mind. Greg sat next to her, Snap and Pop curled up in his lap. Crackle was curled up in Maeve's. She absentmindedly rubbed his back, numb to even the tremors running through him.

I lost Alvie. I let them take him.

She imagined scenario after scenario where she managed to get to him, but with each one, she knew how unrealistic they were. Alvie chose to save them. He chose to sacrifice himself.

A weight settled on her shoulders and she looked up into Greg's eyes as he tucked a jacket around her from the seat next to her. "Maeve, I know this is difficult, but I need you to stay with me. I'm worried you're going into shock."

In Maeve's mind there was a delay between hearing Greg's

words and understanding them. She nodded. Shock. Yes, she was going into shock. How could she not? Protecting Alvie, looking out for him, was her life. Ever since she'd met him that had been the overriding goal of her existence. He was a part of her. Him being gone—it was like someone had taken her arm. She could not wrap her mind around it. In fact, her mind, which she took such pride in, seemed to be shutting down.

Tapping her hand, Greg spoke softly. "Maeve, honey, I need you to say something."

She looked into his concerned face. What did he just say? She couldn't seem to grasp the words. Vaguely she heard a phone ring, but she just continued to rub Crackle's back.

"Maeve," Greg repeated.

She looked up slowly. Everything felt slow, like she was pushing through water. Greg held a cell phone toward her. Maeve just looked at it, not knowing what he wanted her to do with it.

Taking her hand, he placed the phone in it and then pushed it up to her ear. "Guardian gave Chris Tilda's cell phone number. It's Chris."

"Maeve? Maeve, are you there?" the deep male voice cut through the fog in her mind.

I know that voice. "Chris?"

"Oh, baby, thank God. I've been so worried."

Maeve's chest tightened and she grasped the phone.

"Is everybody okay? Where are you guys?" He asked.

The dam inside Maeve burst open. Tears streamed down Maeve's cheeks. "Alvie. They took Alvie."

Greg took the phone from Maeve as she sobbed. The triplets crushed into her, all of them joined in their terror for Alvie. She could hear Greg speaking with Chris and filling him in.

But Maeve just clutched the triplets to her, delving into a deep, dark place. She stayed rocking with them until Greg hung up. He spoke to her and she made some sort of response that seemed to satisfy him. But she had no idea what she said or what he'd asked.

Eventually the triplets slipped into an exhausted sleep and Maeve closed her eyes, too, praying the oblivion of sleep would take this pain away.

Sometime later, Maeve woke. She blinked open her eyes, glancing outside the Jeep in time to see an exit for Denver fly by. She jolted fully awake, grabbing Greg's arm and waking him. "Denver? What are we doing back in Denver?"

Wincing, Greg pried Maeve's hand from his jacket. "Um, we're not. We're heading past Denver to Aurora."

She frowned. Aurora, Colorado was dominated by one landmark—Buckley Air Force Base. "We're going to Buckley? We can't bring the triplets to—"

Greg put up his hands. "Maeve, calm down. We're not turning anyone in."

Adam turned on the indicator and took an exit. He drove down a long road lined with fields on either side. Ten minutes passed before a small town came into sight. Adam pulled into the parking lot of an old abandoned diner. It looked like it had been out of business for years.

Now Adam leaned over and gently put a hand on the back of Snap and Pop, who were curled up with Hope on the floor. Hope lifted her head and licked Adam's hand. Shutting down the car, he turned to Tilda in the passenger seat, who looked to be just waking up herself.

There were no other cars in sight. Without a word, Adam stepped outside and disappeared around the side of the diner. Maeve watched him go, still not sure what to make of Tilda's grandson, but she could feel his concern for the triplets.

Tilda turned to face her. "He's just making sure no one's around."

"What are we doing here?" Maeve asked.

Greg pointed toward the windshield. "Waiting for him."

A white Camry pulled into the lot. She frowned, leaning forward. Snap's head popped up from the floor and she scrambled into the driver's seat, leaning against the steering wheel to peer out of the windshield with a happy cry.

She looked at Greg, who nodded at her with a smile. With a gasp, Maeve was out of the car and sprinting across the empty lot.

She threw herself at Chris as he met her halfway across the lot, crushing herself to him. Maeve felt her knees weaken and Chris's arms tightened in response. She breathed him in, filling in one of the missing pieces in her heart.

"I've got you, Maeve," Chris whispered, "and we'll get him back."

Maeve nodded into his shoulder. But couldn't say anything past the sobs in her throat.

CHAPTER 54

PAGE, ARIZONA

Norah sprinted through the trees, her heart pounding. Bob had found her again, which meant either someone had tracked her by satellite or Bob was just really good.

And Bob was not that good.

Iggy kept pace with Norah, sometimes even moving ahead. Norah was amazed at how quickly he moved. She couldn't say he was running, because it was more like he leapt six feet at a time. He used his large hands occasionally to lock onto a tree and propel himself forward. If she weren't so terrified, she would be fascinated.

But fascination was not the dominant emotion right now. Bob chased after them like a bull, and every few seconds he took a shot. His aim was crap when he and his target were moving, but he wasn't shooting to take her down, although she knew he'd be pretty happy with a lucky shot. No, his goal was to terrify her and keep her off balance.

And it was working.

A bullet crashed into the tree near her, splinters of wood digging into her arm, and she cursed once again that she hadn't checked for her weapon as they'd escaped the car. All she had was an empty holster.

But despite her fear, she'd been counting. Bob had one bullet left, and then he'd have to change out the magazine. That was her chance.

A rock outcropping stood ahead. *Or maybe not*, she thought, an idea forming. "Keep going, Iggy," she said as she ducked around the rocks and then climbed it silently.

Bob came tearing through the woods. She'd always warned him that he needed to be more aware of his surroundings. He always bulldozed right into situations anyway. And right now, she was very glad he was a stubborn S.O.B. who never accepted criticism, constructive or otherwise, from anyone.

She stayed low, keeping her eyes and ears peeled as she silently pulled her belt free. She wound the ends around her fists as she waited. Soon she was rewarded with Bob's big frame coming into view, his eyes locked ahead of him. She waited, calming her breathing.

When he passed, she didn't let herself hesitate. Leaping from her perch, she looped the belt around his thick neck and yanked him to the side. He slammed to the side with a yell, his head slapping the ground hard, his gun flying into some nearby bushes.

She rolled to her feet as Bob scrambled to his feet, his face red with anger, his stance wobbly. "You traitor. You found that thing. What the hell did you think you were doing?"

"It's not like the others. It's not violent. It doesn't deserve to die," Norah said, hoping maybe she could somehow convince him.

"You don't get to make that decision," he snarled.

Reality 2, optimism 0, she thought, narrowing her eyes at her partner. "I won't let you take him."

"I was hoping you'd say that." He sprang at her.

But Norah was ready for him. She slammed the ball of her foot into his chest and felt a rib snap as Bob stopped, his eyes growing large as he dropped to his knees. Norah grabbed the back of his head and slammed her knee into his face. He pitched forward, unconscious. She shook her head. He always thought his strength made him a better fighter. *Idiot*.

She checked his neck, but he was breathing, which was more than he planned on leaving her doing. She started to follow Iggy's trail when a man in all black stepped out from behind a tree in front of her. She put up her hands. "Whoa, hey. What's going on?"

Two more men stepped out behind and beside her. Norah's gaze shifted from one to the next. The man in front of her spoke into the mic on his collar. "We've got Tidwell. No sign of the subject. Instructions?"

The reply came back quickly. "Terminate."

CHAPTER 55

"Terminate." Norah's heart pounded at the word.

The man in front of her waved his weapon toward her. "Get on your knees and turn around."

Like hell. If they were going to kill her, she was damn well going to make them look in her face. She glared at him. "Why are you doing this?"

"Orders. Now turn around," he said his voice hard.

Meeting his gaze, she shook her head. "No."

The man shrugged. "Fine."

She tensed waiting for the bullet. Then the man behind her screamed. She whirled around as he grabbed his neck, blood pooling through his fingers before the second man went flying back with a yell.

Norah's eyes widened. What was happening?

The man in front of her yelled, his aim shifting to his own men. Norah lunged for him, pushing aside his gun hand as she buried her shin in his thigh. His knees buckled. She elbowed him twice in the face, then wrenched his weapon free from his hands and slammed the butt of it into the side of his skull. His eyes rolled up into his head and he dropped.

She turned, the weapon trained on the path behind her as two other men in black barreled down it toward her. She let off a burst of fire, catching one in the shoulder. The other dove behind the rock outcropping. A shadow shifted along the top of the rocks. Norah watched in disbelief as Iggy leapt from the rock, landing on the other man with a growl, a set of talons that extended from his hands digging into the man's neck. He rode the man to the ground.

Norah's mouth fell open and she stared at Iggy, her whole body shaking. "Iggy?"

The snarl on his lips disappeared and his eyes went wide. He stumbled back from the man and looked down at his hands as the talons retracted. *He's a tiny Wolverine.* He stepped toward her and she backed up, raising her weapon.

His little mouth made an 'O,' and his shoulders drooped. One of the radios of the dead men sprang to life. "Alpha team, report. Alpha team."

Trying to digest what she'd just seen, Norah swallowed hard. Iggy, cute little Iggy, had killed those men. Iggy stepped toward her and Norah backed up again, maintaining the distance between them. "Iggy, we need to go."

He just looked at her, his eyes incredibly large and his small mouth turned downward. Once again the loneliness she'd felt when she'd first met him washed over her. Norah looked at the men behind him. Her gaze stopping as she looked at her partner, and she knew without a doubt he'd planned on killing her. Iggy had been in the clear. If he had kept going, they wouldn't have caught him. He'd come back for her. He'd come back to protect her. She knelt down.

"It's okay, Iggy. It's okay." Iggy hesitated for only a moment before running for her and throwing himself into her arms. Norah held him close as he trembled. "It's okay," she said again as she stood, Iggy still clinging to her. "Let's go."

Those men were going to kill her. No conversation, no

questions, just death. And Iggy had saved her. She stepped past the downed men, not looking at them, knowing she had crossed a line. She had declared her loyalty.

And she did not regret it.

CHAPTER 56

GLENDALE, COLORADO

The triplets let Chris have Maeve to himself for a full two minutes, which for them was pretty good. Chris hugged each of them individually, and some of the fear that had clawed at him since Lancaster abated. But one look at Maeve's face told him how hard the last day had been. Even the triplets' joy was tinged with sadness. They missed Alvie. Their little family wasn't whole without him. And Chris promised himself he would do everything in his power to get Alvie back.

Now Chris walked toward the old Bronco with Snap and Pop perched on his shoulders, Crackle tucked into the nook of his arm, and his other hand firmly holding Maeve's.

Chris felt a huge relief at being back with them, although the idea of Alvie in the hands of Drummond shot cold fear right through him. But the coldness of Maeve's hand and the fear in her eyes reinforced that he could never let her know how terrified he was.

As they approached the car, Greg, who was leaning against the hood, waved. "Well, looks like they missed you."

"I assure you, the feeling is completely mutual. Hey, Crackle, I need my arm." Instead of climbing down, Crackle climbed up Chris's chest, placing one leg on either side of Chris's head and his hands on Chris's head. Chris extended his hand to Greg. "Glad to see you're alive." And Chris really was. Greg was the eccentric uncle in their little grouping.

"Me, too," Greg returned the handshake.

The handshake was firmer than it used to be. Apparently those workouts were having an effect, Chris thought before he spoke. "And thank you for everything. If you hadn't shown up …"

Greg waved away his words. "Not me. That was all Tilda and Adam."

As the woman herself walked around the car, she raised her eyebrows at the triplets perched on Chris. She extended her hand. "Matilda Watson. Everyone calls me Tilda."

Stronger grip, Chris noted. "Thank you for your help, but my family is one short. Do you have any idea where he is?"

Tilda hesitated.

"You know," Maeve said.

"Yes," Tilda nodded slowly. "But there's something else we need to handle first."

Wrenching her hand from Chris's grasp, Maeve stepped forward. "No, there isn't. Where is he?"

"I believe he's been taken to a facility in New Mexico. But we'll need help to get him out. We'll need Guardian," Tilda explained.

"Then contact him," Greg said.

"Actually, Guardian is the one who directed all of us here to Aurora," Tilda said.

"Why?" Greg asked. "What does he want?

"Help. Guardian lives in Aurora. He thinks Drummond is on to him. He sent me his address," Tilda explained.

Maeve shook her head. "We don't have time for this. Alvie—"

Chris took her hand. "Maeve, Guardian got me here, got all of you here. We're going to need his help to rescue Alvie. So we'll grab Guardian and then we'll get Alvie, all right?"

She looked up at him and nodded.

And Chris prayed he was telling the truth. He turned to Tilda. "Okay. Where's Guardian?"

CHAPTER 57

PAGE, ARIZONA

Norah and Iggy ran, staying to the woods, almost parallel with the highway. There had been some signs of life, but she hadn't headed for them, knowing they'd probably expect her to do just that. She could hear traffic somewhere in the distance to their left, but she saw no bright lights indicating a town. From what she remembered of the map of the area, there wasn't a lot around here. Heading to the road would only leave them exposed.

Iggy perched on Norah's shoulder for parts of the run, and Norah felt a little like Luke Skywalker training with Yoda. It managed to bring a small fangirl smile to her face despite the terror of what they were facing.

Her former partner had tried to kill her. And Bob was not someone who acted on his own, which meant her former agency was now locked against her.

As for who those other guys were, she had no idea. They wore no identifying insignias on their clothes. But the way they moved, and as organized as they were, meant that they were well trained. She had a sinking feeling they might be the extra help Sanders had been trying to bring in.

Ahead, Iggy swung from one branch to the ground, then launched himself back up to another. He moved quickly and was surprisingly strong for his size. But why wasn't he in the database? She didn't think it was too much of an assumption to say he was an alien. Obviously he was a high priority for them to send a special team.

Or I'm the special target. When she'd joined the D.E.A.D., the need to keep their work from the public was hammered home over and over again. The public fear and panic that would be generated by the acknowledgment that these creatures existed was argued to be society destroying. *And apparently they no longer trust me to keep my mouth shut.*

She could understand that, but what she couldn't understand was why a kill order was the first approach to dealing with her. She'd known she was risking arrest. She'd known there would be penalties. But she didn't think she'd be killed. *What the hell have I stepped in?*

When she'd first joined, she'd of course been familiar with all the stories of the men in black. She'd never put too much stock in those stories. She thought nervous citizens caught up in a cold-war mentality had exaggerated the interactions. She knew after Roswell eyewitnesses had been visited and pressed to stay quiet. And there'd been the odd tabloid-style story now and then. But the men she'd run into were deadly in their intent. And they *were* all dressed in black.

So maybe I need to rethink my views on MIBs.

And the more she thought about the over-response to her actions, the more she wondered what exactly had been done to some of the civilians who had come in contact with the aliens from Area 51. She'd never followed up on them after a case. But what were the chances she was the first one whose existence the government had decided was too risky?

She pictured Sandra and her son, Luke. Both had had face-to-face contact with a Blue Boy, and Norah was glad she hadn't mentioned that the boy had been in contact with the winged creature before the attack. But as soon as she got out of this mess, she was going to be sure to contact Sandra and tell her to be on her guard. She might be jumping at shadows, but she'd rather needlessly warn them than chance something happening to them.

Ahead, Iggy stopped, crouching down low on a branch. A halo of lights could be seen in the distance. Norah hadn't heard anyone behind them for a while, but she knew they had not given up. She climbed up the small rise ahead of her and Iggy joined her.

"It's a rest stop," she whispered. Iggy tilted his head, looking at her.

"People stop here for snacks and to take a break before continuing on their travels."

"Ig?"

She gave a small laugh, thinking that she might actually be beginning to understand the differences in Iggy's utterances. "I don't think we have time to stop for something to eat. Remember, bad guys?'"

He still looked at her and Norah realized he probably hadn't understood her. He seemed to understand some basic words but not long statements. She sighed as he continued to look at her with what she thought of as his hopeful face. She crouched next to him, undecided. They needed to move, but skulking around in the trees wasn't going to work for long. They needed a car. But if she stole one they'd hear about it. She could hitchhike if she figured out a way to hide Iggy, but that presented a whole other host of potential problems.

The snap of a branch behind them caused her to whirl around just as a red dot landed on Iggy's back. "No!" She grabbed him and flung both of them over the ridge, rolling as bullets tore up the ground behind her.

She got to her feet with Iggy perched low on her back, his arms on her shoulders. The area in front of them was two hundred yards of open space and then the brick travel center. An SUV swerved into the parking lot.

No, no, no. Norah picked up her pace, stretching out her stride as she raced toward the travel center. People had caught sight of her and stopped what they were doing to watch, at least until the bullets hit the pavement. Then everyone began to scramble for the doors with a scream.

The SUV barreled across the parking lot toward them and then screeched to a halt, blocking their access to the building. Norah veered left, not even slowing. She heard the doors of the SUV slam shut behind her and then the sound of heavy-booted feet giving chase. Ahead, another SUV pulled around the side of the building and headed right for them.

Oh God. We're trapped.

CHAPTER 58

UNDISCLOSED LOCATION

Guardian flew into the room. The alarm had gone off for Tidwell while Guardian was heading home. Guardian leapt into the chair and pulled up the data for the last twenty-four hours. Satellite imagery depicted the fight between Tidwell and her partner. Tidwell could have killed Maxwell but had chosen not to. Interesting. Compassion.

And then the other men had shown up and the Maldek had sprung into action. *It has bonded to her.* Guardian watched Tidwell back away from the Maldek. *She's scared.*

But then Tidwell opened her arms and the Maldek flew into them. Guardian nodded. Partnership accepted. Guardian fast-forwarded quickly through the run through the woods, all the while keeping track of the other screens. This would be Guardian's last day in this office. Quickly, all the necessary code that would allow Guardian into critical systems was reviewed. Good. No issues.

D.E.A.D.

Guardian's gaze shifted back to the screen with Tidwell and the Maldek. *Oh no.*

Guardian's hands flew over the keyboard after a quick check of the clock. There wasn't time. They would be here soon. But Guardian had one last thing to do.

CHAPTER 59

PAGE, ARIZONA

Norah's mind scrambled as she ran. She thought of and discarded scenario after scenario as she bolted along the parking lot of the rest stop. There was an SUV behind them along with men on foot. Another SUV coming at them from the front. The wall of the travel center was to her right with no entrances, and there were men in the woods beyond the parking lot to their left.

There's no way out of this.

The engine of a tractor trailer blared to life from the parking lot to their left. Its tires squealed and it burst across the parking lot, slamming into the side of the SUV in front of her and pinning it against the building.

Holy shit.

Behind her she heard a yell and whipped her head around as a gunman was tossed in the air by a sedan. The man bounced off the roof and the sedan just picked up speed. Two other gunmen fired at the sedan, but it just kept going for them. It slammed into one and the other dove for the side, but the car turned, running over him with a sickening thump.

She turned and ran for one of the downed men who had gotten to his knees. She kicked him in the face and he crashed back down again. Iggy leapt from her shoulders and onto the car that was silent. She retrieved the weapon from the man she'd kicked, a P90, which thankfully she was familiar with, and grabbed the extra magazines from his pockets.

Three more gunmen emerged from the trees. *Oh, come on.*

"Iggy, let's go!" He leapt from the hood and into her arms. She swung him around to her back as she broke into a run. A car engine sounded from behind her.

Norah did not turn to look. She just picked up her pace. She looked over in shock as the sedan that had taken the men out slid up silently next to her, its window lowering. She started to veer away, then she realized there was no one driving the car. A tinny voice spoke over the radio. *"Get in, Agent Tidwell."*

Like hell. Norah veered away, but bullets slammed into the ground on her right. *Shit.* Left with no choice, she threw Iggy through the open window and dove in after him.

As soon as she was in, the car sped up and flew down the ramp and onto the highway. Norah righted herself and stared at the steering wheel that was shifting as the car sped down the highway. The car was a Tesla Model S. She knew they had self-driving capabilities, but she also knew someone had to tell the car to drive.

"Who's driving this?" she asked, feeling like a crazy person.

The large screen that served as the Tesla's dashboard went blank before the answer appeared.

__I am Guardian.__

Well, that's not creepy. Iggy leaned toward the screen and Norah pulled him back, having a vision from a horror movie flash through her mind where an evil presence reached through a screen.

"Where are we going?" Norah asked figuring whoever was driving this thing had to be listening.

To Leander

She jolted in surprise. "What? Where is she?"

Where she needs to be.

And now we've moved on from creepy to cryptic. "Did you control those other cars back at the rest stop?"

Yes.

"Why?"

The screen was blank for a moment, and Norah was worried for a moment that Guardian wouldn't respond.

The Maldek needs to be protected.

Norah glanced down at Iggy, who had climbed into the driver's seat. Maldek? Was that what he was? She'd never seen that name in any of the files. But she'd heard it before.

She thought back to when she had first started to work for the D.E.A.D. She had started researching everything she could find on alien life. She'd started with the reputable scientists and agencies—Carl Sagan, NASA, well-respected theorists. But soon, she'd made her way through all of their work and had delved into the less-reputable sources. And one of those sources had talked about a race of alien beings known as the Maldeks.

According to a Native American man named Morning Sky, his grandfather had communicated with an alien named Bek-Ti. While Norah couldn't recall exactly where Bek-Ti was from, she did remember the discussion of Maldek. Maldek was said to be a planet located between Mars and Jupiter that was destroyed by a hostile alien race. Some Maldekians escaped and took refuge under Mars's surface, where the Martians had also taken refuge. The ice comet that destroyed the planet of Maldek had apparently also destroyed Mars's atmosphere.

The story had stuck with her for two reasons. One, she knew Mars had once in its distant past had a habitable environment similar to Earth's. And two, she'd read in a number of arguments that the asteroid belt located between Mars and Jupiter was actually the remains of a planet destroyed billions of years ago.

So the argument from Bek-Ti did actually have some factual basis. And now Norah was staring at a small green guy. He was obviously proof of life beyond this planet. Was it possible that was where Iggy was from? How did he end up here? Were there other Maldeks out there? Was someone looking for him?

We will arrive at our destination in seven hours and thirty-four minutes.

Norah wasn't sure she could trust Guardian, but she also knew she did not have a lot of options right now unless she wanted to fling herself and Iggy from a car moving seventy miles per hour down the highway. She picked up Iggy from the driver's seat and crawled over into it herself, placing Iggy on the passenger seat. She might not be driving, but she would feel better if she was at least sitting in the driver's seat in case something went wrong with Guardian's control.

Or in case I need to try and wrestle control away from him ... her ... it.

It was strange watching the steering wheel shift without anyone touching it. She reclined her seat a little more, stretching out her legs. Right now there was nothing she could do. And her time in the Marines had taught her that you should sleep when you could. She closed her eyes but opened them a few seconds later as Iggy climbed into her lap, settling in. He looked up at her and paused as if asking if it was all right.

Needing a little contact herself, she gently rubbed his back. He leaned against her, letting out a sigh. Norah closed her eyes, her hand resting on Iggy's back. Images from the rest stop and the earlier fight flew through her mind.

No, think about it later. You need to sleep. You don't know what's coming, and the only thing you can do is at least try to be rested.

With effort, she forced her mind from the violence. Instead, she thought of the last show she'd watched. It was *Ted Lasso* in the motel room with Iggy. She started replaying the episode in her mind from the opening sequence.

And she was sound asleep well before she reached the closing credits.

CHAPTER 60

AURORA, COLORADO

Adam drove slowly through the residential neighborhood.

"Look out!" Maeve called from the backseat. Adam slammed on the brakes as a boy who couldn't be more than six cut out onto the road on his bike.

Greg's voice came through Maeve's earpiece. He and Tilda were a few miles away with the triplets while Adam, Chris, and Maeve made the approach. "Are we sure this address is for Guardian? This is not exactly the locale I expected for a big-time hacker."

"Yeah, no kidding," Chris said. They were about two blocks away from the address Guardian had sent. Guardian's home was smack dab in the middle of a cookie-cutter neighborhood only four years old. Each house was identical to the one next to it. And almost every house seemed to have a swing set in the backyard.

"Are we sure Nadine is Guardian?" Greg asked.

"Maybe she's a friend," Chris said as Adam pulled up to the side of the road, two houses down from their destination.

The house they were heading to was owned by a Nadine Johnson. There wasn't a lot on Nadine online. Her internet footprint was practically non-existent. But they did learn she used to be in a big-name law firm in Denver. She took some time off from that and now she worked in the legal department of the NSA.

But there was nothing in her academic record or work history that indicated an affinity for computers. From the DMV photo they'd found online, they knew she was an attractive African-American woman in her mid-thirties, with dark hair and dark eyes. She wasn't smiling in the photo, but Maeve didn't think that said anything about the woman. After all, who was happy about spending time at the DMV?

"You ready?" Adam asked.

Maeve nodded. They'd agreed she'd make the approach, thinking she'd be the least threatening. "Greg, you know the plan?"

He sighed. "My part's not that difficult. I hear anything scary and I take the triplets and Tilda and beat a hasty retreat. I'm a little more worried about your part."

"We'll be all right," Maeve said.

"Give me two minutes." Adam stepped from the car. He was going to find a spot close to the house where he could keep an eye on Maeve. Chris hadn't been thrilled that that duty had fallen to Adam but had agreed to stay in the car, ready to move if they needed to.

"You sure you're up for this?" Chris asked.

"The sooner we get Guardian or Nadine or whoever, the sooner we get Alvie back," Maeve said.

"Be careful," Chris warned.

"I will." Maeve promised, before she stepped out of the car, pausing for a second to take stock of her surroundings. Three kids played basketball in a driveway a few houses down. Another homeowner pushed a lawnmower over their lawn. And a woman jogged by while pushing a toddler in a stroller. *Just a normal day in suburbia.*

A dog barked somewhere in the distance, followed by squeals of children laughing. A light wind ruffled Maeve's hair. She was having a tough time accepting how normal everything was around her right now. People were just living their lives, no worries about the government tracking them down and destroying their family.

An image of Alvie flashed through her mind. Her knees weakened and she stumbled before straightening herself. She blew out a breath. *Get Guardian and then we get Alvie. This is for him.*

Straightening her shoulders, she headed up the path to the yellow, two-story colonial house with a well-manicured lawn. She reached up and rang the doorbell, then took a step back.

The door swung open and a young girl with her hair worked into four braids stood in the doorway behind the screen door.

Must be Nadine's daughter. Maeve opened her mouth to speak, but the girl beat her to it. "Hi. I'm Penny."

Maeve smiled at the friendly little girl with the bright eyes behind her glasses. "Hi, Penny. I'm Maeve. I'm looking for your mommy."

Penny frowned, tilting her head. "You are? Does Mommy know you?"

"Not yet."

"Hm." Penny stepped out of the doorway.

Although Maeve waited for a moment, she heard no further sounds. She knocked again. "Hello?" she called through the screen.

"Hold on," a woman called.

An African-American woman in her thirties appeared at

the door, a dish towel in her hands. She dried her hands as she spoke. "Yes?"

"Nadine Johnson?"

"Yes," the woman drew the word out.

"This might sound weird, but do you work for the NSA?"

The woman stepped back, alarm flashing across her face. "Who are you?"

"I'm Maeve Leander. We received your message. We came to—"

The woman shook her head. "Message? What are you talking about? I never sent you any message."

Maeve frowned, watching the woman, who looked completely confused by Maeve's words and even a little scared. What was going on? Maeve spoke slowly. "We received a message from someone called Guardian. They gave us this address and said they needed help."

The woman shook her head. "I don't know what you're talking about. I never sent you any message, and I certainly don't know anyone named Guardian. I think you need to leave."

Nothing about the woman's demeanor suggested she was lying, but Guardian had sent them here and Nadine worked for the NSA. That couldn't be a coincidence. "I'm sorry to have bothered you. But you're sure you don't—"

"I'm Guardian."

Maeve turned slowly to look at Penny, who'd returned to the room. She walked up behind her mother, pulling a suitcase.

Nadine turned as well, her mouth gaping. "Penny, what are you talking about? You invited this woman here?"

"We need to go." Penny said to her mother before she turned to Maeve, meeting her gaze for only a moment. "They're coming."

CHAPTER 61

Maeve stared at the little girl. She was even smaller than she'd realized. She was barely four feet tall and incredibly skinny. She couldn't be any more than nine. "How old is she?"

Nadine reached out a protective arm, stepping in front of her daughter. "Twelve, not that it's any concern of yours. Now you need to go before I call the police." The door slammed in Maeve's face.

Stunned, Maeve stepped back. Guardian was twelve? That had to be a mistake. Maeve tapped the mic on her collar as she headed back to the car. "Guys, did you get that? Do we have the wrong place?"

Greg answered her. "No. Nadine *and* Penelope Johnson both work at the NSA. Penelope was hired two years ago."

"But she would have been *ten*," Maeve said.

"I know." Greg's exasperation came through loud and clear. "But that's what my research is telling me."

Lowering her voice as she stepped back, Maeve shook her head not sure what she could do. "It has to be a mistake.

Maybe somebody switched the names or something. There's no way that little girl—"

Tires squealed in the distance as a dark Suburban turned onto the street, moving fast. "Guys?"

"Get out of there, Maeve!" Chris yelled.

Shooting a terrified look at the car barreling down the street, Maeve turned and ran right back to the Johnsons' home.

From behind the door, she could hear raised voices. Yanking open the screen, Maeve shoved open the heavy front door. Nadine jumped back, pulling Penny protectively behind her.

"An unfriendly SUV is heading right here. You are in danger. We need to go," Maeve said.

Nadine shook her head. "We're not—"

"They're coming to kill us," Penny said, the words all the more chilling due to the lack of emotion in them.

Nadine gaped at her daughter. "Why would you say such a—"

Outside, the squeal of brakes cut off her response. Chris's voice burst out through her earpiece. "Maeve, get them out the back. I'm on the street behind you."

Maeve whipped around as three men took up position in front of the house. *Oh God*. Maeve kicked the front door shut. "Get down!" She slammed into Nadine, pushing her to the ground and yanking Penny down with them.

Gunfire cut through the front of the house, destroying the windows and splintering the front door.

Scrambling toward the kitchen, Nadine pulled a screaming Penny with her. Maeve followed them, sliding through the kitchen door and around the cabinets. The gunfire cut off and Adam's voice came through her earpiece. "Get them out the back. Now."

Latching onto Nadine's arm, Maeve hauled her up. Penny

had scooted into a corner and lay curled in on herself. Maeve grabbed Penny's arm and she screamed, cringing away.

"Maeve, where are you?" Chris yelled.

"Still in the kitchen. Having a problem here." Maeve tried to grab Penny again, but she kicked out at her, keeping her back.

Adam crashed through the front door. He grabbed the suitcase and sprinted into the kitchen. "Get the mom—I've got her."

Maeve turned to Nadine, who stared her, eyes wide. Not bothering with any explanation, because honestly, what could she say?, Maeve just hustled her out the back door. Penny screamed again but went silent as Adam hoisted her over his shoulder.

As Maeve ran through the Johnsons' backyard, she pulled Nadine with her and through the neighbor's yard behind them. Standing behind the hood of the truck, Chris waved them on, taking aim behind them. He let off a series of shots that caused Nadine to cry out.

But Maeve just barreled forward, all but throwing Nadine in the back of the car. Adam lowered Penny in beside her mother as Chris jumped into the driver's seat. Maeve dove in after the Johnsons as Adam took the passenger seat.

Jumping back into the driver's seat as Adam offered cover fire, Chris tore out from the curb. Turning to watch through the rear window, Maeve's heart raced. But no one seemed to be following them. She let out a shaky breath.

"You guys okay?" Greg asked in her earpiece.

With a small, slightly hysterical laugh, Maeve ran a hand over her mouth. "Oh, sure, right as rain."

"Meet you at the rendezvous, he said."

"Okay," Maeve replied. Her heart pounded as Chris sped down the residential streets.

Chris checked the rearview mirror. "They're not following us."

"I disabled their car," Adam said.

"How?" Maeve asked.

Adam turned, his voice even. "Bullets."

Chris grinned. "Well, let's hope they came alone."

And it appeared they did. But it was another twenty minutes before anyone relaxed.

But not Penny. The longer they drove, the more agitated she became. Then she began to shriek. Nadine leaned down, struggling to open the suitcase.

Maeve reached down to help her. "What do you need?"

"Her headphones and tablet."

Unzipping the case, Maeve handed Nadine both items, which luckily had been right on top of the suitcase's contents. Nadine positioned the headphones on Penny's head and a few moments later she calmed. Nadine handed Penny the tablet and Penny's hands flew over the screen.

The traffic light in front of them, which had just turned red, shifted to green. The next five lights all turned green or stayed green as they approached.

Maeve met Adam's gaze. "I guess she *is* Guardian."

"I don't understand what's going on," Nadine said, looking from Maeve to the front seat. "Who are you people?"

Her heart went out to the woman. She seemed to have absolutely no idea what her daughter had been up to. And now she'd been yanked into a world that Maeve, who'd grown up with Alvie, still struggled at times to believe.

"I'm afraid you two are now part of a government secret." Maeve paused, not sure exactly how to start. She struggled to come up with a way to ease the woman into it. But honestly, Maeve had been through too much in the last few days to finesse this conversation.

Oh, screw it. "Nadine, do you believe in UFOs?"

CHAPTER 62

DULCE, NEW MEXICO

His team had missed Guardian. He was still trying to wrap his head around the fact that Guardian was a child. A female child, no less. But after Penny Johnson had been picked up by Leander and company, there'd been no sign of her.

Or them, for that matter. The little girl, a girl in *pigtails*, had hidden all of them completely. It was humiliating. His phone beeped and he yanked it out with a growl.

It was a text: *He's here.*

And just like that, Martin's mood shifted.

He felt like humming. No, singing. He felt like singing. They had Subject One in custody. Control of this particular subject had been a decades-long quest.

To the determined go the spoils, he thought with a smile as he made his way down the hall on the seventh level, the facility's lowest level. This was where cryogenic storage was located. He visited this level once a day. It helped him think.

He punched the elevator button and the doors opened

immediately. Stepping in, he punched the button for the first level as the elevator doors closed soundlessly. He tapped his foot as he watched the number change on the display above the doors. With a ding, the doors opened, and he moved briskly down the hall. Security personnel nodded at him as he passed, but he ignored them. He pushed open the door just as the truck was pulling to a stop in the large loading area.

When the facility had first been created, there'd been little more here than a large cave. The cave had been hollowed out to allow large trucks and it had been extended another half mile into the mountain. Lights shone brightly across the space and a dozen guards had arranged themselves around the back of the truck.

The subject had been driven by truck the entire way. Construction, of all things, had forced them to take a longer route. Anticipation rolled over Martin. He made his way to the truck as the door was opened. Inside were six more guards and a containment unit. Four men carried it out and laid it on the waiting stretcher.

"Open it up," Martin said.

His security head unlocked the crate, pulling back the lid. Martin peered in at the creature. He was small, smaller than Martin had expected. Perhaps he'd built him up so much in his mind he'd expected more. But he just lay there, his small chest rising and falling. Even though he was close to thirty years old, there was a childlike quality to his appearance. No doubt that was what had led to the bond between the creature and both mother and daughter Leander.

Fools.

A man in a white coat walked around from the front of the truck. Dr. Mikhail Svenson, second in charge of science division. In his late fifties, Svenson had been with Martin for years. He rarely left the facility. He even slept there. The man was a true patriot.

"When was he last dosed?" Martin asked.

"Before transport. He should wake up within ten minutes or so."

Martin smiled. "Perfect."

"Do you want him to be brought to the third level?" The doctor asked.

Martin didn't answer right away. Normally a new subject was brought to the third level for a full round of testing. Each new subject spent about two weeks there before they were brought down to the fourth floor for mind-control experiments and then finally to the sixth level for genetic experiments and aggression analysis. The sixth floor was where all the fun happened.

The history on this particular subject, though, was already well documented. He was probably the most well-documented subject in U.S. custody.

Martin nodded. "Yes. But just get baselines and verify they're consistent with his files. I want the testing to start first thing this afternoon."

CHAPTER 63

WALSENBURG, COLORADO

They drove for three hours without stopping. When they did stop, only Adam got out. He ordered enough food at a travel stop for all of them. Carrying the bags of food and another smaller bag from the convenience store, he got back in the car.

Chris turned onto a gravel drive twenty minutes later at Adam's instruction. The drive was long but finally ended at a ranch house. Lights were on inside and Maeve's heart lifted. She needed to see her little guys. She glanced at Nadine. "You ready for this?"

Maeve and Nadine had spoken for an hour straight after they were in the clear. Maeve answered all her questions the best she could, but she could tell the woman was struggling. Apparently Nadine did not believe in aliens and thought UFO sightings were cases of experimental aircraft or crazy people.

So convincing her that the U.S. government had held aliens for years in a secret program had not exactly been an easy sell. The gunfight had helped sell the fact that the government was currently trying to kill her and her daughter. But Maeve could tell Nadine was still trying to come up with any other scenario that fit the facts in front of them.

Nadine gave Maeve a look just shy of a smirk. "Meeting alien-human hybrids? I'm not sure anyone's ready for that."

"How do you think Penny will handle it?" Maeve asked.

"I think she'll handle it better than me," Nadine said, her gaze straying out the window, her voice sounded lost. "Apparently she's had more time to acclimate to this than me."

"I know it's a lot, but—" Maeve paused, then shrugged. "Actually I have nothing to say beyond that. It's a lot."

The front door opened and Greg bounded out of the house, Hope right on his heels. Maeve had asked him to keep the triplets inside. She figured making the introduction in a house might make it less surreal.

Maeve stepped out of the car and Hope jumped at her. Maeve rubbed her sides. "I'm happy to see you as well, little buddy."

"How about me?" Greg asked.

"You, too, big buddy." Maeve hugged him.

"We're going to walk around. Make sure we're all good." Chris gestured to Adam, who was already walking down the drive.

Tension curled inside Maeve but she nodded. "Okay. Be careful."

"Always." Chris kissed Maeve's cheek before he headed down the drive, Hope trotting behind him.

Maeve introduced Greg to Nadine. Penny still sat in the car, her attention focused on the tablet's screen.

"So that's Guardian." He paused. "I thought he'd be taller."

Maeve hit him in the arm.

"Ow." Greg rubbed the spot.

Penny looked up from the tablet, the screen reflecting in her glasses for a moment before she took off the noise-cancelling headphones and stepped out of the car. "Where are the triplets?"

"Inside," Maeve said.

Penny headed to the house. Nadine shrugged at Maeve with a bewildered look on her face before hustling after her daughter.

"Um, that was a little strange," Greg said.

"Really? After everything we've seen, you think *that* was strange?" Maeve asked.

He shrugged. "What can I say? Now normal is the new strange."

Maeve laughed before heading to the house. "You're not wrong."

CHAPTER 64

DULCE, NEW MEXICO

There was an energy in the lab today as Martin stepped in. On the one hand, it all looked the same. The subject cages, four on each side, were lined up against the walls. Tables lined the inner layer, covered in computers, medical equipment. And then there were the stretchers, dunk tanks, and assorted other equipment that lined the back wall.

All the equipment was on wheeled pallets to make it easier to move them around the lab. A dozen lab assistants, most with white coats over their blue scrubs, were working at different lab tables lined up in rows in the center of the lab. The glass windows of his darkened office were straight in front of him, twenty feet above the space.

And yet, as normal as the scene appeared, there was almost a tangible spark in the air. A new subject always had that effect. And this subject had been coveted for a long time. It had been a waste of both time and money to coddle Subject One all these years.

While Martin had at first supported the idea of seeing if a

bond could be established between Subject One and the deceased Dr. Leander, once the bond had been established, they should have moved on to the next stage of testing—seeing what the subject would do in support of that bond. But with a Leander running the project, that had never happened. Now Martin could test the subject to his heart's content. *But first things first ...*

And first for this subject was establishing a pain threshold. He didn't think the creature's threshold would be too high. After all, he'd hardly been exposed to hardships in his life. But how much pain could he tolerate for himself and how much would he tolerate for someone else? Now that was an interesting question.

He frowned, thinking of the restraints placed on the experiments at Wright-Pat. They'd have no such problems here. He'd chosen his scientists because of their interest in expanding the boundaries of science and because they were not hampered by the restrictions of conscience.

His director of the department, Belinda Piatto, looked up from her microscope as Martin stepped through the sliding doors. Fifty-seven, with degrees from Harvard and Princeton in medicine and zoology, she was a tall, stately woman with an impressively no-nonsense attitude to life. She nodded as he made his way over to her. "You're just in time. We were about to unbox the subject."

"Where's Orion1?" Martin asked scanning the space.

"In a holding cell." She gestured toward the door at the back right-hand corner of the room.

When subjects were not being used, they were held back there in a long line of cells. There were currently thirty-eight subjects in their custody. Most had been transferred from Area 51 before Project Vault had been conducted. Martin glanced at the two subjects that were being held in containers along the walls. They were both hybrids of the Gray species.

"Before we unbox the subject, have Orion1 brought in. And make sure his control collar is fully charged," Martin said.

He'd reviewed the recordings from Area 51 and had seen the big Gray demonstrate what Martin thought might be protectiveness toward Subject One. First in the hallway and second, outside, when Orion1 had distracted the guards to allow Leander, Subject One, and the triplets to escape. He could be reading too much into it, but the latter act had shown uncharacteristic behavior on the Gray's part. It simply did not 'throw fits' like it did in that instance.

And he wanted to see if he was correct in his interpretation. The large Gray had been in what could only be described as an unemotional countenance since he'd been in custody.

Belinda arched an eyebrow at the unusual request. "May I ask why?"

Normally Martin did not like people questioning his orders, but he knew Belinda wasn't asking to be disrespectful. She was looking for the scientific angle of the request. "I believe there may be a connection between Orion1 and this subject. I would like his responses observed and recorded."

"Interesting. Very well." Belinda waved over her assistant, who had been standing back awaiting her orders. "Have the big Gray brought in." She paused. "Put him in Cage 3."

Martin nodded in approval. Cage 3 would provide the Gray with a perfect view of the subject. Martin rubbed his hands in anticipation.

It looks like Christmas has come early for me.

A few minutes later, Orion1 was led into the lab. The Gray was six feet tall, with a large, wide head. Two black eyes dominated its face while the nose, really just two small holes, was overlooked unless you were looking for it. The face was almost triangular, coming to a dull point at the chin with a small mouth.

The anatomy of its throat and mouth made talking impossible. But it was intelligent. It just communicated another way, although it had refused to communicate with them since it had been taken into captivity. Every once in a while, though, Martin would sense the Gray probing his mind.

It had long, thin arms and a thin body, but it was, like Subject One, surprisingly strong. Two security officers led it in, but Martin knew it could easily overpower them if he wished. Apparently it did not wish to. Even now, it made no effort to resist its captors. Truth was, it had always been a model prisoner.

But Martin had never let any of his people let their guard down around it. The Gray was biding its time. Even now, it glanced around the room, taking in exits, personnel, weapons. Martin did not know what profession the Gray held in its own society, but Martin would not be surprised to learn it involved security. Martin could see the cool calculation in its eyes as it was led from the holding cell. The same look it had every time it was taken out.

And one day, Martin knew it would make its move. But so far it had shown no indications of trying to leave. The Gray was smart. It knew this room was only one of many. There were five other levels it would need to get through to reach the surface. And then it would have open ground to contend with. No, the Gray wouldn't move until it knew exactly what it was doing, how it was getting there, and where it was headed.

Not that there hadn't been attempts to rescue it. There'd been a few over the years, although they never resulted in more than increased sightings over the locations the Gray had been held. But those sightings had made them wonder how those crafts were finding the regal-looking Gray.

That was when Belinda had realized that the Gray emitted a small electromagnetic signal. Unless you were looking for it, you would never find it. Protocols had been put in place to make sure the Gray's signal was blocked. After that, it had been moved and there'd been no more sightings, no more rescue attempts.

The Gray glanced at the other two creatures along the walls. They each bowed their heads slightly toward it. Martin always marveled at that. They all bowed to the Gray, even the ones created in the labs. Somehow they knew it was more.

Martin knew there was a hierarchy within the alien species. Different ones were held in more regard. Some, like the Maldek, were little more than pets. But if the other creatures' attitudes were an indicator, the Gray here was alien royalty. Catching him had been a coup, one the United States government did not truly appreciate. So Martin had overseen his captivity. He'd even had to remove a few individuals who argued the Gray should never have been held to begin with.

The Gray had revealed little about itself. It had never communicated anything beyond pain. Its most common emotion seemed to be disinterest.

But Martin had a feeling all of that was about to change. He knew the second the Gray realized Subject One was in the lab. The Gray was halfway across the room when it stopped, its small nostrils sniffing, its large eyes going even wider. Its gaze zeroed in on the container holding Subject One.

In a blink, the Gray swung at the two men holding it, knocking them down while pain lanced through Martin's brain. Next to him, Belinda screamed as well. Martin dropped to the ground, barely able to think beyond the pain. It just hurt so much—as if his very brain was screaming to get out. From his peripheral vision, he saw the Gray move with shocking swiftness across the room, straight for Subject One.

Spots danced in front of Martin's eyes, and he felt the trickle of blood from his nose and ears. He reached for the control in his pocket, his hand feeling so very heavy. His breaths stuttered, pain beginning to spread from his head down through his chest.

Desperately, Martin's finger felt the edge of the control. He slid his hand down and pressed the button. The pain stopped immediately as the Gray let out a scream. Martin kept his finger on the button, letting the Gray scream and scream until the remote slid from his hands and Martin slipped into darkness.

CHAPTER 65

WALSENBURG, COLORADO

The introduction of Penny and Nadine to the triplets went surprisingly well. The triplets were sitting with Tilda on the couch, waiting for them. They smiled at Maeve and jumped to their feet, but Maeve waved them back down, thinking less enthusiastic hybrids would be easier for the Johnsons to accept.

Nadine and Penny walked slowly into the room. Nadine's eyes were huge; her hand flew to her mouth. "They're—oh my God."

Penny had no expression on her face. She simply studied them in silence.

"Penny?" Nadine asked.

"They're bigger than the last time I saw them," she said before walking out of the room. She headed to the dining-room table, pulling out her tablet.

"Uh, so that went well?" Greg said.

Tilda stood up. "So it appears. Adam dropped off the food, so let's eat."

The triplets looked at Maeve, who smiled before kneeling down and throwing open her arms. They sprinted over to her. Maeve hugged them tight, even as she saw Nadine stumble into a club chair with a gasp.

Greg patted Nadine on the shoulder. "Don't worry. You get used to the cuteness. Now, how about some dinner? I know I can eat."

Penny had had no trouble with the triplets' existence, but as Maeve watched Nadine, she knew her mother was a different story entirely.

Nadine sat at the dining-room table, not touching her food as everyone else dug in. She just couldn't seem to take her eyes off the triplets. But then Chris had entered with Hope. The triplets ran to Chris, who flipped each of them in the air. A smile broke across Nadine's face and she finally turned her attention to the food in front of her.

A half hour later, the food was eaten and the dining room tidied up.

Tilda turned to Nadine. "I think we need to have a chat with your daughter."

Nadine shook her head. "No, she has nothing to do with this."

Maeve kept her tone non-threatening. "I think the time for denying her role in this is past. And there are lives on the line here. We need to know what she knows."

Nadine pursed her lips.

Chris stood up. "Well, I'm going to give these rug rats a bath and put them to bed. Greg, how about you help me?"

"Uh, sure." Greg got awkwardly to his feet, scooping up Crackle. "I call dibs on this one."

Crackle happily scrambled onto Greg's shoulders. Snap

and Pop sprinted for the stairs, Chris right behind him along with Hope. Maeve smiled as she watched them go before turning to Nadine.

"The triplets are really cute," Nadine said, turning her gaze from the stairs.

"Yeah, they are," Maeve said. "And I need your daughter's help to keep them safe."

Nadine looked at her daughter, who seemed to be ignoring them. She bit her lip, and Maeve wasn't sure if she should try a different tack to convince her. She turned to Tilda, who shook her head, warning Maeve to stay quiet.

Okay. Maeve crossed her arms over her chest and waited. The minutes stretched on as Nadine weighed the situation in her mind.

Every once in a while her gaze would shift to the stairs. Finally, she nodded. "Okay. But I'm staying in the room."

"Sure, no problem." Maeve took a seat back at the table and Tilda sat down next to her.

Nadine hovered for a moment before she sat next to Penny. "Honey, Maeve and Tilda need to ask you some questions."

Adam slipped in quietly behind them, staying by the open doorway behind Penny and her mother. He reached up and took off his sunglasses. His eyes were a striking blue. Maeve had never seen eyes so bright.

No wonder he keeps on those glasses. Those eyes are damned distracting. Without the glasses he looked younger, more vulnerable.

Penny looked at Tilda and then Maeve before she fixed her gaze on the tabletop. "Okay."

Maeve let out a breath. "Why did you warn Tilda that Greg and I were in danger?"

"Agaren would want me to," Penny said.

Tilda gasped, turning a few shades paler.

"Who's Agaren?" Maeve asked her.

"He's a Gray." Tilda leaned forward. "How do you know Agaren?"

"He's my friend." She turned to Maeve. "And he's locked in Dulce with your friend."

Maeve frowned. "What do you mean he's your—"

Penny's head whipped up and she turned to her mother. "It's bedtime. I need to go to bed."

"Of course, honey." Nadine's tone was calm, but Maeve could read the unease on her face.

Tilda shook her head. "We just have a few more—"

Nadine stood. "No. Penny's bedtime is 9:30. We stick to that schedule."

Tilda frowned looking like she was about to argue. But Maeve stood, beginning to understand the unusual girl a little more. And she knew that getting to bed was very important for both mother and daughter at this time.

"There's a bedroom down the hall. I'll show you," Adam said.

Nadine jumped, and Maeve realized she hadn't known he was there. Penny turned as well, staring into Adam's eyes. Neither of them spoke, but something passed between them.

Penny nodded. "Okay."

He led them down the hallway, stopping to pick up Penny's suitcase by the front door before continuing to the bedroom.

Watching them go, Maeve wasn't sure what had just happened and she was too tired to figure it out. Adam reappeared. As he passed Maeve he nodded, his sunglasses back on as he headed back outside.

Maeve turned to Tilda. "Who's Agaren?"

Looking shaken, she sank into a chair. "He's a large Gray," she said again. "I never imagined—"

"Can't sleep, can't sleep." Penny's loud, anxious words drifted down the hall, getting louder and louder. Maeve looked at Tilda for a moment before the two of them hustled toward the bedroom.

The young girl paced across the room, her arms moving erratically in agitation. "Can't sleep. Can't sleep."

"What's wrong?" Maeve asked.

Nadine looked on, helpless. "This room. I knew this was going to be a problem. At home, she has a white noise machine that she sleeps with. It calms her. And she has these star stickers all over her ceiling. She needs that consistency. I can download an app for the sounds on my phone, but the stars, I don't know how to make that happen."

The front door slammed and Maeve jumped as Adam walked in, carrying a navy-blue nylon bag. He ignored Penny, who watched him with big eyes, her hands flailing. Adam pulled a bed tent from the bag. There was something glowing inside. Maeve inched forward and realized stickers had been applied to the top of the tent.

He waved Penny over and she moved slowly toward him. She looked inside and then shook her head. Adam pointed at one star and Penny nodded. He unpeeled it and placed it in a different position.

Penny's shoulders dropped, and then she scampered into the tent. She reached up and started rearranging the stars. Adam pulled a sheet of stickers from his back pocket and stood, patiently waiting for her to finish. She reached out a hand and he placed the stickers in it.

Nadine stood watching, her face shifting from shock to relief, and then tears appeared in her eyes.

Tilda walked up to her. "Adam will superglue the stickers in place in the morning so they stay where they're supposed to be."

"How did he know she would need this?" Nadine asked.

"He must have seen her room. He's"—she paused—"sensitive to things like this."

Maeve watched the strong man patiently wait as the tween rearranged the stars to her satisfaction and she realized he must have peeked in the house to get the layout before she'd gone to the front door. And somehow, he'd known this was important.

Maeve tugged on Tilda's sleeve. "We should go."

"Yes. Nadine, do you need anything?" Tilda asked.

She shook her head, her attention on her daughter. "No, actually, I think we're good."

"Okay. Good night," Maeve said quietly.

"Good night," Nadine said, finally looking at the two of them. "And thank you for saving us today."

Together the women made their way down the hall. Tilda started for the stairs. "Well, I think I'll call it a—"

"Oh, no," Maeve said. "I'm going to help the boys put the triplets down and then we are going to talk. I want to know what you know about the big Gray."

"Agaren," Tilda said softly. "His name's Agaren. Do what you need to do. I'll be waiting in the kitchen."

CHAPTER 66

DULCE, NEW MEXICO

The Gray had knocked Martin and the rest of the lab staff out for two hours. Martin awoke swinging at the doctor leaning over him. The doctor managed to leap back just in time.

Martin growled, sitting up. "What the hell happened?"

The man watched him anxiously. "Sir, you've had what can only be described as a psychic attack. We will need to run some tests to determine—"

"Run them on someone else," Martin growled before he stood, swaying for a moment.

The doctor grabbed his arm, steadying him. "Sir, you really need to lie down and let us finish examining you."

Martin looked down at the man's hand still wrapped around his upper arm. Slowly the doctor removed his hand, taking a step back.

Martin nodded to where Belinda lay a few cots away. "Make sure Dr. Piatto is all right. I need her in the lab."

"But, sir—"

Ignoring him, Martin headed for the door. The Gray had attacked him. While on the one hand he was annoyed at how quickly and how completely he'd been taken down, the other part of him was ecstatic.

Now that *ability could be useful*. If he could figure out how to manipulate it, recreate it, it would be a weapon worth something. Today was turning out to be more rewarding than he'd planned.

He headed to his office and downed a handful of painkillers while calling for the report on the Gray. Martin pulled his chair over to the large picture window overlooking the lab. He took a seat, its legs creaking. His head still felt woozy.

Scanning the lab, he looked for the big Gray. It had been placed in a cell along the wall.

To Martin's annoyance, it was sitting with its back straight, looking no worse for wear. It met Martin's gaze and Martin could feel the challenge in it. Martin tried to maintain contact, but his vision began to darken.

Damn it.

He pushed himself back from the window, out of the Gray's view. He leaned his head back as the room began to spin. And the twin feelings of fear and powerlessness rolled through him. A cold sweat broke out across his body.

No, I am in charge now. He fought off the dizziness, but it was too much, and the darkness claimed him again.

CHAPTER 67

DURANGO, COLORADO

Norah slept for most of the drive. The car had glided off the highway to a charging station. Guardian hadn't sent a message, so Norah thought perhaps the stop was pre-planned, which meant Guardian might not be watching right now. Norah had contemplated making a run for it, but honestly, where was she going to go with Iggy? She had no allies. Leander was probably her only hope.

And now I'm Princess Leia looking for Obi-Wan, she realized. So instead of running when they stopped, she'd gone to use the facilities and get some food for her and Iggy. There'd been money in the car. She felt a little bad about taking it, but being she already had their car, she figured the forty bucks wasn't going to make the owners hate her any more.

As soon as they finished the charge, they got back on the road. She'd picked up a disposable phone and she'd scrolled through different news sites to see if there were any reports on the attack at the travel stop. There was one small article which mentioned a drunk driver.

She shook her head. *Well, that was covered up quickly.* The rest of the trip she simply stared out the window, watching the scenery fly by. She wanted to call her mom and just tell her she loved her. But she knew they'd be watching her mom and monitoring her calls, and she could not risk putting her in danger.

Taking a stuttering breath, she realized she was probably never going to see her again. That these right now were probably her last few hours alive. She might be able to hide out from Bob, but the entire United States government? She knew she would not be able to hide from them.

Tears sprang to her eyes and she wiped them away. She knew she was doing the right thing, but it didn't make it any less crushingly despairing that this was what doing the right thing had come to.

Iggy made a small, mewling noise, and Norah looked over at him, giving him a small smile. "Hey, buddy. Just feeling a little sad."

He crawled into her lap with a deep sigh. "Ig."

The world continued to fly by through the window as Norah hugged him to her, resting her head on the top of his as She let her tears fall as she said goodbye to it.

CHAPTER 68

WALSENBURG, COLORADO

The triplets went down relatively easily. But once Maeve had them all tucked in, they'd looked up at her and an image of Alvie appeared in her mind along with a sense of uncertainty. Maeve's breath caught at the triplets' silent question, and all the fears she had for him rushed to the surface.

Chris sat down on the other side of the bed and spoke quietly. "Alvie *is* in trouble. But we *will* get him back. That's why we're here. So you three get a good night's sleep because tomorrow we all have work to do, okay?"

They nodded back at him. Maeve leaned down and kissed each of them, rubbing a hand through Hope's fur as she dozed at the end of the bed. Hope gave her a lazy tail wag in response.

Maeve paused in the doorway, watching them. Picturing Alvie, tears pressed against the back of her eyelids.

How am I going to save you? How am I going to keep them safe? She thought.

He wrapped an arm around her waist, leaning down to whisper in her ear. "We will get him back. You need to focus on that."

Leaning back against him, she nodded, knowing he was right. But it was hard to keep the fears at bay when the world was quiet. It was easier to shove her concerns and fears away when they were moving and dodging. But now? Now she couldn't get Alvie out of her mind. He'd never been alone. Not once in his whole life. What was he thinking? What was he feeling? Her heart ached imagining his fear and loneliness.

"Come on," Chris pulled her gently from the doorway. "Let's let them sleep. You said we needed to speak with Tilda."

Maeve took a shaky breath, trying to calm the fears building up internally. *Focus on the now.* "She knows about the big Gray from 51. She says his name is Agaren. Penny seems to know him, too."

Chris's eyebrows rose. "How's that possible?"

"I have no idea."

Chris kissed her gently before taking her hand. "Well, let's go find out."

Greg and Tilda were speaking quietly at the kitchen table when Maeve and Chris walked in.

Greg stood up. "Hey, I made some coffee—decaf. You guys want some?"

"That would be great. Thanks," Maeve said as she took a seat.

"Me, too," Chris said, sitting next to Maeve and looking around. "Where's Adam?"

"He's outside. He likes to make sure everything's buttoned down for the night before he turns in," Tilda said, her hands cupping her own mug.

"Where'd he serve?" Chris asked as Greg placed mugs in front of him and Maeve.

Maeve nodded her thanks, noticing the slightest of tension in Tilda's eyes and hands.

"The army. Now, you wanted to know about Agaren." Tilda took a deep breath. "Agaren is a Gray alien in U.S. captivity."

"Wait, how then does Penny know him? Does he get some sort of weekend pass from captivity?" Greg asked.

"If only. I've been thinking about that since Penny mentioned him. I can guarantee she has not physically met him. But Agaren ... he has a number of abilities. I think Penny may have stumbled upon him and figured out a way to communicate with him. As to exactly how she does it, I don't know," Tilda said.

"You speak of him like you know him," Maeve said.

"Gray aliens have been part of the lore about visitors from space almost since the very beginning. But most people don't realize that there's no single Gray race. There are four. Agaren is part of what is considered a ruling caste in the universe."

"A ruling caste?" Chris asked.

"This world's history is not what your books have told you. It's much longer than most of us realize." She took a breath. "But if I tell you, you cannot unlearn it. You cannot unhear it. Once your eyes have been opened, it will all change. You have to be sure it's what you want."

Maeve met Chris's gaze. He took her hand and gave it a squeeze. She turned back to Tilda. "Tell us."

"There *is* order in the universe. We humans are bumbling through it as if it's this big empty space—it's not. Battles have been fought and lost time and again. We know of eight-five different species that exist out there. They are much more evolved spiritually, physically, and technologically than humans. We are not even close."

Maeve knew the Earth was four and half billion years old. The universe, though, was almost three times that age. There could be civilizations out there that were billions of years more evolved than humans. It was a terrifying thought. And within the last few years, more and more planets had been discovered that exist in a Goldilocks zone—places in space that are not too hot and not too cold. In fact, in 2017 alone, seven Earth-like planets were found in orbit around a single star forty light-years away. Scientists believed any of those planets could be life-sustaining.

But now there was even evidence that extraterrestrial life may have existed a lot closer to home. It's known that billions of years ago, Mars was covered in oceans and that it had an atmosphere similar to Earth. And water vapor plumes have also been spotted on one of Jupiter's moons, Europa, and Saturn's moon, Enceladus, calling into question our depiction of moons as desolate, cold celestial bodies.

Even our own planet had confounded well-established perceptions. For example, fossilized evidence of life on Earth had been found dating back to 3.7 billion years ago. The discovery had pushed back the start date for life on Earth by 220 million years, which meant there was life on Earth at around the time there was the same potential for life on Mars, before its environment degraded. Many were surprised by the evidence, but what most people didn't realize was that many of the ideas of what the solar system look like were developed before we were capable of sending probes out into the universe to actually see it. Now that those probes are reaching farther into our own solar system, the more we are beginning to realize that it's not quite as dead as we had imagined.

And the truth was, earlier in America's history, there was strong support for the plurality of worlds—the idea that planets across the galaxy and our own solar system contained life. In fact, up until the latter half of the twentieth century, that was as an accepted belief. It seemed odd that as soon as what many considered evidence of extraterrestrial life became documented, the belief in extraterrestrial life began to reduce. Was that fear or the result of a well-aimed disinformation campaign?

"What does this ruling caste of Grays want?" Chris asked.

"Nothing at the moment. We are young. They are waiting to see which way we break—aggression or peace."

Maeve thought about the state of the world and she had a feeling she knew which way the human race was leaning. "Why are they waiting?"

"The Grays—they are hoping we choose peace. They are"—Tilda paused—"not allies, because that would assume an equality we have not earned. They are more like mentors, guides, hoping we choose the right path."

"If there are so many more advanced races out there, why haven't we seen them? Why haven't they taken us over?" Greg asked.

"Oh, they've been here. The governments of the world have tied themselves in knots trying to explain away their existence. But as we evolved, as our technology evolved, they've visited less. The Grays are almost like an intergalactic police force. They have kept the Earth from being dominated by any one species. Because they've seen the destruction that can be wrought when the wrong species takes over a planet."

Greg swallowed. "In the sciences, there are arguments that our development was guided. That it was not merely a matter of survival of the fittest."

Tilda nodded. "Before the Grays arrived, our genetic code was indeed manipulated."

"So we're an alien experiment?" Chris asked.

"Yes. But I think that's a longer conversation for another time," Tilda said.

Maeve was intrigued by the idea, but she knew Tilda was

right. That was a conversation for another day. "So Agaren is also a prisoner?"

Tilda's voice turned hard. "Until Alvie, he was Drummond's prime acquisition."

"In the files, they don't indicate which crash site he was taken from," Greg said. "He was only called Orion1."

Tilda looked at each of them in turn, as if weighing the impact her next words would have. "That's because he didn't crash here. He landed at Holloman Air Force Base in 1955."

"Wait, landed? Intentionally?" Chris asked.

Greg looked stunned. "I can't believe that story's true."

Chris looked around the table. "What story? What happened at Holloman?"

"In 1955, at Holloman Air Force Base, the United States government made official contact with a UFO," said Tilda. "And President Eisenhower was there for its arrival. In fact, Air Force One was on the same runway. After the UFO landed, a man exited Air Force One, walked over, and entered the alien craft. The man was inside for forty-five minutes. Some say it was even Eisenhower himself."

"That can't be true," Chris said.

"The landing was recorded. Nixon was going to release the tape. In fact, he wanted to be the President that told the world that aliens were real. He wanted to cement his place in history. He contacted two documentary filmmakers to create *UFOs: It Has Begun*, narrated by Rod Sterling. Nixon gave the filmmakers access to the Air Force and Department of Defense personnel. At the end of the documentary, the recording of the landing at Holloman was going to be revealed. But by the time the documentary was completed, Nixon's fortunes had changed and the recording was not released. Instead of being a groundbreaking documentary, it was just another UFO documentary with lots of theories and little proof."

No one said anything as Tilda finished. Finally, Chris broke the stunned silence. "But why? Why meet with them at all? Why take the chance?"

"At the time, the United States government believed the choice was work with them or be taken over."

"Why would they think that?" Chris asked.

"You have to understand that prior to the creation of NASA, many people in government thought it was only a matter of time before we were invaded by outer space. There had been troubling incidents beginning in the forties with the crashes in Roswell, and the reported air raid of Los Angeles in 1942. But even more recently there were troubling incidents like the blackout of 1965. The whole of the Northeast and up to Canada went completely dark, and no explanation was ever provided. But there were multiple reports of UFOs seen up and down the coast right before the power went down. When the atomic bomb was being created, UFO sightings were so commonplace that people stopped reporting them. And the incident at Malstrom Air Force Base in 1967 just reinforced that view and the President's decision."

"What happened at Malstrom?" Maeve asked.

"Eighteen of our nuclear weapons were taken offline, rendered completely unresponsive to all commands. UFOs had been reported in the area. But we believe it was a warning to not use the weapons. For some in government, they took that as an indication that aliens didn't want us to use such destructive weapons. For others, they interpreted it as a threat."

"How did you interpret it?" Greg asked.

Tilda smiled. "Well, I had a little inside knowledge, so I knew they were trying to discourage us from going down the nuclear weapons path."

"Inside knowledge? What does that mean?" Chris asked.

Tilda hesitated, and Maeve had the sense she was trying to figure out how exactly to answer that question. "Aliens have been visiting Earth long before history was written."

Chris raised an eyebrow. "The Ancient Alien stories are true?"

Tilda gave a small laugh. "Some of their interpretations are a bit of a stretch, but they are not all wrong. But those visits, those interactions, continued into the modern day. And they have been working with the United States governments since Holloman."

Greg glared. "So let me get this straight. We worked with aliens—peaceful, altruistic aliens—and then a few years later, we captured a bunch and recreated them? How the hell did that happen?"

"There was an incident," said Tilda. "We made an attempt to incorporate the larger government into our work. We thought it would be a chance to move forward. We had a president in office who believed in UFOs, who we thought would be receptive to the program and the progress we'd made."

"Reagan," Maeve said.

"Yes," Tilda replied.

Maeve knew Reagan had mentioned UFOs and aliens more than once in public speeches. There were even reports that he'd seen UFOs personally on two separate occasions, one landing on the road in front of him as he and his wife Nancy were on their way to a party at Lucille Ball's house.

"So what went wrong?" Chris asked.

"In a word, Drummond." Tilda practically spit out the name. "Somehow he got himself on the team that was brought over from the State Department. I'm not sure how he did it, but while he was there a firefight ensued between the humans and the aliens we had been working with peacefully for thirty years. At the end, a dozen humans and six Grays were dead. Three Grays escaped and one was taken into custody."

"You were there?" Chris asked.

Tilda nodded. "I was wounded. I was later reported dead, and I went to ground. Drummond and his boss, Robert Buckley, made sure all resources were cut from our group. And the people known to be associated with our group seemed to keep running into accidents. So we moved deep into the shadows."

"Your group? Who's your group?" Greg asked.

"We are a government watchdog, I suppose you could say. We didn't want to let anyone know we were still operational. Luckily, we had not told the government the extent of our activities, so most of what we did, and continued to do, they were unaware of."

"So why are *you* so interested in the big Gray?" Chris asked.

"Because he saved my life. He saved a lot of people's lives. And I owe him for that," Tilda said. "Agaren is a good man. He was a leader of his people. He sacrificed himself so that the remainder of his people could escape. And he's been in captivity ever since."

Greg's eyes nearly bugged out of his head. "We've held him for close to forty years?"

Tilda nodded. "I've been trying to find him since then. So have his people. None of us have been successful. It wasn't until Area 51 that we caught sight of him again. And I will get him out of there. I owe him that."

Maeve remembered the connection Alvie seemed to have with the Gray. And what had seemed like approval directed at Maeve. "He saved us at 51. We were nearly caught. He distracted the guards, pulled the attention back to himself."

Tilda gave a small smile. "That sounds like Agaren."

"I had a sense that he approved of us helping Alvie and the triplets, even though it meant leaving him behind. Do you know why that would be?" Maeve asked.

A crease appeared between Tilda's eyes. "He has a large heart. But I think there may be more there. Alvie, after all, in many ways, is a thousand years old. Agaren did not tell us everything, but I think there may have been something in play for Alvie, in his first existence."

Maeve did not like the sound of that. "What did they want with him?"

"I don't know. And it was really more of a feeling I had than anything Agaren specifically conveyed. He's very reserved in what he reveals. It makes him an excellent poker player."

"You played poker with him?" Greg asked.

Tilda nodded. "Yes. I even managed to win a few hands."

Chris put his hands on the table. "Okay, so, fascinating as all this is, I think we're getting off track. Agaren was seen at 51. I take it you believe he and Alvie are being held at the same location?"

There was no hesitation in Tilda's reply. "Yes."

"And where's that?"

"Dulce, New Mexico."

Greg's eyes nearly bugged out of his head. "That place exists, too?"

Tilda nodded. "It was created in the 80s. One of many DUMBs created back then."

"Dumb?" Maeve asked.

"Deep Underground Military Base," Greg said.

"So you think Alvie's in an underground base?"

"Yes."

"Why there?" Chris asked.

Tilda hesitated. "I've learned that Martin Drummond has been made the new head of D.E.A.D., and the facility at Dulce has just been declared a D.E.A.D. facility."

Maeve shivered at the name.

Greg slumped back in his chair. "So Alvie and your buddy Agaren are in a federally protected facility sitting underneath a mountain."

Maeve looked around at the serious looks on everyone's

face. *Oh God. How are we going to do this?* "How many levels deep does the facility go?"

"Seven. It links up with the underground tunnels Greg just mentioned." Tilda paused. "Do you guys know about the tunnels?"

The tunnels—giant tunnels far below the Earth that linked military bases along the western portion of the United States. Maeve pictured the last time she'd been in one. She, Chris, Alvie and the triplets had been in a desperate race through the tunnels to escape the bombing at 51. She swallowed, her stomach rolling at the memories.

"Yeah. We're familiar with the tunnels."

CHAPTER 69

WALSENBURG, COLORADO

Everyone was up and ready to go before Maeve had even opened her eyes. Adam and Tilda had taken off for the safe house near Dulce with Penny and Nadine an hour before she'd awoken.

Last night, they had discussed what the next steps would be. The first step was gaining as much information on Dulce as possible. Tilda said she already had people working on it and resources put into place, although she didn't elaborate on either. But Maeve at least trusted that she was committed to getting Agaren and Alvie out.

They had all headed to bed shortly thereafter, but Maeve tossed and turned. The U.S. government had been working with aliens and then had taken one of those aliens captive. At the same time, they'd been creating or recreating aliens in their labs. To say the revelations had shattered Maeve's already tenuous faith in her government was an understatement.

And then there was the immediate problem facing them—Alvie was being held in an underground base hidden under a mountain. How were they ever going to get him out? And even if they managed to rescue him, then what? Where could they possibly hide him and the triplets that would be safe?

Her thoughts circling around and around in her mind, they only grew more dire as the night wore on. And it wasn't until just before dawn that she dropped off to sleep. By the time she'd stumbled down the stairs, her gang was already in the car. Greg handed her a bagel and a coffee and steered her to the backseat of Chris's car, where the triplets were already sleeping. It was way too early for them to be up.

Polishing off her bagel, she drank just a little coffee before curling up with her little ones on the backseat. Two hours later, Maeve's eyes popped open as Chris hit a particularly deep pothole.

He glanced over his shoulder. "Sorry about that. But we're almost there. Only another thirty minutes."

"Okay," Maeve said, straightening slowly so as not to wake Snap, who was sprawled across her lap. Crackle lay curled up on the other side of the seat with Hope, while Pop had crawled into the passenger seat and laid on Greg's chest. Both of them were sleeping.

For a moment, Maeve met Chris's gaze in the rearview mirror and they shared a smile at the peacefulness of the moment. But then Chris's gaze shifted back to the road and Maeve's shifted to the scene outside her window.

The mountain in the distance looked ominous with the gray storm clouds above it. It was the Archuleta Mesa, and underneath all the towering rock was the base that held Alvie. There were no lights, no indications of any sort of activity. Doubts crept through her. What if they were all wrong? What if Alvie wasn't here? What if he was halfway across the country? Across the world?

She took a breath. No, he was here. He had to be. Besides,

Guardian said he was. And that pint-sized girl was scary smart.

The mountain itself had been the subject of speculation within the UFO world. Cattle mutations were reported in the area surrounding the mesa. Strange lights were also reported in the sky along with black helicopters.

Something was going on around the mesa, but the government adamantly denied any involvement. Although if Drummond was involved, it was possible those denials weren't lies. They just didn't know what Martin was up to.

And how exactly did he fit into all of this? She knew he'd resigned from his position as the director of BOSAC after 51. But somehow despite all the devastation he'd caused, he was back in the government's good graces. The man was a cockroach.

How, though, did he manage to be in charge of the Dulce facility? Did that happen before he became the head of the D.E.A.D. or after? Was it a government facility? A private facility? The more Maeve learned about the country's involvement in the space program, aliens, and UFOs, the more she realized was hidden from view. Take Tilda.

She knew a great deal and yet she was no longer with the government. Yet it was obvious she still knew what was going on and had significant resources. So who exactly did she work for? And what did they want?

God, it was all overwhelming and terrifying and mind numbingly confusing. *And my strange little family is caught in the middle of all of it.* A tremor ran through her as she looked around the car. She would trade her life for each person here, and she knew they would do the same. She just prayed it didn't come to that.

CHAPTER 70

DULCE, NEW MEXICO

Martin had been watching Orion1 through the window in his office for the last hour. Last night he'd woken up hours later, confusion his first emotion. The lab's lights had been dimmed. He'd made his way to his couch after downing more painkillers and slept until morning.

When morning dawned, he'd felt like his old self. He'd ordered a large breakfast and finished every bite before grabbing a shower and a change of clothes.

Refreshed, he returned to his office to see the reports from yesterday awaiting his attention. As suspected, the Gray had attacked the medullas of all the people in the lab—over twelve people simultaneously incapacitated. The scope of its ability was mind-blowing. It had been kept under sedation since then.

Belinda had not been released until this morning. An overabundance of caution on the doctor's part as far as Martin was concerned, but since he could see her in the lab now, he supposed it was all right. After all, Martin had been in no shape to observe the experiments yesterday, and missing them would have been a shame.

He moved closer to the window. This time the big Gray did not look up at him, his attention completely focused on the container holding Subject One.

Why is he so important to you?

Promising himself that today he would find out, Martin headed for the door.

A few minutes later, Martin walked into the lab. Orion1 sat there quietly, unmoving as he watched Belinda. Although she looked a little paler than normal, she still moved efficiently through her tasks. The creature was tense, which Martin could not ever remember seeing before. Each time Belinda or one of her assistants went near Subject One's containment unit, the large alien tensed even more.

Why are you so protective of him? he wondered as he met the Gray's gaze. Of course, there was no response. For years, it had failed to respond, no matter the provocation. Martin narrowed his eyes. *Until yesterday, until you saw Subject One.*

But as interesting as that development was, it was not the subject of today's experiment. No, today's experiment was all about Subject One. And Martin had made sure controls had been put in place to prevent the large Gray from attacking them like it had done before. But Martin still wanted it here. He wanted to see how it responded.

"Are we ready?" Martin asked as he came abreast of Subject One's container.

One of Belinda's assistants—Martin had never bothered learning the man's name—nodded. "Yes, the subject has begun to stir."

Martin peered through the glass window on the top of the container. Sure enough, Subject One was opening his eyes. Martin met his gaze and smiled. The creature reared back and

Martin smiled wider. *Fear. Good.* He gestured to the unit. "Open it up."

The assistant called over another assistant as Belinda joined them.

"Get readings before you open it," Belinda said, taking a seat tiredly on a stool.

"Yes, Doctor," assistant one said, turning to his tablet.

"How are you feeling?" Martin asked Belinda as the two assistants continued to document the subject's physical state.

"Fine. Although I had no inkling of Orion1's abilities. I'm caught between admiration of his ability to hide his skill and concern as to what else he's hiding. Not to mention, the attack clearly shows a vulnerability in both our defenses and our testing."

And this was why Belinda was critical to his mission—she always understood what was important.

"We're ready, Doctor," assistant one said, turning to them.

With a nod from Martin, Belinda waved her hand toward the containment unit. "Let's begin."

The assistants unsnapped the container lid and lifted it up. Subject One's head whipped from side to side, his whole body shaking, his fear an almost tangible thing.

The assistants reached in and lifted out the stretcher Subject One was tied to and placed him on the gurney that had been set up. More straps were added when he was placed on it.

As soon as Subject One had been lifted from the container, the Gray lunged from his bench but didn't touch the glass separating him from the room. Orion1 knew from experience how painful the electric jolt would be if he did so. But he stood there, his gaze on Subject One, his face a mask of concentration.

Subject One stopped shaking his head, turning toward the Gray. Martin frowned. What was happening? "Dr. Piatto?"

She shook her head. "I'm not sure. It appears to be some sort of telepathic connection. The Gray is calming him."

"How's that possible? The case should block any signal."

"Yes, but again, we don't know everything about these creatures. What's happening now is unique."

Martin watched the two creatures. Subject One's heart rate slowed and some of the tension seemed to have eased out of the big Gray. "Interesting," he murmured. "Well, let's get started. Are we recording?"

"They've been going since we brought the subject in," assistant one said.

"Good. Commence," Martin said.

The assistants placed electrodes on Subject One. The subject began to squirm, making a mewling noise. Martin stepped forward to get a better view.

The assistants stepped back and Belinda nodded at Martin. "We're ready."

Belinda stepped to the console. "We'll start with a simple shock and see how he responds." She turned the dial.

Subject One didn't even move. He looked completely unfazed.

Martin frowned. "How much was that?"

Belinda stared at the console. "300 volts. There should have been some response."

"Raise the voltage," Martin ordered.

"Clear," Belinda said.

She pressed the button. Once again, Subject One didn't respond, but the Gray reared back, sitting heavily on the bench. Martin tilted his head, watching it.

Belinda frowned, looking between Subject One and the panel in front of her. "I don't understand. He has to have pain receptors. It would have been documented if he didn't. Check the leads." The assistants jumped forward, but Martin shook his head, speaking quietly. "It's not him. It's the Gray."

"What?" Belinda asked.

"Go again. Same voltage." Martin turned his back on Subject One and watched the Gray. As soon as Belinda initiated the shock, the creature tensed and shook, its hands curling into fists.

"It's protecting him," Martin murmured.

Belinda stepped next to him. "I've never seen that before. I'm not even sure how it would work."

"Let's see if it works when the Gray is farther away. Maybe it requires line of sight," Martin suggested.

"Possibly." She waved her assistants over. "Move the Gray to position one."

The assistants moved the case thirty feet away. The Gray could not see Subject One or even his container.

"Have a camera trained on the Gray," Martin ordered.

The assistants hustled to get the camera set up, and after checking the feed, nodded at Martin. "Good to go."

Martin moved over so he could see the Gray in its container. Its eyes were closed and it sat on the bench at the back. Martin signaled for Belinda to begin. The Gray jolted, its mouth opening as a sweat broke out on its forehead.

Martin smiled.

Well, now, aren't you just full of surprises?

CHAPTER 71

DULCE, NEW MEXICO

The sky was overcast as Chris pulled to a stop in front of the safe house. It was an old, white farmhouse with a long porch, a barn, and a garage. A fire pit sat thirty feet from the front door and the yard had no grass, just dirt, although there was a ring of trees offering cover.

Maeve stepped out of the car and stretched as Adam stepped from the barn. "Is it okay for the triplets to run around?"

"Yes. I'll keep an eye on them," he said.

"All right, guys. Don't go too far." The triplets bounded from the car, Hope traipsing after them, her tail wagging feverishly. Maeve watched them as they somersaulted across the drive with a smile.

"I'll go with them and see what security Adam has set up." Chris kissed her on the cheek before heading out. Maeve frowned, watching him go. Worry accompanied her gaze. They still didn't know why the other security protocols had failed.

"You made it."

Maeve turned to Tilda as she stepped outside. "So it seems. Penny and Nadine all right?"

"Nadine's sleeping. I don't think she got much sleep last night. Penny was working on pulling out some information on the base."

Greg walked up to them, wiping his mouth and twisting his back. "Man, that was not a comfortable sleeping position." He rubbed his chest. "Did someone sleep on me?"

Maeve smiled. "Yes, Pop."

"Huh, well, that explains that dream. So, what's new?" Greg asked.

"Not much. Come on in." Tilda waved them inside.

Maeve and Greg followed her in. The house was a wide-open ranch that looked like it hadn't been updated since the 1970s. Even the kitchen looked original.

"Stylish," Greg murmured. "Well, I'm going to check out the plumbing." He headed down the hall.

Maeve caught sight of Penny sitting at the dining-room table. "Hi, Penny."

Penny said nothing. She just continued typing away on her screen.

Her arms full of blankets and sheets, Tilda bustled in. "Just got these out of the dryer. I'm going to drop them in the bedrooms down the hall."

"Great. Thanks."

Maeve turned back to Penny, glancing at the screen. It was a satellite image. "What are you working on?"

"Checking the security measures I established. They're working." She shifted screens and rows of computer code appeared.

Her mind still on Chris's comment, Maeve nodded. "Hey, Penny. Back when Alvie was taken, Adam said the security protocols failed. That somehow they had gone down. Do you know what happened?"

Penny didn't look up as Tilda slipped back into the dining room. "The protocols didn't fail."

Maeve frowned. "But they found us. And we had no warning."

Her fingers flying over the keyboard, Penny stayed silent.

Maeve looked from Tilda to Penny and it all clicked into place. The security not working. The perimeter alarms being down. Their eye in the sky failing to catch the government forces sneaking up on them.

"Penny," Maeve said slowly, "you didn't let them find us, did you?"

Penny looked at Maeve without expression. "Of course I did."

CHAPTER 72

Maeve stumbled back and Tilda gasped next to her. The sheer magnitude of what this young girl had done robbed Maeve of her voice for a moment before the memory of Alvie falling to the ground brought her voice back with a vengeance. "Why? Why would you do that? They *took* him. You sent them after us and they *took* him."

Penny tilted her head as if she didn't understand Maeve's confusion. "It was the only way."

Staring at the young girl, Maeve was barely holding on to her anger. "The only way? The only way for what?"

"To save my friend," Penny said calmly. "He's been there for years."

"How exactly did you meet him?" Tilda asked.

"Through the cameras. People don't understand him. They don't understand me." Penny returned her attention to the computer.

Maeve stepped forward, but Tilda grabbed her arm, shaking her head. She nodded toward the doorway. With a glare at Penny, Maeve followed Tilda out, her whole body shaking. Penny had intentionally let Alvie be taken. Tilda led Maeve through the dated kitchen and out the back door.

Shock was splashed across Tilda's face, but Maeve had to ask. "Did you know?"

Tilda shook her head. "No. I wondered why Guardian hadn't warned us Drummond's people were near, but I never imagined she'd somehow befriended one of them through the cameras. I never imagined she would risk all our lives to …"

A chill crawled over Maeve's skin and wrapped her arms around herself. *My God, the power Penny has is incredible.* She'd moved all of them like human chess pieces to get them here. And she displayed no understanding of how horrific those acts were.

"I didn't know, Maeve. I would not have allowed Alvie to be taken. Yes, I want this lab shut down. Yes, I want Agaren free. But not this way," Tilda said.

And despite the doubts she had about the woman's motives, Maeve believed her. "But why let Alvie be taken? I mean, we don't have to be here. You would have come for the Gray no matter what once you learned where he was."

Pausing, Tilda stared past her as she answered with a frown. "But we might not have been successful. Penny brought not only you but the triplets into this. Fighting for them, keeping them safe, reuniting Alvie with them, that is motivating. And not just for us."

"What do you mean?"

"The Gray has been in captivity for decades. He's never tried to leave. But Alvie will tap into his protective instincts. Somehow Penny knew that. She knew Alvie being taken would tap into all of our protective instincts."

Although she saw the logic, it did not tamp down her anger. "So now what do we do?"

Tilda looked toward the mountain. "We figure a way to shut the mountain down and get Alvie out."

D.E.A.D.

Maeve glanced back at the house. Penny was their ace in the hole for this mission. But what would happen if things went wrong? Which one of them would she sacrifice next?

CHAPTER 73

Tilda had said she had people coming in for the infiltration, which was going to happen tonight. Not that they had a plan, but Tilda said they'd have one along with enough resources by the afternoon.

Maeve was trusting her basically because she didn't see another option. And besides, Penny's actions had drained her of any ability to rationally determine who was trustworthy and who was not.

Now Maeve sat outside the house on a log, staring up at the sky. Chris and Adam were off in the woods helping the triplets release some energy. Greg was taking a nap. And Maeve just needed a minute to deal with Penny's revelation. She was having trouble wrapping her head around the idea that a twelve-year-old girl had done all of this. She'd placed all of them in incredible jeopardy. And Alvie, good God, what were they doing to him?

She put a hand to her mouth and swallowed down her fear. She couldn't give in to it, not now. Alvie needed her. And if she started to let her imagination get away with her, she'd be no good to anyone.

D.E.A.D.

"Dr. Leander?"

Maeve turned as Nadine walked toward her, her steps uncertain. "Hey, Nadine. How are you feeling?"

"A little spacey, to be honest." She gestured to the log next to Maeve. "May I?"

It was on the tip of her tongue to say no. Maeve really wanted to be alone. But Nadine looked lost and she could empathize with that feeling. "Sure."

Nadine sat down, and neither of them said anything. But the tension grew until Maeve let out a breath and moved to get up. "I'm going to—"

"I know what Penny did," Nadine said quickly.

Maeve sat back down again. "Which part?"

"Your friend, Alvie. I know she arranged for him to be taken."

Maeve sucked in a breath.

Nadine continued. "I don't really know what to make of all this. The triplets, they're cute and they seem sweet, but at the same time it just all seems so …"

"Unreal," Maeve finished for her.

"Yeah," Nadine flicked a glance at her. "Do you feel that way, too?"

Maeve shrugged. "I grew up with Alvie. My mom raised us together. He's always just been mine. I never really questioned his existence in my life any more than someone would question the existence of a brother or a sister, you know?"

Nadine nodded.

"But when I learned of all the others, even with my exposure to Alvie, it was shocking," Maeve said. She struggled to find the right way to describe her feelings back then. "It was . . ."

"Unreal," Nadine finished for Maeve this time.

"Yeah," Maeve said with a sigh.

"Is Alvie like the triplets?" Nadine asked.

Maeve hesitated, not quite sure how to answer that. She didn't think Nadine would be up for a lecture on cloning. She seemed to be struggling with what she knew right now. So all she said was, "Yes. They're a lot alike."

"I'm sorry for what Penny did. I'd say she's sorry, but I don't think she is." Nadine sighed. "I love my daughter, but her way of thinking is very foreign to me sometimes."

"She's autistic?"

Surprise flashed across Nadine's face. "Most people don't recognize that. They tend to think autism is more of a boy issue."

Despite the fact that one in sixty-eight children was diagnosed with autism, Maeve knew that autism was woefully underdiagnosed in girls. Most of the characteristics of autism used in diagnoses were created through studies of boys. Girls, however, presented much differently than boys. In fact, brain scans of girls with autism do not appear similar to boys with autism or girls without autism. Instead, they appeared like that of non-autistic boys in the areas of socialization. As a result, intelligent females with autism often imitate social behaviors that they don't feel to blend in, making their diagnosis difficult. Autistic girls with lower IQs were more likely to be diagnosed earlier than girls with higher IQs.

"She's high functioning. It took years to get a diagnosis. Females often present different from males, which I didn't know. I just knew there was something different about her than kids her own age. Girls with it are actually more social, but they still have the obsessive traits, the difficulty reading social cues, and the hand flapping. My husband, he couldn't handle that Penny was different. He would get mad when she said things in public that embarrassed him. He left when she was six."

"I'm sorry," Maeve said.

Nadine shrugged. "Some men are just not meant to be fathers, especially not to a special-needs kid."

Immediately, Maeve thought of Chris, who'd embraced his role as the father in their unusual little family. She knew how easily he could have cut and run. But he hadn't. He stayed. "How'd Penny end up working with the NSA?"

Nadine smiled, but there was a wistful quality to it. "She started reading before she was two. I had a hunch and brought home math cards one day and she would point to the correct answers. Jerrold and I thought we had this genius on our hands. And we did.

"But then just after her second birthday, her behaviors changed. She would have these fits, and there was nothing we could do to calm her down. And she'd repeat these behaviors over and over again. It was the hand flapping that made Jerrold crazy. One day, he hit her, he was so mad. And that was the day I kicked him out. She hasn't seen him since. He doesn't even call on birthdays or holidays. It's like he just wrote her off."

It was impossible to not to feel for the woman. Maeve couldn't imagine how devastating that must have been.

Nadine continued. "I bought her her first computer when she was seven. She took to it like a duck to water. We had her in a private school at that point, but it wasn't really working. She was struggling too much. A lot of the kids were intellectually challenged while Penny was the opposite. She needed more challenge intellectually but less socially. Nowhere seemed the right fit. I knew she was having a tough time. But then one day I came home and she was staring at the wall. She wouldn't move, she wouldn't respond. She just stared. She wet herself. I was so scared." Nadine's bottom lip trembled.

She took a breath to compose herself before continuing. "I took her to the hospital and she was admitted. She spent a week there and they filled her with different drugs, trying to get the right combo. But it only seemed to make it worse."

Nadine looked away. "I was up for partner in my law firm at the time. I had been so focused on achieving that goal that I hadn't noticed she was slipping away. I knew what she needed and I knew the hospital, the schools, they couldn't give it to her. So I quit and I started homeschooling her. It worked. She came back. Math, science, I couldn't keep up with her. I ended up taking her to the community college so she could take classes. And one semester, I signed her up for a management information systems course. By the end of the semester, government agencies were lining up on our doorstep trying to get her to work for them."

"I didn't want to let her at first. She was just a kid. But computers, they gave her a joy that nothing else did. Something about all that information and being able to control it, understand it—I think it gives her a purpose. She struggles in so many ways, but never there."

"So I asked her what she wanted to do. And she told me she wanted to work for the NSA. She was ten. So every morning I drive her to the NSA building at Buckley. I started working for them as well. Nothing too serious. I review employee contracts and some other legal agreements. But I get to be in the same building as her in case there's a problem and I actually get to use my law degree."

"Did you know she was contacting people outside the agency?" Maeve asked.

"No, but then again, I never knew what she worked on. She has a higher clearance than me. I thought, at worst, she was intercepting emails or something. But tracking down aliens? No, that never crossed my mind."

Maeve knew Nadine had had it rough but still … "Why do you think she did this?"

She gave Maeve a sad smile. "That's actually why I came

out here to speak with you. I don't always understand her motivations, but this one ... I think I do. This Gray—he's important to her. I know it seems crazy. She's never met with him, never spoken with him, but somehow she's connected with him. And that's not something she's been able to do with many people."

"Because of the autism," Maeve said.

"Yes and no. Friends are something Penny has never been able to make. It's not just the autism that makes it difficult, it's how smart she is. She just can't fit in with kids her age. She's never going to giggle over boys or wander the mall with friends to find the perfect outfit. She doesn't understand why girls would do that. But she wants to want to do that."

"And she thinks of the Gray as a friend," Maeve said.

"Yeah," Nadine said.

Maeve still smarted at what Penny had done to Alvie, but she could feel Nadine's anguish for her daughter. She gave her a small smile. "On the bright side, I think we can all agree that Penny takes loyalty to friends to a whole new level."

Shaking her head, Nadine returned the smile. "Yeah, it's a weird sort of good sign. But I know that Penny has put us all in the crosshairs. And I'm guessing whatever you all have planned next will be dangerous."

"It will be," Maeve said.

Nadine's eyes were serious. "Tilda said there are some people that can help if things don't turn out the way we hope."

"Yeah, she mentioned that."

"I promise you, I will get the triplets there and make sure they're safe. After all this, it's the least I can do."

"Thank you," Maeve said.

Nadine nodded, standing up. "Okay. I'm going to go see if I can get Penny to eat and maybe the triplets. Do they eat normal food?"

"They really like mac and cheese."

"Penny, too. Well, I'll make a lot." She headed back for the house.

But Penny was already heading out the door, Tilda right behind her. "She's almost here," Penny said.

Frowning, Maeve stood, wiping off her pants. "Who?"

Tilda grinned. "An ally, apparently."

CHAPTER 74

DULCE, NEW MEXICO

It was almost midday when Norah and Iggy crossed into Dulce, New Mexico. Although Guardian hadn't told them where they were heading, she'd figured it out a few hours ago. It was the only place that made sense. After all, if you're in New Mexico and wondering about aliens, Dulce was pretty much the only option right after Roswell. But she couldn't figure out why Leander would be here.

The Tesla pulled off the highway and onto a small side road. Soon they were heading away from any sort of civilization, and wide-open spaces greeted them. Norah took out the Glock and checked the magazine again, even though she'd checked it half a dozen times so far.

The Tesla slowed down and turned onto a dirt road. The car bucked a little at the uneven surface and Iggy, who was perched on the back of Norah's chair, gave a little cry. She reached up and patted his arm. "It's okay," she said, hoping she wasn't lying.

They drove along for another five minutes, Norah only getting more tense. Then Iggy let out a growl as the Tesla came to a stop. A thick copse of trees surrounded them, but there was no sign of life.

The hairs on the back of Norah's neck stood straight up. Somebody was watching them.

Get out.

The words appeared on the dashboard display.

The doors unlocked. Norah silently cursed herself up one side and down the other. What the hell had she been thinking, blindly following a voice on a car? She was in the middle of nowhere. A perfect place to ambush her and Iggy without anyone catching sight.

"God damn it," she muttered. She looked up at Iggy. "You stay behind me, okay?"

Iggy just looked at her. She sighed, wishing she knew whether or not he understood her. Taking a breath, she cracked the door open. It sounded like a gunshot in the quiet woods.

She'd just stepped out of the car when a voice yelled out. "Gun!"

"Shit!" Norah dove for the ground, slamming the door shut to prevent Iggy from escaping as she hightailed it around the front of the car. "Guardian!" she yelled. "Guardian sent me."

No gunfire answered her. A male voice called out. "Who are you?"

"Norah Tidwell, formerly with D.E.A.D."

"Formerly?" he asked.

"Well, they tried to kill me the last two times I saw them, so yeah, formerly." She took a breath. "I'm looking for Dr. Maeve Leander."

The voice took on a harsher tone. "Why?"

Norah sighed. "Because she once told me that not all aliens were evil. And I need her help protecting one."

She could hear arguing not far from her, though she couldn't make out the words. Then a female voice called out. "Agent Tidwell?"

Norah looked toward the spot where the voice had come from but couldn't see anything. "Leander?"

"My friends here won't let you come any closer until you throw down your weapon."

Norah hesitated, but she was outgunned. And she recognized Leander's voice. "Okay. I'm throwing it out." She tossed the gun toward the light.

"Come out with your hands up."

Oh, this might have been a really big mistake. Norah closed her eyes with a groan. As Norah stood, movement to her left drew her attention.

A small figure darted from the shadows and stood in front of Norah. She backed up, hitting her lower back against the car, her eyes wide. It was an alien. It looked like some sort of Gray but not like any of the ones she'd seen. It looked a little more human somehow. She sensed no threat from the creature. It reached up and took her hand.

Two more appeared behind it. Norah's eyes grew wider. "Um, Leander?"

"Agent Tidwell, I'd like you to meet Snap, Crackle, and Pop. And somehow you seem to have earned their approval." Maeve Leander stepped out from behind a tree.

Norah felt the tension leave her shoulders, knowing the danger had passed. "I could really use your help."

"We're not really in a position to help anyone right now." A man she recognized as Chris Garrigan stepped out from the other side of the car. She hadn't heard him approach.

The triplets stepped away from Norah and moved quickly

to the car door, bouncing up, trying to see inside. A mewling sound came from inside the car followed by an excited cry. "Ig! Ig! Ig!"

Maeve frowned. "What's that?"

"That's Iggy," Norah said, meeting Leander's curious gaze. "And he's the reason I'm here."

CHAPTER 75

Maeve was having a tough time believing that Agent Tidwell was sitting across from her right now. Norah had looked equally shocked when Greg appeared, hale and hearty. But that was nothing compared to the shock on all of their faces when they met Iggy.

Norah explained how she'd come across Iggy and what she'd done to keep him safe. And Maeve was impressed. The woman had guts and conviction. Right now, Iggy was jumping around with the triplets and Hope. But every few minutes he would run back to Norah and sit in her lap for a few seconds, as if to assure himself that she was still there. And he was awfully cute with those big eyes and big belly. He would let out this little purr each time he snuggled into Norah's lap. For being together for such a short time, he'd most definitely bonded to her.

And yet again it was Guardian who had brought her to them.

What were you thinking, Penny? Maeve would like to just ask her what her overall plan was, but she didn't think that would get her the answers she wanted. From studying her actions, it seemed Penny's goal was protecting aliens, in spite of what she'd done to Alvie.

But even that, looking at it from Penny's perspective, she could see. Penny thought that having Alvie get pinched was the best chance for the rest of them to save the Gray. It was just the emotional cost of that action that the young genius did not understand.

And the emotions of the bond between Iggy and Norah was probably beyond Penny's understanding as well.

Iggy tottered off after the triplets again, this time into the living room. Greg watched him go with a giant smile on his face. "You have your own personal gnome. Do you realize how cool that is?"

"Iggy's a pretty special little guy," Norah said with a smile but then her smiled dimmed. "But that hasn't stopped my old agency from trying to kill him ... and me."

"If it makes you feel any better, the government's trying to kill us, too," Greg said.

Norah's voice was Sahara dry when she spoke. "Believe it or not, that doesn't make me feel better."

"Yeah, it probably wouldn't make me feel better, either," Greg muttered.

Maeve took pity on Greg before he could shove his foot any further into his mouth. "I didn't see anyone that looked like him in the files."

"He's not in the official files. I checked," Norah said.

Tilda watched the little guy with a look of awe. "He's one of the purebreeds. He's a Maldek. They're one of the less intelligent species. They were home guardians, similar to dogs. Affectionate, but passionately protective when bonded."

"He attacked three of the special-ops guys who came after me. He could have left me and run. But he came back for me." There was wonder in Norah's voice.

"I think he chose well," Maeve said.

Meeting Maeve's gaze for a moment, Maeve could see the confusion in the former agents eyes. "Guardian led me here, and I'm having a hard time believing you just happened to be in Dulce, New Mexico, given all the rumors about this place."

"It's not a coincidence," Greg said.

"There's someone here we need to get," Chris said.

"Who?" Norah asked.

Maeve explained about Alvie and Agaren.

Norah's jaw dropped open. "You're going to break into a mountain facility? With three aliens, two special-ops guys, two scientists, a tiny baby hacker"—she turned to Tilda—"and no offense, but a little old lady? Are you all nuts?"

Tilda grumped. "I'm more than a little old lady."

Wincing, Norah dipped her chin in acknowledgement. "Like I said, no offense, but short of a small army, how the hell's that going to work?"

"Well, you forgot one important key element," Maeve said.

"Oh? What's that?" She asked.

Greg grinned. "One former D.E.A.D. agent."

Norah crossed her arms over her chest. "Oh, well, silly me. Now it will be easy."

"Well, that's not everybody we're bringing," Tilda said, just as Maeve heard the crunch of tires on gravel.

"Who's this?" Chris asked.

"Reinforcements." Tilda stood and headed for the cars.

Norah watched the approaching cars through narrowed eyes. "I think I'll go hang with the aliens, just in case."

"Yeah, I'll help," Greg said.

Chris leaned down to Maeve, slipping keys into her hand and nodding toward the triplets. "Things go badly, you get our gang out of here."

"Including Greg?" She asked.

"Only if you have to," he deadpanned.

But despite his attempt to lighten the situation, she could

sense his concern. Maeve stared after Tilda, who stood calmly waiting to greet the five SUVs. She knew Tilda was used to keeping secrets, but she really needed to learn which info to keep to herself and which to share with the other members of her team.

The SUVs pulled in and six people got out of each. The people headed straight for the back of the vans and began unpacking crates. One shook hands with Tilda and followed her back over to the fire. The African-American man was in his late forties or early fifties, with hair that was graying at the temples and a pear-shaped body. Chris swore quietly next to her.

Before Maeve could ask, Tilda stopped in front of them. "Dr. Leander, I'd like you to meet Jasper Jenkins, one of my people."

Jasper smiled at Maeve and extended his hand. "It's a true pleasure to meet you, Dr. Leander. What you've done with Alvie is nothing short of a miracle. And getting Alvie and the triplets out of 51, I don't know if anyone could have done any better."

"Uh, thanks?" Maeve accepted his handshake.

Jasper grinned at Chris. "Good to see you again, Chris."

"You know him?" Maeve asked.

"Apparently not," Chris said, even as he extended his hand. "The Jasper I met could barely figure out which end of a gun to fire with."

Jasper winced. "Yeah, sorry about that. When Tilda sent me to keep an eye on you, we thought it was best if I appeared non-threatening, just a bumbling military bureaucrat."

Maeve looked between the two of them. Chris's recertification had occurred on a military base. There were dozens going through the process. Tilda had somehow arranged for Jasper to be one of them, which meant the woman had resources and lots of reach. Maeve glared at Tilda. "*Who* exactly are you?"

"I will be happy to explain that all to you once we get this place shut down," Tilda said.

Maeve crossed her arms over her chest. "But why are you so interested in it? This goes beyond Guardian pushing you to — Actually, why would she contact you at all? I mean, myself, Chris, Norah, even Greg have direct contact to critical individuals in this fight. Who do you have?"

Tilda's eyes went cold for just a moment before they cleared. It happened so quickly Maeve wasn't even sure she'd seen it. "I have a dog in this fight, too. And I have been part of this fight decades longer than you. You want to question my fealty, go ahead. But I don't need you for this, Dr. Leander. You need me." Tilda spun on her heel and headed for the SUVs.

Blowing out a breath, Jasper ran a hand through his hair. "Look, you guys have been thrown in the deep end here. I get that. But Tilda, she has been in this fight forever. She's one of the good guys. And honestly, isn't anyone better than Martin Drummond?"

Maeve had to admit that was true.

"Look, let's get them out. Then we can all sit down, cards on the table, okay?" Jasper asked.

Maeve looked at Chris, who nodded back at her. "It's not like we have another army we can call up to help out," he said.

Jasper grinned. "It's grudging, but I'll take it."

And Maeve couldn't help it. She smiled.

"Look, all joking aside, this is a big moment for all of us. We've been trying to pin down Martin and his project for years. All of us take this seriously. And we know it's personal for you both. We won't let you down. Now, I'm going to organize my guys. Team meeting in five?" Jasper asked.

Chris nodded before Jasper headed for the SUVs. Chris reached over and took Maeve's hand. "What do you think?"

"I think he's right and you're right. We don't have a choice.

But I would feel better if we knew what exactly Tilda's role in all of this was."

"After. Right now, it doesn't matter. All that matters is getting Alvie back," Chris said.

Maeve leaned into Chris. "But then what, Chris? How are we going to keep them all safe?"

Chris didn't say anything, and Maeve hadn't expected him to. She sighed. *Right. One major problem at a time.*

CHAPTER 76

The people who accompanied Jasper had brought a small arsenal with them. While Maeve knew the odds were low of them all escaping unharmed, the addition of eighteen heavily armed commandos to the group did make her feel better.

Tilda approached Maeve and Chris. "I just want to apologize to you two. For me, keeping secrets has been a way of life for more decades than I'd like to admit. Believe it or not, I am just as personally attached to this situation as you are. I can't tell you more than that. But I do promise that I know, in some ways more than you, how important Alvie's survival is."

More than us? Maeve opened her mouth to question Tilda about her odd statement, but Chris cut her off. "Bileris?"

Maeve's gaze shot to the man walking toward them—his face was one she recognized. "Agent Bileris?"

The Secret Service agent smiled. "Maeve, I keep telling you to call me Mike."

Maeve stared at him, struggling to figure out how the hell he was standing here. "Whose side are you on?"

"I'm on the side of doing the right thing," he said.

Tilda nodded at him. "I put Mike in place years ago to be our eyes and ears inside the executive branch. When you fell into the lap of the executive branch, it was fortuitous."

Chris's voice was incredulous. "Fortuitous? That's the best you can do? Who the hell are you, lady? You put a guy in the White House and another in the middle of a military complex. That takes power and connections. So I repeat, who exactly are you?"

"You two know some of the government's secrets about at involvement with E.T.s. I assure you, what you know is not even the tip of the iceberg. And this is one very large iceberg. But time is of the essence now." Tilda looked at Maeve, her gaze full of compassion. "Martin's not known for his slow-moving approach or his empathy. Forgive me for being blunt, but Alvie will not be being treated kindly. The sooner we can get him out, the better. Or we can wait until we have had a long, drawn-out conversation about the other space program. It's your choice."

Maeve knew she was being manipulated, but Tilda's words conjured up images that stole Maeve's breath.

Chris grasped her hand, nodding at Tilda. "Alvie's the priority. But as soon as he's safe, we talk."

"Agreed. Now let's discuss how we're getting him out. Penny has an idea." Tilda headed toward the front porch where everyone had gathered.

Bileris winced and gave them a helpless shrug before following her. Her men parted as she made her way to the front of the group. It was obvious her people respected and trusted her.

But can I? Maeve thought.

"You okay?" Chris asked.

"No," she said, pulling her gaze from Tilda to look at Chris. "But I will be once we get Alvie back."

"Then let's go get him back." Taking her hand, he led her toward the group.

As Maeve walked with him, her mind chose to focus on a phrase that Tilda may have accidentally used, although the more Maeve thought about it, the more she thought its use was intentional. Tilda was warning them or maybe giving them a preview of the revelations to come.

The ones about the U.S.'s *other* space program.

CHAPTER 77

Tilda stood on the porch of the farmhouse speaking with Jasper and Nadine. Tilda's people stood speaking quietly with one another, a few feet away. The group was impressive looking. Each of the people Tilda had brought looked similar—not in coloring or height, but all had roped muscle arms, sharp cheekbones that suggested carbs were not a big part of their diet, and an almost coldness to their gaze. Which, being they were on Maeve's side, gave her a sense of comfort.

They spoke to the extent of Tilda's resources and the possibility that the United States had a second space program. There'd been rumors of the possibility for decades. So was that what all of this was? Evidence of that program?

Nadine slipped back into the house and now only one person stood out amongst the group of focused individuals. Greg, who sat on the ground in the front row in a bright yellow shirt, drawing something in the dirt. Chris headed for him and as they approached, she could make out what he'd drawn. It was E.T. using a phone to call home. Catching Maeve's gaze, he quickly wiped it away with a sheepish shrug as he got to his feet.

Maeve stepped next to him and whispered, "I liked it."

He smiled at her.

Maeve checked that the triplets were far enough away that they wouldn't overhear anything. They were playing near the barn with Iggy and Hope. Norah was with them and she continually scanned the area. And she wasn't their only sentinel. Adam was there keeping watch as well. Maeve felt better seeing him there. She wasn't sure why she trusted him, but she did.

"Okay, now that we're all here, let's get started," Tilda said, and all talking stopped. Tilda explained that Penny had somehow managed to dig up the blueprints for the facility. Maeve wasn't sure how, but Penny said they were accurate. Maeve believed her. And while the blueprints were a good start, they only seemed to emphasize the impossibility of the task ahead of them.

The entrance was through a cave at the base of the mountain that was of course, well-guarded. The facility itself then consisted of eight levels built underground. Level One housed security and communications. Two, housing; Three, labs; Four, mind-control experiments; Five, alien housing; Six, genetic experiments; Seven, cryogenic storage, and Eight, an underground rail system. Level Six was the most likely location for Agaren and Alvie.

But it was Level Seven that made Maeve swallow hard. The words immediately conjured up an image of Alvie frozen in death in a silver coffin.

"Where did she find the plans?" Greg asked.

Tilda shrugged. "Not sure. But there are some online sources that argue for the same layout. We should be open to the possibility, however, that changes have been made and be ready to adapt. Now, our people will take care of the security forces at the gate and Level One while Leander and Garrigan, along with a small detail, head to the lower levels. Other details will secure each floor. Jasper will explain that part of the mission."

Standing, Jasper explained the facility's security in detail. With each layer of security discussed, Maeve felt her hopes dwindling. The place was a fortress.

Apparently Greg had the same thoughts. He raised his hand.

Jasper smiled. "Yes, I believe the overanxious Ph.D. in the front row has a question."

"I am not overanxious," Greg muttered, only loud enough for Maeve to hear. To the group, he said, "So how exactly are we going to do this? Not to doubt the Rambo-like skills of everybody here, but storming this particular mountain and fighting through what's no doubt dozens of security personnel seems a tad bit suicidal."

Tilda smiled. "It is. Which is why we are not going to do that."

"Okay," Greg said. "So what are we doing?"

"We are going to get all of them to leave," Jasper said.

Silence greeted his response.

"And how exactly are we going to do that?" Mike asked, and Maeve felt better that it wasn't just her and her people feeling confused.

"Jasper?" Tilda asked.

He nodded. "Dulce is like any other government facility—they have codes for everything. Codes for lockdown, codes for a breach. You name the problem, they have a code for it. Penny was able to get into their security system and she will set off Code 478."

Jasper paused.

"Which is?" Chris asked.

"Glad you asked," Jasper said. "It's a biological release. As soon as people hear that code, they will be running for the exits. Protocol requires them to be at least two miles from the facility. So we simply hide outside, wait until everyone zips by us, and then head in."

"They'll all go?" Greg asked.

"No. But there will be only a few security guards left behind. We can handle them. And Penny is also going to disable the phones and cameras so they can't see us or warn one another," Jasper explained.

"Huh, that's actually pretty good," Greg said, his surprise evident.

Tilting his head, Jasper smiled. "Thanks,"

Chris frowned. "Wait. How long will that buy us?"

"About twenty minutes," Jasper said.

"I take it back. That's not good at all," Greg muttered.

"It *is* a small window," Jasper conceded. "But if we move quickly, we should be all right."

"But," Tilda cut in, her voice serious, "no one should underestimate this threat. Drummond's not someone who will go down easy. He undeniably has backup security in place. It could be technological or even biological."

"The alien attacks," Greg whispered.

Tilda responded as if he was talking to the group. "Yes. Martin has always been interested in defensive weapons. He has made no secret of the fact that he wants to create soldiers that can fight for us in the event of an alien attack. Dr. Schorn knows this better than anyone here. We should be prepared that he has something along those lines in the mountain."

"Always wanted to fight me some aliens," someone behind Maeve said, and a few others laughed.

"If Penny can shut down the cameras, can't we also take a sneak peek at what he's got in there?" Chris asked.

Jasper shook his head. "Only to a limited extent. She's apparently made forays in before but kept them to thirty seconds to not be noticed. Any longer than that and she'll be noticed. So if we sneak a look first, we'll tip them off. But she can let us know if she sees anything when we're inside. And she will be able to verify the location of our targets once we breach."

"I guess that's better than nothing," Maeve said.

"Not by much," Greg muttered.

This time, Tilda pretended she hadn't heard him. "We watch each other's backs. We get our targets out. If all goes well, we'll be in and out in twenty minutes. Now, we're heading out in one hour. Penny will take down the system as soon as we're in place, so everyone, make sure you are ready to go. The first group leaves in fifteen."

If all goes well ... Tilda's words echoed through Maeve's mind, along with a sense of foreboding. When had anything gone well before?

Greg let out a breath. "Well, I think I'm going to go throw up, and then I'll be ready to storm the mountain."

Maeve laughed. "Good. I'll probably do the same."

He gave her shoulder a squeeze and walked away. Maeve watched him throw a stick for Hope on the way to the barn. He was a good guy. And Maeve would do a lot to protect him. Just like Penny would do a lot to protect Agaren. And Maeve knew she owed the Gray.

She looked toward where the mountain stood, seeing no hint of the insanity underneath it. And Alvie was locked up in the middle of it with that bastard Martin.

Hold on, Alvie. I'm coming.

CHAPTER 78

Norah took the Heckler and Koch MP5 apart and then put it back together in the kitchen of the farmhouse. The familiarity of the routine calmed her. She'd used an MP5 in Afghanistan. This one was a little heavier, but still familiar. Nervousness trickled through Norah and she shoved it aside, knowing being a little nervous was good. It kept you aware. A lack of nervousness led to complacency, which meant death.

A group of twelve had already left to secure their hiding spots outside the base. They'd make sure the spot was safe before the rest followed them. Penny was going to offer them camera coverage to get into position. The rest were getting the gear together and loading the trucks. Norah figured she had maybe ten minutes.

Chris stopped next to her, watching as she slid the fifteen-round magazine into place. "So who'd you serve with?"

"Marines, two tours," she said.

"You sure you're up for this? You will be going against American citizens."

She shrugged. "Yeah, well, they are part of another group of American citizens that tried to kill me. So yeah, I'm good."

"Seriously, Norah, you don't have to be part of this fight."

Sighing, she placed the MP5 on the table and wiped her hands. "Yeah, I do. This guy Drummond, he's not representative of the America I signed up to protect. And Iggy, the triplets—they don't deserve to be killed or locked up in cages."

Nodding to the car, Chris said, "You could stay with the van, make sure—"

Norah cut him off. "I've killed twelve aliens, hybrids, or whatever they were. I was told they were dangerous. I never doubted that. After all, it was my government that sent me out after them. And then I met Iggy. I was told he was dangerous, too. But he's not, at least if you're not trying to hurt me. How many of the ones I killed were only as dangerous as Iggy?"

"I get that. But from experience, I can tell you that they're not all like Iggy."

"Maybe," Norah said picturing some of the dicier cases she'd been involved in. "But I should have made sure, and I have to live with that. So maybe helping you guys free Alvie and this Agaren guy, maybe it will make it a little easier to look myself in the mirror."

Chris watched her for a moment before nodding. "Okay, you and Greg will stay on the first floor. Get Greg to the communications room. Do not go further."

"Got it." Then she lowered her voice making sure there was no one around before she spoke. "But why are we bringing the professor along?"

Chris grinned. "We need some computer work and it's either him or a twelve-year-old. So Schorn it is."

She glanced over to where Greg sat on the couch, nervously drinking a Gatorade. "Does he have any training?"

"The best MIT could offer," Chris said dryly.

"Yeah," Norah said drawing out the word. "You sure we wouldn't be better off with the twelve-year-old?"

Flicking a glance at the scientist, she watched as the man wiped at a spot where he'd just spilled the Gatorade he'd been drinking.

Chris nodded at him. "Greg will surprise you. He will be scared out of his mind and will probably either wet his pants or throw up, probably both, but he will still get it done. You can count on him."

Norah wasn't so sure about that. But she sighed. "Okay."

Although she knew Chris could tell she wasn't convinced he merely nodded. "Ten minutes," he said before heading toward the house.

"Got it," Norah replied, nervous energy cutting through her.

Iggy wandered into the living room behind the triplets, looking around anxiously. Then he caught sight of Norah and made a beeline toward her.

She grinned as he used the table leg to fling himself on the table. "You are some amazing little gymnast."

He pointed at the gun in the holster at Norah's waist.

"Yeah. I need to talk to you about that. Come on." She held out her arms and he leapt into them. She headed back outside, wanting a little more privacy than the farmhouse could offer for this conversation.

He leaned his head on Norah's shoulder with a sigh as she walked outside with him. She knew he liked playing with the triplets and Hope, but it was obvious he still liked her best. And Norah admitted she liked that. But it was also going to make this next conversation a little more difficult.

As Norah rubbed Iggy's back, he gave off a soft purr. She smiled at the sound. He almost sounded like a cat. She took a seat on the log over by the fire pit, ignoring the bustle of people by the rocks and the engines idling in the background.

Instead she sat there with Iggy snuggled up in her lap for a few moments, just letting herself enjoy the moment.

She looked up as the rest of Tilda's people started heading for the SUVs. She watched them for a moment. A secret space program. She'd like to have been surprised, but after everything she'd seen these last few months, surprise was not really in her bag of tricks. But she did worry about what this secret space program's end goals were.

And what they meant for Iggy.

She could tell Maeve had the same fears for Alvie and the triplets. But for both of them, there were simply no other options. They were going to have to trust Tilda and her people.

Maeve stepped off the porch. Chris followed her with the triplets all balanced along his shoulders. Hope trotted along after them. *They're a family*, Norah realized as Chris held Maeve's hand and they headed toward the van.

The group looked good together, natural. Greg stepped out behind them and looked around before his gaze fell on Norah. She nodded to indicate she'd be right there.

Adam appeared from the woods and walked over to Tilda. They conferred for a moment, Adam squeezing her arm gently before heading to the driver's seat of the nearest SUV. Norah frowned. He was the one part of this whole equation she didn't understand. He kept himself apart from everyone except Tilda. It was obvious they were close. But Norah had a feeling that relationship was not what everyone assumed.

Norah watched them all head for the SUV. She was officially out of time. She leaned back a little and Iggy looked up at her. "Ig?"

She forced a smile to her face and an upbeat tone into her voice. "Hey. So I'm going to have to go away for a little bit to help out a friend. I'm going to need you to stay with Nadine and the triplets."

Iggy frowned up at her. "Ig?"

"Keep an eye on the triplets and Penny. Keep them safe, okay?"

"Ig?"

Norah sighed. This was stupid. He didn't understand what she was saying. She hugged him tight. "Be good, okay?"

He snuggled into her. "Ig."

Norah let out a breath, her chest feeling tight. "Yup. Ig."

CHAPTER 79

Saying goodbye to the triplets nearly killed Maeve. Chris had suggested she stay behind. But it was Alvie. How could she not go? Besides, if there was any sort of medical situation with either Alvie or Agaren, Maeve was the person best equipped to handle it.

But leaving the triplets, that was not something Maeve took lightly. Tilda had assured Maeve that the triplets would be protected if something happened to her and Chris, that she had people in place to whisk them away.

But that, if anything, scared Maeve even more. She was essentially handing her children over to strangers. She'd given Nadine a letter to give to John Forrester. He was still the commander of Wright-Pat, although she knew he'd been offered a position in Washington D.C. She knew John would look out for them. She hated dragging him into this, but if the worst happened, she needed to know they would be all right.

Now she stood outside the van Tilda had arranged. The back was chock-full of computer equipment, most of which Maeve did not recognize. But Penny had practically squealed when she'd

D.E.A.D.

seen it. She was inside now, making sure everything was ready. One of Tilda's men would stay with the van and keep everyone far from the action and get them out of there if necessary.

Maeve knelt down and the triplets swamped her, pressing into her. Maeve bit her lip, trying to keep back her tears. But even without the physical proof, the triplets knew how she was feeling. Snap looked up into Maeve's face and placed her small hand on Maeve's cheek. A feeling of love wafted over her. Maeve smiled, even though she wanted to cry. "I love you, too." She looked at Crackle and Pop. "All of you. Now take care of one another. And listen to Nadine, okay?"

They all nodded back at her. Nadine stepped up. "Okay, guys, let's get in the van."

The triplets looked at Maeve, and she knew they didn't want to go. She kissed each of them on the forehead. "It will be okay. Go on now."

One by one they leaned up to her, pressing their forehead against hers. And Maeve struggled even harder to keep the tears back. She stood wiping at her eyes as Crackle disappeared into the back of the van. Norah walked over and placed Iggy inside before hurrying away, a shine in her eyes.

Guess I'm not the only one.

Nadine closed the doors and then walked over to Maeve. "I'll take care of them."

Reading the promise in the woman's eyes, Maeve nodded. "I know. Thank you."

Nadine headed to the passenger seat. The van started up and then pulled down the drive, filled with one special-ops soldier, one alien, three alien-human hybrids, one child genius, and one lawyer mom.

Greg walked up and put an arm around her shoulder. "They'll be okay."

Not saying anything, she nodded numbly. Her watch

beeped and she looked down at it, even though she knew what it meant. A chill crawled over her. *It's started.*

"Yeah, it's just us we need to worry about," Maeve murmured.

Greg groaned. "I can't believe you said that out loud. That should be an inner thought. You should be telling me we're going to be fine. That Martin's people don't stand a chance."

Maeve turned to face him. "We're going to be fine. Martin's people don't stand a chance."

He nodded. "See? That's what I'm talking about. Bald-faced lying, that's all I'm looking for."

CHAPTER 80

Martin sat in his office. It had been a satisfying afternoon of testing. The Gray had managed to protect Subject One, even when out of eyesight. In fact, it wasn't until he was three levels away that his protection failed.

Of course, he could have simply been exhausted. So they had halted the testing, or at least that portion of the test. They continued the pain reception tests on Subject One. He was more sensitive than most of the other creatures. That would need to be addressed in future iterations of the subject. Once both subjects had rested, they would commence the testing again tomorrow.

The implications of Orion1's ability were staggering. If they could send soldiers into battle where the soldiers did not feel pain but their controller did, it could change everything. *I know quite a few governments who will be very happy to hear about this development.*

"Sir!" Hamish banged into the room, nearly tripping over his feet in his rush.

Martin glared. "You knock first."

"I know, sir, I—" Hamish stopped talking, walked back to the door, and knocked.

Martin shook his head. For a genius, the man was an absolute idiot. "What is it, Hamish?"

"I figured out where Guardian is heading."

Martin straightened. "Really?"

The analyst nodded and held a flash drive up. "Can I link this to your monitor?"

"By all means," Martin gestured to his desk.

Hamish sat across from Martin and started fiddling with the keyboard as Martin stared at the screen. A map of the southwestern United States came on screen with thousands of blue dots. He frowned. "What am I looking at?"

"These are all the stationary cameras in this part of the United States—street cameras, bank cameras, private, everything. I was able to figure out which ones Guardian has been shutting down." He hit a button and about half of the cameras disappeared, but the dots still covered most of the map with no obvious pattern.

Martin waved his hand at the map. "This tells me nothing."

"I cross referenced to see how long the cameras were shut down for. Most of them were shut down for a specific amount of time—twenty-three seconds. But some of the others were down for longer."

"Meaning there was something on the screen that they needed to make sure was off the screen before they brought the camera back online." More of the dots disappeared. Martin frowned, the group's destination clear. *I should have known.*

"They're heading here," Hamish said.

Martin grabbed the desk phone and dialed the front gate. He started to punch in the number before he realized he hadn't heard a dial tone when he picked up. He disconnected the call and then listened. Nothing. He slammed down the phone and pulled out his cell. 'No signal' flashed across his screen.

"They're not heading here," Martin said softly. "They're already here."

"What?" Hamish grabbed his tablet, his fingers flying across it. "There've been no alarms. They're not on any of the screens."

"I'm guessing Guardian has something to do with that," Martin murmured.

Hamish paled. "Wh-what should we do?" Before Martin could respond, an alarm rang out, followed immediately by an automated announcement over the PA system.

"Attention! Attention! A biological contaminant has been detected. All personnel must evacuate immediately. I repeat, a biological contaminant has been ..." The message continued to repeat and the red emergency lights flashed on and off.

Grabbing Hamish by the shoulder, he pushed him toward the desk. "Shut the warning off."

"But the contaminant—"

Martin cut him off. "There *is* no contaminant. It's them. They're in our system. Get them out of it."

Hamish quickly moved to Martin's computer, his eyes focused, his hands flying across Martin's keyboard.

Shifting over to the window, Martin looked down into the lab. The lab assistants were hastily backing up their data. Some were already running for the door.

"I can't do it from here. I need my equipment."

Martin turned at Hamish's voice. "Then go, and contact security. Make sure they are aware of the breach and have them send a detail to me."

"Yes. Yes, sir." Hamish scrambled out of the room.

Heading back to his desk, Martin leaned down to the bottom drawer. Opening it, he pulled out his Sig Sauer. After checking to make sure the magazine was full, he tucked it into the back of his pants.

Crossing the room, he pulled on the painting of *The Miracle of the Snow* that hung there. The painting had been rendered in the fifteenth century and depicted a day when it snowed in Rome in August. But more surprising than the weather, Jesus and Mary are depicted looking down upon Rome, a legion of UFOs trailing behind them.

UFOs had appeared in many works of art over the centuries, but most had turned a blind eye to their appearance. *For hundreds of years, we ignored them. And one day soon, we will be forced to pay for that willful blindness.*

The painting swung open, revealing a safe behind it. Martin punched his code into the keypad. The light above the keypad turned from red to green and the door popped open a few inches. Martin pulled it the rest of the way. He pushed past the emergency cash and reached for a small metal box. He pulled it out, along with a headset, and placed them both in his pocket before closing the safe door.

It was smart emptying the facility, leaving only a skeleton crew. And taking out communications was even smarter. By the time Hamish got back to the communication level, most of the facility would have evacuated.

It was a stroke of luck for them that Hamish had been with Martin. Of course, if he hadn't been, he'd be heading for the door along with everyone else.

Hamish would alert the security, but Martin had another security protocol in place that he knew would prove even more effective. He smiled. He'd never had to chance to try this particular weapon out in the field before.

No time like the present.

CHAPTER 81

The alarm had been sounded inside the base. Maeve took a deep breath. The first team was set up five hundred yards outside the entrance of the facility and had managed to go undetected. Penny was keeping an eye on the communications and her camera work had raised no flags.

Maeve sat in the back of the truck between Norah and Greg. Chris was by the door and another six people were with them. As soon as the facility was clear, they would speed toward the entrance and it would begin.

They all had earpieces and mics, although each teams were routed to only certain members. Tilda was staying outside the facility and running point. All communications would go to her and she'd send out what info was needed by each group leader. Everyone speaking to everyone else would only lead to confusion.

Chris was listening intently to his piece. He put up a hand and everyone turned to him. "The first of the vehicles are leaving the base. Two minutes."

Everyone tensed, listening for any indication that their

position had been discovered. Heavy trucks could be heard in the distance but all kept going.

Greg's leg tapped nonstop next to her, his head whipping from side to side as he looked out the windows on each side of the truck. "So, this is good. So far not a single casualty. We're doing great."

Maeve just patted his thigh. Greg's leg seemed to bounce even faster in response. "I mean, hey, we've got a twelve-year-old genius watching over us. No problems there, right?" He said with a onerous laugh.

"Greg, you need to calm down. It's not too late if you want to stay back," Maeve said.

His head whipped over to her. "What? No, I'm good. Just excited to get started."

"Well, you're about to get your wish," Chris said. "The first trucks have left the entrance. Five minutes is their evac time and then we go in."

"Okay, good," Greg said, nodding continuously.

Taking Greg's hand, Maeve squeezed it. "We got this."

"Yup, yup, we do," Greg said, swallowing hard.

"Okay, folks, showtime," Chris said as the truck headed out from their hiding spot and toward the cave entrance.

CHAPTER 82

By the time Martin reached the lab, the personnel had already been evacuated. The emergency announcement had cut off a few minutes ago, which told Martin that Hamish had made it to his control room, although the red emergency lights continued to flash.

And although the personnel had evacuated the lab, it was not completely empty. The experiments in the cages along the wall became agitated as Martin stepped into the room. But then they quieted, moving to the back of their cages.

One stayed in the same position, though, curled up in the corner of his cage—Subject One. Martin glared at it as he hurried past. All this trouble caused by one stupid lab experiment. They never should have allowed Alice Leander to treat the thing like a child. If they'd treated it like a research subject, he would not have to deal with people breaking into his facility to rescue the damn thing.

As he walked across the deserted labs, he could feel the creatures' eyes on him. He could feel their hate. Not that it mattered. They were never getting out of those cages. Unlike at

51, none of these cages were linked to any computer. They had to be opened the old-fashioned way.

Orion1 moved to the bars to watch Martin's progress. He'd been placed as far away from Subject One as possible. Martin did not want the Gray to be able to offer Subject One any comfort. It was a petty move, but after the Gray's attack, he was feeling more than a little petty. Martin felt the Gray's gaze on him and the telltale flutter against his brain.

They're coming for him. The words wafted through Martin's mind. He turned slowly to Orion1. The Gray had never used words before. Of course, Martin had never allowed him to get beyond the initial probing of his mind's defenses before he shocked it into submission.

Martin stopped and crossed to the cage. He was in a hurry, but he'd make time for this. He looked into the Gray's black eyes. He stood, unblinking, staring back. "Then they'll die," Martin said, "just like they should have months ago."

You underestimate them, Orion said.

"No, you underestimate *me*." He pushed the bottom of the control on his wristband. The Gray shook and fell back. He seized for a few seconds before stilling.

"Just in case you get any ideas." With a smile, Martin turned his back on him and headed to the door at the back-right corner of the room. He keyed in his code and pulled it open when the light above it turned green. He walked down the flight of metal stairs and keyed into another door at the bottom.

Stepping through the door placed him in a long, dark hallway. A control desk was positioned to his left. The technician at it jumped to his feet. "Director Drummond, I didn't realize you were coming."

"Have there been any problems?"

"No, sir, all the subjects have been quiet. Although they started to get a little restless just before the alarm went off."

D.E.A.D.

They know they're here. "We've had a breach. They've gotten into the complex. Are the creatures ready?"

The man paused for a moment before nodding, and Martin could tell he was holding back a smile. "Yes, sir. I personally charged their collars this morning and they passed their last obedience test with flying colors. They are ready."

"Good." Martin held out his hand. "Let me have your controller."

The man did not hesitate. He reached down, plucked it off the desk, and placed it in Martin's outstretched hand. Martin slipped it into his pocket before pulling out his own controller and putting the headset on, taking a moment to adjust the mic. Martin moved toward the side of the hall as he turned the controller on. Then he walked up to the first cage. The Kecksburg-AG2, nicknamed Hank by Greg Schorn, was perched on a ledge six feet off the ground. The Kecksburg leapt down from his perch and ran for the glass wall.

"Stop." The creature went still.

"Raise your right hand." It raised its right hand.

"Good." Martin walked down the hall and performed the same ritual with each of the other four.

After the fifth creature followed his commands, he nodded. *Excellent.* He hit the release button on the bottom of the controller. Each of the creatures sprang for the hallway as the doors slid open with a swoosh of air.

They looked at Martin and then turned for the technician. The first sprang toward him and the technician let out a scream, diving under his desk.

"Stop." Martin ordered.

All the creatures went still. "It's all right," Martin said. "I've got them."

The technician stood up slowly, still shaking. He licked his lips nervously, looking between the creatures and Martin.

"Thank you. Um, what … what are you going to do with them?"

Martin ignored him, shifting to the telepathic command mode. *Line up*.

Four creatures moved forward to join the first one, standing shoulder to shoulder. Martin smiled. This program had been a special pet project. These creatures were the first in a long line of weapons that could be used against any threat, human or otherwise. Strength, speed, viciousness, and no moral qualms getting in the way—perfect soldiers.

They had been tested over and over again and had responded beautifully. Martin believed that to be due to the creatures' love of the hunt and the kill.

And Martin had provided plenty of opportunities for them to indulge that passion. But if they failed to follow even a single order, they were denied the next hunt.

And that's all it took to keep them in line. They wanted to kill. As long as you gave them targets, they were perfectly obedient. Martin pictured the technician in his mind.

Step forward. The creatures did, and the technician took a step back. "Director Drummond?" He asked a tremor in his voice.

Martin sent the image of the technician to the creatures again. *Kill*.

The creatures pounced, slicing the man across the chest. The technician screamed, falling back. As one, they landed on him, each grabbing a leg or arm. They pulled and ripped, their actions frantic. Martin took a step back to avoid the spray of blood.

One minute was all it took to reduce the technician to unrecognizable pieces. Truth was, the man was dead five seconds after they attacked. But Martin thought they deserved a little fun.

Stop.

The creatures stepped away from their new toy. Martin smiled as they turned and looked at him.

One stepped forward, baring his teeth. *No.* Martin hit a button on the controller. With a scream, the creature fell to the floor, convulsing. A toxin was working its way through the creature's system. It would paralyze him for eight hours, bringing him to the brink of death while pain cascaded through him. The other four immediately backed away, lowering their heads.

With a smile, Martin sent images to the creatures' minds. *Leander, Garrigan, Schorn, Matilda.* He focused on the images over and over to make sure the creatures had them locked in.

Then he reached for the control panel on the wall next to him and opened the door leading to the stairwell.

Find. Kill.

CHAPTER 83

Adam was in the first truck that entered the tunnel to the facility. Maeve could hear the gunfire even over the roar of the engine and the blood in her ears as they sped through the gates of the base's entry. At first, the tunnel had the craggy look of a large natural cave. But then, about two hundred yards in, the rock walls became smooth. And Maeve knew if she ran a hand against those walls, they'd be as smooth as glass. With a shudder, Maeve realized they looked just like the tunnels under 51.

Norah leaned over. "What kind of machine could make this type of tunnel?"

"Giant U.S.-government-patented tunneling machine," Greg said.

Norah raised her eyebrows. "Seriously?"

Maeve nodded. "Seriously."

Chris's voice came over the earpiece. "Alpha group has cleared the initial lines of security. The entrance level is secure."

Maeve tried not to think about the people who'd been killed to make that happen. They rounded a bend in the gravel road and entered a large cavern, double the width of the tunnel and just as deep. A loading dock dominated one side, and a security station stood along the right-hand side of the small building there.

As soon as the truck stopped, Chris had the door open. "Let's move."

Everyone quickly exited the truck. Once they'd stepped from the trucks, Maeve saw Norah transform. She was just as serious and focused as Tilda's commandos. And being she'd be looking out for Greg, Maeve felt reassured.

Adam strode over from the security station and nodded at Maeve. She swallowed hard, seeing the bodies lined up in front of the building behind him.

Gunfire blasted through the air, coming from somewhere inside. Jasper walked over, a nasty-looking semi-automatic cradled confidently in his arms.

Agent Bileris was with him as well and gave Maeve a nod. "Bravo team has already headed down. They'll have Level Six secured by the time we get there. And Guardian verified that our two subjects are in the lab there."

Butterflies fluttered through Maeve's stomach. *We're almost there, Alvie.*

"We've shut down the elevators. The west stairwell is clear for at least three levels. That's where we're headed." Jasper strode for the open double metal doors built into the rock face.

They all fell in line with him. Three commandos plus Chris hustled forward, taking the lead.

Greg fell in step next to Maeve. "Seriously, Tilda has her own private, highly efficient army. She's pretty badass. I want to be as cool as her when I'm seventy-eight." He paused. "Actually, I'd like to be as cool as her now."

Despite the nerves, Greg's words made her smile. "Any chance we could table this conversation for a time when we're not infiltrating a terrifying subterranean base run by a madman?"

He winced. "Oh, yeah, sure. Sorry."

Ahead, Chris entered the stairwell and Maeve's breath caught. But no gunfire answered him. Before she knew it, she was stepping into the stairwell as well. Emergency lights flashed, bathing the area in red light.

At the second level, Norah grabbed Greg's sleeve and pulled him into the hallway. Two commandos disappeared with them. Maeve ignored the worry that spread through her and continued down the stairs. Ahead, Chris called a halt. They were outside the fourth level. He tilted his head, listening to his earpiece. "Say again, Bravo leader?"

Whatever the reply was, it was not good. Chris tapped the mic at his throat. "I've lost contact with Bravo leader. Everyone be on guard."

They continued down the stairwell, this time moving more slowly. Maeve watched the fifth-floor landing appear. *Only one more to go.*

Chris held up a hand halfway down the stairs to the sixth level. One of Tilda's men broke the silence. "What's that?"

Maeve strained to hear. It sounded like muffled gunfire and a scream. Mike pulled Maeve against the wall, stepping in front of her while Jasper stepped behind her, his focus on the stairs they'd just climbed down.

The door to the sixth-level landing burst open and a creature stood staring up at them. Its skin looked like an alligator's and its lips moved as if it were chewing on something.

With a start, Maeve recognized they were human fingers just before they disappeared into the creature's mouth.

CHAPTER 84

Guardian sat in the van, her gaze shifting between the six screens displayed in front of her. Three of the screens were split screens, providing her with nine views of the facility. The first floor had been cleared easily. Guardian shifted her gaze to the evacuated employees. Their communication with the base was still cut off. They had no idea what was happening. *Good.*

The triplets leaned forward as Penny tapped a command to reinforce the communication firewall she'd created. Normally Penny did not like when anyone watched her. But she didn't mind the triplets. They weren't looking at her in awe or disbelief. No, she knew what they were doing.

They were learning.

Pop squeaked, and a vision appeared in Guardian's mind. A Kecksburg-AG2. Guardian's gaze whipped to the screen in the bottom-right corner. "Oh no."

In the driver's seat, the man started the engine.

"What's going on?" her mother asked.

"Something's gone wrong. I'm moving us farther out," he said.

"Hold on. The triplets are out of their seat belts." Nadine hustled back and tried to usher the triplets to their seats, but they resisted, their focus on the screens.

The driver went back to help. He reached for Pop, who scrambled out of his way. And then the man stopped, looking around. "Hey, where's that little green guy?"

Nadine looked around. "Oh my God. He was here. Where'd he go?"

Penny scrolled through the screens, her eyes constantly shifting between the images before she stopped. She pointed at the screen. "There he is."

CHAPTER 85

Norah hustled down the hallway, her senses on high alert. Aggie, a tall, red-headed guy with an abundance of freckles and their team leader, called through her earpiece. "Communications room is two doors down."

There were only four of them on Charlie team. Her, Greg, Aggie, and a tall muscular female who every one for some reason called Kitten. Personally, Norah thought Tiger or Lioness might have been more appropriate for the tough-looking woman.

They'd seen no one so far besides the security in the entrance. Aggie put up a hand and everyone stopped. Norah kept an eye on the hallway behind them, but it remained silent. This level was probably one of the first emptied when the alarm went off, being it was so close to the surface.

The light on the security box next to the communications door bloomed green and Aggie opened the door. Kitten stepped in, her weapon at her shoulder, Aggie right behind her. Seconds later, they gave the all clear.

Greg glanced in the door and Norah had to refrain from

pushing him into the room. The doctor was a little skittish. Assuring himself that the room was in fact clear, he headed for the console on the other side. Penny had given him a USB drive that should allow him to access the other hard drives within the facility. The facility did not allow any outside access. But once Greg was in the system, the USB should allow them to copy all the drives.

Greg quickly sat down and got to work. Norah stayed by the door while Aggie and Kitten each took up point at either end of the hall. There was no noise except for the sound of Greg typing away at the computer, mumbling to himself. "Almost there. Sixty-five percent copied."

Norah felt tense, even though the area remained quiet. She rolled her shoulders, trying to reduce the tension, but it didn't help. The hairs on her arms stood up. She narrowed her eyes, tapping the mic at her collar. "Aggie, everything good?"

"All quiet," the man Sid.

"Kitten?" Norah asked.

"Quiet here, too. Wait—"

Norah straightened.

"Kitten?" Aggie called.

Gunfire blasted from down the hall, followed by a scream. "Kitten!" Aggie yelled.

"Greg, we need to move," Norah said, her tone urgent.

Sweat had broken out along the man's forehead. "I know, I know. Almost there. Eighty-nine percent."

Aggie came tearing down the hall. "Norah?"

"I can't see anything," she said.

"Stay with Schorn." He bolted past her, disappearing down the hall. Seconds later, more gunfire sounded. "Norah, it's coming. You—" Aggie's voice cut out.

"Done!" Greg yelled, pulling out the USB and standing.

Norah didn't even look at him. She trained her rifle down the hall. She could hear the heavy footsteps and the sound of something clicking as it walked. She let out a breath, trying to calm her breathing.

"Norah?" Greg asked quietly, but she didn't answer. She didn't take her eyes off the hallway. Which was why she had a perfect view of the creature as it stepped into view. It opened its mouth in what Norah thought might be a smile. But not one of friendliness.

No, this was a smile of victory, given right before it raced down the hall toward her.

CHAPTER 86

The Kecksburg paused for a split second on the landing, and Maeve had the horrifying feeling it was trying to decide who to kill first. "Fire!" Chris yelled, pulling the trigger.

The sounds in the stairwell were deafening. The flash of muzzle fire mixed with the flashing of the emergency lights made the scene look like something out of a nightmare. The creature leapt forward, its large talons clamping around the head of one of Tilda's men. With a vicious yank, it ripped the man's head right from his shoulders. Maeve stumbled back up the stairs in horror, her whole body shaking. Bullets slammed into the creature and it jolted back. But it kept its gaze focused on its target.

It kept its gaze on Maeve.

A second creature shoved through the door behind the first.

"Back up! Back up!" Chris yelled. Mike grabbed Maeve, shoving her up the stairs and keeping himself in front of her.

Jasper didn't take his gaze from the creatures or let up on the trigger. "Get to the other door!"

Maeve stumbled up the stairs and grasped the handle of

the fifth-level door, yanking it open. Mike shoved her inside, staying in the doorway. "Come to me!" he yelled.

The rest of their group backed up, but during her short dash up the stairs, she saw two more were down. Only Jasper and Chris were left standing, and both creatures, while injured, weren't slowing.

Jasper dropped to one knee, lining up a shot.

"Damn it, Jasper. Move!" Mike screamed.

But Jasper stayed where he was and got off one shot—right through the creature's eye. It toppled over.

"Oh yeah! Come on, Chris, let's get out of here." Jasper ducked through the doorway.

Chris was the last at the door. The remaining creature leaped at him and Chris flung himself backward through the door as Mike slammed the door shut.

The group stood breathing heavily as the creature threw itself against the door. "That's not going to hold for long," Jasper said.

"No, it's not." Chris tapped his mic. "Control, we need another access route. The west stairwell is blocked."

"Hold," came back the terse reply, loud enough for Maeve to hear it.

They all stood around in silence, the only sound their ragged breathing and the creature crashing into the door over and over again. Jasper leaned against the wall. "So, anyone know any good jokes?"

With a groan, Mike shook his head. "Jasper, you have horrible timing."

Chris held up a hand and everyone quieted. "Roger, Control. Be there in two." Chris started heading down the hall at a jog and everyone fell in behind him. "Penny's opening the elevator doors. We're going to climb down one level and when we reach Level Six, she'll open the doors for us."

"Nothing like a good climb in an elevator shaft." Jasper rubbed his hands together.

But Maeve just swallowed hard. She'd seen enough movies to know that climbing in an elevator shaft never led to anything good.

CHAPTER 87

Norah tossed the grenade from her belt down the hall. Kicking the door shut, she dove for the floor. "Get down!" She yelled.

Debris crashed into the door and Greg peered out from behind the desk. "What the hell was that?"

Standing, Norah winced as her knee twinged. She'd knocked it into the edge of a table leg. "Hopefully pieces of a walking alligator."

Greg paled noticeably. "Do you mean a six-foot-tall, highly muscular, bipedal creature with an alligator-like skin?"

She eyed the strange little scientist. "I take it you've seen one before?"

He swallowed hard. "Uh, yeah. And I can honestly say that grenade probably didn't kill him. Hank's really hard to kill."

Norah moved to the door. "Hank?"

Shaking, his eyes wild, Greg's head turned from side to side. "Well, the original Hank was called Kecksburg-AG2. But I called him Hank. Hank One is dead. But he had a few brothers. And I'm guessing you just met another one of his family members."

Norah tapped her mic. "Aggie? Kitten? You guys there?"

Only silence answered her.

"They're not okay, are they?" Greg asked softly.

Norah shook her head. "I don't think so. Tell me about Hank."

"Well, Hank was really good at tracking … and killing. I'm guessing that is something Drummond was looking for in his little army of aliens," Greg said.

Staring at him, Norah's mouth dropped open. "You think that thing was under control?"

The scientist shrugged but the nervous energy coming off him in waves counteracted the nonchalance of the move. "Probably. Or maybe he just escaped and was killing on his way out. Did I mention the Hanks really like to kill things?"

"Yeah, you mentioned it." Norah pulled the door open. Blood and guts were smeared against the door.

Greg peeked around her shoulder. "Actually, I think maybe I was wrong. I think you got it."

"Yeah, but I also took out the hallway leading to the stairs we were supposed to exit through. We're not getting out that way. You have the USB?" She asked.

Greg nodded.

"Well, let's get out of here." She tapped her mic. "This is Norah with Charlie team. I've lost contact with Aggie and Kitten. I'm bringing the professor topside."

"Roger."

Greg grinned as Norah looked over at him.

"What?"

"You called me 'the professor.' He was my favorite character on Gilligan's Island."

She glared at him. "Focus, Greg."

"Right, sorry, just glad Hank's in pieces," he said quickly.

Norah shook her head, stepping out into the hallway.

"Control, this is Norah. The hallway's blocked. We're going to be coming out the eastern hallway."

"Roger. We've seen security movement. Keep your eyes peeled."

"Will do." She turned to Greg. "Come on. I've had enough of this base." She hustled down the hall. Greg jogged right behind her. She paused at the other stairwell door.

"Great. More stairwells," he muttered.

Norah looked back at him. "What do you mean?"

He shrugged. "I've just found from experience that they tend to be the physical manifestation of terrifying nightmares."

"Ohhh-kay. Just stay with me. We'll be out of here in a few minutes." She pulled the door open, peeking outside. Gunfire raked the door and she slammed it shut, shoving Greg back against the wall. "Shit."

Greg latched onto her arm and pulled her down the hall. "Okay, digging through rubble it is," he said, his words coming out fast.

They sprinted down the hall. Ahead, the rubble moved. "Someone's pushing through," Norah said, picking up her pace.

"No!" Greg grabbed her arm, pulling her back as a dark arm with long talons punched through the debris.

CHAPTER 88

A team of four security officers had reached Martin and they all looked shaken. Six had been dispatched, but they had met up with one of Martin's Hanks, and now there were only four.

I will have to figure out a way to get them to be more selective in who they kill, Martin thought idly as he hustled down the hall toward the lab, his security surrounding him.

Gunfire sounded from down the hall as Martin ducked into the lab. *Damn it.* "Grab those containment units." Martin pointed to where the units were pushed up against the wall.

The guards quickly wheeled them over to the cages. "Put one down there, the last cage on the end," Martin said as he stopped in front of the big Gray's crate. He reached out and punched in the code for anesthetization. The Gray leapt to its feet, its eyes glaring with hate at Martin before they closed and it dropped to the floor.

"Get him in the unit," he ordered.

He ran down to the other unit. Subject One sat against the bench along the back, staring at Martin with terror in his eyes. Martin punched in the same code and Subject One toppled over to the ground. Martin opened up the cage when the gas had cleared and picked him up, surprised at how light he was, even though he knew the hybrid had hollow bones, just like Orion1.

The containment unit was already open. Martin placed the subject inside. "Go help get the other one restrained," Martin ordered the guard with him. The guard hurried over to do his bidding and Martin locked Subject One in place. He pulled out his phone and dialed Hamish.

"Sir?" Hamish squeaked.

"I need control of the freight elevator."

"I don't think I can—"

"Get me control, Hamish. *Now.*"

"Yes. Yes, sir. Give me just a ... there. I should be able to keep control until you reach the surface."

"I'm not going to the surface." Martin disconnected the call.

He leaned down, his face close to Subject One's as anger rolled through him. "You have cost me a great deal of time, money, and pain. And once I have you settled, I am going to return the favor." He slammed the unit shut and locked it. Then he pushed the unit toward the freight elevator.

Yes, I have plans for you, you little bastard.

CHAPTER 89

Maeve stood crouched on the ladder in the elevator shaft. Chris and Mike were on the other side of the door. The doors slid open. The two of them peered through, gun muzzle first. Chris swung out into the hallway. And then Mike did the same.

"We're good," Chris said. Jasper walked along the metal framing of the elevator shaft and grabbed Chris's hand, pulling himself into the hall. Maeve did the same and Chris held her for a moment longer than necessary. "You good?"

"Yeah," she said, feeling a little breathless from the climb and the fear.

"Then let's go get our boy," Chris said.

Nodding, Maeve stepped away from him. Mike headed down the hall. The lab where Alvie was being kept was at the end of the hall, around the corner. Maeve had to fight down the urge to sprint down the hall and burst through the doors.

But getting herself killed would not help Alvie. And he would never forgive himself if she got hurt trying to help him. But it was still difficult to keep her movements restrained.

Mike looked around the corner and held up a hand. "I see

four, no, five humans. They're at the far wall. It looks like there's an elevator back there." Chris tapped his mic. "Control, is there an elevator in the lab?"

"There's nothing on the blueprints. They're loading two containers on," came the reply.

Chris swore.

"Alvie." Maeve jumped forward, but Jasper grabbed her, holding her back.

"Move! Now!" Chris ordered. He and Mike burst through the doors, Jasper following them.

Across the room, the men opened fire. Maeve bit her lip, diving into the room and taking cover behind some shelving. *Please, please don't injure the containment units*, she prayed as her group returned fire.

"Elevator's closing!" Mike yelled.

Maeve peered around the shelving in time to see two of the guards drop; the other two were inside the elevator as it closed. She stood up. "The train. They're taking Alvie on the train. We need to get down there."

"What do we do about these guys?" Jasper waved to the cages along the wall.

Turning, Maeve took in the four aliens locked inside. Her attention on the back of the room, she hadn't even realized they were there. Maeve didn't know what they were. Or what they were capable of. But she knew one thing—she couldn't leave them here. "Those cages are on wheels. You need to get them out."

She got to her feet, running to the door. "Tell Penny to bring the elevator back online. We need to stop Martin." She didn't wait to see if anyone responded. She just sprinted through the doors down the hall.

CHAPTER 90

Greg's heart stopped the moment he saw that way-too-familiar arm extending through the rubble. But luckily his mind kept working. He grabbed Norah's arm and shoved her through the nearest doorway, slamming the door shut behind them. It was a supply closet with no exit.

Norah whirled on him. "What are you—"

He raised his finger to his lips, shaking his head.

Nodding, Norah leaned toward the door. Greg leaned against the door as well. He could just make out the sound of Hank's nails on the tiles outside. He prayed that it hadn't seen them slip into the closet. If it had, Greg had just sealed their deaths. Their sense of smell wasn't great, though, so if it hadn't seen them, they might have a chance.

He held his breath as the creature grew closer and his chest began to feel tight. He exhaled sharply, throwing a hand over his mouth to muffle the sound. Norah stood next to him, her ear to the door, her breath enviably even.

The cadence of the creature's footsteps ticked up and a yell sounded from the end of the hallway, followed by a barrage of gunfire.

"Yes," Greg whispered.

Norah smiled at him, but this time she put a hand to her lips. A long, drawn-out scream sounded, making the hairs on Greg's neck stand up. And then more gunfire, but it sounded farther away.

"They're drawing him away. Let's go," Norah said quietly. She cracked the door open and looked down the hall. "Okay." She stepped out, keeping her weapon trained behind her. "Get through the hole that thing created."

Greg needed no further urging as he scrambled up the pile of debris, his pants leg snagging on a piece of rebar. He ripped it free and squeezed through the opening. The hallway stayed silent as he dropped down to the other side. A few seconds later, Norah appeared, climbing through the same hole.

Together they jogged quickly toward the other stairwell.

"Well, that was—" Debris tumbled from the pile behind them. Greg whipped around as the Hank's head popped through the opening.

"Run!" Norah yelled.

CHAPTER 91

The elevator doors swooshed open. Martin slammed the emergency stop button, locking the doors open before he pushed the container with Subject One out onto the train platform.

I should have trained a dozen Kecksburgs, he thought with a growl.

He couldn't believe Maeve Leander was here. Didn't the woman know when she was outmatched? He glared at Subject One's container. *I should have thrown you in a cage the day you were born.* He needed to get these two specimens out of here, and then it would not be a complete loss.

"Where the hell's the train?" Martin barked.

"Two minutes out," one of his guards said, his eyes shifting back and forth between the two other entrances to the tracks.

"God damn it," Martin growled. He pulled out the controller. He checked the screen. Only two of his Kecksburgs were still alive.

Come to me, he ordered one of them. He felt the pull of the creature.

The seconds seemed to crawl by. He would not lose his

prize possession. Not after he'd just managed to acquire it. He knew he was on the cusp of a weapon that would truly save the human race. He glared at the containers. Why the hell didn't people understand that?

Lights appeared down the track. He'd placed a safeguard on the track so it could be manually overridden from this station. But to do so, you had to be here. There was no way to hack into it from some other location. He smiled.

Time to go.

CHAPTER 92

Norah sprinted up the stairs, yelling into her mic. "We've got a ... thing ... on our tail!"

"It's a Kecksburg-AG2!" Greg yelled as he ran up the stairs next to her. The exit door ahead of them burst open.

"Move!" Adam yelled as he threw a grenade behind them. Norah grabbed Greg's shoulder and threw him through the doorway, then dove in after him.

She slammed onto Greg's back as he hit the ground and quickly rolled off him, taking aim behind her. Adam flew through the doorway after them as the stairwell exploded behind him.

Keeping her attention and weapon trained on the doorway as she got to her feet, Norah backed up slowly. "Did you get it?"

His weapon also trained on the doorway, Adam was backing up as well. "I don't think so."

"Great." Greg's voice was shaky as he spoke from slightly behind her but he held the Sig Sauer Chris had handed him before they left the farmhouse confidently in his hand.

She had to admit, she was impressed he was still there. She'd expected him to run. *I guess Chris was right.*

"Okay, so, weak spots," said Greg, "Eyes, mouth, and, well, that's about it. His skin is pretty damn tough and his talons ... well, just stay as far from them as possible."

Adam nodded next to her at the same time as Norah. "Got it," she said, adjusting her grip.

The creature burst from the doorway. Norah opened fire, as did Adam and Greg. The creature veered to the left, leaping up onto a guard shack and then jumping down to the other side.

Damn, that thing's fast. Norah whirled, trying to follow it, but she kept missing it. Neither of the other two was doing any better. It leapt onto a truck and swung behind it. There was a scream and then everything went quiet.

"Where is it?" Greg whispered.

"Don't know." Norah scanned the area. Adam went to one side of the truck and Norah circled around the other. The two of them met on the other side over the body of one of their men. His throat had been slashed open and he stared unseeing into the air.

"I'll check down by the entrance." Adam started to move quickly away from the truck. Norah searched the area, feeling as if the creature was nearby.

Gunfire burst out from the other side of the truck. "Greg!" Norah sprinted back toward him.

Hank swung from the loading dock, Greg's bullets seeming to do nothing. Its feet slammed into Greg, throwing him back onto the ground with a thud.

Norah brought up her weapon and opened fire. Hank turned and hissed, rushing toward her. A shape dropped from the top of the truck and landed on the creature's neck.

Norah's heart leapt into her throat. "No!"

Iggy dug his talons into either side of the Hank's neck. The

Hank reached up and swiped at him, cutting Iggy across his midsection.

But Iggy raised his hands and once again plunged his talons into the Hank's eyes before toppling off the creature.

"Iggy!" Norah burst forward, firing nonstop as the Hank toppled forward. Adam did the same as he sprinted back toward them from the other side of the truck.

Norah slid onto her knees at Iggy's side, pressing her hands to his wound. Blood seeped through her fingers. "No, no, no." Tears pressed against her eyes.

Vaguely, she heard Chris's voice over the earpiece, saying that Martin was escaping into the tunnels underneath the mountain and asking Penny to open up the elevators. But she didn't take her gaze from Iggy.

He opened his eyes. "Ig?" he whispered softly before closing them.

Greg knelt on Iggy's other side, opening a first-aid kit on the ground next to him. "Move your hands, Norah."

She shook her head. "No. He's bleeding too much."

"Norah, let me help him," Greg said.

Norah looked up at Greg and then nodded. Greg pressed the bandages to Iggy's chest and she heard him telling Penny to find Iggy's file and tell him about his blood. Norah didn't understand half of what the two of them were saying to each other.

She grasped Iggy's hand. "I'm here, Iggy. I'm right here."

"Adam, we need to move him," Greg said, looking up, and then he frowned. "Where is he?"

"He was just—" Norah shook her head. "I don't know."

CHAPTER 93

Maeve, Jasper, and Chris stood in the elevator as it descended. Mike had stayed behind to start removing the aliens. It only had to go two floors, but it felt like they were traveling miles. *Why is this taking so long?*

"When the doors open, be ready to fire." Jasper looked at Maeve. "Will you be able to shoot someone?"

She glared at him. "Just try to stop me."

Jasper nodded with a grin. "Well okay then."

The elevator dinged, indicating they had reached their destination. They all flattened themselves against the sides of the elevator as the doors opened. Chris peered outside. "Clear."

Maeve and Jasper followed Chris out into a short, dull, yellow hallway. It looked like it belonged in a parking garage. Through the small window in the door at the other side, she could see the top of a two-car train as it approached.

Oh no.

Chris peered through the window. "Train's stopping. They're on a platform a hundred yards to our left. Martin, two guards, and two containers. There's no cover between here and there."

"Well, let's go. Team Save the Aliens to the rescue," Jasper said, grasping the door handle. He nodded at Chris and swung it wide.

Just as the train pulled into the station, Chris darted out. He got off the first shot, catching one of the guards in the shoulder before he could react.

As Jasper stepped out, he pulled the trigger as well, but Martin leaned out from behind a pillar and fired. Jasper crashed to the ground. "No!" Maeve yelled, pulling the trigger on the man on the platform. He jerked and then collapsed.

Chris was already moving forward. "Check Jasper!" he yelled.

Maeve darted to where Jasper lay.

Blood trickled down the side of his head from where the bullet had grazed him. Luckily it didn't look like it had done much damage, but he'd slammed his head into the ground pretty hard.

Crouching down, Maeve placed her fingers on the man's neck. His pulse was strong. A lump had formed, but she didn't think it was a life-threatening injury. Hopefully he was just knocked out. She looked up to where Chris was exchanging gunfire with Martin. Alvie and Agaren's containment units were on the platform in between the two of them, and Maeve cringed each time she heard the ping of metal.

Jasper did not look like he was getting up anytime soon. Maeve rolled her shoulders and then placed her hands under his arms.

Okay. I got this. She straightened as Chris let out a yell. "Maeve, look out!"

Her heart rate spiked as a shadow leapt onto the top of the train only fifty feet away. It was a Kecksburg. It stared at her, tilting its head. Maeve scrambled for her gun and leveled it at the creature, pulling the trigger, but all she got back was an empty click. She was out.

The creature raised its head and let out a scream before it leapt from the train. Maeve stared at the arc of its jump, knowing she might be able to get out of the way, but that would mean leaving Jasper behind.

And she just could not do that.

She pulled him back against the wall and scooted in front of him, pulling Jasper's knife from the holder at his belt. The four-inch knife was nothing against that thing's talons, but she wouldn't just stand there and let it kill her.

She braced herself as it landed ten feet in front of her.

CHAPTER 94

Maeve tensed, her palms slick with sweat. The creature stared at her and roared. It crouched, about to leap, when gunfire blasted into the creature. It leapt back, turning toward the source with a hiss. Maeve whirled around as well, as Adam strode forward, a large weapon Maeve didn't recognize in his arms. Adam stalked toward the creature. He must have come down the stairwell near the other elevator.

Adam continued to back the creature toward the train. "Get Jasper out of here," he ordered, not sparing her a look, his focus locked on the Kecksburg and Martin.

The Kecksburg leapt back on top of the train car. Blood poured from the wounds in its left side. Adam shifted his aim to Martin, who dove away from the doorway, the shot exploding the window.

Maeve hauled Jasper toward the freight elevator as Chris ran out and pushed one of the containers into the elevator. Maeve managed to get Jasper inside and then ran for the other unit. Chris joined her as Adam stepped in front of them. The Kecksburg leapt down from the train. It caught a blast in its midsection, which sent it flying back toward the train. It landed in the doorway as the doors started to shut. But the creature's body kept them from closing fully and kept the train from leaving.

"Adam, come on," Maeve yelled as they got the second container into the elevator.

He pulled the trigger, but the weapon was empty. He tossed it to the side. He pulled two long serrated knives from his belt. "Chris, get them out of here," Adam yelled.

Chris pulled Maeve into the elevator.

"What about Adam?" she asked.

Jasper moaned from the floor. "He'll be all right. Do what he says." With a long look at Maeve, Chris turned off the emergency brake and the doors slid closed.

Maeve lurched for the doors. "No, we can't—"

Jasper shook his head with a wince. "Trust me. Adam's got this."

Maeve stared at him in disbelief. Adam was facing down a Hank and Martin with only two knives. How the hell could he have that?

CHAPTER 95

As soon as Adam shot past him, Martin bolted into the other car to get the train moving. It would be a tough loss, losing his prized specimens, but losing his life would be a much tougher loss to swallow.

He'd only gotten a glance at the man, but it was enough for him to recognize him as Tilda's grandson, Adam. And he was proving to be every bit as tough as his grandfather had been. Martin initiated the command to get the train moving, but an error message appeared. *Damn it.* Something was blocking one of the doors.

He picked up his Sig Sauer and strode back to the other car. Pushing through the door, he saw the Kecksburg lying half in and half out of the train car. The doors were opening and slamming closed on it.

On the platform, the elevator doors closed. He looked around but saw no sign of anyone else. They all must have taken the chance to escape. He strode down the car toward the creature. He'd have to open the doors and order it to move. Hopefully it could still move on its own. He really didn't want to test his control by having to move a wounded Kecksburg.

The creature's left side was bloodied and its head whipped back and forth. One arm looked broken and the other flailed around uselessly.

A prickling sense of unease rolled down Martin's back and he turned to the other side of the car. A man kicked in the already spider-webbed glass.

With a yell, Martin rolled away from the glass and crawled down the car. Adam hit the ground and rolled into a crouch. Before Martin could get fully to his feet, Adam slammed his foot into Martin's chest, sending him flying onto his back again.

Martin saw stars but still managed to bring his gun hand up, firing wildly. Adam leapt back, diving and rolling behind a row of seats.

"You bastard." Martin got to his feet, anger rolling through him. "You've cost me everything. Why couldn't you and Tilda just leave well enough alone?"

Martin pulled the trigger over and over, emptying it into the seat's back. He turned when he was abreast of it and peered over. Adam was gone.

What the—

Adam leapt up from three seats ahead, his knife flying through the air and catching Martin in the shoulder. With a scream, Martin fell back, his gun flying out of reach. He crawled along the ground toward the doors where the creature was caught. He latched onto the door, holding it open long enough for the creature to slide its body far enough to get its good arm out.

Adam stalked down the car toward him. Somewhere in the fight, the man's sunglasses had gone flying.

Martin stared into his face, disbelief flowing through him. "No. It's not possible. Joseph?"

"You don't know me," the man said. But Martin knew that wasn't true. His eyes were not deceiving him. This was Joseph, in all his youthful vitality.

But Joseph should be nearing eighty years old now. Martin stared into the man's eyes and fear slid down his back at the cold, reptilian look in the man's eyes.

No, it can't be.

The man's gaze locked on Martin so he didn't notice the shift in the position of the Kecksburg. It reached out, whip fast, and grabbed Joseph's legs, yanking him back. Joseph plunged his knife into the creature's arm. The creature roared, yanking itself from the train doors and flinging Joseph toward the elevator doors as the train doors slid closed.

The train jolted forward and Martin grabbed onto the seat, pulling himself up. On the platform, Joseph and the Kecksburg circled one another. Martin kept his gaze on the man.

It's not possible. It's just not possible. How did I not know?

CHAPTER 96

It felt like the elevator took forever to reach the surface. Chris contacted their team to let them know they were coming up and that they would need help. Maeve unstrapped Alvie and checked his vitals. He was breathing. She did the same for the big Gray. His pulse felt strong as well.

"They okay?" Chris asked from over by the control panel.

"I think so," Maeve said.

"We're going to have to move quickly as soon as these doors open. There's not much time left," Chris said.

"Okay." She paused. "What about Adam?"

Jasper still sat on the floor, and Maeve knew his world was still spinning. When he spoke, his voice was a little slurred. "Don't worry about Adam. He's been around a while. He knows how to take care of himself."

Maeve studied Jasper, getting the feeling there was something she didn't understand. But right now she supposed there was probably a lot she didn't know. So she closed up the container with the big Gray. It would probably be easier to roll him out. But she pulled Alvie from his container and clasped him to her, breathing him in. Tears threatened to fall, but she willed them back. They'd have to wait until they were safe. And they weren't safe yet.

The doors slid open and Maeve tensed. But the faces outside the doors were ones she recognized. Mike moved in quickly. "I've got Jasper." He pulled Jasper up, carrying him over his shoulder.

"I can walk!" Jasper yelled.

Mike didn't slow down. "Shut up, Jasper."

Two others hustled in and started pushing out the big Gray's container. Chris nodded to Alvie. "You want me to—"

She shook her head quickly, clutching Alvie to her. "No. I've got him." All of them hurried toward a waiting truck. Three minutes later they were pulling out of the entrance. Chris sat next to Maeve, who clutched Alvie protectively to her.

"Do we know how everyone else is?" Chris asked.

"We lost four of our people," Mike said, his voice somber.

Oh no. Maeve clutched Alvie tighter. "I'm so sorry."

Mike nodded his acknowledgment of her words. "Greg and Norah are all right. But Iggy—he was hurt."

Maeve frowned. "Iggy? But he wasn't supposed to be anywhere near this."

"No, he wasn't," Mike agreed. "But apparently he tracked Norah down. And he arrived just in time. A Kecksburg was about to make mincemeat out of her and Greg."

Maeve pictured the adorable little alien. "And Iggy stopped him?"

"Guess you don't want that guy on your bad side," Mike said.

Shaking her head, Maeve tried to picture it but she couldn't. The truck picked up speed, jolting all of them. Chris steadied Maeve and Alvie looking at Mike who was listening intently to something over his earpiece.

"What's going on?" Chris asked.

Mike's voice was level even though his Adam's apple bobbed. "We have an inbound chopper."

"Ours?" Chris asked.

"No. The D.E.A.D.'s. We need to get out of the area before they arrive," Mike said.

"What about the rest of the employees from the site?" Maeve asked.

"Still in the dark but getting antsy. Their communications are still blocked, but they'll send someone soon to see what's going on," Mike said.

The truck made an abrupt turn and everyone on the back swayed to the side. Mike held his finger to his earpiece, listening. "Shit."

Maeve frowned. "What's—"

But the explosion next to the truck answered them.

The chopper had found them.

CHAPTER 97

The truck shook as the explosion rocked them. "Damn, that was close," Mike murmured.

The truck swerved back and forth. Jasper groaned. "Oh, I think I'm going to be sick."

"Don't suppose you guys have anything that will take down a chopper?" Chris asked.

"Sorry. Fresh out," Mike said.

"So what's the plan?" Maeve clutched Alvie to her.

Nervous energy rolled through Mike's voice. "We're veering away from the group and heading toward a populated area. Hopefully blowing up a truck in the middle of Main Street will not be something they are looking to do."

"How far away is the nearest town?" Chris asked.

Mike met Maeve's gaze. "Five miles."

"Oh crap," Jasper said, sinking to the floor of the truck bed. "So we're just hoping whoever's flying that thing is a really bad shot?"

"Yup." Mike glanced out the back of the truck. He frowned. "Oh no."

"What?" Chris looked out as well. "Is that another one?"

"I think so," Mike said his voice grim.

We're not going to make it. Maeve held Alvie tight, leaning her forehead into his. *I love you, Alvie. Whatever happens, I don't regret coming for you.*

"Wait, that's not a chopper," Mike said frowning.

Maeve's head popped up and she stared into the sky as the other dark image came into view. She stumbled toward the back of the truck, which was weaving ferociously. Chris grabbed onto her and Alvie, anchoring them in place.

The winged creature from the ranch soared into view. It glanced down toward the truck and Maeve looked up at it. Then it was flying past them. "That's the guy from the ranch! The one who saved us," she exclaimed.

"What's it doing?" Mike asked.

"I think it's going for the chopper," Maeve said, hoping she was right and hoping it survived the encounter.

The gunfire that had been aimed at the truck cut off. They all scrambled forward, trying to get a look at the battle in the sky. The creature dove low and came up underneath the chopper, out of range of any of its weapons. It didn't slow, slamming its shoulder into the underbelly of the helicopter. The chopper shuddered and one of the gunmen fell from the open doorway with a scream.

The pilot tried to wrangle back control, but the creature slammed into the chopper again with both feet, leaving a dent in the underbelly. Then it flew down and, picking up speed, crashed into the side of the chopper.

The chopper tilted sideways. The creature flew back, its giant wings keeping it afloat as it watched the chopper try to right itself. But there was no time. It was on its side and the ground was coming up fast. With a loud crash, the chopper slammed into the ground, fire erupting into the air as metal debris scattered into the air.

Maeve gasped. It had all happened so quickly.

"Glad that guy's on our side," Chris muttered.

"Yeah. But why is he?" Mike asked.

The creature turned, flying toward their truck. About twenty feet up, it made two slow circles above the truck before flying off. Maeve watched it go.

"Thank you," she whispered, knowing that would not be the last she saw of it.

CHAPTER 98

They did not return to the safe house after leaving the underground facility. Tilda had arranged for each of them to take a different route back to a new location. Maeve's group took two separate flights, lifting off and landing from grass fields, not airports.

It had taken seven hours to complete the trip. By the time they arrived, it was pitch black and Maeve couldn't see much of their surroundings. Alvie clung to Maeve's hand as they stepped off the plane. He'd barely let go of her since he'd come around. She could feel his pain at what had transpired and she didn't know how she was going to help him through it.

Now they were bundled in the back of an old army truck that bucked and shook as they drove along an uneven road. But soon the uneven road smoothed out. The ride became soothing and Maeve closed her eyes. They jolted open again as the truck came to a stop. Chris rubbed his eyes next to her, having also fallen asleep.

Maeve gently rubbed Alvie's back. "Alvie, honey, we've stopped."

He awoke slowly, his eyes blinking a few times. She put her hand on his cheek. "It's okay."

He leaned into her for a moment before pulling back. Maeve led him to the end of the truck, where Chris helped them both off. There were two large buildings that reminded Maeve of military barracks. Maeve's feet had just touched the ground when she felt a burst of joy through her mind. She smiled as the triplets bolted out from the closest building. They sprinted across the space and threw themselves at Alvie. Chris put a hand on Alvie's back to keep him upright. Tears crested in Maeve's eyes at the reunion. This was how it was supposed to be—all of them together.

Chris put an arm around her. "We did it."

She looked up at him and smiled. "Yeah."

Greg jogged his way over to them in a mismatched pair of pajamas. He hugged Maeve and shook Chris's hand.

"How's Iggy?" Maeve asked.

Greg grinned. "He'll be okay. A couple of stitches and he's been put on bed rest. But being that Norah has apparently decided to stay snuggled up with him while he rests, the little guy looks perfectly content."

Relief flowed through Maeve at the news. "Good."

"You guys are all in the room next to me." Greg paused. "You're okay with all being in the same room, right?"

"Oh, I am very okay with that," Maeve said as the triplets ran for her and hugged her tight. She laughed, pulling them to her. Yes. Right now life was as it was supposed to be.

She looked up as headlights shone from down the road. Another truck appeared. It pulled up a few feet away and Adam stepped out of the back along with Jasper and Agaren.

As the Gray stepped down, he looked over at Alvie and the triplets. All four of them rushed over to him, and hugged him. The Gray went still and then gently rubbed each of their heads.

"What is that all about?" Chris asked.

"I have no idea," Maeve said quietly. "But I think everything we know has just changed."

EPILOGUE

SEATTLE, WASHINGTON

The Seattle skyline twinkled back at Martin from behind the picture window in his living room. He sipped his tea, trying to establish some calm. It had been a week since the incursion into the Dulce facility. He'd managed to regain control of it, but those who'd infiltrated it had escaped and he hadn't seen any sign of them. And worse, they had gotten away with his two most prized subjects.

His research was backed up, but it was going to take time to get back to where he was. He was most disappointed that his new security animals had been destroyed. They had shown a great deal of promise. Of course, they had ultimately failed.

He shook his head. And all because of the stupid bond between Leander and Subject One. Years ago, he'd mulled over the idea of killing Maeve Leander when she was a child. At the time, the concern had been that Maeve's existence would pull her mother's attention from the A.L.I.V.E. Project. But that fear had proven unfounded. Maeve's bond with the creature had only deepened Alice Leander's commitment to the project.

And Martin had never worried about the bond between Maeve and Alvie, probably because he'd never had such a bond with anyone, not even his own daughter. It had never crossed his mind during those early years that it would one day be a problem.

The doorbell rang and Martin narrowed his eyes. No one knew about this house. There were zero links between him and this place. He picked up his Sig and turned on the TV to the security camera footage. A tall blonde woman wrapped in a fur coat stood there with a muscular blond man in leather, both in their thirties. The woman smiled and waved at the camera.

A small tingle of fear slid over his skin as he moved to the door and opened it. "Tatiana, Dietrich. What a nice surprise."

Tatiana leaned up and kissed him on the cheek. "Martin, darling, we heard about your unfortunate loss and rushed right over to extend our sincerest condolences. And, of course, to offer whatever aid we can." A wave of expensive perfume hit him as Tatiana brushed past him into the living room, not waiting for him to invite them in.

Dietrich closed the door behind them and gestured for Martin to precede him into the living room.

Martin smiled at him but tensed as he turned his back to the man. Tatiana stood in front of the picture window. "This is a beautiful view. I can see why you would want to keep this place secret."

"How did you find out about it?"

Tatiana gave him a flirtatious pout. "A girl can't reveal all her secrets, now can she?"

"Can I get either of you something to drink?"

She took a seat on the couch with a sigh. "No, no. We won't be staying long, will we, Dietrich dear?"

Dietrich dear said nothing.

"Anyway, we wanted to make sure that all of your research remains intact after all this unpleasantness. It would be a shame if we had to report back that our investment has been squandered."

Martin refused to allow the fear that was crawling through his stomach show on his face. "Of course the research is secure. We did lose some subjects, but there is some intelligence that was gained that I feel could outweigh that loss."

The smile dropped from Tatiana's face. "I can't imagine that's true. You know how we feel—"

Martin cut her off. "An old friend has reappeared."

Tatiana glared at him, and he knew she was debating whether or not to reprimand him for cutting her off. Curiosity won out. "And who, pray tell, might that be?"

"Matilda Watson," Martin replied.

Tatiana's eyes flashed and Dietrich let out a small growl. Tatiana put up a hand to silence Dietrich. "You're sure?"

"Very. And she had Joseph with her," Martin said.

Tatiana's eyebrows rose at that announcement. "Did she really?" she asked quietly.

Martin said nothing because he knew the question wasn't aimed at him. Tatiana stared out the window and Martin could practically see the gears shifting in her mind. Finally, she stood.

"Well, this is a most interesting turn of events. And you may be right. This information may just make up for the loss of the research subjects." She walked up to Martin and patted him on the cheek. "Aren't you a lucky boy? Of course, we'll need to speak with you about this in detail when we substantiate it."

Martin gave her a brief nod. "Of course."

She waved at Dietrich. "We're leaving."

Dietrich still said nothing, simply followed Tatiana out of the room. Martin heard the front door open and then close. He released a breath and a sweat broke out on his brow. He grabbed the remote with a shaky hand and watched as Tatiana and Dietrich got into a Mercedes and pulled away.

Martin glanced up to where the cameras sat in the corners of his living room. Camera 3 had the best angle. He brought it up, rewinding the recording to when Tatiana and Dietrich had walked in. He paused it when Tatiana looked straight into the camera. Then he zoomed in. They did a good job of camouflaging who they were. It was almost impossible to differentiate them.

He focused on Tatiana's eyes. Always the eyes. They never were able to hide the eyes when on camera.

On screen, Tatiana blinked, and for a split second, her irises changed shape, elongating and looking exactly like the eyes of a snake.

"There you are," Martin whispered.

NEXT IN THE A.L.I.V.E. SERIES

www.vinci-books.com/rise

Where do you hide when the world is searching for you?

Turn the page for a free preview.

R.I.S.E. - PREVIEW

CHAPTER 1

Huntsville, Alabama
1961

Janet Fairfax took the rollers out of her daughter's hair, arranging the curls around her face. Face to face, they sat at the makeup table, an almost identical pair in profile. "Now, just don't let them see how smart you are. And don't tell them when they're wrong."

Matilda Fairfax looked up from the book in her lap. It was Wernher von Braun's *Project MARS: A Technical Tale*. "Mother, they want me to work for them. I'm pretty sure they want to know I have a brain in my head."

Janet's lips tightened, a sight Matilda was all too familiar with. "Matilda, this may be your last chance to find a husband."

Matilda opened her mouth to respond, but her mother held up a hand, holding her off. "No, you listen to me. I know you're a smart girl. But you are going to be a lonely girl. You need to find yourself a man. And no man is going to marry a woman who reads books on rocketry for fun."

Then he's not the man for me, Matilda thought but wisely kept to herself. This was an old argument.

Not that Janet didn't love her daughter. Matilda knew her mother loved her. She just didn't understand her. For Matilda, though, being married was not the ultimate goal in life, which set her apart from most of the girls her age, and all of their mothers. She wasn't against marriage, necessarily. She just wanted to marry a man who viewed her intelligence as a benefit, not a character flaw.

For Janet Fairfax, however, a high IQ was the equivalent of having a scarlet letter branded across her chest. Matilda was her only daughter. It had been bad enough when, as a toddler, she'd started correcting her father when he explained how things worked. But then Matilda had skipped grades and never seemed interested in playing with any of the girls. She tinkered away in the basement, building little contraptions. Janet knew how much those little contraptions meant to her daughter. But she also knew how difficult life could be for a woman on her own.

Janet turned the chair around so that Matilda could see her reflection in the mirror. Soft curls framed her delicate face. Her blue eyes peeked out from underneath her fringe. A blue ribbon was tied up on the side of her head. The blue of her dress further accentuated the blue of her eyes.

Her mother smiled. "You look lovely. And I have no doubt that you will find a husband on that base."

Matilda rolled her eyes. A husband was not what she was looking for. But her mother looked happy. And Matilda had to admit that she did look pretty for a change. So she said nothing except, "Thank you, Mother."

* * *

There wasn't much that happened in Huntsville, Alabama. It was a small town in rural America. It had its share of problems and had been a military manufacturing hub in 1940. In 1941, however, it became a central research area for the U.S. rocket program. In 1950, Huntsville led the field in rocketry, leading to the development of the Redstone, Jupiter, and Pershing missiles.

But the residents liked to think that Huntsville, Alabama, was the smartest town in all of America. Why? Because Huntsville, Alabama, had the George C. Marshall Space Flight Center (MSFC), the U.S. government's civilian rocketry and spacecraft propulsion research center.

Von Braun had actually come to Huntsville two years before the Marshall Space Center was created. He and his team of scientists had worked at the Redstone Arsenal, where they successfully developed a modified Redstone rocket called a Jupiter-C to launch Explorer I, America's first orbiting satellite. It was at Marshall that the Saturn V launch vehicle, the super booster that would propel Americans to the Moon, was developed under the guidance of Wernher von Braun.

Huntsville was also as red-blooded and patriotic as any other city in the United States. There'd been some grumbling when the first of the German scientists had arrived. But as success built upon success, the grumbling slowly began to go quiet, especially when it came to beating the Russians into space. There wasn't an American alive who didn't want the U.S. to beat the Russians to the Moon.

And all of those hopes were pinned on the man who President Eisenhower had named to run NASA: Wernher von Braun.

And Matilda was about to meet him.

She smoothed down her blue dress, pressing down the edges of her white collar before running a quick hand over her hair. She'd chosen the blue dress with the white polka dots, but now she was rethinking her choice. Maybe she should've gone with something a little more somber. After all, at eighteen, she would be one of the youngest employees at NASA.

This dress probably makes me look like I'm on my way to an afternoon at the movies.

She took a breath, pushing away her doubts. She wasn't one who was normally bothered by self-doubt. Since the age of three, she'd been telling people what they were doing wrong whenever they did it wrong. It had not endeared her to her teachers ... or her parents, for that matter. But her chess teacher had been thrilled, and once it was understood that her brain worked at a much higher level than those around her, she'd been forgiven oversights of decorum ... for the most part.

At the age of seventeen, Matilda had already graduated from college. While she'd been written up in the paper and the town had proudly proclaimed her the new genius on the block, her mother had mourned the fact that she would never find a husband.

Matilda, though, worried she would never find a job. Women in the sciences were not common. A woman as young as she was in the field? Well, Matilda had never heard of any.

But both mother and daughter had been elated when Matilda had been invited to apply for a job at the Army base. Matilda because she couldn't believe that Wernher von Braun had actually extended the invitation to her personally. Her mother's excitement had a decidedly different angle: She had visions of handsome, muscular soldiers surrounding her daughter day and night. She overheard her mother talking to her father, saying that if Tilda couldn't find a husband on the Army base, then there was simply no helping her.

Tilda tried not to let the remarks sting, but being she was still thinking about it weeks later, she supposed she'd failed on that count. She shook her head. This was not the train of thought she should be thinking about right now. Reaching up, she pulled the bow out of her hair and shoved it into the pocket of her dress. Then she smoothed down her hair once again. That was better. Less like a girl out for an afternoon on the town and more of a woman ready to take on whatever task was set in front of her.

Or at least, that's what she hoped.

As she reached Room 217, she paused in front of the door. It was at the end of the hall and looked just like all the other doors on the floor. But Tilda knew this door was different. This door was the door to the future that she'd dreamed of. Taking a breath, she knocked.

"Come in." The voice was strong and masculine, with a very heavy Austrian accent.

She pulled open the door and stepped into the room. There was a desk sitting in front of her that was empty, the door beyond it open.

"Come on back."

Walking past the desk, she stood in the open doorway. The man behind the desk looked up with a smile. Blond hair and bright blue eyes looked back at her warmly. The man stood up and walked around the desk, towering over Tilda. "Miss Fairfax, it is a pleasure to meet you."

As she reached out her hand, she marveled at how at ease she felt in the man's presence. This was a man who was her intellectual superior. For once in her life, she would not be the smartest one in the room. And more than anything, she was looking forward to learning from him. "Dr. von Braun, it's a pleasure to meet you as well."

The scientist, who had just one month ago created the Mercury 3, the rocket that sent the first American astronaut, Alan

Shepard, on a suborbital flight on May 5, 1961, the scientist who America had pinned its hopes on getting to the Moon before the Russians, smiled back at her. "Please call me Wernher."

He gestured to the corner of the room. She was so focused on von Braun that she hadn't realized there was someone else in here with them. Although as she got her first look at him, she wondered how that was possible.

He was the most beautiful man she'd ever seen.

Tall with a muscular build, his cheekbones were sharp under piercing blue eyes. They were so blue she wondered about the lighting or if she was turning into one of those women from the romance novels her mother read.

"Matilda Fairfax, I'd like to introduce you to Joseph Watson, my right-hand man. We three are going to accomplish great things together."

CHAPTER 2

Present Day
Canso, Nova Scotia

Nervousness ran along Dr. Maeve Leander's skin like an electrical current. She knew it was a delayed reaction to everything that had occurred in New Mexico. An image of the Kecksburg charging at her wafted through her mind.

She cringed, closing her eyes as if she could hide away from the image, but it was just replaced by others: Alvie in the containment unit, about to be loaded onto a train headed to who knew where by Martin Drummond; the large winged creature that attacked the chopper that had nearly taken Maeve, Chris, and a dozen others when they'd burst free from the Archuletta; and finally, Agaren, the large Gray whom Maeve had first seen at Area 51 when he'd caused a distraction allowing Maeve, the triplets, and Alvie to escape detection, and whom they'd liberated from Dulce as well.

Those hours leading up to that fight, and through it, had felt like the longest in Maeve's life. Afterwards, they had spent hours shifting from cars to planes and back to cars again before coming to a small camp that looked like a deserted summer camp rather than a safe house.

Dr. Greg Schorn, one of Maeve's closest friends and former colleague from Wright-Patterson Air Force Base, stepped out of one of the SUVs carrying Iggy, the Maldek who'd saved his and Norah Tidwell's life. Greg met her gaze, the moonlight flashing off his glasses. He gave Maeve a tight smile before carrying the wounded Iggy into one of the buildings. Norah walked quickly next to them and disappeared into one of the cabins.

Maeve had looked over the wound, and despite the amount of blood, it was actually pretty shallow. If they kept it clean, Iggy should be all right.

The triplets were chasing Hope, their black-and-white Labrador retriever mix, in the area in front of the cabins. They had too much energy after being cooped up for too long. Alvie was with them but not joining in. The triplets were Alvie's clones, created at Area 51 only a year ago. Alvie was twenty-nine years old, but his height of just under four feet made him seem so much younger. He had a disproportionately large head that came to a point at his chin. He had two large black eyes over two holes that served as his nose and a very small mouth.

And he was gray in color. The triplets looked identical to him except for Snap, the only girl, who had thin wispy white hair.

Alvie and Maeve had been raised together as brother and sister, although somewhere along the way, her role had shifted to a more maternal one. It was an unusual upbringing, but she could not imagine her life without him.

And now, she couldn't think of anything she could do to help him.

The triplets had been spared most of the danger, but Alvie had been held by Martin for days. And Maeve held no illusions that he was treated well during that time. The burns on his body were evidence of the cruelty he'd been exposed to. Maeve watched Alvie, but for the first time in their lives together, he was keeping his thoughts from her. He had been doing so ever since she'd removed him from the containment unit.

Maeve tried not to feel hurt, but it wasn't working. But she knew Alvie had been through a lot. He needed time to process. Alvie was not fully human. He was half human and half gray alien. And all good. Cruelty wasn't something he was used to.

And while he hadn't shared what had happened, she knew it was harsh. She wasn't sure what kind of lasting damage Martin Drummond had done to him. Although Maeve wasn't a violent woman, she promised herself that Martin would pay for what he had put her family through.

An arm slipped around her waist. She looked up into Chris Garrigan's blue eyes. A former Air Force captain, he had been in charge of Alvie's security at Wright-Patterson. And he was also the reason she, Alvie, and the triplets were still alive. "He'll be okay. We just need to give him time."

Maeve leaned in to Chris, soaking up his warmth. She nodded her head but couldn't speak past the ball of emotion that suddenly appeared in her throat.

A throat cleared behind them. Maeve glanced back at the round African American gentleman who stood there. Jasper Jenkins cleared his throat again. "Sorry to interrupt, but I thought you might want to get everyone settled."

Her gaze shifting to the triplets and Alvie, she squeezed Chris's arm. "Let them play a little longer. I'll go see what the situation is."

Chris kissed her cheek. "Okay."

Jasper led Maeve into one of the cabins. She braced herself, expecting spiderwebs, rat droppings, and dirt. She was pleasantly surprised. Someone had recently cleaned it. She could still smell the lemon cleaner. There were two bunk beds and two cots, along with a bathroom at the back. A small stack of clothes had been placed on the bunk at the front.

"This is great. Thanks." Maeve sank onto the nearest bunk, looking through the clothes. There were pajamas and new sweats for all of them, which was good because they were all desperately in need of a change of clothes.

"There's shampoo, soap, and everything else you'll need in the bathroom. If you need any—" Jasper's words cutting off, his eyes widening as he stared behind her.

Maeve looked over her shoulder.

Agaren stood in the doorway. He was six feet tall, with a large triangular-shaped skull and gray skin tone. His black eyes offered no clue to his thoughts. But the slightest movement of his small chin toward Jasper told Maeve he was communicating with him.

"Um, yeah, so I'll leave you two alone?" Jasper looked at Maeve for confirmation.

She stood. "It's fine."

Agaren stepped into the room and to the side to allow Jasper to pass. Jasper paused in the doorway before heading outside.

Nerves fluttered through Maeve's stomach. She gripped her hands tightly behind her back. "How are you?"

"Good. It is good to be free. Thank you."

It was shocking hearing the words coming out of his

mouth. Maeve had assumed that his communication would be telepathic as well. "You speak?"

The large gray inclined his head. "It took a great deal of time to figure out how to. It is a very rudimentary form of communication, but eventually I was able to master it. Although it is not entirely comfortable."

Maeve wanted to be insulted by his interpretation of speech, but the fact that he was correct stopped her. Although humans did believe that they communicated mainly through speech, nonverbal communication was more indicative and communicative of how humans actually felt and what they intended than the spoken word.

Plus, being Maeve now understood how Alvie and the triplets communicated, she had to admit it was a much more comprehensive way of getting one's thoughts across. She could feel how Alvie felt when he asked questions that conveyed so much more than just the question itself. She could tell when he asked why if he was curious, scared, excited, or all of the above. With humans, if you just went from the spoken word, all you knew was that they were curious. But really, could just one characteristic describe the motivation for a human's behavior or questions?

"I am all right with telepathic communication. I've had a great deal of practice," she said with a small smile.

Yes, you have. Alvie is a remarkable individual, he said switching to telepathic communication with a feeling of gratitude.

Although worried about Alvie, the first feeling she felt when thinking go him was love. He was her heart. "He is. I care a great deal about him."

And he you.

There was a link between Alvie and the alien in front of her. Unlike Alvie, Agaren was pure Gray. He'd been captured by

Martin decades ago and held all that time. Yet he had approved when she had protected Alvie over him. She looked him right in the eyes. *"Who is he?"*

Agaren did not feign ignorance at what she was truly asking. *He is the key to humanity's peace or their destruction. I fear now that recent events have pushed your fate closer to annihilation.*

Mouth dropping open, it was a struggle to hold back the shiver his words elicited. "Why?"

I am part of a council. Our job is to monitor Earth and its development. You are a very young planet. Only a few billion years old. Yet your species has been invasive. You have overtaken all of your resources, using them to the brink of depletion. You have destroyed large swaths of your own population. Your aggressive ways concern the Council and have for centuries.

Once again she wanted to argue, but she knew what he said was true. When *Homo sapiens* became the dominant hominid on the planet, they had destroyed much along their way. Australia had been teeming with giant animals before humans stepped foot on its shores. Two thousand years later, all those large beautiful beasts had disappeared. The same phenomenon was observed in Madagascar.

In fact, there had been three waves of extinction tied to human behavior. The first wave of extinctions was caused by the spread of foragers. The second wave accompanied the spread of farmers. And the third wave has proven the deadliest to the planet, caused by pollution spewing into the environment at an unprecedented rate.

Experts estimated that at humankind's current rate of resource consumption, we'd kill off between 200 and 2,000 animal species annually and that climate change would result in between 10 and 20% reductions in global production of food in the next five to twenty-five years, not to mention the coastal areas that would become flooded and areas of the world that, due to the heat, would be completely uninhabitable for humans. So Maeve could not argue that the Council had no right to be concerned.

Agaren's voice once again appeared in her mind. *I must return to the Council and explain about my absence. They will know what I have experienced, what I have seen. There is no way to keep it from them, and I would not want to anyway. Truth is always the way forward, but I fear it will push them away from humanity.*

"What happens then?" She asked.

They may decide that humans no longer deserve to be protected. That they are an invasive species that needs to be, at the very least, contained, at worst, removed.

A chill rolled over Maeve and this time she did shiver, wrapping her arms around her stomach. "Removed?"

He nodded. *It has happened before. But you and Alvie, the other humans who have risked much to protect him and his clones, you are the hope. I will stress this with the Council.*

"And if they don't take your word for it?" She asked.

There have been twenty-three hominids on this planet. Homo sapien sapiens will fall like the others.

Maeve sucked in a breath.

The door opened, and the triplets rushed into the room. They sprinted for the nearest bed, clambered on, and began to jump with happy squeals.

His head tilted to the side, Agaren watched them for a moment before walking over to them. The triplets all went still, looking up at him with their small mouths hanging open.

Raising his pointer finger, Agaren pressed it gently to the middle of each of their foreheads. Snap, Crackle, and Pop all smiled and closed their eyes. Pop opened his eyes first and reached up for Agaren. The slight widening of Agaren's eyes indicated his surprise at the motion. After a moment's hesitation, he reached out his arms.

That was all the encouragement Pop needed. He hopped

into them. For a moment, Agaren stumbled back before his arms closed around the little alien hybrid. And then a smile formed on his face as well.

Alvie appeared in the doorway. Agaren stared at him, and the hair on Maeve's arms stood on end. She knew they were having a conversation. Maeve said nothing, just watched in silence. Then Alvie broke the contact. He walked over to Maeve and took her hand, which gave Maeve the distinct impression that he had just picked a side.

Maeve prayed that for his own sake it was the right one.

CHAPTER 3

Seattle, Washington

A soft rain fell against the hood of Martin's white BMW X6. It had rained every day since he'd been back in Seattle. After that first night and the visit from Tatiana and Dietrich, he'd thought about leaving. But he knew that wherever he went, they would follow. There was no getting away from them.

There never had been.

He pulled into a parking spot in front of the old warehouse. It had been erected in 1973 as a furniture manufacturing building before it had finally gone bust in the late 1990s. It had sat empty and abandoned for nearly twenty years before Martin purchased it and had it refurbished. It was one of two dozen hubs he'd created across the country.

The one in New Mexico had been the largest. Losing that base stung, but they had all the data. He supposed that was the most important part. And the destruction of the base had also offered some new data. Creatures that they had had locked away for years had suddenly come to life. A few had escaped the facility, but most had been killed.

Martin sat in his car, drumming his fingers on the steering

wheel. The creature he truly wanted had not been killed in the explosion. No, the one they called Alvie had been rescued. *Damn you, Tilda.*

He'd honestly thought she was dead. Matilda Watson was good. He would give her that much. And being he'd thought she was dead for years, his new goal was to make sure she lived up to that belief.

But it wasn't the sudden appearance of Tilda that weighed on his mind. No, it was the resurrection of Joseph. Seeing him at the train station had been like seeing a ghost. He hadn't aged a day. Which could mean only one thing …

Stepping out of the car, he hurried into the warehouse. He pulled open the old door, noting the cobwebs in the corner of it. He hurried through the old factory's reception area. Plastic chairs served as a waiting area for former clients while an old linoleum desk stood directly across from the main doors. The sign for Hanley's Furniture was still displayed behind it. Another door led into the old warehouse.

Martin pushed through and stepped into a different world. Steel reinforced walls surrounded him on four sides. An airlock door was directly in front of him. After an eye scan and entering a password, the door slid open. While from the outside the warehouse looked like a decrepit old building, the inside had every modern convenience. In fact, the outside was simply a shell. They had cleared out the entirety of the inside of the warehouse and built a new interior, complete with walls and ceiling.

And while the area around the warehouse may have looked abandoned, he had been under surveillance for two blocks. Every car and pedestrian within five miles of the warehouse was inspected. If the individuals continued on their way, they would never think the derelict warehouse was anything but abandoned. But if anyone dared to try to enter the warehouse or even its property, well, that would not end well for them.

Entering the main hub of the warehouse, the low hum of computers and work greeted him. On the far wall to his right were servers encased in refrigerated glass containers. In front of them were a dozen cubicles where his analysts worked. On his left was a long line of glass walls holding his office, and then in the back was his small apartment. On the other side was a small lounge area. It contained three leather couches, a couple of beat-up chairs, and a small kitchen area.

He ignored all of the analysts and headed for his office. He stepped into the room, tapping a button on the console on his desk that would darken the glass around him. No one would be able to see in, but he would be able to see everything happening outside the room. Shaking off his jacket, he hung it on the stand by the door.

Stacy Mal hustled in. She placed a coffee on the desk in front of him. At forty-two years of age, Stacy still dressed like the college kid she had been when Martin had recruited her. She wore her blonde hair in a ponytail, a Harvard sweatshirt, jeans, and Converse sneakers. From the back, she could easily be mistaken for a college kid. But from the front it was clear from the lines in her face that she had lived a life.

Placing two files on the desk in front of him, next to the coffee, she said, "I have something for you."

Martin took a seat behind the desk and pulled one of the files close. He scanned the filename: Sandra Gillibrand. It took him a moment to place it. The case out in Kansas. It had been a D.E.A.D. case. Two science experiments from Area 51, the Blue Boys had targeted the son at the home. It was the farthest east the creatures had traveled. Sandra Gillibrand was the mother and had taken down one of the Blue Boys, not an easy task.

But the second one had been taken down by a creature that

had never been meant to escape Area 51. It should have died there.

I should have killed it years ago. Out loud he asked, "What did you find?"

"You know the basics: Sandra Gillibrand, single mother, former Marine, widow. Luke Gillibrand, age ten, autistic. Nothing for the last ten years sent up any red flags. They've been struggling financially, she has a strained relationship with her parents. And Luke has had some trouble at school due to behavioral issues."

"Aggression?" He asked.

"No. He's been targeted by bullies," she said.

Martin rubbed his eyes, trying to tamp down his annoyance.. "Why are you bringing this to me?"

She spoke quickly. "I did a search on Luke's father. He died in Iraq before Luke was born. Luke never met him."

A headache was building behind Martin's eyes. He scrounged in the desk drawer to his right for some ibuprofen. Latching on to the bottle, he said, "Yes, and?"

"And his career was pretty unremarkable except for one thing: He was part of a project called Antaeus," a small smile crossed her face as she watched him expectedly.

Popping two pills, he swallowed them down with some coffee. Antaeus was an interesting choice of names. In mythology, Antaeus was the son of Poseidon and Gaia. He was incredibly strong when physically connected to the earth. "I'm not familiar with the project."

"I thought as much. It was actually a project spearheaded and designed by Robert Buckley," she said, landing the name without realizing how much of an impact it would have on Martin.

But Stacy had all of his attention now. Robert Buckley, his former mentor, had taught Martin almost everything he knew. But Martin had slowly outpaced him, developing his own base of knowledge and cache of secrets. And apparently, Buckley had kept his own secrets as well, including Project Antaeus.

She continued. "Antaeus involved trying to create a more advanced soldier. The soldiers were given shots under the guise of vitamin supplements, to enhance their abilities. Then they were studied over the course of a year."

He grunted. Another Captain America attempt. "And the results of the study?"

Stacy shook her head. "A complete failure. Most of the soldiers were killed in action by the end of the year. But even before that, they showed no greater ability, no higher kill rate, no improvement at all in their functioning."

Martin focused on one word in her statement: most. "What about the ones that didn't die?"

She spoke quietly. "They're all dead now. If they didn't die in Iraq, they did when they got home."

Martin met Stacy's eyes. Apparently Buckley made sure that all traces of the project had disappeared.

"But I believe they overlooked one piece of evidence: Luke." Stacy pointed to a line on the file he was reading.

It was the dates that the project had run and then been officially abandoned. Martin looked up and smiled. Sandra Gillibrand became pregnant while her husband was on leave, and while he was part of the project.

"What was in the supplements?" Martin asked as he sat back at his desk.

She nodded to the folder on the desk. "It's in the other file. Buckley created the supplement from some sort of sample they had at Wright-Patterson Air Force Base."

Martin went still. *No, that bastard. He wouldn't.*

Pulling the file to him, he quickly scanned through the data, his anger rising. If Buckley wasn't dead, Martin would take great joy in killing him all over again. He closed the file.

"I'm going to need a strike team. Tell them to bring me Luke Gillibrand. I want him unharmed."

Although Stacy nodded, she asked, "What about the mother? She'll defend him."

Martin waved her away. "She's unimportant. If she gets in the way, kill her."

www.vinci-books.com/rise

FACT OR FICTION?

Thank you for reading. I hope you enjoyed yourself. As with the Belial series, a lot of reading and research goes into the creation of a book from the A.L.I.V.E. Series. D.E.A.D. is no exception. So on to the facts!

Feral Children. The information on feral children is accurate. research does indicate that there is a small window of time for a child to develop language. If they do not have a chance to hear language, their ability to be able to speak is greatly reduced if not eliminated. In addition, young children who spend as little as a year in the wild can have difficulty re-assimilating into society. The examples used in the book are real children-the boy who took on bird characteristics when forced to live with only birds, or the young boy who was raised by monkeys is accurate. Other children have been taken in by dogs, wolves, and an assortment of other animals, suggesting some in the animal kingdom are much more compassionate than humans.

Solitary Confinement. Solitary confinement is a hallmark of American correctional institutions. It is also incredibly damaging to our humanity. Being isolated from people and social connections can negatively affect an individual's brain. As mentioned in *D.E.A.D.*, solitary confinement has actually demonstrated an ability to alter an individual's brain. It has permanent effects.

Not mentioned in this novel, however, is that early prisons involved cells where people were isolate. No one spoke, no one communicated. People were expected to simply think about what they had done, to be penitent. It's actually where the term penitentiary comes from. The first penitentiary in the U.S. was called the Walnut Street Prison. Most people went insane or committed suicide.

Maldek. Now this is a tough one. As was the case for Agent Norah Tidwell, I read a great deal from academic sources on aliens and UFOs before turning to what we will call less academic sources. One of the latter sources was an account written by a man about his grandfather's interaction with a stranded E.T. named Bek-Ti. According to Bek-Ti there was a planet in between Mars and Jupiter called Maldek that was destroyed by a hostile alien race. Mars environment was irreparably damaged by the same attack resulting in the destruction of its atmosphere. According to the tale, some surviving Maldekians took refuge under the surface of Mars with other Martian survivors.

Is this true? I don't know. But there is some scientific support for some of the propositions, such as Mars having a habitable environment and there being a large asteroid belt between Jupiter and Mars. Maldek will actually be discussed in more detail in R.I.S.E, the third book of the A.L.I.V.E series.

FACT OR FICTION?

Buckley Air Force Base. Buckley Air Force Base is an actual base in Aurora Colorado. Following 9/11, some operations for the NSA were moved to Buckley AFB. And Buckley itself does have a space orientation. It houses a space-based missile warning system, space surveillance operations, as well as providing space communication and support functions.

Dulce Underground Base. There have been rumors of a government underground base in Dulce, New Mexico that is connected to UFOs for decades. Strange lights, black helicopters, cattle mutilations have all been observed. In addition, a number of people have come forward claiming to have worked at the facility and provided information about the facility inside. Whether or not those reports are accurate are a matter of debate.

Chris's Defense Proficiency Requirement. I completely made this up. I have no idea if there is any sort of requirement for military personnel on unusual assignments.

President's and UFO's. For this one, it is a little difficult to pin down what is true and what is not. So I'll tell you what I know. I read the information on JFK and his interest in linking up with the Russian space program in a couple of different books. At the time of his death, he was on the outs with the U.S. space program and as a result had made overtures to Russian leader Nikita Kruschev to achieve a joint mission to reach the moon. After the third offer, Kruschev did allegedly agree and a few days later, JFK was killed.

Reagan was focused on UFOs and alien life during his terms. He made a number of references to an alien force attacking Earth being a unifying force to bring all the countries of the world together. His famous reference to it was in a speech to the UN in 1987. But allegedly he had a similarly private conversation with Gorbachev.

Orion. There is an Orion constellation which some argue the builders used the same angles when building the three largest pyramids in Giza, Egypt. According to Egyptian mythology, Osiris was one of the creators of humanity and he came to Earth from Osiris.

Werner von Braun. Verna Van Braun was the father of rocketry. He was originally a German scientist who came to the United States through Operation Paperclip. Many argue we would not have gotten as far with the space program without him.

Winged Aliens in Space. According to multiple sources, Russian cosmonauts did report seeing winged seven-foot tall aliens outside their craft on a mission in 1985. As mention in *D.E.A.D.*, they also reported an orange cloud engulfing their ship prior to the sighting.

Life in Space. Scientists now contend that there was water on Mars billions of years ago and that it had an environment similar to Earth. Some even argue it was at one point closer to the sun, making it more temperate. And water fumes have been found on the moons of both Saturn and Neptune. In addition, lights have been spotted on the moon that do not currently have an explanation.

Holloman Alien Landing. There is a Holloman Air Force Base. Now the question is, did the landing occur? There was a documentary that Nixon allegedly supported. He had planned on using it to announce that we were in fact not alone in the universe. He wanted to cement his place in history. But once he cemented his place in history a different way, the documentary went from earth-shattering revelations to standard revelations. Some eyewitnesses did step forward to claim that they had seen a UFO land on the runway and someone enter it from Air Force One. There have been other claims over the years that the United States has been working with aliens, many of them revolving around the base in Dulce, New Mexico.

Belief in Life on other Worlds. It is interesting that the belief in UFOs and aliens was readily accepted up until the mid-twentieth century. Many of the founding fathers and early American religious leaders in fact believed in the plurality of worlds-that we are not alone in the universe. It seems shortly after Roswell, that there was a shift in the perception of aliens and UFOs. And I find that timing rather interesting.

Alien Incidents. There was a 1965 blackout that took out power up into Canada. UFOs were reported prior to the blackout and a believable official cause was never released. There was also some sort of incursion into Los Angeles in 1942 that resulted in an air raid alarm being sounded and gunners taking aim into the night sky. And recall this was at a time period right after Pearl Harbor, so the military was extra vigilant about the possibility of air incursions.

P.S. A Little Extra Trivia For Fans of The Belial Series. When I was researching UFOs, I came across a few surprising supporters. One name that leapt out at me was Cotton Mather, the reverend who helped lead the charge for the Salem Witch Trials. Around 1647, Mather recounted the sighting of a UFO in the air of New Haven Connecticut.

ABOUT THE AUTHOR

Author, Criminologist, Terrorism Expert, Jeet Kune Do Black Sash, Runner, Dog Lover.

Amazon best-selling author R.D. Brady writes supernatural and science fiction thrillers. Her thrillers include ancient mysteries, unusual facts, non-stop action, and fierce women with heart.

Prior to beginning her writing career, RD Brady was a criminologist who specialized in life-course criminology and international terrorism. She's lectured and written numerous academic articles on the genetic influence on criminal behavior, factors that influence terrorist ideology, and delinquent behavior formation.

After visiting counter-terrorism units in Israel, RD returned home with a sabbatical in front of her and decided to write that book she'd been thinking about. Four years later she left academia with the publication of her first book, *The Belial Stone*, and hasn't looked back.